BORDER BRIDE

ARNETTE LAMB

POCKET BOOKS

New York   London   Toronto   Sydney   Tokyo   Singapore

An *Original* Publication of POCKET BOOKS

POCKET BOOKS, a division of Simon & Schuster Inc.
1230 Avenue of the Americas, New York, NY 10020

Copyright © 1993 by Arnette Lamb

ISBN: 0-671-77933-8

First Pocket Books printing September 1993

10 9 8 7 6

Cover art by Lina Levy

Printed in the U.S.A.

MALCOLM REACHED OUT AND GRABBED HER ARM.

When he stepped toward her, his foot tangled in the sheets. Before he could get his balance, he fell, pulling her down with him. Twisting, he managed to land on his back with Alpin sprawled on his chest. Her elbows poked him in the ribs. He winced and grasped her upper arms.

"What are you doing?" she demanded.

"Me? You're the one on top, but that was always the case with us, wasn't it?"

"You cannot seduce me." She tried to jerk away.

He held her fast. "Admit it, Alpin. You always wanted the upper hand."

"We were children then, playing games and squabbling. You hated me. And I . . ." Her gaze slipped to his mouth. She swallowed. "And I was . . ."

"You were what?"

"I was naïve about how far our playing would go."

He shifted beneath her. The movement gave vivid proof of just how much he'd changed over the years and how much he did want her.

"Now you know where such playing can lead. . . ."

Books by Arnette Lamb

Highland Rogue
The Betrothal
Border Lord
Border Bride
Chieftain
Maiden of Inverness
A Holiday of Love
Betrayed
Beguiled

Published by POCKET BOOKS

To Heather Lee Elizabeth
and her new parents,
Candy and Marvin Purdue

Acknowledgments

Very special thanks to my literary helpmates, Joyce Bell, Susan Wiggs, and Barbara Dawson Smith.

And to the agent to die for, Denise Marcil.

And to my wonderful editor, Caroline Tolley, for her insight and her intuition.

Prologue

Lady Alpin MacKay itched to yank off her mourning veil and fan her heated cheeks. And she would, once her visitor stopped eulogizing her late guardian, Charles, and started reading the will.

"A sober man and a defender of the true faith," the lawyer, Othell Codrington, was saying.

Sober? thought Alpin. Poor Charles had drowned his sorrows in rum.

"A widower to envy . . ."

A man to pity. After his wife, Adrienne, passed away, Charles had spent a decade grieving himself to death. As an impressionable girl, Alpin had longed to find a man who would love her as deeply as Charles had loved his wife. But she also wanted a man who would not break under tragic circumstances. Years and the reality of island life had crushed her romantic dreams.

"A man shrewd in business, yet fair . . ."

A misconception. For ten years Alpin alone had managed

1

every detail of the vast plantation, from the purchase of biscuit flour to the harvesting of the cane.

". . . gone to a greater glory . . ."

And to the company of his beloved late wife. Thank God.

A soft breeze wafted across the veranda and filled the air with the sweet aroma of boiling sugar. Alpin sighed. Paradise Plantation would belong to her now—the spacious two-story house, six and one-half acres of manicured lawns, one thousand acres of fertile fields recently denuded of muscovado sugarcane; fifty-six English servants, eighty slaves, scores of thatched huts, a dozen narrow barrack houses, four water wells. The wicker chair on which she sat. The copper tub in which she bathed. The mosquito netting draped over her bed. The carriage, the cart, the chicken roasting on the spit. The precious mill with its twin chimneys spewing smoke into the tropical blue sky. Hers.

The promise of independence sent her spirits soaring. Life on the plantation would continue as it had. But not for the slaves. Five years ago she'd persuaded Charles to free them. The neighboring planters had been outraged. Under pressure, Charles had yielded to the conservative element. Now Alpin MacKay would stand fast in her beliefs.

A drop of perspiration made a slow, ticklish slide from her temple to her jaw, down her neck, and inside the collar of her black fustian dress. Ignoring her discomfort, she stared at the leather satchel perched on the solicitor's lap. Would he never read the will?

When he paused to draw breath, she said, "You're very kind, Mr. Codrington, to save me a trip to Bridgetown. And you must be highly skilled, for Charles said he would trust his affairs to none but you."

The attorney sat straighter. Sweat streamed from beneath his powdered wig and soaked his lace-trimmed cravat, turning the gentlemanly concoction into a soggy knot of wilted ruffles. "That ever was the case, my dear. Charles made an impressive go of it here." He cast a covetous gaze toward the mill. "Although none of us have ever seen the enterprise."

Let this city lawyer and everyone else think Charles had

2

managed Paradise and modernized the mill. Alpin needed no praise for her work, only peace of mind and security. Soon she would have both. She fought the urge to drum her fingers impatiently. "As you say, Charles was a gentleman among men and concerned about the welfare of those in his keeping."

"I met him five years back—before he added that new contraption to the mill." Codrington opened the satchel, which contained dozens of papers. He withdrew a be-ribboned document bearing a golden seal the size of a fig. "His generosity was a testament to his Christian convic-tions." A benevolent smile curled the lawyer's lips and revealed several missing teeth. "He's left you a generous stipend."

She needed no allowance. Profits from the sugar would more than support her. Dumbfounded, she repeated, "A stipend?"

Like a child reading a primer, he traced each line of the document with his forefinger. "There are the usual bequests to servants. A fellowship for his club. Ah, yes. Here it is. 'One hundred pounds a year to my cousin, Lady Alpin MacKay.'"

Icy fingers of dread crept over her skin. Her throat grew tight. "And . . ."

"And passage home."

Never! she silently raged. Charles had provided the funds for a visit to the Borders of Scotland and England, but only if she wanted to go. Which she didn't. "How considerate of him."

A sand fly landed on Codrington's nose. He swatted it away. "You may, of course, take any family heirlooms."

Knowing the veil concealed her wide-eyed astonishment, Alpin put all her effort into keeping her voice calm. She would cut cane to earn her keep before she'd depend on any man again. "What of Paradise Plantation?" She held her breath. If Charles had foolishly gambled it away or mort-gaged it . . .

Codrington batted the fly again. "I am at liberty to say only that five years ago he transferred ownership of all his worldly possessions. A tricky matter for some in my profession, considering the distance and correspondence required, but quite simple for me. Mr. Fenwick will continue to oversee the estate until the owner decides what to do with it."

Fear buzzed in her ears, obliterating the pounding of her heart and scattering her thoughts. Paradise gone. Impossible. This was her home. Where would she go? She could challenge Codrington, but to what end? She would expose her bitterness. Jeopardize any chance of righting this wrong.

Right it! Keep your wits. There's time aplenty to learn the facts and think out a plan. Henry Fenwick was a capable and kind overseer, but he despised the ruling class of Barbados.

She took a deep breath and put on a cheery face. "To whom did Charles transfer ownership?"

In a protective gesture, Codrington closed the flap on the satchel, fastened the buckle, and folded his hands over it. "The transfer was a private transaction between gentlemen. I'm sworn to secrecy." He handed her the will. "Have you mastered reading, Lady Alpin?"

In four languages. But the slimy toad needn't know that. Let him think her ignorant; his own superiority might loosen his tongue. "The art of deciphering words can be difficult."

Benevolence lent him a pitying air; his mouth went slack, his hands relaxed. "I understand. And I suppose I can tell you that by transferring the plantation to another party, Charles was repaying an old debt of gratitude."

Gratitude? To whom? How could Charles have been so cruel as to leave her with only a paltry stipend? She had forgone marriage to shoulder his responsibilities. And for what? To care for a man who had nursed a broken heart from a bottle and passed his wealth on to someone else? Her sacrifice had been for nothing. Someone else owned Paradise.

Her stomach roiled. Who?

The answer lay in that satchel. Why else would Codrington guard it so fiercely? A name. She needed a name. Hatred filled her. If she could examine those papers she'd have a target for her ire. She knew the way. Once she had Codrington away from the house, she'd excuse herself for a female necessity.

But first she had to get his attention. She swept off the veil. He stared, gape-mouthed.

"Is something wrong, sir?"

He fumbled with the satchel. "I, ah . . . You, uh . . . It's just that Charles told me . . ."

"Told you what?"

"He told me that you were unmarriageable—more . . . mature. I expected—" He cleared his throat. His gaze fell to her breasts. "May I say you have preserved yourself admirably."

The clumsy comment, delivered with a lustful leer, disgusted Alpin. Because she was small, people always thought her younger than her age. As a girl she had hated being mistaken for a child. Now she could use her youthful appearance to her advantage.

"How very thoughtful of you, Mr. Codrington. Would you like to see the mill?"

He jumped up so fast, the satchel fell to the floor, forgotten.

Twenty minutes later, her fingers trembling, she opened the pouch and scanned the legal documents. At the sight of the name on the transfer papers, she tossed back her head and groaned through clenched teeth. Her childhood rose up to haunt her.

By the time she replaced the papers and returned to the mill and her guest, Alpin had made her plans. She breathed deeply of the spicy smells of Barbados, but her thoughts had already turned to Scotland and Kildalton Castle. She was about to mount the next siege in the years-old war with the scoundrel who now controlled her destiny.

Kildalton Castle
Summer 1735

"And if I refuse?"

Craning his neck, the soldier squinted into the dim interior of the falcon mews. "She is prepared for a refusal, my lord, and up to her old tricks, I trow."

Malcolm's hand stilled, his fingers holding a scrap of meat above the open mouth of a hungry owlet. The wounded mother owl looked on. "How is that, Alexander?"

"Lady Alpin said if you doona come and greet her personally, she'll carve out your eyes and feed them to the badgers."

Malcolm dropped the meat into the hungry maw. Childhood memories flashed in his mind: Alpin splintering his toy sword and throwing it down the privy shaft, Alpin howling with laughter as she locked him in the pantry, Alpin hiding in the tower room and crying herself to sleep, Alpin coming after him with a jar of buzzing hornets.

A shudder coursed through him. Years ago she had played havoc with the life of a gullible lad. The world-wise man would now play havoc with hers. "I wonder what she'll do if I call her bluff?"

Alexander Lindsay, trainer of archers and master of the hunt, moved cautiously down the aisle between roosting falcons, agitated kestrels, and a trio of golden eagles. The predators paced on their perches, wings stirring the air. When he reached Malcolm, Alexander doffed his bonnet and revealed a pate as bare as the pinnacles of The Storr. Still squinting, he looked in Malcolm's general direction. "I only brought the message, my lord. 'Twas not my place to interrogate your guest."

"Guest?" Malcolm laughed. The wide-eyed and downy owlet peeped for more food. Smiling, Malcolm tore another piece of meat from the carcass and fed it to the eager bird. "Tell the lady Alpin I'm busy. And report to me the moment Saladin returns from Aberdeenshire."

Alexander eyed the owl with wary curiosity. "To be sure, the sentry will signal at the first sight of the Moorish lad. But Lady Alpin, she also said if you wilna come, she'll change her mind about forgiving you for what you did to her years ago in the tower room."

"She'll forgive *me?* Blessed Saint Ninian, she's twisted the events of the past. Send her on her way to her kin in Sinclair."

"Aye, sir. England's the place for her kind." Alexander strolled out the door and closed it behind him.

Sinclair Manor, a short hour's ride away, south of Malcolm's Scottish holdings and beyond Hadrian's Wall. In England. Alpin would hate it there. She always had. Only now she couldn't don the clothing of a bootboy and seek sanctuary here in Malcolm's Border fortress. As a lad he'd borne the brunt of her wrath. He'd been seven years old and she six when she was justly deemed uncontrollable and exiled to the island of Barbados. Years of separation had dulled the enmity Malcolm felt toward her. But five years ago when he learned of her disloyalty to her island guardian, Malcolm had put in motion the wheels of revenge.

Long ago she had taken from him his heart's desire. Now he'd taken hers.

A grinding ache, bone deep and soul scouring, held Malcolm immobile. Sensitive to his moods, the birds grew restless, their deadly talons clicking on perches of rough-hewn oak. The worried owl tried to draw her chick beneath a protective wing. Malcolm felt cheated, self-betrayed, for he made a practice of leaving his cares outside this dark sanctuary. Today he'd brought them inside with him.

He'd also maneuvered Alpin MacKay into a corner. Since receiving word of Charles's death, Malcolm had expected news of Alpin's return to the Borders. In a week or so he'd pay a call on her at the home of his English neighbor. Then he'd watch Alpin squirm like a mouse impaled on a claw.

Secretly pleased, he forced away the old pain and spoke reassuringly to the distressed owl.

The door swung open. Sunlight flooded the room, making the owl hiss and the kestrel squawk. The owlet pecked Malcolm's finger. He drew back his hand, his senses fixed on the figure of a woman standing in the doorway.

"Hello, Malcolm." Her panniered skirt almost filling the opening, her features obscured by the brightness of the light, Alpin MacKay stepped into Malcolm's private haven.

Darkness settled over the mews again. Malcolm watched her blink, trying to focus her eyes. Alpin's expertise lay in deceit and avarice. Which would she practice first?

Despite his memory of past injustices, Malcolm couldn't help but admire the pleasant changes that had occurred in his childhood nemesis.

He remembered a scrawny hoyden nicknamed "runt" with a grudge against the world, her matted hair trailing to her waist, and a spotting of freckles like measles dotting her nose and cheeks. Alpin MacKay had matured into a vision of petite femininity. No taller than his chest, she looked small enough for him to carry on his hip, her neck slender enough for him to circle with one hand.

She wore a gown of sunny yellow satin, the bodice cut square across the top and dropping to a point below her narrow waist. Her dress was modest, but even a monk's robe could not have hidden the bountiful charms of Alpin MacKay.

"Where are you, Malcolm? I can't see." Her alluring violet eyes surveyed the mews. "Say something so I can find you."

The rich, husky timbre of her voice also seemed at odds with the caviling shrew he was certain she'd become. But he'd changed, too, as she would soon discover.

He tossed the rabbit carcass to the watchful mother owl, then walked to the door. "I'm here, Alpin." He touched her elbow.

She jumped back, her skirts tipping over an empty bucket. "Oh!" Delicate fingers curled around his forearm. "Please don't let me fall."

As a child she had always smelled of the food she'd filched and the animals she'd rescued. As a woman she smelled of sweet, exotic flowers blossoming in the tropical sun. The idea that anything about Alpin MacKay would please him shocked Malcolm more than her presence in his sanctuary. She should have gone to Sinclair Manor to await the return of the uncle she hated. Events of late had left her nowhere else to go. Malcolm had planned it that way.

"I doubt you'll fall," he said. "You were always nimble on your feet."

She laughed, tipped back her head, and squinted up at him. "That was before stays, skirts as big as hayricks, and modern shoes. Are you standing on a box?"

"A box?"

Her expression softened, but her eyes were still adjusting to the darkness. "Either that or you've grown as tall as an oak."

He stared at the crown of her head and the thick coil of braids she'd made of her hair. Wisps of mahogany-hued ringlets framed her face. "You don't seem to have grown at all."

She pursed her lips. "I expected a more original observation from you, Malcolm Kerr. A kinder one, too."

She could expect whatever the hell she wanted, but James III would sit on the throne of the British Isles before she'd get honest pleasantries from Malcolm Kerr. "Why, I wonder," he mused, "for kindness was never the way between us."

"Because—because we've known each other for so long."

"A circumstance," he murmured, "that brought me great heartache and other assorted pains as a lad."

"Oh, come now." She leaned into him, her shoulder pressing against his ribs. "Surely after more than twenty years you've outgrown your hatred of me. I've certainly outgrown playing tricks on you."

Tricks? She had a gift for understatement. "But you haven't outgrown threats, unless carving out my eyes and feeding them to badgers is your usual way of greeting an old acquaintance."

She bristled with indignation, a trait she'd mastered before she lost her milk teeth. "You are *not* an acquaintance. You're my oldest friend. And I was only jesting."

"I'm relieved, then," he mocked and threw open the door. Shielding his eyes from the sunlight, he stepped outside. Alpin's closed carriage stood across the castle yard. A group of curious children had gathered around the conveyance. Releasing her, Malcolm turned and plunged his arms into a barrel of rainwater so cool it chilled his anger. He began scrubbing his hands. "It's nice of you to visit. You had a pleasant voyage?"

"Visit?" Lifting her chin, she cupped her hands over her eyes to shield them from the sun. "I've come all the way from Barbados to see you, which I haven't had the opportunity to actually do, what with the darkness in there and the sunshine out here, and all you have to say is some insipid nicety before sending me off?" A sheen of tears glistened in her eyes. "I'm wounded, Malcolm. And perplexed."

Guilt pricked his conscience. He hadn't witnessed the trouble she'd caused in Barbados, and Charles hadn't supplied the details. Malcolm believed it, though, for Alpin MacKay could turn a May fair into a bloody feud. But this snip of a woman couldn't threaten him now. Since his father's elevation to marquess of Lothian, Malcolm, as earl, ruled all of Kildalton and half of Northumberland. His enemies feared him. His clansmen respected him. Alpin MacKay, the woman, suddenly intrigued him. "I had no intention of wounding you."

She smiled and rubbed her eyes. "I'm relieved," she said in a rush. "I have a million questions to ask you and at least that many stories of my own to bore you with. You can't believe how different Barbados is—" She stopped, her eyes wide in surprise.

"What's amiss?" he said, thinking he'd never seen a woman with lashes so long and skin so sweetly kissed by the sun. He knew her age to be twenty-seven. She looked nineteen. Where had her freckles gone?

"My God," she breathed, her gaze scouring his face. "You're the image of my Night Angel."

Malcolm's admiration turned to puzzlement. "Night Angel. Who's that?"

She stared at the old tiltyard, concentration evident in the pucker of her chin, the crease in her forehead. Then she shook her head as if clearing her thoughts. "'Tis nothing but my memory deceiving me. Your hair's so dark and—and yet you favor Lord Duncan."

At the mention of his father, Malcolm thought again about the misery this selfish woman had visited on everyone who had ever befriended her. But now was not the time to reveal his feelings or his plans for Alpin MacKay. Now was the time to bait a line with friendship and go fishing for her trust. "Mother would certainly agree that I favor Papa."

"You mean Lady Miriam. How is she?"

Thinking of the gracious woman who'd indulged his childhood fantasies and encouraged him to become his own man, Malcolm smiled. "My stepmother is still the fairest of women."

Alpin turned to the castle entrance, excitement dancing in her unusual eyes. "Is she here?"

"Nay. She and Papa are in Constantinople."

"I'm disappointed. She was always kind to me. I did so want to see her. Is she still a diplomat?"

Pride and affection warmed him. "Aye. Sultan Mahmud

wants peace with Persia. He asked King George to send her."

A sigh lifted Alpin's shoulders and drew his attention to the symmetrical planes of her collarbones and the thin gold chain that disappeared into her cleavage. "Must be grand to be so valued," she said. "Imagine the king asking favors."

The soldiers on the wall had turned to stare. The fletcher stood in the doorway of his shop conversing with Alexander Lindsay. Passersby slowed, their curious gazes darting from their laird to his lovely visitor. Malcolm reached for a towel. "I think she would prefer a sojourn in Bath to a summer in Byzantium."

"I prefer the Borders. It's wonderful to be home." Alpin scanned the battlements, then the castle towers. "Have you brothers and sisters?"

Home? He considered challenging her absurd declaration, but decided to cast out another line of cordiality. "Aye, I've three sisters."

A dimple dented her cheek. "Oh, how wonderful for you. Are they here?"

He almost laughed and revealed how peaceful his home had become without his gregarious siblings. He had no business speaking so casually to Alpin MacKay. He did have business with her, however. The very gratifying business of retribution.

He tossed the towel aside. "Nay. The eldest married the earl of Hawkesford last fall. The other two are with Mama and Papa."

Alpin threaded her arm through his and strolled across the yard, pulling him along. "I can't imagine why they'd want to leave this place."

Looking down, he could see the mounds of her breasts and a familiar Roman coin at the end of the chain. His mind fogged with hazy images of a skinny ass and stick-thin legs shinnying up the drainpipe on the castle tower. Lord, she'd changed. "You always hated Kildalton Castle."

"Oh, Malcolm. I was such an angry child." Her guileless expression softened his heart. Her lush assets had an opposite and unwelcome effect. "I had nothing, no one, back then. It seems so safe and protected here now, as if your Scottish ancestors are standing guard over everything and everyone."

"Well, aye," he found himself saying. "Kildalton Castle has a way of capturing your soul."

"See?" She hugged his arm. "I knew we were still friends, and I'll wager the gifts I brought for you and Saladin that you're a romantic at heart."

Malcolm's wariness returned. He could think of no good reason for her to befriend him, let alone his confidant, Saladin. "How did you know Saladin lived at Kildalton?"

"The two of you are the talk of Whitley Bay. Is Salvador here?"

She spoke of Saladin's twin brother. "Nay, he's with my stepmother."

Her lips pursed with regret. "I'll miss seeing him again."

She'd ever been a solitary child. Before his death her guardian in Barbados had lamented in his letters to Malcolm that he feared she'd never find a kindred spirit. Now she was destitute. What farce did she play? "You've had quite a change of heart," he said.

"Of course I have." Her hand touched his. "I'm a woman now."

He didn't need his father's fake spectacles to see how gloriously maturity had embraced her. "You used to call me a sniveling cur."

"You used to call me 'runt.'" She looked at his arms, his chest, his neck. An artless feminine smile again produced the dimple. "Don't expect me to call you names now. You're a formidable presence, Malcolm Kerr."

If he didn't know better he'd think she was flirting. The prospect both baffled and inspired him. He stared at the ancient coin. "You're an interesting surprise, Alpin MacKay."

"Oh! Do you truly think so?" She squeezed his hand and turned her attention to the row of new barracks against the castle wall. "Wasn't the butcher's shop there?"

He felt as if she was coaxing him out on a branch and

planning to hack away at the limb. With her, he knew the feeling well. Memory stirred his ire. "Aye. The butcher used to be there. You tossed his knives into the blacksmith's forge and set fire to his chopping block."

"You remember?" She shook her head and set the curls at her temples to swaying. "I was so selfish."

"Except to strays and injured beasts."

A wistful smile enhanced her youthful appearance. "I couldn't bear to see any animal hurt. What ever happened to Hattie?"

"Your three-legged rabbit?" Years ago in an attempt to win the favor of Malcolm's father, Alpin's uncle had forced her to give up her pet to Malcolm. Alpin had been so forlorn. An hour later she had rallied, and in a wickedly premeditated move she had wrecked Malcolm's future. Even now the wound smarted. "Hattie turned out to be an exceptional breeder." The irony of the subject made him grin. "Sweeper's Heath is overrun with brown rabbits."

"I'm so glad you cared for her. Thank you. Will you take me to Sweeper's Heath? I'd love to see Hattie's offspring."

Like a blow from a well-trained opponent, reality struck him. Her guardians were dead. The plantation in Barbados she had called home for over twenty years now belonged to Malcolm. But she couldn't know that. The transaction had been a private affair.

"Will you, Malcolm?"

"That depends. Why are you here now?"

New tears filled her eyes. "You mean why am I here *at last*. Oh, Malcolm. I begged Charles to send me home. There was never enough money, he said. Then after dear Adrienne died he hardly spoke at all. The rum finally killed him, you know. He did leave me a stipend. So I dashed out straightaway and bought passage on the first packet home."

"Come now, Alpin," he scoffed. "You hated the Borders."

"I hated everything and almost everyone then, or have you forgotten?" As if brushing away a pesky insect, she waved her hand. "Enough about me. I've a surprise in the carriage."

Malcolm shortened his long stride to match her quick,

determined steps. He wondered what sort of wounded creature she'd brought. As they approached the carriage he noticed the trunks and hatboxes fastened to the boot. "You haven't been to see your uncle?"

She sent him a puzzled frown. "Do you know, it never occurred to me to go to Sinclair Manor. I only thought of coming to you."

He'd schemed to return her to Sinclair Manor and under the control of the uncle she hated. If she thought to avoid her fate, she'd be disappointed, another prospect Malcolm relished. But where did she intend to stay? Surely she was just stopping by Kildalton to pay her respects. He lifted an eyebrow. "Why would you come to me?"

"Oh! I've been too bold." She ducked her head, but not before he saw a flush stain her cheeks. "Island life loosens the manners and the tongue, or so the visitors say. It's just that you and I were so close when we were young. I couldn't have survived Sinclair without knowing you were only two hours away."

Years before, she'd driven a knife into his pride. Did she think to twist it with sweet words and false sentiment? She would wither into a hag before she succeeded. "We were close all right, especially when you held a dirk to my throat and tied me to a tree." He shuddered at the thought of what had come after.

She reached for the carriage door. "Let's not squabble. I'm harmless now, I assure you."

Oh, aye, he thought, as harmless as Eve with a bushel of quinces. But he was no naive Adam, languishing in Eden and yearning for forbidden fruit. He *was* a lord of the Border, perilously trapped between Jacobite clan chiefs to the north and loyal English subjects to the south. He had not needed another pretty diversion. He'd wanted retribution. So he'd meddled in Alpin's future and reduced her alternatives to none.

"Perhaps," he said, watching her fondle the brass handle, "you would care to join me for supper before you continue on your way."

Her hand stilled; then she brought it to her side. "Con-

16

tinue on my way?" She again craned her neck to look at him. "I came to see you, Malcolm. I thought you would want that."

Oh, he did, but their meetings would be at his convenience and in her uncle's English manor house. "You can't expect to stay here at Kildalton. 'Tis unseemly. After we've eaten, I'll have Alexander escort you across the border to Sinclair."

"My staying here is unseemly?" She chuckled. "Thank you for attempting to flatter me and guard my reputation, but I've been on the shelf for so many years, I'm dusty. Unless you are concerned about *your* reputation. Have you turned out to be a rogue, Malcolm?"

He braced his hands on his hips and laughed so hard the tassels on his sporran quivered. "If I have, Alpin, you can rest assured I'll keep my lusty proclivities on a short leash. But what would a spinster be knowing about rogues?"

Her mouth dropped open, and she slapped her hand against her cheek. "It's your wife, isn't it?"

Humor vanished. The old enmity returned in full force. Because of her, he would never marry. She couldn't know that, but if the gossips in Whitley Bay had told her of Saladin's presence in Kildalton, they must also have told her that Malcolm had no wife. A situation the other clan chiefs longed to change.

Unable to meet Alpin's inquisitive gaze, he stared at the kilt-clad soldiers on the battlement. "I have yet to wed." *Thanks to you.*

"And you're so blasé about your bachelorhood. Unless . . ." Deviltry twinkled in her eyes. "You can't be waiting for me to fulfill that childish bargain we made years ago."

Memory failed him. "Which bargain?"

"You wanted a baby brother. You made me promise to give you a child. I thought 'twas a matter of spending the night alone at the inn in Bothly Green."

"I assume you now know it takes more."

Ignoring his innuendo, she said, "In exchange, you agreed not to tell your father or my uncle that I was hiding in the tower room. You reneged. They found me and sent me to Barbados."

Bitterness engulfed him. "I did not tell my father that you had run away from Sinclair Manor, nor did I tell your uncle you were here."

The intensity of her gaze captured him. "Truly?" she asked, disbelief in her husky tone.

"Truly. My father heard you in the tunnels and discovered your hiding place. You shouldn't despair at the prospect of falling under the baron's protection again."

Her confident stare and winsome smile unnerved Malcolm.

"I couldn't possibly go to Sinclair," she said. "Charles left you his plantation and all his possessions. As one of his possessions, I now belong to you."

2

"**Y**ou *belong* to me?" The voice of the ninth earl of Kildalton almost broke.

Alpin had expected to feel elation at catching him off guard, and she did. She hadn't counted on feeling admiration, hadn't anticipated the feminine yearning that pulled her stomach tight. But what woman wouldn't appreciate a man as handsome as Malcolm Kerr? Interest sparkled in his oak brown eyes, and a hint of a grin played about his lips. Lord, he could turn a nun's head.

Fearful that he would discern her reaction, Alpin thought of the eighty slaves at Paradise. They depended on her, needed her.

"You're smiling," he said. "You *want* to belong to me?"

Let him think her a meek female—for now. She shrugged. "According to Charles's will you're responsible for my welfare."

"Well, now." He smiled and folded his arms over his chest. "'Tis a truly interesting turn of events."

She couldn't contain her own surprise. "You're pleased?"

19

"But of course," he said, like a wolf wooing a lamb into slavering jaws.

His cunning tone alarmed her. In defense, she tensed and stepped away. Just as quickly, she relaxed. They were both adults now. She was not some retiring English rose pining for a notorious Scotsman with an appealing smile and an ancient title. She was a woman with a purpose and a plan.

Gossips in the port city of Whitley Bay had told her of his ascension to laird of clan Kerr and earl of Kildalton. Prior knowledge of his elevated rank was unnecessary, for Malcolm Kerr wore authority and confidence as effectively as he wore Highland dress. Gazing at his back and observing his masculine swagger, she began to believe the rumors about his easy way with women.

She moved around him. "Splendid. You can have your housekeeper show me to my rooms. Is Mrs. Elliott still with you?"

He watched her a moment more, that peculiar smile lingering on his lips and disturbing her composure. "Unfortunately no. She's in Constantinople with my parents. Since you belong to me, I'll have someone bring in your things." Over his shoulder he called out, "Alexander!"

The soldier who'd greeted Alpin hurried across the yard. Balding and a head shorter than Malcolm, the soldier wore a plaid similar to the bold red and green tartan of the Kerrs.

As he approached, a memory stirred, nudging Alpin to again remember her visits to Kildalton years before. Alexander Lindsay. That was his name.

He joined them, his mouth drawn in a disapproving pucker. She smiled and said, "Hello, Mr. Lindsay. A very long time ago you helped me bury my pet badger. Do you remember?"

He stared down at her; yet his pale blue eyes seemed distant. "Aye. We laid the toothless beast to rest in the old tiltyard."

Time had dulled that particular knife-sharp pain. Others still hurt, but none so deeply as the loss of her home, a wound inflicted by Malcolm Kerr. Thoughts of taking Paradise from him soothed the ache.

"Malcolm demanded the hide to use for a sporran," she said. "He threatened to dig up poor Abercrombie. I cried, but he wouldn't stop teasing me. You sent him to Lord Duncan for discipline and had Mrs. Elliott make me a sleeping potion."

Disarmed, Alexander swallowed hard. "A noble beast for certain, my lady."

"Lord Malcolm? A beast? I do hope not."

"Nay—" Alexander whipped his gaze to the laird of Kildalton, who chuckled.

"She's having you on, Alexander. Everyone knows I'm a lambkin at heart when it comes to the fairer sex and God's creatures." Sending Alpin a sidelong glance, he added, "Have you a lady's maid in that carriage?"

The rumble of his voice, flavored with a slight burr, reminded Alpin of her miserable childhood in the Borders. Barbados had been her salvation. Now she must find a way to convince Malcolm to return it to her.

"Yes. Her name is Elanna." Alpin knew the woman would cause a stir; she had planned it that way.

"Assist the lass, Alexander," said Malcolm. "And have someone bring in their bags."

Then he took Alpin's arm and leisurely walked across the yard and up the steps to the keep. Studying his large hand, she wondered how the reed-thin lad had grown into so magnificent a man. His broad shoulders and thick neck would rival an oarsman's. His slender waist and long, muscled legs bespoke hours spent on horseback. He'd lived a privileged life, free of worry, while she'd fretted over crops, battled disease and the forces of nature to build a secure future for herself. It wasn't fair that the fruits of her labor should fall into his hands. Codrington's explanation rang in her ears: in transferring ownership of Paradise to Malcolm, Charles had repaid a debt of gratitude. But what had Malcolm done to earn such generosity?

He opened the huge double doors and waved her inside. "You're suddenly quiet, Alpin. Why?"

His question jarred her from speculation. Inside the castle she couldn't help comparing the stone fortress, with its heavy Jacobean furniture and expansive rugs, to the airy simplicity of Paradise.

She scanned the familiar entryway, looking for a safe subject. She found it in the appointments. "I don't remember so much armor on the walls of Kildalton. Was it here before?"

"Nay." He paused to touch a worn and dented leather shield bearing a blazing sun, the emblem of clan Kerr. "After Lady Miriam ended the war between my father and your uncle, Baron Sinclair, Papa took these fighting implements from the soldiers. They've become heirlooms."

Battle axes, lances, and helmets covered the high stone walls of the entryway. Two benches with needlepoint cushions sat below the leaded windows that looked out onto the yard. Tables with urns of freshly cut heather lined one wall, tapestries depicting the May Day and a country fair graced the other. The staircase curved up to the second floor.

Light from a chandelier in the shape of a cinquefoil illuminated the room. She spied a familiar weapon. "You used to wear that sword."

He chuckled. "You mean I used to drag it around. As a lad I couldn't wait to wield it. Papa drew a mark on the wall in my room and said I could start soldiering when I was as tall as the mark. I measured myself every day until . . ."

She glanced up. He was staring down at her, his jaw clenched tight, a guarded expression in his dark brown eyes.

"Until . . . ?" Their gazes locked. "Who's quiet now, Malcolm?"

He smiled without joy. "Until I was about your height."

That wasn't what he was going to say. She was sure of it. He was hiding something. "Are you mocking me again?"

"Nay." He guided her to the stairs. "I was wondering what has made you so defensive."

Had honesty been her purpose she would have answered that it was necessity, for never in her life had anyone except the Night Angel, the avenger of her youth, bothered to take her side. As far back as she could remember, she'd been either a poor orphan with nowhere to go or a poor relation without tuppence to her name. When she finally found a home, Malcolm had fallen heir to it.

She laughed to conceal her bitterness. "Actually, I like being small, for when I trip I don't have far to fall."

"A clever rhyme."

"My lord . . . ?" A housemaid about fifteen years old approached them. The fair-haired girl had eager hazel eyes and a country-fresh complexion liberally dotted with freckles. She wore a plain brown dress so new the seams still puckered, and a starched white apron and mobcap.

"Excuse me, my lord. No one's come to apply for the position of housekeeper."

"Thank you, Dora," Malcolm said. "This is Lady Alpin. Please prepare one of the guest suites for her and her maid."

Dora bobbed a curtsy. "Which suite, my lord? With Mrs. Elliott gone, there ain't none to say."

"Alpin, you once boasted that you knew every nook and cranny of Kildalton. Have you a preference?" he said.

Sarcasm laced his words, but she ignored his reference to her skulkings in the past. "I don't remember, and I'm not particular, so long as the room has a fireplace. I'm used to sunnier climes."

"Then you shall have the sunniest and warmest rooms here." To Dora, he said, "The large suite on the second floor—where the earl of Mar always stays."

She gasped and darted a worried glance up the stairs. "There's no linens on the beds, my lord, what with Mrs. Elliott gone and the new housekeeper quittin' and all."

He tapped his teeth together for a moment. Patiently he said, "Then fetch the linens and whatever else the room needs. While you're doing that, I'll show our guest where it is."

"Aye, sir." She walked away mumbling, "Candles and towels, and plenty of peat. Oil for the lamps. Water for the basin . . ."

"After you." He extended his hand toward the stairs.

As she climbed the stone steps, Alpin passed dress shields bearing brass plates with the names of the lesser clans that

23

aligned themselves with the Kerrs: Lindsay, Elliott, Armstrong, Maxwell, Johnstone, and Ramsay. Hundreds of men swore fealty to Malcolm. They would follow him into battle should he need an army. They paid him a laird fee.

With so many contributing to his wealth, what would he do with the gift of Paradise? Surely he had no interest in a plantation half a world away. He could probably buy a score of Paradises and not put a dent in his gold chest.

She longed to ask him what he planned to do with the island property, and she would, once she'd set her plan into motion by ingratiating herself with him and insinuating herself into his life.

At the top of the stairs he ushered her to the left. A door behind them opened.

"Malcolm . . . ?"

The sultry voice stopped him. Alpin glanced over her shoulder. Her breath caught.

In an open doorway stood a woman *en déshabillé*, her arms bare, a Kerr tartan covering her from breasts to knees. Her mane of golden blond hair hung in wild disarray. Tall and lithe and perfectly comfortable with herself, she yawned.

His mistress, thought Alpin with more jealousy than she expected. Eligible bachelors of means were rare on the island of Barbados. She'd had a gentleman caller once, but Charles had been so embarrassingly drunk that the fellow had never returned. After word got out, no other man had bothered to court Alpin.

Malcolm cleared his throat. "Good afternoon, Rosina." Ruefully he added, "May I present my guest, Lady Alpin MacKay, late of Barbados."

The woman's pale eyes widened, then fastened on Alpin. Blushing, Rosina gave Malcolm an apologetic smile, murmured "How provincial," then stepped back and closed the door.

Alpin started walking again.

"I suppose you're appalled," he said.

"Hardly. I'm disappointed."

24

"You are. Why?"

"Because you're not very good at keeping promises."

He stopped in front of a door at the end of the hall, his eyebrows raised in question. "I'm not?"

"No. You promised to keep your lusty proclivities on a short leash."

A devilish smile enhanced his dark good looks. He bent from the waist, his shoulder-length black hair grazing his cheek. "What length *leash* would suit you?"

He was saying one thing and meaning something else. She didn't know him well enough to understand either. For some reason she looked at the door where the woman had been, then at the door before her. "I'm not sure. Perhaps a furlong."

He chuckled. "I could make a bit of mischief and more with so mighty a leash."

Feeling out of her depth, she took the offensive. "Making mischief always was your strong suit."

"Just as teaching me to kiss was yours."

Outrage barreled through her. "That's hogwash, Malcolm Kerr. Every time I saw you, you tried to paste your sloppy lips on me!"

Calmly he said, "You started it."

"I did not!"

"Aye, you did." Leaning against the door, he folded his arms over his chest. "'Twas Adrienne's birthday party. You were five. I was six. You'd seen her kissing Charles and talked me into trying it with you. I liked it and tried to recapture the experience numerous times."

His recollection reminded her that they'd once been friends. But not for long. "According to rumor, you've made a vocation of kissing any woman who'll let you."

A rakish grin gave credence to his vile reputation. "Just don't forget 'twas you who lured me onto the path of sin."

Delivered with quiet intensity, the sermonlike words made her laugh. "Go ahead, Malcolm. Condemn me for your ill-gotten fame. Just remember. Only one of us enjoys sloppy kisses."

All his humor vanished. "No man has ever made you feel desire?"

No man had bothered to come close enough, she almost yelled. Her experience with kissing had begun and ended with Malcolm Kerr. The confession sounded so pitiful she wanted to cry. His concern seemed so earnest she looked away. "Is this my room?"

"Alpin . . ." he entreated softly. "You're dissembling."

Putting as much scorn into her voice as she could muster, she said, "Oh, please, Malcolm. Unlike you, I don't reveal the details of my affairs or flaunt them before strangers."

He pushed open the door. "Of course. How indiscreet of me, a stranger, to ask."

She glided past him. "Indiscretion. Another of your sterling qualities."

"Why do I doubt you're as prim and proper as you let on?"

Even with her back to him, she felt his keen gaze and had the strangest notion that she had unwittingly challenged him. The possibility gave her pause. At length she faced him and said, "Because you wouldn't know prim-and-proper if it crawled into your sporran."

His eyes narrowed and he looked into his chieftain's pouch. "Prim-and-proper would never crawl in here."

Aghast, she said, "I should slap you."

"But you won't. Make yourself at home, Alpin. Should you decide about the length of that leash, I'll be in my study."

More annoyed with herself than with him, Alpin stifled the urge to slam the door in his face. Putting on a sweet smile, she closed the door. Her suite contained a sitting room, a bedchamber and privy, and a smaller room for her maid.

She walked to the open windows and sighed with relief.

Moments after her arrival she'd feared Malcolm might send her away. Through careful maneuvering she'd ensconced herself in his household and found living proof of his scandalous reputation. Lucky for her and her cause, he'd be so preoccupied with his lusty proclivities and his gorgeous mistress that Alpin would be free to put into motion the next step in her plan.

She gazed down on the castle yard and smiled. A gapemouthed Alexander helped Alpin's maid from the carriage. Battle-hardened soldiers, laundry maids, and even the children of Kildalton stared in disbelief at Elanna.

His mind a muddle of conflicting thoughts, Malcolm stared at the bar of sunlight seeping beneath the door to Alpin's room.

Alpin's room. In my own castle.

Having her here meant he could make her life miserable on a daily basis. He could avenge the stinging blow she'd dealt him so long ago. The prospect should have made him smile. But the moment their conversation had turned to the innocent, fumbling kisses they'd shared as children, he'd sensed a vulnerability in her. Did she pine for an island beau or had she been truthful when she claimed to have had affairs?

He tried to picture her writhing naked with a man, the nipples of her luscious breasts standing at pert attention, the lavender of her eyes darkening with desire. But he realized he knew little about the woman she'd become, wouldn't know the truth from a lie on her lips. In his occasional letters Charles had seldom mentioned her; the grief-stricken widower had been consumed by the loss of his wife.

He put aside his confusion; now that she belonged to him he had all the time he needed to learn about Alpin MacKay.

He remembered her shock at seeing the nearly nude Rosina standing in the open doorway of his bedchamber. Petulant and eager to return to her native Italy, Rosina had taken her anger out on his staff.

His patience grew thin. Same as his mistresses before her, Rosina was supposed to have stayed at Carvoran Manor, his estate near Hadrian's Wall. But the moment his father and Lady Miriam had left for Constantinople, Rosina had moved into Kildalton. He usually shared this castle with his

27

parents and his younger half sisters; he simply didn't want Rosina intruding on his privacy or influencing his impressionable siblings.

Rosina was an accommodating and inventive bedmate, and she served a necessary role in the current political problems, but as a constant companion she bored him to tears and disrupted his household. Eager to lessen the complications of his life by one, he went to his bedchamber.

He found her lounging naked on his bed, practicing one of her more seductive moves. She trailed a long tapered fingernail from her thigh to her navel.

Smiling, she stretched her arms over her head. Holding the submissive pose, she purred, "Come back to bed, my lord. I find I like it here."

The old hunger roiled in his gut and lower.

He stared at her navel and the webwork of tiny lines, a memento of the stillborn child she'd borne her former lover. She'd bear no bastards for Malcolm. Alpin MacKay had seen to that.

He walked to the bed and sat, the mattress shifting beneath his weight. The heady smells of the past night's lovemaking blended with her signature scent: roses. She even tasted like freshly crushed petals. "As much as I would enjoy whiling away the day, I cannot."

Rolling to her side, she bent one knee, giving him an unobstructed view of her femininity. "You're angry with me because I dismissed the housekeeper yesterday."

He was angry, but taking her to task always proved futile.

"Only a fool would call my mood angry, Rosina, especially after the dessert you fed me last night."

She cuddled her cheek against her shoulder. "You kept me awake until dawn." Her hand dipped lower. "But I'm rested now."

Temptation dragged at him. He had assizes to conduct. Judgments could wait until tomorrow. Saladin *could* return today. If so, Malcolm could hear the report at supper. Alpin would be at the table. Alpin.

Rosina reached for his hand. "You'll find another housekeeper," she said without a trace of an accent.

She struck a nerve, but the argument was old and unwinnable. Rosina wouldn't lift a finger. "I could use your help these days."

She huffed and indignantly challenged, "Do you want a mistress, a clerk, or a housekeeper, my lord?"

He almost confessed that he wanted all three—and more. But he knew well the difference between dreams and reality.

"What I want, Rosina, is for you to return to Carvoran Manor. Alexander will take you there."

Anger flared in her eyes. "I think I shall return to that rustic hunting lodge you call a manor." She jumped from the bed and strolled naked across the room. When she reached the washstand, she picked up the water pitcher and shook it. "This is empty. There are no clean towels, and that lazy Dora hasn't brought me anything to eat."

With no housekeeper, Malcolm needed someone to take the staff in hand. With Alpin MacKay here—He stopped the thought. A solution blazed in his mind.

Rising from the bed, he walked to the door. "I'll tell Alexander to saddle your horse. You'll have to pack yourself."

Rosina stared, her shoulders slumped. "You're truly sending me away?"

"Aye." He opened the door.

"What about the messages Saladin brings from the north?"

"I'll bring them to you, as always."

Cupping her hands beneath her breasts as if offering them to him, she said, "Will I see you before then?"

Under normal circumstances he would have taken her in his arms. Instead, he lied. "Of course. You're too beautiful to leave to your own devices."

"Devices?" she hissed.

He stepped into the hall and pulled the door closed just as the pitcher crashed against it.

Alexander stood at the top of the stairs. "The lass is in a temper."

"She'll get over it. Take her back to Carvoran Manor, and send her a bolt of blue China silk and a case of sherry."

Alexander toyed with a carved thistle that decorated the wooden banister. "Aye, my lord, but there's something you ought to know. . . ."

Past surprises and short on patience, Malcolm again lamented the absence of Mrs. Elliott. At least he could depend on her. "What is it, Alexander? And if you tell me the men are complaining because the neeps 'n' tatties were cold or the mutton tough, I'll put them to clearing fields."

That brought a smile to the soldier's face. Standing straighter, he hooked his thumbs in the belt that secured his kilt. "'Tis Lady Alpin's maid. She's . . . ah . . . not what you'd expect."

A commotion sounded on the stairs. Malcolm walked to the landing, but stopped in his tracks.

Gliding up the stairs was the most unusual woman he'd ever seen on Scottish soil. Standing as tall as Alexander, the maid wore a gathered skirt and full-sleeved tapered bodice of cotton batiste dyed yellow with bold slashes of red and blue. A matching turban covered most of her black hair. Atop the turban she carried a small barrel.

On the landing, she curtsied and inclined her head, her swanlike neck making the simple gesture of obeisance an exercise in grace. So keen was her balance, the keg barely moved.

Stupefied, Malcolm studied her ebony skin and deep brown eyes, his mind awash with thoughts of his friend Saladin. What would the Moor say when he returned to find a nubile African woman in Kildalton Castle?

Considering the chaos his own life had become, the answer made Malcolm smile. "You are Elanna, I believe."

"Betcha that. The gods, they sing happy, happy song on the day I was born."

Her speech contained a number of accents; beneath the musical quality of her Barbadian English, he heard a clipped, guttural sound. "I hope you aren't homesick for Barbados."

"I am Ashanti," she said, lifting her chin. Then she held out the barrel. "I make you a gift of the water of Barbados."

Alexander intercepted the barrel, tucking it under his arm as if it were a sack of wheat.

"You were born in Africa?"

She stood as still as a statue. "Same as many Ashanti girl children, I was stolen from my people. In Barbados market, Bimshire Charles bought me from a slave trader."

Fascinated by her innate pride, Malcolm said, "What is Bimshire?"

"Bajan name for Englishman."

"Bajan is the language of Barbados?"

"You plenty smart white man."

According to Charles, Alpin had badly botched the matter of freeing the slaves at Paradise Plantation five years ago. Since she obviously owned this woman, Malcolm read the worst into the vagary. Alpin had been disloyal.

Thinking of the number of women in his household, he decided to put aside his curiosity over Alpin and Elanna until Rosina was gone. "You'll find your mistress at the end of the hall."

He motioned toward Alpin's room, then made his way to the solitude of his study. Saladin would return to find a woman of his own race at Kildalton. One look at her and the chaste Moor would lose his heart.

Grateful that he would never fall prey to love, Malcolm eased into his favorite chair. His thoughts strayed to his favorite pastime: the domination of Alpin MacKay.

Alpin hung the last of her dresses in the wardrobe, her attention focused on the back panel of the clothes closet. She rapped lightly with her knuckles until the sound rang hollow. Then she searched for the latch that would open the door to one of the many hidden tunnels in Kildalton Castle. Her fingers touched metal. Applauding herself, she slid the panel aside and peered into darkness. The musty smell brought back memories of her childhood.

"Why you always call that Lord Malcolm a sniveling cur?" demanded Elanna. "He's a mighty pretty man."

Shelving thoughts of her lonely past, Alpin closed the

panel and turned to her friend. "His looks don't change what he is. A scoundrel."

"Betcha that." Elanna leaned over the bed and peered up at the canopy. "Nice needleworking here. You tell me what he was like before the mischief gods took his soul."

Objectivity didn't come easy to Alpin, especially where Malcolm was concerned. But her friend deserved an honest answer. "He was actually a sweet lad who hated his name."

Elanna paused in her inspection of the mattress. "What does 'Malcolm' mean?"

"He's named for a former king of Scotland."

She sat on the feather tick. "You said Alpin was also the name of a Scottish king. This is true, too?"

"Yes. We were both named for rulers of this land."

Elanna shook her head. "Fancify that."

"'Tis the only thing we have in common. And as a child, Malcolm refused to answer to his name."

"What did they call him?"

"A different name for every day of the week. He would read about famous men in history—kings or philosophers, warriors or monks. Then he would choose one and become that man for the day—even down to his clothes."

Picking up her leather case, Elanna put it on the bed and opened the latch. "You mean fancy pants and curly white wigs?"

Alpin remembered the day he'd pretended to be Charles I. Refusing a wig, Malcolm had worn a paper crown. At the time she'd run away from Sinclair Manor and was living in secret in the tower room. No one suspected her presence at Kildalton, because she ventured out of the secret tunnels only at night. "No. I don't recall him ever wearing a wig. He once chose Caesar, though. You should have seen him wrapped in a sheet and wearing a crown of rowan leaves."

Elanna tossed sacks of herbs onto the bed. "You sing happy, happy song about those times."

"Yes. I liked him," she said, and meant it, now that she knew he wasn't the one who had told her uncle where she was hiding years before. "But that was long ago. Now he's a greedy, self-serving wretch."

Waving a bundle of dried sticks, Elanna said, "You could dose him with my squat-in-the-bushes tea."

Alpin laughed. Elanna had an herbal concoction for everything from a broken heart to a wandering eye. "Perhaps I will." Then an idea struck her, a way to secure Malcolm's trust and her future.

She walked to the bed. "Did you bring the ingredients for your come-to-me sauce?"

Elanna's dark eyes glittered with interest. "Betcha that. I brought plenty." Then her excitement faded. "It's no good without fresh figs or mangoes to hide the bitter taste. I only brought dried fruit."

"Will berries do?"

Elanna shrugged. "Maybe so. We could make a juice."

An aphrodisiac for Malcolm would suit Alpin's plans.

3

Malcolm sat in his study, the now cold midday meal before him on a tray. He sawed at the braised rabbit, but no matter how small he cut the pieces, the meat was still too tough to chew. The brown bread would have been a welcome change, but only to a sailor six months at sea.

Giving up on the hare, he stuck his fork into a glob of what could have been perfectly cooked pearl barley or horribly overdone peas. He braved a taste and discovered barley with too little onion and too much salt and nutmeg. Nutmeg! His tongue grew quills.

Reaching for a mug of beer, he washed down the lumpy mess and cursed Rosina for running off another housekeeper. His stomached growled. At the rate he was eating, he might as well share Saladin's Muslim fare. But a diet of nuts, berries, vegetables, and rice did little to quell his hunger.

He'd have traded his herd of fat Spanish cattle for a banquet of roast suckling pig, baked quinces, potatoes with parsley and butter, crusty bread, and a trifle big enough to fill a bucket. For that he'd have to wait until his parents and

Mrs. Elliott returned. His mouth watering in vain, he slammed down the mug, pushed away from the table, and began to pace the study.

Like his father, grandfather, and all the previous earls of Kildalton, he conducted the commerce of his kingdom from this room. On Malcolm's twenty-first birthday, his father, now the marquess of Lothian, had abdicated his lesser titles, then retired to a life of diplomacy and making his marchioness happy.

As a lad, Malcolm had basked in the glow of his father's and his stepmother's love. By example, they'd shown him the closeness a man and a woman could share, the mutual respect, the ability to forgive and forget. Alpin had cheated him of the chance to have a family of his own. He was destined to be a bachelor forever.

Even so, as a youth, Malcolm had prowled the better drawing rooms of Edinburgh, London, and Paris on a futile search for a woman and helpmate of his own to love. But when none of his mistresses conceived, he faced the grim truth that he would never wed. Only dishonesty would gain him a bride. He could not live with that bit of fraud.

A familiar sadness pulled at him. He stared at his boots and noticed a worn spot in the rug. Three times he'd witnessed his father pacing this very floor when Lady Miriam had begun the travail of childbirth. He'd seen tears of both joy and relief in his father's eyes when each of Malcolm's half sisters had been delivered safely. Their hungry wails still echoed in Malcolm's ears. Of late, he could certainly sympathize.

He strolled to the wall housing a succession of family portraits. The latest featured the entire family. The first pictured Malcolm, his father, and a very pregnant Lady Miriam.

The years had passed and Malcolm's father never pressured him to find a wife. So he'd settled cynically into the role of bachelor earl. Lairds of Scotland's finest clans, eager for an alliance with the Kerrs, paraded their marriageable daughters before him. He put on a show of playing the marriage game, but Malcolm couldn't deceive the innocent girls who honestly wanted a husband to give them children. The sad and secret truth was that the ninth earl of Kildalton couldn't provide the tenth.

But perhaps—He halted the thought. Now was not the time to embrace a futile dream. The northern clans bristled under the stern and unfair rule of George II and turned their attention toward Italy and the exiled James Stewart. "The king across the water," they hailed him, and styled themselves Jacobites in his name. If the Hanoverian currently occupying the throne of the British Isles didn't show more concern for the welfare of his Highland subjects, Scotland was in for trouble that could make the Battle of Flodden look like a petty squabble.

A Lowlander and laird of the Borders, Malcolm felt squeezed between the two factions. He couldn't take sides. His birth mother had been English and had willed him her dower lands, a substantial portion of Northumberland. He couldn't turn a blind eye to his English subjects. Neither could he turn his back on his Scottish kinsmen. So he performed the most neutral service he could: he kept Rosina, the Italian mistress, who spoke fluent Scottish and ferried messages between the Highland clans and their estranged monarch.

No one suspected Malcolm's involvement. For decades his family had sold salt to the Highlands. Each time his friend Saladin took a load of the precious commodity north, he also passed letters to the Jacobites and accepted their replies, which Rosina then delivered to James Stewart either in Rome or at his summer estate in Albano.

When Saladin returned from this latest trip, Malcolm would carefully lift the seals, read the correspondence, make notes, and advise his stepmother accordingly. He would not be an unwitting partner to treason. He would interfere only if the clans began to speak of war. Still, if he were caught in the act, he would be hanged for a traitor and his estates forfeited to the Crown.

A knock sounded at the door. It was probably Alexander bringing word that either Saladin had been spotted by the lookout or Rosina had been returned to Carvoran Manor. Malcolm said, "Come in, but only if you've got a leg of mutton and a mountain of fresh haggis."

Alpin breezed into the room. She'd changed into a full-skirted pink gown with lace trim at the rounded neckline and on the short puffy sleeves. The springtime color complemented the honey hue of her skin. She'd be a scandal in Edinburgh or London, for proper young ladies avoided the sun. But then, Alpin MacKay had never been one for convention.

Her gaze fell on the table. She smiled and, with mock severity, said, "Now, why would you be wanting more food, Malcolm? You've hardly touched what's on your plate."

His empty stomach growled again. "My stepmother's sleuthhound wouldn't touch this fare. But try it, if you've the courage."

Her chin came up a notch. Malcolm applauded himself; she could never refuse a dare.

She tore off a piece of the hare, popped it into her mouth, and began to chew. Her eyes grew wide, and she almost gagged, reminding him of the time as children they'd hidden beneath a banquet table and sampled caviar.

She swallowed and wiped her hands on his napkin. "I take it your cook hates you."

"She loves me like a son, but she's gone to Constantinople."

She looked down at the tray, but not before Malcolm saw her eyes light with interest. What was she thinking? That he might die of starvation? Probably so.

Picking up the bread, she tapped it on the pewter plate. It sounded like a hammer on an anvil. "I'm surprised Rosina doesn't take better care of you."

He almost said that Rosina's talents lay abovestairs, but despite his distrust of Alpin, he couldn't bring himself to embarrass her with so crude a remark. Besides, he honestly didn't think she would understand sophisticated sexual banter. "Rosina has left us as well."

She moved from the table to the bookcase and leaned

close to read the titles on the leather-bound spines. "Then the subject of you leashing your lusty proclivities is moot—unless you have another mistress hiding somewhere."

Malcolm choked with laughter, thinking that the wicked lass had become a clever woman. But just how clever? And how many affairs had she truly had? He searched for a lover's mark, but found none. She didn't carry herself with the same feminine assurance he'd seen in kept women.

"Did I say something wrong?" she asked.

"Nay. I'm more concerned with keeping my belly filled and preventing mutiny among my clansmen."

"Mutiny?"

"Aye. The men are hungry for a decent meal. Tell me, can you manage a household, Alpin?"

She pulled out one of the books and opened it. With her fingernail she scraped a glob of old candle wax off the page. "I remember reading this story when I was hiding here years ago." A wistful smile made her look even younger. "It's about a goblin that snatches up children who refuse to go to bed." Her expression turned grim. She snapped the book shut and returned it to the shelf. "I'm sorry I got wax on the page of your book."

Malcolm pictured her at six years old, huddled in the windowless tower room of Kildalton Castle, a candle in one hand, a monster story in the other. Sympathy swamped him.

"Lord," she said, "I was a fanciful child."

She'd been cruel and spiteful to everyone who crossed her path—even those who tried to help her. "Fanciful?" he challenged. "You dumped soot in the flour bin."

She frowned and scratched her temple with unfeigned surprise. "Did I? I don't remember that."

What she'd done as a child he intended to avenge. Her past misdeeds could be an effective weapon, but he mustn't let them overshadow the recent crimes of a selfish woman who had no respect for human beings. "You haven't answered me. Can you manage a household as large as Kildalton?"

Her eyes met his. "Yes. As soon as you present the servants to me."

The reply reeked of honesty and confidence. He could help her by introducing her to the servants. He could threaten to dismiss any who dared to gainsay her. He could make her life easier, but he wouldn't.

"Dora can show you where the stores are kept," he said, "and acquaint you with the staff, such as it is . . . later."

She continued to peruse the bookcase, but stopped when she noticed a bell hanging from a cord about a foot over her head. "What's that?" she asked.

It was a contraption his father had devised years ago when he'd caught Malcolm snooping in the secret tunnel behind the bookcase. The bell was tied to a fishing line that was attached to the tunnel entrance, a door near the lesser hall, twenty-five feet away. Malcolm answered her with a lie, saying, "It's a Mecca bell. When Saladin made his pilgrimage he brought it back for my father."

She crossed the room and lifted herself up on the window seat. Her tiny slippered feet and delicate ankles dangled below layers of lace-trimmed petticoats. She folded her hands in her lap. "You used to tell stories about all of the things you'd do when you became the earl. Is it what you expected? Have you accomplished all you wanted to do?"

Surprised by her interest, Malcolm picked up the tankard and drank. Through the glass bottom of the mug he could see his plate and the stringy rabbit. "Being at peace with my English neighbors enables me to put my energies into the commerce of Kildalton." Dissatisfaction among the Highland clans complicated his life, but he didn't feel comfortable telling Alpin about Scottish problems.

"You must involve yourself with the tenants," she said. "I've never seen such prosperous farms in the Borders. I remember the people being poor—at least those between here and my uncle's property in England."

He felt a deep sense of pride in his accomplishments, yet he spoke offhandedly. "We've worked to breed better and stronger draft horses, fatter cattle, and we import Spanish steel for scythes and plowshares."

Again she scratched her temple. "Spanish steel," she

murmured, her eyes distant. "It's worth the extra price? It doesn't rust and it keeps a sharp edge?"

Amused by her interest, he took a knife from his desk. Drawing the blade from the leather sheath, he handed it to her. "Be careful," he said, stepping back. "You might cut yourself."

She grasped the bone handle and tested the blade with her thumb. Her eyebrows rose in surprise, and she let out a soft whistle. "In Barbados, we use a big knife called a machete to harvest the cane."

"We?"

Her brows fell. As haughty as a duchess, she said, "I mean the slaves do, of course." She quickly sheathed the blade and pitched it to him.

He put up his hand and caught the knife, the leather casing slapping against his palm. She had a strong arm and an excellent aim. But then, Alpin had been deceptively robust as a child. Even now he doubted she weighed much more than six stone. But was she still deceptive and conniving? He intended to learn everything about her, from her plans for the future to the name of her exotic fragrance. "Tell me more about the sugarcane and your life in Barbados. Frankly, I'm surprised you didn't meet some dashing sea captain and marry there."

Mischief, or perhaps anger, flashed in her eyes. Then she laughed and flattened her palms on the window seat. Bracing her arms, she tipped back her head and studied the stuccoed ceiling. "Most of the eligible Englishmen who came to the island were second or third sons without a farthing to their name. They gambled or speculated with what little they had. Few of them made a successful go at anything more than betting on a winning cock."

Seeing her posed as she was, Malcolm had an unobstructed view of her slender neck. Suddenly he thought those second and third sons foolish. Still, she had professed to having affairs, in the plural. He couldn't resist saying, "Did you ever wager on a cock?"

She stiffened. "Ladies do not attend cockfights."

"If Alpin MacKay has grown into a proper lady, the Hanoverian king is fluent in Scottish."

She laughed. "I truly am a lady."

"I see." Mature? Aye, she was that, but he doubted she acted like a lady. "You used to wear breeches and ride bareback."

She grew serious, her eyes luminous, her lips softly parted. "I also used to live in the stables at Sinclair Manor, or have you forgotten that?"

Taken aback, he returned the knife to a drawer in his desk. "I thought you preferred your menagerie of wounded creatures to your cousins."

"I traded one set of creatures for another. That's why I ran away and came here."

She'd made Malcolm's life a living hell and had sown the seeds that would destroy his future. He buried the old hurt behind a halfhearted smile. "I caught you stealing food from our kitchen."

She shivered and rolled her eyes. "I was so frightened I almost wet myself that night. You said they would hang me and use my ears for fish bait."

"It was the only time I had the upper hand with you, as I recall."

Blinking, she said, "Is that truly what you believe?"

Some of their childhood confrontations did seem humorous now, as he looked back on them, and he took a moment to wonder if he wasn't planning to deal too harshly with her. "What do you believe?"

Then she leaned forward and, over the rustling of her petticoats, said, "I *know* that you held me down and kissed me, and you made me promise to give you a child."

Like the waning sunlight outside the window, his objectivity faded. "Rest assured, that's one promise you'll never keep, Alpin."

Her inquisitive gaze roamed his face, his neck, and his legs. A flush stole up her cheeks. "I never presumed that you expected me to . . . that we would . . . that . . ." Flustered, she toyed with the gold cord on the drapes.

Amused by her discomfiture, he blithely said, "What did you never presume?"

Palms up, she opened her mouth, then closed it. At last she said, "That we would consummate the promise. I'm here because, as usual, I have nowhere else to go, Malcolm. Charles knew that when he transferred the plantation to you."

"How did you find that out? 'Twas supposed to be a private transaction between men."

"But it concerned me. Charles assumed you would do the honorable thing and make me your ward. We could be friends. I've even agreed to become your housekeeper." More forcefully she added, "I will not accept charity or be a burden to you."

Damn. He hated feeling guilty. All contrition, he said, "How can I call you a burden if you earn your own way?"

She swallowed, her gaze darting from the globe to the desk to the tray of inedible food. "Very well. I suppose we should discuss my salary."

Malcolm hadn't considered compensating her. He had other plans where she was concerned. "Since you belong to me, as you so vividly put it, I'm responsible for clothing you and furnishing whatever essentials you need."

She swung her feet. The gesture made her seem endearingly young. "The same as you do for Mrs. Elliott?"

Affronted by the analogy, he said, "I hardly provide Mrs. Elliott with silk gowns or a dressmaker to sew them."

She plucked at the skirt. "It's cotton, not silk. And Elanna will make my gowns and hers."

The black woman. "I must say I'm disappointed that you perpetuate the institution of slavery. I had expected more humanity from you."

Her eyes narrowed, and she knotted her fists so tightly her knuckles gleamed white. "I detest slavery, and anyone who says differently is a miserable liar. Elanna is a freedwoman."

Malcolm had misinterpreted Charles's vague reference to Alpin causing trouble over the slaves in Barbados. If she was to be believed, she and Charles had differed on the slavery issue. Malcolm realized he'd gotten their positions cross-wise; Charles was the one who had favored slavery.

Well, Malcolm decided, at least Alpin had one redeeming quality. "Did you persuade Charles to free her?"

Again, her eyes met his. "Yes. In lieu of several years' salary as his housekeeper. Elanna will earn her way."

Knowing a slave could sell for as much as twelve hundred pounds, Malcolm figured Charles was either very foolish or very malleable. But neither rang true, for according to the records and the bank drafts the lawyer Codrington regularly sent to Malcolm, the plantation had made a handsome profit every year for the past decade. The last harvest proved particularly fruitful; Malcolm had used the proceeds to build a new bridge over the river Tyne. "Charles was a generous guardian."

"I'm a very good housekeeper." Her grin gave him a peek at her dimples. "I trust you'll pay me accordingly."

Malcolm felt he had little choice in the matter, and yet the idea of paying her, the woman who had made his life miserable, rankled. He was a Scotsman, though, and knew how to be thrifty. "I'll pay you fifty pounds a year."

"Two hundred," she said, as serious as a tinker with only one skillet in his wagon. "Plus a suitable wardrobe."

He took the few steps that separated them. Towering over her, he said, "One hundred."

Seemingly unperturbed, she said, "One fifty and any essentials I may require. The wardrobe, of course. Sundays for my own and a free week each year beginning on my birthday. And the stipend Charles left me."

If she could haggle as successfully with the butcher, she might save Malcolm money. "You will pay your own maid."

"Of course. I always have."

"Done." He extended his hand.

She took it, her long, slender fingers curling around his. He stared at her wrist, her elbow, and her arm, and noticed again the sun-washed color of her skin. He thought of her breasts and pictured them milky white, a stunning contrast to the rest of her. Stark white sheets would be a perfect foil for her chestnut hair and lavender eyes.

"What are you thinking, Malcolm? That you've made a poor bargain?"

He shook off the erotic images and cursed himself for having lustful thoughts of Alpin MacKay. "Nay," he said. "I'm thinking that you have."

Pulling her hand free, she hopped down from the window seat. "I never make poor bargains. Now tell me what you like to eat, when you like to eat it, and how many people I must feed."

For the next hour Alpin wielded a quill as he rattled off an extensive list of delicacies even the king's own steward would have been hard-pressed to provide. So transparent was Malcolm's attempt at intimidation, she wondered if he didn't suspect her motives or honestly dislike her. But she'd done no more than pull a few childish pranks when they were young. Surely he'd forgotten and forgiven those. He'd merely grown into an unhappy, beleaguered man who couldn't even have fun at a carnival. He couldn't know she planned to marry him and demand Paradise as her wedding gift. Once the papers were signed, she'd leave the Borders behind and take ship home.

"You'll supervise the housemaids, make certain my bed is made each morning and my shirts and tartans cared for properly."

He was, she decided, full of himself. Oh, he cut a fine figure, slouched comfortably in a wing chair, his chin resting in his palm. Still wearing the perfectly pleated kilt, he crossed his well-muscled legs and oozed enough charm to set a dozen simpering females to swooning. More than his aura of power, he exuded a lazy sensuality. His marvelous brown eyes danced with interest, and his straight nose and fine high cheekbones spoke of centuries of Scottish nobility.

She hid her opinion behind a bland smile. "Will there be anything else, my lord?"

"Aye." He plucked at the tassels on his sporran. "Tonight I've a craving for roast suckling pig, baked quinces, potatoes with parsley and butter, crusty bread, and a trifle big enough to"—he slid her a measuring glance—"to fill a washtub."

Wanting desperately to be away from him and his despotic ways, she replaced the quill, folded the paper, and got to her feet. "Will nine o'clock be soon enough?"

He looked at the lantern clock. It was just after six. "You can't manage it that fast, can you?"

With all the melodrama she could summon, she sighed and held out her arm. "Certainly I can." When he didn't immediately rise, she said, "I was thinking about a raisin and fig sauce for the pork." And a good dose of Elanna's come-to-me juice.

He licked his lips, but stayed where he was.

"Or," she drawled, pointing at the food tray, "I could warm up that rabbit."

Eyes narrowed, he said, "Blackmail is a poor way to start our business arrangement."

Despair weighted her shoulders. She couldn't woo him if all they did was bicker; even the strongest love potion couldn't turn enmity to affection. But if Malcolm didn't show his support for her by presenting her to the staff, she'd have an uphill battle gaining authority over the servants. Her arm ached, but she refused to drop it or lose the battle of wills they waged. "I only have myself to ransom. Now will you introduce me to the staff?"

His steady gaze held her immobile. "I've work to do here. The household ledgers need balancing. Even the grain stores haven't been inventoried since Mrs. Elliott left in February."

Another concession, but she could use the additional duties to her advantage. "I'll do your ciphering. I'm very good with numbers." Seeing his skeptical frown, she said, "And I'm honest. You can trust me."

He cleared his throat and pushed to his feet. As his hand closed over hers, Alpin had the distinct impression that Malcolm didn't trust her at all.

4

Malcolm's mouth watered as he gazed at the feast before him, the exact foods he'd requested. "Did Lady Alpin prepare this?"

"Aye, my lord. She and the African." Dora shook her head and ran her finger along the edge of Malcolm's desk. "Who'd've thought a real lady'd roll up her sleeves and sweat over a cooking fire?"

Real lady. The changes in Alpin still baffled him, but not enough to make him forget the past or alter his plans for her future. He had plenty of time, though, and other priorities, namely the Highland Jacobites and their obsession with putting James Stewart on the throne. Pray Saladin returned with communiqués that reflected a new moderation or at least the status quo on the part of the northern clan chiefs. "Where is Lady Alpin?"

Dora rubbed at a stain on her new apron. "Counting the stores in the pantry and waiting for her bathwater to heat." Whispering, the girl added, "She bathes every night and said so in front of the whole staff. The maids, you know—not the bootboy or any of the lads."

He speared a slice of roasted pork. Steam, fragrant with figs and raisins, filled his nose. An image of Alpin, naked in the wooden tub, filled his mind. Expectation of both lightened his mood. "She'll soon have you taking to a tub of an evening."

As he expected, Dora huffed up like a gentry matron who'd been pinched on the fanny. "I'd sooner be tied to my papa's plow and dragged to Edinburgh wearing nothing but my shift."

"'Twas only a jest, lass."

"Oh." Blushing, she went back to worrying the stain. "My lord . . . ? Is it true that Lady Alpin lived here once, when you were a lad?"

The savory meat almost melted in his mouth. "Aye. She ran away from her uncle's house."

"The bootboy said Mr. Lindsay said that old Angus MacDodd swore she greased your saddle and put thistles 'tween your sheets."

He'd forgotten many of Alpin's harmless pranks. For years he'd lived with the repercussions of her one unconscionable sin. He swallowed hard and felt the bark of a tree at his back and across his chest the ropes that secured him to the trunk. Alpin had stood over him that day, a storm of anger in her eyes, a jar of buzzing hornets in her hand.

"Take back what you said about my dress," she had demanded, shaking the jar.

"Never," he'd spat and kicked dust onto the hem of the only dress he'd ever seen her wear. "You look worse than a pukey lass. You look like your uncle's lapdog all dressed up in satin and bows."

Tears had filled her eyes. "I hate you, Malcolm Kerr."

"My name is Caesar," he had announced.

Then she had lifted the hem of the toga he wore, twisted the lid from the jar, and tossed it under his costume.

The tickle of insect legs on his private parts turned to stabbing, biting, excruciating pain. When the swelling started, he thought it would never stop, and by nightfall his balls were as big as the blacksmith's fists.

The midwife had said he would never sire a child. His stepmother had vehemently disagreed. Her staunch belief had proved fruitless, for none of Malcolm's women had ever conceived. Only his parents, Saladin, and Alexander knew the awful truth. If it became public knowledge—Nay. He stopped the thought, couldn't bear the disappointment his people would feel.

"Was she the meanest child in Christendom?" Dora asked.

Unable to gloss over Alpin's past, he said, "Aye. She was a fair hellion."

"Never know it now, my lord. Right businesslike she is and don't take no sauce from any of the staff." Dora chuckled. "She sent prissy Emily away a while ago. Caught her in the barracks playing kiss-the-freckle with Rabby Armstrong."

With one less maid, the barracks wouldn't get cleaned. The soldiers would complain. Malcolm would have to discipline Alpin. She'd get angry and storm off to her uncle's, a place she'd run away from years ago. Precisely where Malcolm wanted her. Yet the prospect of having Alpin under his roof and his thumb—hell, under him in bed—held a certain appeal.

Using only the edge of his fork, he cut another bite of meat, his thoughts fixed on the confrontation.

The next afternoon he found Alpin in the barracks, bending over a cot and stripping off the sheet. Half a dozen soldiers, as cocky as swains on Laird's Day, lounged nearby, their gazes, some hungry, some curious, fixed on her.

Was she flirting with his men? Anger ripped through him. So the wicked child had become the coy woman. But as he leaned his shoulder against the doorjamb to listen and watch, he realized she was telling his men about the time he'd fallen off his stilts and tumbled into the well.

Wearing a worn blue dress, without panniers and volumi-nous petticoats, she looked more like an industrious parson's daughter than the businesslike housekeeper Dora had described. What struck Malcolm most forcefully was the ease with which she commanded attention and the unholy joy she derived from telling the tale.

Plumping the straw-filled leather mattress, she said, "After he rescued Malcolm, Lord Duncan asked him if he was troll hunting or practicing his part in the May Day parade. Malcolm stiffened his spine and said he was merely thirsty all over."

"Our laird can bandy words with the best of them," Rabby Armstrong boasted. "I expect Lady Miriam had a thing to say about our laird nearly drowning."

The men laughed. Two of them moved to help her. She waved them away.

"She did indeed. Volumes as I recall." Alpin stared out the window. "Then she taught us both to swim."

Malcolm remembered. Once the lessons were over and the adults gone, Alpin had insisted on swimming in nature's garb. She'd been tiny and rail-thin, with a chest as flat as oatcakes and nipples like pink buttons. She'd given him his first full-blown hard-on. Then she'd laughed and warned him that he might catch a fish with his fat worm.

Did she swim naked on the tropical island? No, she'd been too busy standing by and watching poor Charles drink himself to death. Had her unhappy childhood hardened her to the suffering of others? Probably so, for she hadn't shown a glimmer of sadness over the loss of her generous guardian. The thought disappointed Malcolm. She put on a show of kindness, but inside she was heartless. Charles had welcomed her when no one in the Borders would risk taking in a stubborn, wicked child. He had provided for her and even arranged for Malcolm to carry on in his place. He would care for her all right—in his own way.

"He didn't go near the well for a long time after that," Alpin was saying.

Malcolm stepped into the room. "As I remember the incident, you pushed me into the well and threw my stilts down the privy shaft."

She looked up, a surprised smile curling her lips. "Come

49

now, my lord. Admit that I had no choice, not when you swore to beat me with them."

"You made certain the occasion never arose."

"A lass needs leverage, and if I didn't know better, I'd suspect you intend to blame me for every ill that befell you in childhood."

Not all, he thought. Only the one that had left the deepest scars, the one that robbed him of the chance to have a family of his own to love. "Let's just say I was a healthier lad when you stayed at Sinclair Manor."

"Don't deny our friendship," she scoffed. "That's why you always wanted to play bride-and-groom with me."

One of the soldiers said, "The laird never plays that game. He won't be tricked into marriage. Not until he's sowed his wild oats with willing women."

Alpin flipped her long braid over her shoulder. "Who said I was willing?"

Another round of laughter filled the room. Malcolm felt humiliated, for he had tried in his silly, childish way to befriend her with affection. He tipped his head toward the door. "I'm sure Alexander has something for you swains to do."

Rabby Armstrong got to his feet. "But, my lord . . ."

In a softly threatening tone, Malcolm said, "Such as keeping watch for Saladin and sounding the horn when he arrives."

"Aye, sir." They mumbled good-byes and filed out the door.

Alpin moved to the next cot. "You shouldn't have sent them away. They're assigned to the night watch and need their rest."

Her imperious tone caught him off guard. "You were disturbing them more than I."

"Jealous, my lord?"

"Nay. I'm angry. You shouldn't have dismissed Emily," he shot back.

"Dora told you what happened?"

Malcolm shrugged. "I would've found out anyway. Now

explain yourself, if you please. Emily's worked here for two years."

Blithely she said, "She behaved badly with Rabby."

"Ha! Alpin MacKay accusing someone else of bad behavior." The irony made him laugh. "Kiss-the-freckle is a harmless game."

Holding the wadded-up sheet to her breast, she turned. "Not if you have freckles where Emily does."

Chagrined, Malcolm said. "And where is that?"

She sent him a withering glare. "Use your manly imagination."

He was, but his fantasy centered on the woman before him and the shapely body hidden beneath the serviceable dress. "Above or below the waist?"

"That depends on where your brains are."

He sputtered, trying to remember the last time he'd been outwitted by a woman. Seeing her sly smile, he suspected she took pride in putting men in their place. Odd, for at seven and twenty she should be desperate for a husband.

She sighed and wiped her brow. "I didn't dismiss Emily permanently. I only sent her away for the afternoon. She's caring for Mrs. Kimberley's children so the woman can come and bake for us today. Henceforth Emily will work in the castle proper." When he didn't comment, she added, "With your approval of course."

So blunt she was and almost fearless. In some aspects she hadn't changed. "Of course. Did you speak so frankly to Charles?"

She flung the sheet across the room, missing the pile. Lips pursed, she said, "I seldom found the time to speak to him at all."

Her vehemence didn't surprise Malcolm. The implication in her voice did, for when it came to Alpin, Charles had surely been a paragon of charity. "I suppose you'll tell me you worked harder there than here?"

She whirled. "I worked as hard as anyone. I had no . . ." She clamped her lips together.

"You had no what?"

"Nothing."

"I can't believe Alpin MacKay is afraid to speak her mind."

She toyed with her bracelet. "I'm not afraid."

"Then finish what you were going to say."

"It's unimportant."

He found himself softening toward her. "We're friends, remember?"

She sighed. "I worked hard because I had no choice."

Believing her tale of woe could lead to an understanding between them and perhaps something more. Seeing her now, shimmering with dignity, he felt a grudging respect and a sudden craving to know just what the "something more" might be.

He immediately shied away from the thought of sharing intimacies with Alpin MacKay. "I hope you'll show me the same loyalty. You can start by educating me on the operation of a sugar plantation."

She smiled a little too brightly. "You can be sure I'll be loyal, my lord. I'll care for your property as if it were my own."

And he was a Welshman with a name as long as winter. Rising, he picked up the wayward linen and tossed it with the others. The laundry smelled of sweaty men and long hours of labor in the tiltyard. She'd soil her dress if she carried the dirty linens. Bothered that he even cared and still miffed that she'd pranced into his home and charmed his soldiers and his staff, Malcolm suspected she was up to no good. "Someone worked hard at Paradise, and it showed in the plantation's profits."

She mumbled what sounded like "You should know," then snatched up the last dirty sheet and walked to the pile. "Speaking of work . . . If you'll excuse me, I'd like to finish here so I can ride later today. Have you a request for dinner?"

He put his boot on the sheets. "Tell me why the mention of Paradise Plantation makes you so angry that you throw things. Did you hate it there?"

The stormy violet of her eyes reminded him of the sky just before sunrise. "I'm not angry. And no, I didn't actually hate it there." She dropped to her knees and slid her hands under the pile. When he didn't move his foot, she stared at the hem of his kilt. "I'm just busy and eager for a ride on that dappled gray. You're getting manure on these sheets."

He'd come here to exercise his right as lord and master of his domain. Alpin might have a quick wit, but she'd still do as he said. From his vantage point he could see the deep indentation of her cleavage. His plan to make her life miserable took a different turn. He became aware of his own nakedness beneath his tartan. His skin prickled with sensual awareness. "You still haven't told me the real reason you don't want Emily cleaning the barracks."

Alpin sat back on her heels, tried patience smoothing out her features. "It's for her own good. She could get into . . . trouble. She also sets a bad example for the other maids. If she gets away with improper behavior, they'll think they can too."

Improper behavior turned to a lurid picture in Malcolm's mind, with Alpin as the object of his desire. "There's nothing wrong with courting," he said, unable to squelch the odd yearning for that elusive "something more."

"Oh, yes, there is. Fathers send their daughters here to work, and it's up to you, as laird, to see to their welfare, both physical and moral. The same principle applies to the lord who fosters his kinsman's son."

She had a point, but he'd be damned if he'd let her enjoy it. He also realized he wasn't quite ready for the conversation to end. "*You* were here with the men."

She chuckled. "I'm hardly a temptation."

Was she fishing for compliments? What the devil, he'd offer her one. "Then you spent too much time on that tropical island, Alpin. Any of those men would have traded his best mount for the chance to play kiss-the-freckle with you."

A smile curling her lips, she murmured, "I assure you, my lord, that will never happen."

"Lost all your freckles, have you?"

"Malcolm Kerr!" She slapped his calf. "How dare you be so vulgar."

Ignoring her maidenly outrage, he went on. "I seem to remember you had a cluster of them here." He touched his hipbone. "And here." He touched a spot at the top of his thigh. "And we mustn't forget the ones on your back."

"You had them, too, don't forget."

"Where?"

"Stop right now. That's enough. We were talking about Rabby and Emily."

"Leave the lad to me. I'll speak with him."

"I'm sure you will. Lot of good it'll do."

"Are you mocking me?"

"No. I just don't think you'll succeed in controlling Rabby's love life. That would be the pot calling the kettle black."

Gossips in Whitley Bay had filled her head with tales of Malcolm's casual flirtations. He courted the gentry maidens so no one would guess the real reason he dodged marriage; he couldn't, in good conscience, marry a lass and sentence her to a life barren of children.

"What's this?" she asked. "Malcolm the great rogue at a loss for words?"

"Have I tried to seduce you?"

"Of course not," she said softly. "You wouldn't try so farfetched a thing."

"I might."

"Well, don't. We wouldn't suit, not as lovers."

"How do you know?"

"I *just* know. Can we get back to the problem of Emily and Rabby?"

Malcolm intended to show Alpin MacKay how wrong she was to challenge him. "Would you care to make a wager on whether or not I can control Rabby's amorous adventures?"

Tipping her head back, she studied him closely. But when her tongue peeked out and made a slow trek over her lips, leaving a slick sheen, he lost the ability to govern his lustful thoughts. He could make a picnic of her mouth and a feast of her other delights. Wait! his conscience screamed. That's Alpin MacKay you're fantasizing over.

Shocked at his reaction, he folded his arms over his chest and raised his eyebrows. "Well?"

"Why not, my lord?" She shrugged, drawing his attention to the set of her shoulders and the delicate hollow at the base of her throat. "I'll put a keg of rum against your gray mare."

"What? A horse for a jug of spirits? That's hardly fair."

Like a tutor grilling a slow-witted student, she said, "I have six kegs of rum. You have ten times that many horses. All things considered, my ante is as valuable to me as yours is to you."

Her distorted reasoning rattled in his mind and looked for a logical place to settle. But the exercise was unnecessary, for he would emerge victorious. He didn't want the rum . . . unless he could use the occasion to understand his sudden interest in a woman he shouldn't want. "Very well, but only if you share it with me."

She shivered. "A whole keg? We'd both be rotten drunk."

"A drink between friends, then. 'Best friends' is how I recall you describing us. Unless you've changed your mind."

Again she took great interest in her bracelet. "Rest assured, Malcolm, I could never change my feelings for you, even if I tried."

Her cheerful tone couldn't mask an innuendo. Neither could the gleam in her eye. He smiled down at her. "Good. I'm also considering selling Paradise and I'd like to know more about it before I do."

Her eyes grew large, and the color left her face. "You can't sell Paradise. That would be foolish." She grasped his ankle. "Please don't sell it."

"Why not?"

Her gaze darted desperately from the bunks to the floor to the tartans that hung from pegs on the wall. "Certainly you can sell it, since you own it," she said, distracted. "But what about the people there? The servants. The slaves."

She said the last word with so much compassion that Malcolm was again reminded of the trouble with the slaves five years ago. Could Charles have agreed to give Malcolm the plantation out of spite because Alpin had taken the side of the slaves? His first instinct was to reject the idea that the Alpin he'd known was capable of championing a humanitarian cause. But as a child she had loved animals and Malcolm really didn't know her anymore. She had not written to him, and Charles had omitted personal information about her in his letters.

"I haven't decided what to do about Paradise. Why don't you help me? You can tell me all about the place, give me your opinions."

A doubtful gleam sparkled in her eyes. "You will continue to profit handsomely if you keep it."

"Because of the cheap slave labor?"

Squinting in fury, she swore, "'Tis an abomination."

He'd seen that same look in her eyes years ago when he'd threatened to dig up her dead badger and make himself a new sporran from the hide. She had railed at him, called him a slimy cur, and threatened to set fire to his bed, with him in it. Now he couldn't resist egging her on. "Slavery has its appeal." When she gasped, he rushed to add, "If we had it here in Scotland, I'd buy the earl of Mar and put him to work shoeing my horses."

All seriousness, she said, "You're mocking me."

"Nay. I'm trying to learn from you."

She exhaled, as if relieved. "I'm sure you'll do the right thing, Malcolm. But you needn't decide anything about Paradise for now. Mr. Fenwick is a capable overseer."

She was hiding something; he knew it. He just had to find a way to learn all her secrets. "You sound like Lady Miriam."

Humor twinkled in her eyes, drawing attention to her perfectly arched brows and the curling wisps of auburn hair that framed her face. "And you've a bit of the diplomat in you, Malcolm Kerr."

He laughed. "That's because you don't know me."

"Oh, yes, I do." She rose and headed toward the door, her hips swaying seductively.

He reached out and grabbed her arm. When he stepped toward her, his foot tangled in the sheets. Before he could get his balance, he fell, pulling her down with him. Twisting, he managed to land on his back with Alpin sprawled on his chest. Her elbows poked him in the ribs. He winced and grasped her upper arms.

"What are you doing?" she demanded, her eyes wide, her heavy braid draped across his neck.

"Me? You're the one on top, but that was always the case with us, wasn't it?"

"Don't do this." She tried to jerk away.

He held her fast. "Admit it, Alpin. You always wanted the upper hand."

"We were children then, playing games and squabbling. You hated me. And I . . ." Her gazed slipped to his mouth. She swallowed. "And I was . . ."

"You were what?"

"I was naïve about how far our playing would go."

The tension in his limbs suddenly eased; the air between them crackled with anticipation. As naturally as he might reach for warmth on a cold winter night, he pulled her closer, until the sweet rush of her breath fanned his face, until the minute details of her features filled his vision. "Now you know where playing can lead."

"You cannot kiss me."

"I always have."

"No. Yes. I mean, those were different times. We were children. You don't want me now."

He shifted beneath her. The movement gave vivid proof of just how much he'd changed over the years and how much he did want her. "We were friends, nay?"

"Aye," she breathed, wariness turning her eyes the deep hue of pansies. "You were my only friend."

She exaggerated. He could see the deception in every facet of her being. Alpin MacKay harbored deep feelings for him, but fondness was not one of them. Why, then, would she swear otherwise? He had to call her bluff, find out why the woman who'd stolen his chance to sire an heir would work so hard to seduce him today. "I was and still am your best friend."

She opened her mouth but decided against speaking

whatever she had on her mind. Her teeth slipped over her bottom lip, and she stared blindly at the Kerr badge that secured his tartan to his shirt.

Determined to bring his challenge to fruition, he slid a hand over her shoulder and cupped her neck. "Let's renew our friendship."

With slight pressure he drew her mouth to his and tilted his head to one side. She squeezed her eyes shut and locked her lips tighter than a spinster's hope chest. Friends, eh? He'd see about that.

He kissed her softly at first, but when she remained stalwartly unwilling, he used the cheapest trick of seduction he knew. "You kissed better as a child."

She chuckled, her breasts nudging his chest, her hips undulating against his groin. "So did you. Only now you don't have dirt on your face and innocence in your heart."

Somehow she'd taken his dare and turned it back on him. "Neither of us is innocent, Alpin. We've outgrown that." Summoning resolve, he tried to ignore the lust racing through his veins and settling in his groin. "A truce?"

As serious as sin on Sunday, she said, "I think you mean a tryst, Malcolm."

"You like me," he insisted. "In your heart you always have. Why else would you want to make a home here now?" If she accepted that lie, he'd make certain she paid a heavy price for it.

"You're very important to me, Malcolm."

He noted the equivocation and decided to play on it. "Then prove it, Alpin. Give me a kiss of peace."

Now that the moment was upon her, Alpin froze. She had lured him here to flirt with him, to sow the seeds of seduction. The come-to-me potion wasn't ready, but she couldn't back down. She had nowhere else to go. The theme of her life hadn't changed, only now she lay belly to belly with a man she couldn't afford to alienate. Temporarily resigned, she reached up and, with as much tenderness as she could muster, raked an errant strand of hair off his forehead. "If it will ease your mind."

It didn't ease hers, for when Malcolm Kerr began kissing

her in earnest, Alpin received her first lesson in the real art of seduction. He oozed finesse, and with a gentle roaming of hands and soft words of encouragement he inspired her to play the eager student. Too proud to back down and too preoccupied to think of an alternative, she followed his lead and kissed him back.

No childish groping as in days gone by, this embrace spoke vividly of adult need and mature passion. Her breathing grew shallow and her head light, but her body stayed firmly rooted to his. Because he was as large as she was small, he seemed a generous and comfy pillow beneath her. On the heels of that thought, she became aware of subtle changes, of limbs adjusting for a better fit, of his swelling hardness where she'd grown soft, of his languid hands turned possessive in their touch. When his tongue stroked the seam of her lips and prodded them to part, she pulled back and stared, aghast, at him.

His eyes drifted open, the brown irises dark, his expression dangerously provocative. He gave her a lazy smile and murmured, "You're not trying to make peace." Then he pulled her back into the kiss. "You also lied about having had affairs."

After that taunt, she ceased cataloging his every move and made a few of her own. She threaded her fingers into his hair and felt the thick texture of every strand. Her tongue sought his, twirling and exploring, while her mind took note of the slick spiral of wanting that curled around her backbone and sapped the strength from her legs and arms. Like currents under the surf, strong emotions pulled her toward him, promising some mysterious reward.

When his hands caressed her bottom and his hips surged beneath her, she became shockingly aware of the prize he offered. As effective as a slap in the face, the knowledge that she'd excited him chased away her desire. But if he suspected the true nature of her feelings, he would only challenge her again. She must let him think he'd succeeded in his quest to prove that their friendship not only still thrived but that it had deepened into passion. She also had to get away from him. Now.

"I think," she said, drawing back to catch her breath, "that your peaceful intentions have sparked off a war."

"I yield, then." He spread out his arms. "And I propose a treaty of mutual satisfaction. We've already laid the ground-work."

Baffled by his husky whisper and startled at the acquiescence she felt, Alpin squeaked, "You would lie with me?"

He chuckled, the sound a rumble against her breasts. "'Tis where such sport usually ends."

"Sport?" Good intentions fled like gulls before a hurricane.

"Aye, and I expect we'll enjoy a fair dose of that. Shall we say tonight at midnight in my bedchamber?"

"Tonight?" Outrage made her blood boil. "Your mistress just left."

"I want you, and that's all that matters." With his index finger he tapped her nose. "Tonight. I'd take you there now, but Saladin would only interrupt us."

Her mind had become a wasteland devoid of coherent thought. "Saladin?"

He nodded. "I see you didn't hear the trumpet sounding his arrival. I almost missed it myself."

She hadn't heard any horn. But the look on Malcolm's face signaled a warning of its own: she'd gone too far in her attempt at seduction. She'd only wanted to distract him a bit. Now she was in over her head. "Don't you think this is all happening too fast?"

To her dismay, he chuckled again and tucked his hands behind his head. "Absolutely not, and don't bother taking your bath in the kitchen. I'll have the tub sent to my room." He jiggled his eyebrows. "We'll share that as well."

He looked like a fat tomcat after a successful night on the prowl. Precisely what she'd hoped to achieve, but not during their first tryst. She wasn't ready to give herself to him yet. He had to propose marriage first.

She rolled off him and got to her feet. Sucking up her pride she said, "We cannot, Malcolm. 'Twould be wrong."

"Wanting each other is right," he said in a silky whisper. "And you can't deny the desire you feel for me."

"No." Unable to face him, she stared out the window. To her surprise, life in the castle yard went on in normal fashion. A hay wagon lumbered toward the gate; the goosegirl shooed her flock out of the way; the blacksmith banged out his perpetual melody; rowdy children played chase. She was reminded of two other children and a time long ago. But hatred and greed separated them now. "I liked it when you kissed me, but I've changed my mind."

His hands touched her shoulders. "Change it back, Alpin."

"You must promise never to kiss me again." She stepped away.

He followed her, a wall of warmth at her back. She felt the rush of his breath on her skin. "I promise I'll do more than kiss you." The blast of a horn made her jump. His fingers tightened. "We'll discuss it tonight in my room."

"No, we won't. 'Tis finished here and now."

He released her. She turned and saw the warmth flee his eyes, leaving cold dislike. "Then pack your bags. I'll have Alexander take you to your uncle."

5

At the sound of his retreating footsteps Alpin almost called him back and slapped his face. She should have expected knavery from the beast, Malcolm Kerr. Her better judgment kept her silent. Was it his fault she'd fallen prey to a trap of her own making? Yes. With his tender kisses, he'd put her off guard; then he'd struck a mean blow.

She shivered in fear—fear of yielding to her nemesis, fear of the yearning he aroused in her, fear of being sent away to the wretched house she'd fled at the age of six. A greater dread gripped her. Was she destined to live out her life and never know the love of a man, never see just how far passion would take her?

But Malcolm Kerr wasn't speaking of tenderness or affection in the traditional sense. Sport was what he'd called it. *Sport.*

Her stomach turned sour, and bright girlish dreams faded like curtains too long in the sun. She didn't want romance anymore. In her youth she had. Watching Charles and

Adrienne devote their lives to each other had given Alpin a sound understanding of the meaning of love. It had also shown her the danger of so deep a commitment, for when Adrienne died a part of Charles had perished with her. From then on, he'd been a shell of a man, uninterested in the world around him and blind to the needs and to the future of his young ward.

Alpin's life had changed on that fateful day. She had put her childhood behind her. Rather than swimming in her favorite pool of rainwater, she began devising ways to divert it to irrigate the thirsty fields of sugarcane. Instead of playing hoodman blind with the slave children, she spent her time formulating a plan to set them free.

She became a practical woman, interested only in the basics of life: a roof over her head, enough land to support herself, and peace of mind.

Malcolm Kerr had taken all three. With the stroke of a quill he'd taken her home and her livelihood. With one kiss he'd stolen her self-respect.

Lifting a shaking hand, she touched her lips and remembered the feel of his mouth on hers, melting her resolve and inciting a desire that lingered even now. She could put an end to her torment. She could knock on his door at midnight, lie in his arms, and discover the mysteries his kisses foretold. But from observation, she knew where a tender liaison would lead: she might gain the means to fulfill her dream of returning to Paradise and freeing the slaves, but in doing so she ran the risk of enslaving her heart to a man who wouldn't value it.

Her strong will rebelled against such sentimentality. She had work to do, plans to make. She'd gotten in over her head and suffered a momentary setback. He'd pulled a dirty trick on her. Bravo for him. He'd obviously forgotten that Alpin MacKay was an expert trickster. In her own way she would refresh his memory.

Casting off self-doubt, she scooped up the laundry and took it to the washing shed. Then she went to the kitchen to oversee the preparation of the evening meal.

Alone in the cavernous room, Elanna sat at the oak table, peeling a mountain of turnips. Her eyes, as dark as molasses, surveyed Alpin. "Trouble be coming with you through that door."

Thinking Malcolm had followed her, Alpin flinched and glanced over her shoulder. Except for an industrious spider, expanding an already impressive web, the doorway was empty. "If I were you"—Alpin reached for the broom and destroyed the web—"I'd leave off playing the sage, at least while we're here. These country folks might stone you for a witch."

Elanna held up her hands as if warding off a foe. "Big bad Scotsman put mighty fright in poor slave girl's heart."

Alpin laughed and set the broom aside. "You can also put away your Bajan. You speak perfectly good English when it suits you. And you're free."

"Because of you." Elanna patted the table, her dark skin blending perfectly with the aged wood, her gaily flowered dress adding cheer to the ancient room. "Sit. Tell me what happened to put such fire in your eyes."

Alpin lifted her skirt and stepped over the bench. "You were right about me finding trouble." She picked up a turnip peel and coiled it around her finger. Then she told her friend about the seduction of Malcolm.

"Why worry? You said he always kissed you, even when he was a lad."

"This was a different kind of kiss."

"Betcha that. You don't look like you've been romanced by any boy."

Alpin dropped the peel and again touched her lips. Even the tangy flavor of the turnip couldn't obliterate the warm taste of him. "Now he wants me to be his mistress."

Elanna picked up the knife and stabbed at a turnip. "He's supposed to want to say 'I do, I do' first."

Admitting defeat dulled Alpin's senses and sapped the strength she'd garnered. "I must keep a level head where he's concerned. The scoundrel insisted I share his bed or return to the house of my uncle, Baron Sinclair."

"Ecky-beckie man!"

She referred to the freedmen turned poor white trash in Bridgetown. "Lord Malcolm is hardly a drunken beggar," Alpin replied.

Using the knife, Elanna scratched an itch just beneath her turban. Glancing left and right, she whispered, "He did some kind of begging to get poor Master Charles to give him your Paradise."

The old injustice rose like a sour tide in Alpin. Paradise Plantation rightfully belonged to her. Making a fist, she pounded the table. "I know. But if I share his bed, he'll have to marry me. As his wife, I can lay a claim to Paradise."

"Betcha that. But be plenty careful. You give him all the mangoes, he won't want the tree."

Naively, Alpin had anticipated a proper courtship, then an honorable marriage. She hadn't expected him to be so devious. "He knows we have nowhere else to go. Oh, why did Charles give him our home in the first place?"

Pails rattled in the yard outside the kitchen door. "Shush," said Elanna. "The servants here are loyal to this Scotsman, and they get to gossiping quicker than Master Charles could empty a bottle of rum." A mischievous smile revealed Elanna's pearly white teeth, of which she was inordinately proud. "As soon as you find a way to get in his study and peek at his papers, you'll learn why the plantation fell to him."

Alpin's one small success gave her confidence. "I've already managed that. I agreed to take on the work of steward, too."

"Don't surprise me. You never could sit still for more than a minute."

When Alpin rose, Elanna chuckled. "See?"

Alpin ignored the gibe; she'd heard it too many times over the years. "If you'll watch over the evening meal, I'll get started on the books now."

Elanna grasped her wrist. "What about the other? How can you get him to say 'I do, I do'?"

Alpin hadn't a clue. Worse, part of her yearned to be his lover, to know firsthand the intimacies a man and woman could share. But she wouldn't fall in love with him, not with the one who'd stolen her home and her life's work and taken what little independence she had. "I don't know. I'll just have to be more conniving than he."

"You already are. You outwitted every white man in Barbados. Besting a skirt-wearing Scotsman should be as easy as shinnying up a fig tree."

The reminder of their home buoyed Alpin's confidence. "'Tis a tartan kilt, Elanna, and very traditional in this part of the world. You'll get in big trouble calling it a skirt."

Pulling her generous lips into a pout, Elanna said, "They'll stone me for that, too?"

Amused at her friend's irreverence, Alpin shook her head. "They'll shun you."

"They will not. They're too busy staring at me and murmuring dire threats about what's to happen to me when that man they call Saladin returns." She brandished the knife. "No Bacchra with a Turk's name gonna put a scare in this Ashanti princess. I say, go ahead and burn my free papers before I'll go back to saying 'yes sir, no sir, get it quick right now, sir.'"

Elanna assumed Saladin was a white man; Alpin had never mentioned the Moor. She could explain, prepare her for the shock of meeting a man of her own race here in Scotland. But seeing the stubborn glint in Elanna's eyes, Alpin decided her friend needed a small lesson in humility. "What will you do when he arrives?"

Elanna brushed her thumb over the edge of the blade. "Maybe carve out his liver and make some mighty fine pâté."

Alpin strolled to the door. "Just don't bloody up the floor. We're one maid short."

"Betcha that. Oh . . . what should I cook?"

Over her shoulder, Alpin said, "Lots of vegetables. Saladin doesn't eat meat."

The bench legs scraped against the stone flags. Turnips

66

rolled off the table and thumped loudly onto the floor. "You know him from when you lived here before!"

Alpin grasped the handle and pulled open the door. "Yes. I used to hide his prayer rug and hammer nails with his scimitar."

"Come back here!"

Elanna's angry command ringing in her ears, Alpin strolled rapidly into the lesser hall and made her way to Malcolm's study.

She had just finished comparing last night's inventory of the pantry to the figures in the household ledger when the door banged open and Malcolm came in. Her pulse jumped at the sight of him, resplendent in Highland dress, his shoulder-length black hair mussed by the wind. As a lad he'd been compassionate and imaginative. He'd treated her kindly when others called her a poor relation and a wicked child.

Now he stiffened at the sight of her. Interest flickered in his eyes, then turned to chilly indifference. What had happened to the caring, sensitive boy? How could she trick this cold man into marrying her?

He began stripping off his gloves. "Ah, you're still here."

Seated in his oversized chair, she felt small, defenseless, and her hands shook. She set down the quill before she made an inky mess. Forcing a smile, she tapped the page. "You've too much grain in the inventory and not enough meat in the springhouse, which is too small."

He stared at her breasts. "I never seem to have enough of the things I truly want. But I suspect that's about to change."

Perhaps they would both get what they wanted—a fair trade of sorts: Paradise Plantation for her, another female to conquer and perhaps an heir for him. But he had to marry her first.

"Those are strange words from a man who was born to wealth."

"Money doesn't provide everything."

That was a common belief among the rich, a sad cliché from a man who'd never wanted for shelter on a rainy night. Those less fortunate could struggle to better themselves and he would never understand their ambition, let alone applaud their achievements. "Charles would have agreed with you, but he would have added that money can certainly tip the scales of fate."

"Then I trust you'll provide the needed balance for my scales?"

She'd wanted few things in her life, had received fewer. But the pain of her failed hopes and tarnished dreams would remain a private matter. Still, his cryptic statement deserved a like reply. "I'll be an excellent provider, if you'll trust my judgment."

A noise in the hall drew his attention, giving her a splendid view of his noble profile. She was again reminded of the caped man she had called her Night Angel. "If time permits, we'll add 'earning trust' to tonight's agenda, won't we, Alpin?" Before she could commit the folly of telling him what he could do with his agenda, he waved a hand toward the hall. "Now let me reintroduce you to Saladin Cortez."

Her interest stayed fixed on Malcolm. A worry line marred his forehead, and tension tightened his jaw. Why? What was it about Saladin's return that troubled him so?

The moment the Moor stepped into the room her curiosity fled. A hand's length shorter than Malcolm and much trimmer in build, Saladin Cortez wore the same type of clothing she remembered, except for stylish differences. His cotton turban featured an impressive ruby the size of a pigeon's egg; golden embroidery trimmed his brown tunic and knee pants. He still favored knee-high red boots, but he now wore an exotic pointed beard.

He blinked, his inscrutable gaze focusing on Alpin and revealing his surprise at seeing her here.

A courier's satchel was draped over one of his shoulders, a belt housing his deadly scimitar the other. Although familiar, the weapon looked smaller than Alpin remembered. She glanced at Malcolm's sporran and realized his chieftain's pouch appeared smaller, too. Prior to her recent arrival, the last time she'd seen Malcolm and Saladin they'd been boys wearing the accoutrements of men. Now they were adults carrying the ancient symbols of their vastly different heritages.

"Welcome—" Saladin coughed and sent a questioning glance at Malcolm.

"Aye. She's most welcome indeed," Malcolm said with smooth authority. "Lady Alpin is now our housekeeper, among other things."

Saladin eyed Malcolm with keen regard.

Malcolm eyed the satchel.

Alpin grew uneasy, felt like an outsider. She closed the book, stood, and began tidying the desk. "It's been a very long time, Saladin," she said, at a loss for anything else.

Malcolm ushered his friend into the room and held out his hand. Saladin sighed and, with what she thought was regret, yielded the leather pouch. "Ill tidings, my lord."

Malcolm immediately delved into it.

The Moor faced her. Steepling his fingers, he touched his forehead and bowed. "It has been too long, my lady. May the blessings of the Prophet be upon you."

She murmured her thanks, but her attention strayed to Malcolm, who now frowned as he examined a handful of letters. What kind of ill tidings had he received, she wondered, and from whom? Probably a woman, she decided, and bully for her, if so.

Hoping to put a dent in his armor of self-importance, she said, "Why, how now, Lord Malcolm! 'What see you in those papers that you lose so much complexion?'"

He stiffened and glared at her, his dark brown eyes alive with accusation. "As I remember, you couldn't read the simplest primer when you left here for Barbados. Now you recite Shakespeare and quote boldly from a tale of traitors. I wonder why you chose a passage from *Henry the Fifth*."

She had thought it fitting, but to be truthful, she had wanted to show him that she'd bettered herself over the years. His reference to treason, however, completely baffled her.

To hide her vulnerability, she faked a sulk. "I was trying to impress you, but you've found me out. Whatever will I do now?"

His brusque demeanor softened to a cool regard that threatened retribution. "'I suggest you pray that God of his mercy gives you patience to endure, and true repentance of all your dear offenses.'"

As a child he'd recited the classics with ease. As an adult he infused them with menace. She picked up the ledger and hugged it to her breast. "Endure what, my lord?"

He made a slow perusal of her face, then grinned. "What else? Our ever-expanding agenda."

Feeling adrift in a sea of innuendo, she moved to the door. "Does your afternoon agenda include refreshments?"

"Aye. Beer for me and orange water for my Muslim friend. You'll find the fruit in the root cellar." Looking at Saladin, he added, "And please ask Elanna to serve us."

Alpin crossed the threshold and heard Saladin ask, "Who is this Elanna?"

As Malcolm closed the door behind her, he said, "A surprise, my dear Saladin. A surprise."

Alpin changed her mind about leaving her friend in the dark, saw the harm and disloyalty that could result. After fetching the oranges, she took Elanna aside and told her about Saladin.

The former slave girl looked the same as she had the day Alpin presented her with a certificate of freedom. Her innate poise turned to childish excitement. "He's African?"

Dora stopped mashing summer berries and inched closer. Alpin drew Elanna into the privacy of the scullery. Barrels of salted meat and a batch of fresh basil scented the air.

"He's half African," Alpin said. "His father was a Moor, and his mother a Spanish noblewoman."

Elanna stared, still awestruck. "How did he get here?"

"As children, he and his twin brother Salvador were scribes in the employ of Malcolm's stepmother, Lady Miriam."

Pinching her bottom lip between her thumb and forefinger, Elanna said, "She is the diplomat."

Alpin shifted the oranges from one hand to the other. "Yes."

"Here, give me those before you drop them." Elanna made a sack of her apron. Alpin put the fruit inside. "How old is Saladin?"

"He was twelve or thirteen when I left here for Barbados. That would make him thirty-two or -three now."

"Is he handsome?"

"I'd say he looks impressive. Majestic, if you will."

"Hum." Elanna grew thoughtful. "Must be a poor Moorish man, since he doesn't have a harem here."

Amused, Alpin said, "How do you know if has women or not?"

Elanna shot her a look of superiority. "The maids here were quick to tell you about that girl Emily and her soldier. Betcha they couldn't keep juicy gossip like that a secret if their freedom depended on it."

"They didn't tell you much about Saladin?"

"I didn't ask." She tapped her breastbone. "This African princess learns by watching and listening."

Alpin chuckled. "When you've finished serving them, make the love potion. And be sure to tell me what you think of Saladin."

Explanations were unnecessary. From the moment Elanna stepped into Malcolm's study and spied Saladin, her face mirrored the gamut of reactions, beginning with shock and settling into avid interest. Especially so when Saladin put the tankard to his mouth. His coal black eyes stayed trained on Elanna, and the longer he looked, the more he drank. The tankard was empty when he put it down, but his eyes revealed a thirst no drink could quench.

"More?" asked Elanna, reaching for the pitcher.

In answer he surveyed her from head to toe, his gaze lingering on her neck and hands. "Oh, yes. I believe so."

"You some thirsty man," she said in a regal whisper while refilling his mug.

"And you're an interesting surprise. How did you get here?"

With a coy look, she said, "On a very slow and smelly boat, Your Majesty."

Humor flashed in his eyes. "I'm no king."

She winked at Alpin. "But you're majestic."

"I am?" Saladin asked.

She nodded, giving evidence of what the older Paradise slave women called her sassy ways. "Betcha that."

"Yes, well . . ." He cleared his throat. "You were born in Barbados?"

She set down the pitcher and squared her shoulders. Then, for only the second time since meeting her, Alpin heard her friend say, "I am Elanna, the last Ashanti princess of the Kumbassa people."

Saladin's arm froze, the newly filled tankard an inch from his mouth. "You're African royalty? A slave?"

Pride gave proof to her noble lineage. "You see before you a freedwoman." Her elegant facade crumbled when she playfully added, "Betcha that."

He shook his head. "Curse me for a plaster saint, Elanna, but I doubt any of us ever truly gain our freedom."

She turned to Malcolm. "He's your slave?" she squeaked, her face pinched in disbelief.

Smiling benevolently, Malcolm chuckled. "A slave to philosophy and a servant of theology. That's our Saladin."

"That's no answer," she snapped. "Is he or is he not your property?"

"Not mine or any mortal man's."

She threw up her hands. "You sing a riddle song. I'm going back to the kitchen."

Saladin caught up with her before she reached the door. "I'll walk you there."

She eyed him as a canary would a cat, until he smiled in invitation. A blush turned her dark skin mahogany red. "I suppose it's all right."

"Betcha that," he quipped and, putting a hand at the small of her back, guided her out the door.

Feeling like an intruder, Alpin looked at Malcolm and was

surprised to find him staring at her. Seated at his desk he didn't seem so formidable, but his intense gaze held a menace of its own.

Perturbed, she crossed the distance and leaned close. "Why are you staring at me?"

"Was I staring?" He casually raked the opened letters into a pile and concealed them with a book. Then he propped his elbow on the desk and rested his chin in his palm. His black eyebrows rose in query. "What's wrong with admiring the very attractive woman who's agreed to share the pleasures of the flesh with me?"

She wanted to ball her fists, pound on the desk, and damn him for a rogue and a thief. Instead, she kept her voice light. "You needn't hide your love letters."

"You're not jealous?"

She wasn't in the least, but to keep up the pretense of wanting him, she shelved her indifference and returned to more important matters. "What happened between us in the barracks—Well . . . please understand that I didn't come here to vie for your affection." Softly she implored, "Don't you see that?"

His eyelids drifted shut, the lashes so thick and long they almost fanned his cheeks. "We'll discuss why you came here at length . . . later. After our bath."

Second thoughts plagued her. She needed time to devise a foolproof way of tricking him into marrying her. "What happened was very disturbing."

"A mere fraction of how disturbing the rest will be."

"This is all happening rather quickly, don't you think?"

"You enc 'iraged me, Alpin. Why back down now?"

She had encouraged him, and probably given him the mistaken impression that she was experienced in the art of seduction. Her easy success still baffled her. Could she now appeal to his sense of honor? "Because . . ."

He toyed with her bracelet. "Because?"

Exasperated, she blurted. "Because I'm a virgin."

Hunger gleamed in his eyes. "An enticing element in our arrangement."

He sounded as if he were bartering for a herd of sheep.

He, a rich man with a vast kingdom, made richer by the acquisition of Paradise Plantation. Well, she refused to be an easy conquest. She'd fashion her own bargain, but first she needed more information. "Enticing? What do you mean?"

His fingers began a slow journey up her arm. "If what you say is true, then it might be a considerable enticement—in some circles."

The only circles she could think about were the ones his fingers were drawing on her skin. How, she wondered, could she despise and desire him at once? "Why do you want me? You can have your choice of women."

"Suffice it to say, you have always held a special and unforgettable place in my life."

"A dishonorable place," she grumbled, "is where you'd put me."

"On the contrary. I intend to *honor* you from the delicate lobes of your ears to the dainty tips of your toes."

A tingling started in the parts he mentioned and spread everywhere in between. "I'm neither dainty nor delicate. Save those niceties for your dear Rosina."

"Forget her. She's gone."

"Where?"

He tapped his teeth together. "To Carvoran Manor."

"That's the estate your father was building for you when I left years ago. Is it grand?"

His hand stilled. "Nay. 'Tis nothing pretentious."

She relaxed. "Then tell me where it is and what it's like."

He began turning the bracelet around her wrist. "Remember the dry well near Hadrian's Wall?"

Confident that she had distracted him, Alpin grew bold. "Yes, I do. You once told me a treasure was buried there. I spent two days digging up the place."

Assuming a comically innocent air, he patted her hand. "But you found a pair of knives to add to your collection of sharp weapons."

"Some weapons. They were rusted beyond redemption. Still, it was a clever trick on your part."

His eyes narrowed. "And you keep cleverly changing the subject. Tell me, Alpin," he murmured, "what *do* you want?"

His seductive tone drew her like gulls to fish bait. She let down her guard. "I want a home of my own among people I can trust and call friends."

"I'm your friend, and you can trust me."

He said it with such sincerity that her heart leaped. If she could believe him, she could forgo subterfuge. "I can?"

"Uh-huh. Have you other stipulations before we end our negotiations and cry peace long into the night?"

He seemed so sure of her capitulation, and if there was anything Alpin hated it was being taken for granted. "I have about a thousand questions, and I'm not sure you'll want to answer them."

"You ask a thousand, Alpin. I'll ask one. Will you or will you not be mine?"

She didn't trust him, but if she could convince him that her work and dedication had made Paradise the profitable plantation it was, just maybe he would understand and give her back what was hers by right. Then she wouldn't have to trick him. Besides, she liked it when he spoke softly and smiled in that friendly way. "I'm not sure I should risk losing the good job I have."

"You'll enjoy your new duties, although the hours will be longer at first. Touch me, Alpin."

A warning blared, but she saw no alternative to giving him what he demanded. So she cupped his cheek and was immediately sorry, for the drag of new whiskers tickled her palm and the gleam in his eye dented her resolve. "You might go hungry."

He squeezed his eyes shut and turned, pressing a kiss on her hand. Groaning, he said, "I'm hungry now."

Her stomach bobbed like a keg on the ocean. She fought the urge to surrender and concentrated on the consequences of what he proposed. "What if I conceive?"

His fingers curled around her arm. "You won't," he said flatly.

"How can you be so certain? And, more to the point, how can I believe you?"

He opened his eyes and drilled her with a powerful stare. "Another wager? As I recall, you enjoy a friendly bet."

This was the opportunity she'd been waiting for. As normal as any woman, she felt certain she could bear a child. But could she maneuver him into wagering Paradise Plantation against her fertility? Something held her back, for she wasn't quite ready to reveal her heart's desire. "I'll think about it."

"Do your thinking this afternoon. I expect you to come to me tonight."

She must stall him. She must use her feminine wiles to gain some time. When the easy solution came to her, she almost felt guilty. "Are you offering to marry me?"

His steely gaze wavered.

"I didn't think you were," she said.

Uncertainty gave him a crafty look. "'Tis a big step."

"My point exactly. We should take a few months to think out our decision."

Understanding glimmered in his eyes. "A month," he growled. "No more."

She felt a fleeting relief, but her thoughts soon turned to the grand scheme she must create. "You're very understanding."

"More than you know, Alpin."

She managed a weak smile. "That sounds ominous."

"I know women. I've three sisters, remember? And now"—he placed a final kiss on her hand—"I regret to say, my duties to Kildalton call. Please send Saladin to me."

She thought of the letters and realized he probably had to answer them. Caught up in the reprieve she'd won, she kissed his cheek. "Straightaway, my lord."

As she left the room she began to whistle. Malcolm thought he had her in a compromising position. He did, but he wasn't the only one who could play the game of compromise. Alpin would keep a close watch on him and discover his weakness.

She knew just the way. Kildalton Castle was full of tunnels and secret passages. Years ago a frightened six-year-old girl had taken refuge there. Today those dark corridors would provide a desperate woman with a listening post and, she hoped, the tools to win back her home.

First she had to find the key.

6

"First I've got trouble with Alpin, and now this treasonous rubbish." Malcolm pitched the letter across his study. Broken seal flapping, the paper landed at Saladin's feet. "I tell you, Saladin, if this political maneuvering doesn't stop, John Gordon of Aberdeenshire will find himself dangling from a rope at Tyburn, just as Christopher Layer did."

Saladin picked up the letter and put it on the desk with the other correspondence. "You should rejoice. Swift execution is one of the few admirable elements of Christian justice."

Accustomed to irreverence from his friend, Malcolm took no offence; he groaned. "I can kiss good-bye any hope of a peaceful harvest."

"The rope makers will prosper, and the women will delight. Seeing a man hang brings his comrades to life, no?"

"None of this is humorous, Saladin. King George won't tolerate a challenge to his reign."

"A true English barbarian," he said with glee.

"You should feel right at home."

Saladin sat up straight and pointed to the letters. "Have Gordon and the other clan chiefs committed themselves to usurping the Hanoverian?"

Malcolm slapped the letters so hard his palm stung. "You tell me what you think. You just spent a week with the scheming bastards."

"As much as it distresses me to say, I think you have reason to worry, my friend."

Malcolm braced himself for the worst. "Go on."

"The roebucks are ready for the rut. Your fellow Scots, Gordon and Lord Lovatt, don't seem interested in felling stags. At least not the ones with velvet on their antlers."

Fury tied Malcolm's stomach in knots. His soul begged for an end to the strife among the northern clans. "I knew it. Those stubborn Highland lairds may have cloaked their Jacobite villainy in urbane rhetoric, but the meaning of these letters is clear."

Saladin nodded. "I heard the earl of Aberdeenshire say he'd lost faith in his king across the water ever winning the crown himself."

"Aye. Gordon has given up on James Stewart and invited his warring son to come and take back the throne. Since the death of his mother earlier this year, the prince is reportedly lost and angry." Mystified by the idea of war, Malcolm shook his head. "Another Jacobite rebellion. A Catholic Stewart wearing the crown. Fool's dreams and unlawful acts."

"Don't worry so, Christian."

Malcolm walked to the window and observed the peaceful interplay of his people. If fighting began, his soldiers would be manning the battlements rather than helping the weaver rethatch his roof. Instead of handing out biscuits to the excited bairns of Kildalton, the women would be passing buckets to put out the fires of war.

"Your bonnie prince is just a stripling lad of fifteen years. He can't lead an army," Saladin insisted.

"Charles Stewart is not *my* prince. He's never set foot on Scottish soil. But make no mistake, at five and ten he's a scholar in the school of Mars. Sir Thomas Sheridan has tutored him well enough in that. The lad can't read nor speak ten words of Scottish. He's a soldier."

Saladin joined him and clasped a hand on his shoulder. Offhandedly he said, "It's a grand bluff. I doubt he's an accomplished warrior."

Only Malcolm could best Saladin in a contest of sword-play, and hordes of men had tried. "Then you're in for a surprise."

Saladin grinned, revealing the space between his front teeth. "Thank you and praise Allah, but I must decline." He strolled to the chair and plopped down. "One surprise a day is enough for my humble Muslim soul."

Malcolm eagerly grasped the digression from Scottish politics. "I assume you refer to the lovely Elanna."

Laughing without humor, Saladin stroked his beard and tapped his booted foot. " 'Refer' to her? 'Debauch' comes immediately to mind."

Malcolm eased his hip onto the edge of his desk and studied his oldest friend. Normally stoic and always at peace with himself, Saladin now fidgeted like a criminal in the witness box. "She threatens your vow of celibacy?"

Saladin stared into the cold hearth. "Not if you get rid of her before my evening prayers. Which brings me to the burning question." He faced Malcolm again. "Why aren't they at Sinclair Manor? You arranged for Alpin to live with her uncle, Baron Sinclair."

"Lady Alpin tricked me." He relayed the details of his first two meetings with her.

Saladin roared with laughter. "She hasn't changed."

The fallacy of that statement made Malcolm see red. "Oh, yes, she has. Now she says she's my property."

Saladin swung his legs over the arm of the chair. His red boots contrasted vividly with the deep brown leather. "Ah, English law," he lamented with great sarcasm. "It seems she knows the statutes well."

"Among other things." Like setting Malcolm's blood afire and sending his rational thoughts fleeing out the window. Relief would come, though. Once he had her in his bed, his obsession would end. As would her virginity. A shiver went through him at the prospect of teaching her the ways of love.

"I see." Saladin plucked a blade of grass from his boot. "Alexander said she could cook. That's something in her favor. She's also a beauty—for a white woman. Don't you think?"

Malcolm groaned and said, "She is that, right enough, my African friend. Have you ever seen eyes that color?"

"Not in twenty years, and I don't remember them being so pretty."

"Neither do I."

"Don't tell me you're tempted to seduce her." He jolted upright. "I expected you to marry her off to one of those pox-ridden Campbells you hate so much."

For the first time since Alpin had schemed her way into his home, Malcolm saw a way to put his plans back on course. "I might do both."

Saladin shook his finger in reproof. "Seduction first, my friend."

Infused with assurance, Malcolm kissed his fingertips and flung his hand in the air. "But of course."

Saladin rolled his eyes. "Truthfully, I can't picture Alpin welcoming your attentions. She never did before. What was it you used to say? Oh, I remember." He worked his lips like a netted trout. In a high voice he said, " 'Give me a kiss of peace, Alpin.' "

Disgruntled at the reminder of his foolish youth but unwilling to reveal his feelings, Malcolm shrugged. "She claims I'm her best friend."

"If you believe that, I'll sell you a map to find the Holy Grail."

"And I'll tell her to put pig fat in your oatcakes."

"A truce!" Saladin slapped his thigh. "And curse the luck you have with women. She did you grievous harm and deserves your vengeance, but I never expected her to fall in your arms."

"Must be the will of the gods."

"What does the lovely Rosina have to say about your new best friend?"

"Plenty, but I don't have to listen. I sent her back to Carvoran Manor."

"Prudent—under the circumstances. A wise man always controls his women."

Malcolm's decision to send Rosina away seemed clever in the extreme. "Or keeps a manageable number of them, but that isn't important. Now that you've returned, Rosina will soon be taking ship. Unfortunately these letters must get to Italy."

"Don't be surprised if John Gordon pays you a visit. He seemed especially eager for a reply."

"He's been eager for years, but never enough to come south."

Saladin winced. "He has reason now. He's also withdrawn his approval for the betrothal between his daughter and Argyle's son."

Jane Gordon was the most sought-after heiress in Scotland and, according to some, the richest marriage prize in the British Isles. But in Malcolm's case, Jane was forbidden, because an alliance between the earl of Kildalton and the mighty Gordon clan would unite the Borders and the Highlands, or roughly half of Scotland. The king had forbidden the match years ago. He would suspect trouble if the marriage was proposed again.

"Poor lass," Malcolm said. "Since the day she was christened, her father has been bartering her all over Scotland and France."

"I think he will approach you on the matter. He asked if you had found a bride. When I told him no, he asked about your parents. I told him they were abroad on the king's business. He was silent for some time."

"He was calculating."

"I believe so. He smiled and excused himself. Then he sought out Lord Lovatt, who was playing chess with the earl of Mar."

"Just the three of them together is a bad sign, even if it was hunting season."

"Lovatt lost interest in the chess match."

"I should inform Lady Miriam."

"She taught you well. You've managed to hold the Jacobites at bay since she left for Constantinople. Why bother her now?"

"Because she asked me to get involved in the first place. If this attempt to bring Bonnie Prince Charles into the fray succeeds and reflects badly on her, I'll feel responsible. Her male counterparts in the diplomatic corps are always looking for opportunities to discredit her."

In a deadly whisper, Saladin said, "Lord Duncan will deal with any man who tries to discredit her."

Malcolm had to agree. His father would fight a duel to the death in defense of Lady Miriam. With one look, his father could put the fear of God in King George himself. "True, but if my parents are to suffer the consequences of this dangerous business, and I have no doubt they will, they should at least know the details."

"How will you let them know?"

Malcolm picked up a blank sheet of paper. "A few paragraphs of urbane rhetoric."

Saladin chuckled. "Lady Miriam's first language."

Malcolm joined in the laughter. "Don't forget she interceded many times on our behalf."

"And saved our worthless hides from the strap."

"Enough about our wayward youth. Tell me more about Elanna. Is she truly an African princess?"

"Well, she's willful enough to be an Ashanti."

In light of his own problems with Alpin, Malcolm welcomed the company of another miserable man. "I'm beginning to think all women are willful."

"When you relegate them to the status of temporary bedroom ornaments, some are bound to protest."

From a silver dispenser, Malcolm took a pinch of sand and sprinkled it on his desk. "Pardon me if I question the advice of a man who bedded his first and only woman at the age of fifteen."

"You know my reasons."

"I have always respected your objection to mixing our

races. But it no longer applies. Figuratively speaking, and without offense to the Prophet, the mountain has come to Muhammad."

Saladin slumped. "We're both in for trouble."

"Not I. I have no need for a permanent mate."

Saladin's mouth flattened to a white line. "False, my friend. You've a need, but you're too sanctimoniously noble to take a wife, knowing you can never . . ." He broke off and looked away.

"Give her a child?" Malcolm finished for him. He would never sire a son to wield a toy sword and wage mock battles. He'd never sire a daughter to string flowers and chase butterflies. Melancholy stole his breath, yet he knew the futility in dwelling on the impossible.

Alpin had crippled him.

She would pay. As soon as he put Rosina and the troublesome letters on a ship, he'd renew the conquest of Alpin MacKay.

"Enough about my virtues toward the fairer sex. Let's talk about yours. What will you do about our African princess—"

The bell clanged, signaling that someone had entered the tunnel behind the bookcases. Saladin sprang from the chair. "What the devil?"

"Shush." Malcolm put his index finger to his lips.

Only two keys existed. He rummaged through his desk until he found his. Mrs. Elliott kept the other key. That meant Alpin had it now. She had remembered the layout of the castle yard before Malcolm built the new barracks; she probably remembered the tunnels as well. She'd traveled them often enough as a lass.

He mouthed her name to Saladin.

Frowning, the Moor whispered, "Why? What does she want?"

Malcolm shrugged, then cupped a hand to his ear and pointed to himself and Saladin.

"She's eavesdropping?"

Embittered by her intrusion, yet curious as to what she hoped to gain, Malcolm nodded. Then he carefully considered his options. He had a grand opportunity to fill her head with false information.

Smiling, he whispered, "Let's oblige her, shall we?"

A grinning Saladin unfolded his hand, palm up, to Malcolm.

Moving close so she could hear his every word, he stood before the bookcase and spoke in a loud, clear voice. "Our Alpin has certainly grown into a beauty. Don't you agree, Saladin?"

Standing in an alcove in the dark, musty corridor, Alpin felt the compliment chase away her anxiety. She had come to pry. Instead she'd heard pretty compliments.

"True," she heard Saladin say. "Island life seems to have agreed with her."

"Aye, but she's better off here, where she belongs."

"What are her plans?"

"She hasn't shared them. I like to believe she's content keeping house for me."

When mangoes grow on fig trees, thought Alpin. As soon as she could get him to transfer ownership of Paradise to her, she'd be on the first packet home.

Saladin laughed. "I don't have to guess how you feel about having Alpin so close at hand."

"Having her *so* close at hand does indeed stir my imagination. I just hope she doesn't find out."

"Find out what?" Saladin asked.

Yes, what?

Malcolm said something in Scottish, a language Alpin had never learned.

"We both know you have special feelings for her," Saladin replied in English. "I wouldn't dream of telling her. But I'm sure she suspects."

"How do you know that?" Malcolm snapped.

Alpin stared into the inky darkness, confusion and curiosity running rampant in her mind.

"Because of the way you look at her."

"And how is that?" Although Malcolm spoke calmly, she couldn't miss the accusation in his voice.

"You look like a starving man awaiting the first dish in a

ten-course meal," Saladin said. "Don't glower at me. I didn't write the menu."

"But you glory in my predicament."

"Guilty as charged. Tell me, friend. Does Lady Alpin return your lustful feelings?"

"If she doesn't now, she soon will. I have a plan."

Keenly alert, Alpin moved a step closer. Her toe slammed into something hard and sharp. She had forgotten about the blasted boot scraper. Pain shot up her foot, and she bit her lip to muffle a gasp.

"What was that sound?"

In agony she leaned against the wall, eased off her slipper, and rubbed her throbbing toes.

"What sound?" Saladin asked.

"I thought I heard a noise in the tunnel."

Heart pounding, Alpin held her breath. If only she could see them, but the hidden door had been so well crafted not even a stream of light trickled into the tunnel.

Saladin said, "Hand me that lantern and I'll see what it is."

Alpin shivered, scooped up her shoe, and backed out of the alcove. Once in the tunnel proper, she felt for the wall. When she had her bearings, she touched the key in her pocket.

"It's probably a rat."

"Since when do you have rats in your castle?"

"Since the snakes died, I suppose."

Snakes! Alpin listened for the sound of scaly creatures slithering along the dirty stone floors. Her knees locked.

"What if the snakes aren't dead? What if they multiplied?"

"Impossible," said Malcolm. "They were both males."

"How could you tell? They looked alike, down to the fangs."

Fangs!

"The snake dealer at the market in Barcelona told me so."

"You believed that swindler? He also tried to sell you the crown of Isabella."

"He tried to sell you the sword of your namesake." Malcolm laughed. "You almost bought it."

"Forget the snake dealer and our foolish youthful adventures. Where were we? Oh, yes. You were about to tell me what you have planned for Alpin."

Malcolm's voice dropped to an indistinct rumble. She crept into the alcove again and put her ear to the squat door that she had once walked through with ease. But that was years ago. She had been a lonely, desperate child. She had become an angry, desperate woman—who couldn't hear a blasted word Malcolm was saying.

As soon as he finished mumbling, Saladin whistled and said, "I'm impressed with your clever ideas."

What ideas? Impatient, and feeling the darkness press in on her, Alpin struggled to conquer her fear and quiet her breathing.

"Did you hear something?" Malcolm asked.

"Noise in the tunnel again? Perhaps it's the ghost of the Border Lord come back to haunt us."

"Bah!" said Malcolm. "He never was any more than a ghost."

Alpin knew better. At her first glance of Malcolm Kerr, the adult, she had realized that the Border Lord and her Night Angel were the same man. But why didn't Malcolm, of all people, know the true identity of the legendary dark stranger?

"I always wondered about him," Saladin said. "Was he real or a legend created by parents to make children behave?"

"You wonder about everything from the stars in the sky to the fall of man."

"Please," Saladin drawled. "What were we talking about?"

You were talking about me! Damn that accursed Malcolm. Would he never reveal his plan for her?

"We were talking about vermin in the tunnel. I have an idea." Malcolm's voice grew softer, as if he had moved away, across the room. "You go around through the main door to the tunnel. I'll duck under the squat door here. We'll flush the pest out the back of the tunnel and into the walled garden."

Alpin's heart climbed into her throat. Using the same route Malcolm planned, she could flee, for she'd used the garden door to gain access to the castle years before. She could run down the inky corridor, through the iron door, and out into the walled garden. Or she could follow the tunnel to the stair tower and hide there. But the thought of entering that room she had once called home bothered her more than the prospect of facing down a rat.

"I don't want any rats in the garden. That's where I say my prayers to Allah."

"Just take your scimitar with you. No rat would stand a chance against that blade."

"I'm not going into that tunnel."

"Why not? Are you afraid? I thought Moors were fearless."

"Even if the snakes have died and the rats become shy, I remember your skill at setting trip wires."

Trip wires! Oh, Lord. What had she gotten herself into? And when would they get back to talking about her?

"That was years ago. I dismantled them all."

Saladin huffed in disbelief.

"Would I leave so dangerous a thing where an innocent servant could fall victim?"

"Probably not, but no one ever uses the tunnels anymore. Me included."

"Except those hairy, long-legged spiders," Malcolm said.

Spiders? So what? Alpin wasn't afraid of any spiders.

"Nasty creatures." Saladin's voice wavered with disgust.

"Don't tell me you're frightened of insects."

"I am if it's the same spider that gave Mrs. Elliott that vicious bite a couple of years ago. She nearly died."

Poisonous spiders! Perspiration blossomed on Alpin's skin; yet she felt cold with fear.

Leather creaked; one of the men had risen from a chair. Alpin told herself to stay calm. Even deadly spiders were timid and afraid of people. Right? She wasn't sure, but she was certain she had enough time to make her escape, if she didn't trip and fall into the web of a—

"Why don't I believe those vermin are dead?" Saladin said.

"'Tis baffling to me. I'm a man of my word."

"You're also a bit too eager to get me into that tunnel. I have a feeling you want me to fall on my face."

Hooray for Saladin's skepticism!

"I've outgrown such pranks."

"Swear, then, on your honor as the ninth earl of Kildalton."

As far as Alpin was concerned, Malcolm Kerr had no honor, earl or not. She wouldn't believe him if he swore on the bones of Christ.

"I'm wounded that you don't believe me."

"Let's just say I've known you too long and I'm not completely convinced."

"Wait," Malcolm said. "Sit back down. I'll tell Alpin about the rats. She'll know what to do."

"I never thought I'd hear you sing her praises."

Yes! Now she would learn what was on Malcolm's mind.

"Times change. People change." She could almost see him shrug.

Saladin laughed. "You've certainly got some changes in store for her."

What blasted changes? Would they never stop speaking in ambiguities? It was almost as if they knew she could hear them. That thought made her skin crawl. But she disregarded it; they couldn't have any idea that she stood in the tunnel.

"Where is she?" Saladin asked.

"Riding, I think. She's taken a liking to the dappled gray."

"That gelding's a spirited mount. Do you think she can manage him?"

"I hope so. I'd hate to see the lass hurt. I'm sure the baron would have something to say about that."

The baron! At the mention of her hated uncle, Alpin stomped her foot.

"There's that noise again."

89

"'Tis your Moorish imagination. There's nothing but ghosts of rats and spiders in there."

Alpin shivered.

"What will Sinclair say about her living here rather than with him? He is her only kin."

"He's still in Ireland fawning over a grandchild."

"He's certainly changed, Malcolm—since your step-mother defeated him. He'll want to know that Alpin's here."

"Aye. I may send word to him, but I suppose I should tell Lady Miriam first."

"Will you tell the baron and Lady Miriam what you just told me?"

What did the mighty Malcolm just say?

"Oh, I don't think so," he said, a silky quality in his voice that gave Alpin pause. "I like to keep my plans for Alpin close to my chest."

Alpin thought a dagger would look better there.

"I'll leave you to your correspondence," Saladin said. "It's time for my prayers."

When she heard the door open and close, Alpin retraced her steps and exited the tunnel. Once in the lesser hall she plopped down on the ancient family throne and breathed a sigh of relief. Her excursion into the bowels of Kildalton Castle had gained her little, except the knowledge that Malcolm had some plan for her. She was determined to learn exactly what Malcolm Kerr had on his mind.

Common sense told her she had the perfect tools, but would her conscience allow her to use them?

7

Later that day, with the walls of Kildalton Castle far behind her and the wind snatching at her kerchief, Alpin eased back on the reins until the gray slowed to a walk. Her legs ached from the jarring ride, and a slight soreness in her bottom reminded her that she hadn't sat a horse since leaving Paradise.

Paradise. Swamped by a wave of homesickness, she closed her eyes and conjured up a vision of bright blue skies above a jewel of an island lush with lacy ferns, sprawling bearded fig trees, and an ocean of sugarcane.

Tears rolled down her cheeks. The cool breeze chilled her dampened skin, telling her vividly of the differences between her tropical home and this northern land. She had hated her life here, and when Malcolm's father, Lord Duncan Kerr, had put her on a ship more than twenty years ago, Alpin hadn't looked back. She had embraced Barbados with the zeal of an explorer claiming new territory. Her territory. Her own new world.

People there depended on her. She had given the slaves a

promise of freedom. Upon her return she would again pick up the banner of emancipation. The indentured servants would see their years of toil culminate in the promised gift of a parcel of land and independence. Under the supervision of Henry Fenwick, Paradise would pass the slow months after harvest. If necessary, the planting would wait for her.

When her loneliness grew and a sob welled up in her throat, Alpin knew she must rally her courage. Dwelling on past injustices and future rewards would only hinder her return to Paradise. Still, it seemed unfair that Malcolm possessed so much while she owned so little.

Malcolm.

She felt hollow at the thought of him, of his teasing smiles when she had expected mocking sneers, of his masculine allure when she had believed herself immune to romance. Her remembrances of him centered around dunking in a brisk loch or searching for the perfect skipping stone and, on rainy days, playing peevers and tag in the dark, hidden corridors of Kildalton Castle.

How did he see her now? How did he reflect on their childhood together? He spoke of broken stilts and stolen kisses, but when he pulled her into his arms and lured her with a man's expertise, she sensed an anger she didn't understand. With the ease of a dockside hawker luring passengers from an incoming ship, he was drawing her into a scheme. Yet sometimes his charm and his attraction to her seemed superficial, as if he were still playing one of his many roles.

His reasons for so heartless a ploy eluded her. Unless it was the hornet incident. But she'd been only six at the time. Surely he wouldn't hold a grudge for so many years. She'd done him no lasting harm.

She had been the orphan, the poor relation shuffled from her mother's deathbed to the indifferent care of her uncle, Baron Sinclair. At first her nightmares and weeping had kept the others in her adopted family awake. Their scorn of a bereft child had hurt more than the uncaring woman who'd given her life, then died, a brokenhearted and penniless widow.

To escape the sneers and scolding of her new relatives, Alpin had gathered her meager possessions—a lucky coin, a lock of her mother's hair, and a collection of knives—and staked out a corner in the stable at Sinclair Manor. In the bustling, crowded household, no one had even missed her.

She learned to hear a lullaby in the lowing of a milk cow. She found comfort in caring for sick and injured creatures, not knowing at the time that she herself was one.

Then on a bleak winter's evening, at a spot not far from where she now rode, her Night Angel had found her and taught her that children were supposed to be cherished and nurtured.

Seeing Malcolm as a man, she had at last discovered the identity of the first person to show her kindness. Malcolm's father had cared. The memory of her dark savior sparked her courage.

She dashed away her tears and swallowed her sorrow. The devil take Malcolm Kerr. She could and would make the most of her stay in the Borders. She'd find a measure of enjoyment in the land she'd left so many years ago.

Patches of heather and gorse thrived amid a field of cotton bracken and perfumed the air with the unforgettable scent of Scotland. In the distance Hadrian's Wall snaked across the land like the exposed backbone of an enormous reptile. Once she had frolicked in those Roman ruins.

Hoping to recapture those days she guided the horse onto the narrow road she had traveled often as a child. The freedom road to Kildalton Castle.

A family of red grouse dashed across the path and scurried beneath the protective canopy of a tangle of last year's bramble. A herd of hungry sheep ignored her passing, but a pair of red deer stags, their budding antlers thick with velvet, cocked their heads and stared, then bolted for the cover of a stand of beech trees.

As she approached the crumbling stone wall, she was surprised to find it smaller and more ravaged than she remembered. But back then everything had seemed enormous to a girl called "runt."

Alpin reined in the gelding and slid off the horse's back,

her fingers gripping the saddle, her feet dangling in the air. The jump to the ground jolted her ankles. The horse sidestepped and ambled to a puddle of rainwater. On wobbly knees, she struggled for balance, all the while wishing she were tall enough to dismount with ease.

Laughing at so foolish and senseless a whim, she found a stick and began to overturn rocks. The familiarity of her surroundings warmed her: the old road and the break in the wall, mounds of earth the Romans had moved and nature had sown with weeds, industrious meadow pipits darting overhead and ferrying food to their young while the crafty hooded crows looked on, the constant breeze that even in summer made gooseflesh of her skin.

"Well, how now, Lady Alpin? What see you in those rocks that you lose so much attention?"

Malcolm Kerr.

Even in a raging hurricane, she'd have known his voice.

Grasping the stick tightly, she faced him. And was again startled by his masculine beauty. Dressed in full Highland regalia and seated on a pure white stallion, he looked like a powerful monarch in command of all he surveyed.

"Surely you have a greeting for me," he said.

Her will to resist his allure threatened to crumble much like the wall that served as his backdrop. Appalled at her own weakness, she tucked the stick under her arm and approached him.

"You have my attention now, my lord, and my cheeriest good day."

He doffed his bonnet, replete with three eagle feathers and a smaller version of his clan brooch, a blazing sun cast in silver. "My same to you. What are you doing here? Spying on me again?"

"Again? I was here first. You're spying on *me.*"

He looked away, as if he'd said something he shouldn't. Then he stepped from the horse in a fluid motion that sparked her envy. "A favorite pastime of yours, as I recall."

"As I recall"—she strolled to a spot near the wall—"this was my land." She drew a line in the dirt. "That was yours."

He gave her a cocky grin, his oak brown eyes glittering with challenge. "Then I'm trespassing."

Her heart said he'd become an expert at invasion, but her pride said she could best him at that, too. "One of your minor offenses, I'm sure."

"Oh? And I suppose you're the saint who'll recite all my sins."

"Only a few. I must consult your other women to learn the rest."

"I've not committed a sin with you now that you're a woman. Although I've been trying."

"You're so glib, Malcolm. What are you doing here?"

He pointed over the wall. "I live there, on occasion."

She climbed up the fallen stones and peered over the wall. In the distance, near a loch where she used to fish, she saw a well-traveled road leading to a small estate. She squinted to make out the details, but she was too far away. Then she remembered. "That's Carvoran Manor."

"Aye."

That hollow feeling in her stomach returned. "You keep your mistress there."

"Kept. She's gone."

She pursed her lips to keep from smiling. "Oh. So sorry. You must be bereft."

He twirled the bonnet while his eyes made a lazy inspection of Alpin's riding costume. Uncertain whether he was judging her or her outfit, she grew defensive. At one time her wardrobe had consisted of breeches and tunics he'd outgrown. "Why are you staring at me?"

"Because the sight of you in leather breeches offers much consolation—to my bereavement. Especially from this vantage point."

He was only teasing. She laughed and jumped to the ground. "You're either a prime rogue or a creative jester."

"Perhaps I'm both."

"And perhaps I'm the queen o' the May, instead of a homeless maiden."

His smile faded. "Why do you always do that, Alpin?"

"Do what?"

"Speak bitterly about your life so that I'll feel sorry for you."

Pride made her reckless. "You're mistaken. I don't want your pity or anyone else's."

"Then what *do* you want?"

My home, her soul screamed.

"It's only fair," he said in a chiding tone, "that you tell me. I've never lied to you."

Surprised by his frankness and stumped for an appropriate reply, she surveyed her surroundings. "I want that chest of Roman gold we always searched for."

He grew dead serious, his piercing gaze pinning her where she stood. "I'll find out, you know. You can't hide your secret from me."

The threat in his voice struck a warning bell. "What makes you think I'm hiding something?"

He winked. "I'm your best friend, remember? And I'll be your first lover."

She felt like an animal, caged by his virility and trapped by her own foolishness. "Somehow I have trouble thinking of myself as one of the objects of your lusty proclivities."

Stepping forward, he held out his hand. "'Tis unfair to throw a man's words in his face, and I don't think of you in that way."

"The way you think of Rosina?"

"I don't think of her at all."

"Don't expect me to be flattered. You're fickle."

He took the stick from her hand and tossed it aside; then he grasped her wrists and pulled her close. "Nay, Alpin. I can be loyal to the right woman. Truth to tell, I'm intrigued by what I see and don't see."

He towered over her, but she was growing accustomed to staring at the clan badge that secured his plaid at the shoulder. "What don't you see?"

A bland smile softened his masculinity. "You asked me if I intended to blame you for all the ill that befell me in childhood. I believe the opposite is true."

She fought to keep the sarcasm from her voice. "What could *I* possibly blame *you* for?"

"Let's just say I have the feeling you find fault with me because of my birthright."

He was close to grasping her motive. Dangerously close. "You make me sound shallow and petty."

Bending from the waist, he pushed against her, coming so near she could distinguish each of his eyelashes and feel the warm rush of his breath. "Then show me who you really are. Tell me why you sought my protection."

Stretching the truth seemed appropriate, considering how fast her pulse was hammering and how much she wanted to throw her arms around his neck and make certain he truly forgot his Rosina. "You protect me? You've tried to seduce me at every turn."

"Some things never change, such as your expertise at evasion."

She had to get a distance between them. Knowing she'd start fidgeting if she didn't move, she turned toward the wall. "You know why I came to you."

"Because you had nowhere else to go? I don't believe you. You could have gone to Sinclair Manor."

The cruelty she'd suffered during those years came back in a flood. She whirled on him. "Ha! I hated my life there and ran away every chance I got."

"But you could have at least stopped to visit. And had you, I think you would have stayed at Sinclair Manor."

"I'd sooner go back to living in your tower room."

He shook his head slowly, real disappointment clouding his eyes. "There. You've done it again. I'm sorry, Alpin, that you had to seek refuge in a windowless room. I'm sorry you had to steal food, but it wasn't my fault."

His valid observation gave her pause. She hadn't expected honesty from Malcolm Kerr, but he was correct about her methods; she saw that now. "Thank you for telling me, and it wasn't your fault I ran away from my uncle." It *was* Malcolm's doing, however, that she'd lost Paradise, but she'd live over a tavern and wait on tables before she'd confess that truth. The bleak option seemed ironic in the extreme, for if he did discern her methods, she might as well learn how to tap a keg.

Swallowing her pride, she held out her hand. "Forgive me?"

He took it and with his thumb traced the pads of her fingers. "Apology accepted. You might be interested to know that your uncle's household has changed."

"Certainly," she quipped. "Now his poor relations live in the sty."

"Wrong. Thanks to my stepmother's negotiations, all of your cousins have married well and moved on. Your uncle is in Ireland. You could have a wing in the manor all to yourself."

Suddenly suspicious of his glowing report, she said, "Do you want me to go there?"

His hand slipped up her arm. "Nay. I want you in my bed."

She gasped, for at every turn her confusion grew. "I hardly know you anymore." Yet he seemed to know her very well.

"Another expert evasion. Number two on the day, I believe."

From somewhere behind her, she heard a lamb bleating for its mother. The cry echoed her own emotional turmoil. She might as well blurt out what he wanted to hear and get it over with. "I'd rather stay with you."

He leaned close. She smelled sandalwood, the manly fragrance he'd preferred even as a lad. "Then you'll admit I'm making progress?" he asked.

Even though she willed it away, an embarrassed flush warmed her cheeks. "I'll admit you're making bold."

He assumed an adorable pout that years before had made the visiting noblewomen pinch his perky cheeks. Now it made her want to punch his nose. "When will I ever learn to behave?" he said.

Troubled by the easy way he distracted her, Alpin shrugged at his charming display. "Probably when time stops ravaging this wall." She raked a handful of dust from between the stones. "The mortar is crumbling."

He opened his mouth, then closed it. Giving her hand a squeeze, he said, "That's evasion number three. I believe we were discussing what else you want, besides a home and honest work."

If he thought to befuddle her with seduction, he would fail. Because she intended to control their courtship. "Have you a complaint?"

"Only one." He touched the edge of her kerchief where it covered her ear. "I heard a rat rummaging in the tunnels."

Did he suspect that she had eavesdropped on his conversation with Saladin? No. He was too arrogant to let it pass. He would have confronted her if he'd guessed. Although her excursion into intrigue had been a failure, she might again make use of the tunnels. "I'll have Dora see if the stableman has a good mouser."

"Fair enough. Rodents can be pesky devils—always poking their noses where they're unwanted. Now, tell me what you want from me."

Dissembling seemed her only option. "I want us to get to know each other, as we did before."

"We *knew* each other when I was seven and you were six. We whiled away many an afternoon playing kiss-the-freckle."

Her life had changed the day she met Malcolm Kerr. Twenty years later fate—or someone—had interfered once more. Until she again gained control of her future she would play her evasive game. "We shouldn't have been so brazen."

"You're probably right." He laughed and fell into step beside her. "'Twould seem our destinies are forever linked. From the moment you ran away from home, my life changed."

Happy moments in their past gave her the will to thread her fingers through his. His skin felt work-worn and made her rethink her assumption that he led a privileged life. But she must be cautious in her understanding; she'd learned early in life the high price a gullible girl must pay.

Glancing up, she realized he'd been waiting for her to speak. "Do you remember the time I tried to build a house here?" she asked.

"Aye." He pointed to a pile of smaller stones near the break in the wall. "You were certain you could make your fortune offering refreshment to travelers on this road."

"That's because you told me there was water in that old well."

"I thought there was."

"I spent an entire day down in that hole digging in dry dust."

"I pulled you out and tended your bruised fingers."

He had. She'd been exhausted and on the verge of tears. Then he'd appeared above her, a smile on his face, a quip on his tongue, and a rope in his hands.

"Lord, I was an industrious little beggar," she mused.

"Beggar? Never. You always insisted on doing your share and earning your keep."

"I'm smarter now."

"I know. You're more clever, too."

"You won your share of contests."

He laughed. "Not when the sport required throwing daggers or nocking arrows."

"But you always bested me with a sword."

"Only because I was stronger and bigger."

"As you say, my lord. Some things never change."

He grew thoughtful, his intense gaze following the flight of a hen harrier. "You asked why I doubt you. Here's a case in point. I don't expect you to address me so formally, unless you're mocking me."

He might call her clever, but he took the prize for being astute. "I was, and I'm sorry."

"Then gain my forgiveness by addressing me in a fashion befitting our friendship."

"Yes, Malcolm. Although I'm surprised you use your name. You always hated it. Remember the time you dressed as Caesar and I talked you into letting me tie you to a tree?"

He stopped. "That's number four," he growled.

Thinking his harshness stemmed from patience lost, she

100

dropped his hand and played the role of cowering maiden. "You grant no quarter today?"

His eyes narrowed and his nostrils flared. "I could be persuaded to take a hostage."

Realizing she had angered him, she sought to diffuse his rage. "I think you mean a prisoner."

"Nay. A hostage has something with which to bargain." His gaze moved to her breasts. "You're well supplied with valuable assets."

So much for placating his pride. "I should slap you."

"You could, but then I'd grow more doubtful of your sincerity."

She couldn't alienate him. She only wanted to capture his heart while guarding her own. Once she'd taken possession of her home, Malcolm could do as he pleased. Turning her back, she walked to the old well. "Then you must tell me what I can do to convince you."

He followed her and pulled off her kerchief. "You can begin by letting down your hair and reviving your role as pagan goddess."

In the spring of her last year in Scotland, she and Malcolm had painted their skin and danced naked, enacting an ancient fertility ritual.

"I see you remember," he added. "You're blushing."

"You were playing a Druid priest that day." Seeing his eyes darken with desire, she added, "We performed the ritual in childish innocence."

He grasped her waist and lifted her onto the rim of the well. "A rehearsal of sorts? You outdanced me."

A determined glimmer in his eyes, he spread her leather-clad thighs and moved so close the warmth of his wool tartan heated her skin.

"I haven't danced in years, and you're stronger now," she said.

"I'll take special care to show you the proper steps, and I'll stop often so you can catch your breath."

Her pulse began to hammer. "You're not talking about childish dancing, are you?"

Putting his cheek next to hers, he breathed softly in her

ear. "Take the pins out of your hair and I'll show you exactly what I'm talking about."

Shivers rocked her and she clutched his shoulders for balance. "I'll fall into the well."

"I promise to catch you," he whispered, his mouth perilously close to hers. "I always have."

Beyond denial, she lifted her arms and began pulling the wooden pins from her hair. Hands shaking, she fumbled to complete the mundane task, which now seemed vital to her sanity. His mouth touched hers, his tongue darting forward to nudge her lips apart. She followed his lead, and by the time her hair fell free, her senses were spinning out of control. His exotic scent tantalized her nose while the heat from his body fed the flames of her desire.

He wrapped an arm around her, clutching her as if she were a precious keepsake, and although she felt his free hand unbuttoning her tunic, Alpin no longer questioned the right or wrong of his methods. He seemed her perfect mate, his heart pounding in unison with hers, his labored breathing an echo of her own. When his tongue lunged insistently against hers, she welcomed him, joined in the twirling, darting ceremony.

Just when she thought she might tumble backward into the well, Malcolm traced a line of kisses across her cheek and down her neck. He drew back, one hand splayed at the base of her spine, and again put his other hand to work freeing the tiny pearl buttons of her blouse. She looked up. The hen harrier still glided overhead. The afternoon sun turned a high bank of knobby clouds to a giant sheet of hammered gold.

Malcolm pulled her blouse from her breeches and stared at her exposed breasts. The breeze teased her heated skin.

A softness shrouded his strong features, and his lips were damp from their kisses. "You've been swimming naked as we used to. Your skin is brown where it shouldn't be."

"A gentleman wouldn't mention it" was all that came to mind, for she was caught up in appreciating the way she affected him.

He lifted the old coin she wore on a chain. "Adrienne gave you this. Your heat lingers in the metal."

Lips as sensuous as his should be outlawed, she thought, and words so beguiling should be proscribed. "Yes. It belonged to the Border Lord."

He looked youthful in his skepticism, like the adventurous Malcolm of days gone by. "Nay," he said. "'Twas my father's. He gave her the coin."

He'd been honest enough to point out one of her faults. Now she could be honest with him. "Your father is—or was—the Border Lord."

She expected him to argue and prayed that he wouldn't. They had reached a moment of accord, and although he was her enemy, she wanted this brief respite from their war.

"I wondered when you'd guess his identity. And that's number five, Alpin. The last on the day, I trust."

His provocative tone sapped her will to evade him further, made her eager to extend their truce. Returning his caresses seemed an inevitable move. She reached for the laces on his shirt.

"In a moment, sweet." His eyes held a determined look, and his hand was insistently firm on hers. "I haven't painted you yet. Wait right there."

He stepped back, but held her until she found her balance on the edge of the well. Then he ran to his horse and lifted a wineskin from the pommel. Her feet dangling off the ground, she watched him walk toward her, his silk shirt billowing in the summer breeze, his colorful Kerr tartan lending power to an already formidable presence. How, she wondered, could any woman resist him?

Instinctively she drew the edges of her blouse together.

Twisting off the stopper, he said, "May I offer you drink for your thirst?"

From him, the ordinary question sounded devilishly indecent. She opened her mouth and closed her eyes. When the tangy liquid flowed over her tongue, she thought he'd introduced her to some strange wine. But with the first swallow she tasted berries. And the truth.

She almost gagged on Elanna's love potion.

He grasped her shoulder. "Drink slowly," he said, "or you'll choke."

Sputtering, she wiped her mouth. "Where did you get that?"

A frown creased his high forehead. "From Saladin. He found it in the kitchen and offered me a share."

Her stomach roiled and her tongue rebelled at the earthy aftertaste of the herb.

His eyes grew wide with concern. "What's wrong?"

Nothing, her mind screamed, except that I've slipped a proverbial noose over my own neck! "Nothing's wrong," she said on a nervous sigh, "but I think we would be better off with water."

He sniffed the juice. "Is it tainted?"

Before she could cry yes, he took a sip. Licking his lips, his eyes darting left and right, he said, "Berries. I rather like it." Then he tilted his head back.

Just as he began squirting the drink into his mouth, she yelled, "No!"

He stopped. "No? Why don't you want me to drink this?" Smiling, he added, "Don't fret. I'll save some for you."

A viable reply eluded her. Over the clamoring of her heart, she accepted defeat. "You really like it that much?"

He handed it back to her. "Aye. Don't you?"

Dread gripped her. "Of course," she conceded, and pretended to swallow the dangerous drink.

Her heart sinking, she watched him take back the wineskin and finish off the contents. One small blessing rang in her mind: he had drunk only half of the stuff. A drop of blood red liquid seeped from the corner of his mouth, flowed to his chin, and halted an instant before trailing leisurely over his throat, down his neck, and to his shirt. As if in a daze, she saw the thirsty white silk absorb the garnet-hued liquid.

The leather bag hit the ground with a plop. She glanced up at him and froze, for his eyes held a dreamy quality.

To her astonishment he put his index finger in his mouth, then traced a Celtic cross on each of her breasts. At that moment she understood the true meaning of the word "erotic," and with each symbol he sketched, her need increased. Watching him slip his finger into his mouth for added moisture brought a tightness to her belly and a weakness to her legs.

With great care he illuminated her torso, his touch too soft to tickle, too exquisite to agitate. A parade of sensations marched across her skin and spawned feelings so fresh they glistened like the morning dew. She felt like a treasured prize, coddled, worshiped, and valued, but as he continued his foray into artful seduction, her ethereal thoughts gave way to physical need, and her body yearned for a more intimate touch.

When he finished drawing circles, he fashioned twin blazing suns, his hallmark. Feeling completely possessed, she watched in fascination as he bent his head and took her nipple into his mouth. A cry escaped her lips, and her backbone turned to jelly. Thinking she would fall, she grasped his head and threaded her fingers in his hair. Beneath her thumb, she felt a pulse pounding at his temple in a steady rhythm. As he cherished her breasts, she came to know the slick texture of his mouth, the drag of his tongue, and the even edge of his teeth. Noise ceased, save the gentle suckling sounds he made and the desire that became a living, screaming thing inside her.

Moving from one areola to the other, he tasted and stroked her, his fingers massaging, and when he had taken his fill, he straightened up and rested his forehead against hers.

Perspiration trickled off his brow and over her thumb. A different kind of dampness flourished in her most secret place.

He inhaled deeply and said, "Do you feel properly paganized?"

She smiled. "Devilishly so."

Licking his lips, he nodded, then looked left and right.

A furnace of heat blazed where their skin touched. "Has someone come?" she asked.

He laughed, a pained sound that made his chest heave.

"Nay, and 'tis a definite problem, considering where we are and what you are."

Pulling her hands away, she stiffened her arms and braced herself on the well. After the softness of his hair, the stones felt gritty and cold against her palms. "I don't understand."

Dropping his chin and lifting his brows, he said, "You're a virgin, remember?"

Confusion took the edge off her desire. "You said my virginity was an enticement. I thought you were glad."

"What would please me"—he began righting her clothing —"is to strip off those breeches and love you here and now. But 'twould not please you. Most likely you'd hate me for callously taking advantage of you."

That he cared about her feelings surprised Alpin and reinforced her belief that she didn't really know the man Malcolm Kerr had become. One thing was certain: he wanted to love her, and the thought of doing so brought him great joy. Or was it the berry juice? She didn't know.

Feeling giddy and childish again, she wrapped her legs around him for balance, leaned back and over the lip of the well. The sound of her laughter echoed off the circular walls. "I could never hate you for making me feel the way I do right now."

"You truly want me for your mate."

She'd won. Why else, save true devotion, would he put her welfare before his lust? Jubilation filled her. A heartbeat later a twinge of guilt threatened her high spirits. The potion had induced him to want her, but she'd come too far and risked too much to turn back now. "Oh, yes, Malcolm. You are what I want. All I want," she lied through her teeth.

8

Malcolm almost believed her. But through hazy senses he looked beneath her flush of passion and saw desperation. He knew that old reckless enemy. He'd lived with it since becoming a man. Peace of mind had come on the day when he'd accepted the inescapable and hellish truth that he would never sire an heir.

Alpin MacKay had a demon of her own. She just hadn't come to terms with it. She fancied she'd found a way out of her dilemma, though, and it involved Malcolm. Knowing he was the answer to her problem both disappointed and angered him. He also wondered just how far she'd go. Marriage? Was marriage to him her solution?

To test his theory, he pulled her into a sitting position. His head began to spin, and he planted his feet. "Then I suppose I should begin phrasing my honorable intentions."

So keen was her relief, he might have told her she'd be crowned queen on the morrow. Her lavender eyes glittered with hope. She hugged him fiercely and said his name on a sigh. He could have challenged her easy acceptance. Instead, he fought the lust hammering in his loins and played his trump card. "Who would have thought," he said with an odd and unexplainable whimsy, "that Alpin MacKay would handfast herself to Malcolm Kerr?"

She grew as stiff as a Highland halberd. "Handfast?"

"Is something wrong with that arrangement?" he asked rubbing her back and thinking she should be on it, in his bed.

She softened a bit. "I thought . . . Well, you did use the word 'honorable.'"

"Aye, and I meant it." The lie played tag with his conscience and momentarily disoriented him. He shook his head to clear his thoughts. "Handfasting is probably the most honorable of Scottish customs, for it equitably favors both parties. We'll say our church vows when you conceive—" He stopped, feeling light-headed. Thinking it was the subject matter, he forced back his weakness. "When you conceive my child."

She didn't notice his discomfort, for she blurted, "But it makes me feel that you want me only to produce an heir."

Pushing her back so their gazes could meet, he spoke the bitter truth with absolute sincerity. "I swear to you, Alpin MacKay, getting an heir on you is the least of my concerns. I do have obligations, though."

Her smile could have illuminated a hundred dungeons. Perhaps he'd been wrong in his judgment of her. What if she did truly love him? If so, he'd deal with her affection later. But for now he had too much to learn about the woman and the reasons why she was so desperate to marry him. He also wanted a good night's sleep. "Then you're pleased?"

"Oh, yes, Malcolm." Her voice was breathy. "'Tis my fondest wish."

The words fit their circumstances perfectly, because his passion for her was the one emotion he couldn't disguise. He lifted her and walked toward the horses.

She clung to him like pride to a Scot. He liked the feel of her in his arms. He'd always wanted a mate to share his life, to listen to his troubles, and to help him preserve the noble heritage of clan Kerr. He'd just never had the heart to trick an unsuspecting bride into a marriage that would never bear fruit.

For some reason he couldn't contain his selfish needs. At this moment he wanted her with the hot lust of a green lad mounting his first willing wench. Disgusted with his own vulnerability, Malcolm put her astride the gelding and handed her the reins. "What shall we do now?"

She tossed her head back and, still smiling, surveyed the clearing. "You could show me Carvoran Manor."

Malcolm turned away and fumbled with the reins to his own mount. He'd lied about Rosina; she wasn't leaving for Italy until the morrow. To keep up the pretense of smitten swain, he put on a leering grin and expressed his own fondest wish. "If I take you there, Alpin, you'll be playing the wife before you've enjoyed being the bride."

"Oh." She paused in the process of tying her kerchief, her elbows cocked, the fabric of her tunic stretched across her breasts. The leather breeches hugged her hips and slender legs.

The desire he thought he'd suppressed returned with a vengeance, swelling his loins and cramping his belly. Mouth watering from the taste of her lips, he cursed himself for a noble fool. He should have taken her moments ago and at least fulfilled his body's needs. Since he hadn't, he must take control of himself. "'Tis your choice, Alpin."

"Let's have some fun, then. Like we used to," she said, turning her mount toward the westward path. "I'll race you to Phantom Oak." Slapping the gelding's rump, she held on tight as her horse bolted from the clearing.

"Wait!" Reacting a moment too late, Malcolm sprang into the saddle and took off after her. One thought blazed in his mind: Phantom Oak had been felled by lightning years ago. The great trunk now blocked the old path. She wouldn't be able to see the obstruction, for the tree lay beyond the blind turn around Reiver's Rock, and sunset would soon be upon them.

He yelled her name, but she couldn't hear him over the pounding of hooves. Urging his mount to a flat-out gallop,

Malcolm ate up the distance between them. When he was three lengths behind her, he yelled again. She glanced back, her face alive with excitement. Then she yelped in alarm at his nearness. With another whack to the rump of the gray, she pulled ahead.

And raced headlong into danger.

Using the reins, Malcolm whipped his stallion. The desert bred Barb answered with a burst of speed. Bracken and gorse raced past in a green and yellow blur. Malcolm clenched his teeth against the bone-jarring ride.

Catch her, catch her, catch her, his mind screamed. But Alpin's slight weight allowed her mount to outpace his swifter horse.

Reiver's Rock popped into view, a great boulder half the size of the donjon of Kildalton Castle. Up ahead, Alpin crouched low over the neck of the gray, her leather-clad bottom high in the air, her knees expertly hugging the gray's withers. In front of the rock, the road forked. To the right lay the new path, well worn and wide enough for a cart. To the left, the road became a seldom-used footpath mired in weeds. In years past he and Alpin had run this same race hundreds of times, only the finish had ended in a climb to the top of Phantom Oak.

Today it would end in death.

As he expected, Alpin veered left, as she always had. Malcolm yelled again and gave his horse a vicious kick. But Alpin's mount was too far ahead, the rider too determined. In horror, Malcolm saw her lean to the right, preparing for the turn around the rock.

Panic gripped him. He'd never catch her in time. "Alpin!" he roared. "Stop right there!"

She turned and gave him a sassy wave. She was still looking back at him when she passed out of sight.

An instant later her mount screamed. From Alpin he heard no sound. But as if he were witnessing the event, Malcolm saw the gelding balk at the huge fallen tree. Saw Alpin fly from the saddle. Felt her slam into the oak. Pictured her crumpling to the ground in a broken heap.

Damning himself, her, and every saint that haunted the

heavens, Malcolm hurried his mount around the rock. The winded gray stood before the massive fallen tree. The saddle was empty. Oh, dear God, he couldn't see her!

Malcolm drew rein, then lunged to the ground. He scoured the weed-strewn path and the thorn-covered bracken. No Alpin.

He called her name. Silence answered.

Heartsick with dread, he ran to the wooden step bridge that marched up and over the trunk of the fallen tree. He should have listened to his father. He should have agreed to cut up the tree. He should have cleared the path.

"Stupid, stupid," he swore, cursing louder with each step he leaped, his fists grasping the handrails. Bounding to the top, he stopped.

And saw her. She'd been hurled over the huge trunk and lay on her side, curled into a ball amid a patch of white heather.

He raced to her and fell to his knees. "Alpin. Talk to me." Carefully he touched her back.

No movement, not even the shallow drawing of a breath. "Alpin!"

He'd wished her dead a thousand times, but that was before he'd held her in his arms and kissed her, before he'd seen the vulnerability she couldn't hide. Even though he didn't trust her, he understood her better now. He suspected that few of her hopes and dreams had come true. She had a right to a life, even if she had unwittingly stolen the most precious part of his.

She gasped and coughed until she caught her breath. Then she groaned and uncurled herself. Her kerchief sat askew; her complexion glowed pasty white.

Only slightly relieved, he felt her forehead. "Alpin? Can you hear me?"

Between rasping breaths, she said, "What happened to our tree?"

Our tree. His chest grew tight at the sentiment. "Lightning struck it. Where are you hurt?"

Gingerly she rolled onto her back and cradled her right wrist. "Everywhere."

He took her arm. "Let me see."

"Ouch!"

"Shush. Be still." The sleeve of her blouse lay in tatters, and her skin was gritty with dirt and abraded with angry scratches. The bones of her wrist felt as delicate as the wings of the tiny owlet in his mews. Tenderly he probed for serious injury. "I don't think your arm is broken."

She groaned again and looked up at him, her eyes filled with pain, her pupils dilated with fear. "I can't tell you how relieved that makes me feel. Who built those fool steps up and over that fallen tree?"

"I did."

She closed her eyes. "I should have known." Tears streamed down her cheeks. "Why is it always you, Malcolm?"

Perplexed by the obscurity of her accusation and the extent of her sorrow, he grew defensive. "I tried to warn you. I called out, but you wouldn't heed me."

"I couldn't *hear* you." She blew out her breath and pulled her hand away. Wincing, she rotated her wrist and flexed her fingers. "I probably wouldn't have listened anyway. I wanted to win."

He straightened her kerchief and felt her scalp for lumps. Thankfully he found none, but as he cradled her head he was again reminded of how small yet resilient she was. "Some people never change. You had no business riding so recklessly. You could have killed yourself and crippled the gray. You professed a liking for that horse."

She lifted her gaze and rolled her eyes. "Oh, please. Just this once, I'd rather have your concern than your profundities."

Peeved that she would chide him when the fault was clearly hers, Malcolm said, "I'm concerned all right. 'Tis the duty of a lord to all of his subjects." He held out his arms. "Can you stand?"

"Stand what?" Sniffling and laughing, she dashed away her tears. "If it's to be another of your lectures, my answer is an emphatic no."

If she could find humor in her own brush with death, who was he to be so serious? "Then how about a helping hand or two?"

Flexing her wrist again, she said, "Thank you. This one doesn't seem to be of much use to me just now."

He gripped her around the waist and pulled her to her feet. "It'll be sore tomorrow."

"It's sore now." She swayed.

He steadied her. "Can you walk?"

"Not over that bridge. I don't trust the carpenter."

Malcolm swung her into his arms, and was again surprised at how slight she was. "'Twas my first and last attempt at carpentry."

"I'm so glad." She rested her head on his shoulder. "You're better at . . ."

"Better at what?"

"Never mind."

"Tell me or I'll drop you in the dirt."

"No, you won't."

"Then I'll forbid you to ride the gray."

She studied him for so long a time he grew uneasy. "You'll make a better husband."

That wasn't what she'd started to say. He'd stake his earldom on it. "How do you know I'll make a good husband?"

"You want me. I want you, and I'll give you a castle full of wee Kerrs with hair as black as midnight."

Her useless boast made his anger surge anew, and he caught himself just before he blurted out the truth and contradicted her. Instead, he carried her over the bridge and started to put her on his horse.

"Wait," she said. "I can't go back dressed in these breeches. I must put my skirt on again."

Surprised, Malcolm said, "Imagine Alpin MacKay worrying over appearances."

"I've changed, Malcolm. I'm not a hoyden wearing cast-off clothing and making mischief everywhere I go."

"Pardon me if I'm tempted to argue that point."

Her frown softened into a self-effacing grin. *"Most* of the time I'm so proper you'd find me boring." To his further surprise, she calmly said, "Will you get my skirt? It's in the saddle pouch."

Malcolm put her down and did as she asked, but he still wanted to get a rise out of her. "Much more decorum from you and I'll think island life turned you into a proper lady."

She huffed up. "Oh, stop teasing me and help me get into the thing or it'll be dark before we get home."

He chuckled. "Hold your arms up and I'll slip it over your head."

As he dressed her, he was surprised at the memories the act spawned. "How many times did we unbutton and button, unhook and hook each other?"

The folds of the skirt muffled her laughter. "Every time we went swimming or . . ."

The skirt caught on the fullness of her breasts. Careful not to rip the cloth, he tugged the garment down to her waist. "Or danced our pagan rituals?" he said.

A lovely blush brought the color back to her face. Staring at his lips, she said, "Do you kiss and tell?"

A current of energy crackled between them, and his first instinct was to kiss her again. "Only with Celtic priestesses."

"Forget what I said about you being a good husband." She poked him in the stomach. "Ouch." Cradling her hand, she murmured, "I think you're a libertine."

For some unknown reason he wanted to hold her, just hold her. He must be shaken by her narrow escape. "I think you'd better ride with me."

"I think so too, Malcolm. I feel safe in your arms."

As I feel safe in yours. He cut off the startling thought. Afraid he would start babbling romantic nonsense, he put her on his horse, then mounted behind her and headed home, the gray trotting after them.

No sooner had they passed through the gate than Alexander ran to meet them. Grasping the halter of Malcolm's horse with one hand, the soldier doffed his bonnet with the other. He looked at Alpin's tattered blouse. "What happened to her, my lord?"

A dozen clansmen crowded around. Addressing them all, Malcolm said, "The lady collided with Phantom Oak."

Alexander grimaced and said, "We should've made kindling of that dead tree years ago."

Alpin thrust up her chin and gave Malcolm a knowing glare. "My words exactly, Mr. Lindsay."

Making a basket of his arms, Malcolm twisted in the saddle. "Here, Alexander. Take her before she draws blood with her tongue."

The crowd of soldiers murmured and chuckled. Alexander took Alpin, and as her weight left Malcolm's hands, she said, "You can put me down, Mr. Lindsay."

"Aye, my lady." He set her down.

Malcolm dismounted.

Alexander said, "There's trouble, sir."

Thinking he needed more problems about as much as he needed another woman in his life, Malcolm turned to his first order of trouble. "You go inside, Alpin, and tend to those wounds. You know where Mrs. Elliott keeps the medicinals."

Looking weary, she nodded and walked away.

"What's happened?" Malcolm said to Alexander.

The other men snickered and traded knowing glances.

Alexander cleared his throat. "'Tis the Moor and the African miss."

Irritation sapped Malcolm's patience. To top it off, Alpin had heard and rejoined them. "Where are they?" she demanded.

"Go into the castle, Alpin," Malcolm said through clenched teeth. "I'll take care of it."

Ignoring him, she said, "Where are they, Mr. Lindsay?"

From the stubborn set of her chin, Malcolm knew she'd wait out the Second Coming before she'd leave without an answer. "Tell her, Alexander," he said.

"Saladin has her locked in the walled garden," the soldier said.

"Why?" said Alpin. "Has he gone mad?"

"She's the one who's mad," Rabby Armstrong said. "Angrier than a newly sheared ewe. Wouldn't you say so, Mr. Lindsay?"

Alexander shook his head. "Afraid so, my lord. 'Tis a war going on back there."

Alpin marched across the yard, a limp hampering her steps, her skirt swirling about her ankles. Thinking of the leather breeches that clung to her in all the right places, Malcolm pursued her. Alexander and the others followed.

When he caught up with her, Malcolm said, "You're hurt, Alpin, and your scratches could fester. Go inside. I'll send Elanna to you."

She slowed her steps. "No. I want to see for myself."

They rounded the corner tower. Malcolm leaned close and whispered, "Don't you trust your handfast husband?"

"It's not that. I'm responsible for Elanna. Sometimes she can be contrary."

"She had an expert tutor. Like mistress, like maid. I just hope she's declared a holiday today," Malcolm said.

A larger crowd milled around the side yard adjacent to the walled garden. Saladin sat on the ground, his back propped against the squat wooden door, his legs splayed. Against his cheek he held a wad of gaily flowered cloth that looked vaguely familiar. "Welcome home, my lord," he said.

"What happened?"

"That woman disturbed my prayers."

From beyond the garden wall the unseen Elanna yelled, "Here's what I think of your prayers, Muslim." Bits of paper sailed over the wall.

"That's the Koran she's ripping to shreds," Saladin said, staring at the shower of debris that fluttered to the ground.

"What did you do to her?" Alpin demanded.

"To *her?*" He took the rag from his cheek, revealing a bruise the size of a plover's egg.

Elanna yelled, "Tell them what you did, you ecky-beckie beast!"

"I did nothing," he shouted back.

116

"Ha! And my father was a mosquito-eating Eguafo with boar's bones growing out of his nose."

Malcolm knelt beside his friend. "Tell me what happened."

"She flirted with me and dared me to kiss her."

"You lying blackamoor!"

Sighing, Saladin closed his eyes. "I don't know what came over me. I did try to kiss her, and you see what she did to me. She's big trouble."

"Betcha that, you monkey-faced slave catcher."

"Oh, Lord, Saladin," Alpin murmured. "You've unleashed a wild woman."

"Have I?" he countered smoothly. "A man has his limits. Any other would have done the same when faced with a half-naked woman bearing fruit."

Malcolm wondered where he'd gone wrong, what he'd done to turn his life into a comedy of errors. "My friend, let her out."

"Yes," Alpin said. "Open that door."

"Certainly," Saladin said, as amenable as a missionary with a cause. "When she apologizes."

Elanna laughed. "This African princess will go white like a fish belly all over before she sings sorry, sorry song to some perverted Moor."

Tilting her head back, Alpin called out, "What did he do to you, Elanna? Are you all right?"

"He jabbed his tongue in my mouth. Oooh." Her voice quivered with disgust. "He tastes like that mush he eats for breakfast."

"You served it to me, wench," Saladin snapped.

"You begged for it and more," she shouted.

Saladin scowled and reached for his scimitar. The curved and polished blade glinted like gold in the fading light of sunset. "Stay there, then. Perhaps a night in the open will cool your hot temper."

"Temper?" Elanna said. "You one stupid man, Saladin Cortez. You ruined my dress."

"Malcolm! Do something," Alpin demanded.

117

The men in the yard howled and slapped one another on the back. Malcolm coughed to cover his own laughter. "Did you ruin her dress, Saladin?" he asked, choking.

"I hardly call a short length of cloth a dress." He waved the rag. "And I only took a piece of it."

"The piece covering my breasts! You threw what was left in the fountain," Elanna screamed. "It's wet."

"Fountains usually are," Saladin murmured.

Alpin had heard enough bickering. Her wrist ached. From her scalp to her toenails, she felt bruised to the bone. Considering the amused glint in Malcolm's eye and the way he stood, legs apart, arms crossed over his chest, she suspected he would never force his friend to relent. How could he? Judging from the red stain on Saladin's lips, he'd tasted Elanna's berry brew. At present neither man was blessed with an overabundance of rational thought. But Alpin knew of another way into the garden, a way uncluttered with prideful men and curious onlookers.

Besides, she thought cheerfully, she'd lured Malcolm into proposing today. Why force him to choose between loyalty to his friend and obligation to her?

So she slipped away and went to her room to fetch her ring of keys and a dress for her friend. Taking a lighted lamp from the lesser hall, she entered the tunnel. By the time she made her way to the right corridor, thoughts of a hot, soothing bath and the absence of snakes and trip wires revived her. She passed the alcove outside Malcolm's study and smiled, for now that he'd proposed she wouldn't need to spy on him again.

She passed the darkened stairway leading to the tower room she'd once called home, but refused to dwell on those lonely times. Malcolm was correct, and she refused to pity the frightened child she'd been so long ago.

When she pushed open the iron door at the other end of the tunnel and stepped into the walled garden, her mouth fell open in surprise. Elanna stood on the garden side of the squat wooden door, Saladin's prayer rug draped over her shoulders. Smiling with sweet satisfaction, she ripped out

118

the last pages of the Koran and flung them, along with the leather binding, over the wall.

"You forgot something, Muslim," she trilled and pitched his prayer rug over the wall. Brushing her hands together, the last Ashanti princess of the Kumbassa people strolled toward Alpin. Head high, shoulders squared, Elanna stood as naked as she had a decade ago when Charles had purchased her at a slave auction in Barbados.

But it wasn't Elanna's nudity that shocked Alpin; it was her friend's dishevelment. Elanna looked like a woman who had been thoroughly seduced. Without her head wrap, her shoulder-length hair lay in a wild tangle. Her lips appeared swollen and pouting with sensuality. The haunted expression in her jet black eyes confirmed Alpin's conclusion. She knew the look well, understood the blatant yearning Elanna displayed. Having fallen victim to the charming allure of Malcolm Kerr, Alpin felt bound by the same kind of love spell.

Once at Alpin's side, Elanna touched her tattered sleeve and quietly said, "Island girls got big trouble."

Alpin nodded, and from the other side of the wall she heard Saladin say, "Let's go hunting, my lord. I've a hankering to get away from these women and kill something my religion forbids me to eat."

9

So close their shoulders touched, Elanna and Alpin stood at a window in the upstairs solar. In the darkened yard below, Malcolm stepped into the stirrup and swung himself into the saddle of his white stallion. Torchlight illuminated a score of tartan-clad soldiers who waited nearby, their masculine banter rising in the yard, their horses kicking up dust.

Through the diamond-shaped panes, Alpin saw Alexander approach his laird. Malcolm leaned over and spoke to him at length. She couldn't hear what he said, but he pointed to the tiltyard, to the falcon mews, and waved a silk-clad arm indicating the whole of the compound.

Alexander made a fist, then stuck his thumb in the air. He spoke, held up his index finger, spoke again, then unfurled his middle finger.

Malcolm nodded and continued his instructions.

Alpin fumed, but not because he was leaving; she needed some time to regain her sense of self. Still, he could have consulted her, for she was capable of managing his affairs.

He hadn't sought her out since she left him an hour ago to rescue Elanna from the walled garden.

Since then Alpin had cleansed her wounds and donned her nightrail and robe. She'd changed her mind, too. She didn't want him to go. But Malcolm seemed more interested in hunting than in consummating his handfast marriage.

"So much for passion," she mused.

"Island girls better off alone," Elanna said.

Feeling dejected, Alpin scraped at the dirty glass with her fingernail and wondered if he would even say good-bye.

What would she do if he traipsed off without so much as a glance in her direction? She'd wring his selfish neck, that was what she'd do. It wasn't that she expected a dramatic farewell. But she had a role to play, and how in the name of all that was holy was she supposed to act like a devoted bride if he wouldn't bother to play the smitten groom? Because he wasn't smitten, she admitted silently. He felt only lust, and even that might vanish when the potion wore off.

Rabby Armstrong sprang up in his stirrups and shouted to Malcolm. All of the men looked toward the stables. A moment later Saladin popped into the pool of yellow light. Tail swishing, neck tucked close to its chest, his pitch black mount sidestepped like a winning racehorse on parade.

"My blackamoor one mighty fine man. Betcha that."

Taken aback, Alpin said, "*Your* blackamoor? Do you want him?"

Elanna shrugged. "For a time." Then, referring to an oft-cited tribal custom, she said, "Ashanti princess must look into the eyes of the father of her forever mate."

Alpin watched Saladin effortlessly maneuver his horse through the throng and to Malcolm's side. In an alien land he had made a fine life for himself. "Saladin is bastard-born. He doesn't know his father."

Longing softened Elanna's features, but no amount of discomfiture could lessen her regal stature. "Sorry, sorry, and so I said to him."

"Was that before or after he tore your dress?"

121

"That's *why* he tore my dress." She shook her head slowly. "He goes behind God's back, that one. He's a mighty angry man."

"But you gave him the berry juice."

"That blackamoor *takes* what he wants, anytime, all time."

"How did you stop him?"

Her chin came up a notch. "I didn't."

"He ravished you?"

"No." The finality in Elanna's voice spoke volumes about the episode in the walled garden.

"What made him stop?"

Elanna pounded the stone sill with her fist. "One stupid principle."

"What principle?"

"Too silly, silly to mention tonight."

Even as a lad Saladin had been ruled by his strong convictions and Muslim beliefs. Alpin suspected he hadn't changed. Elanna wanted him. He'd declined. "What will you do?"

Tears glistened in her eyes. "Make him sing sorry, sorry song." Elanna whirled and stomped from the room.

Just as Alpin started to call her friend back, Alexander bowed and stepped away. Malcolm turned toward the keep and, as if he knew precisely where she was, guided his horse to a spot directly below her.

Her heart thumping, Alpin opened the window and leaned out. Lamplight from within the room showered him in a golden glow and turned the sun on his clan badge to a star twinkling in the night. Anticipation of what he would do and appreciation for the starkly handsome man he was made her wish they were lovers in the true sense of the word.

She hated herself for the weakness.

Smiling, he lifted a gauntleted hand and crooked a finger, beckoning to her. He might have slapped her, so sharp was the blow to her pride. How dare he sit that loose-gaited, short-winded nag like a man born to ride and destined to rule? How dare he look so splendid in his role as earl of

Kildalton and laird of clan Kerr? How dare he treat her like a tavern wench and make her yearn for a parting kiss?

Ignoring his summons, she lifted her brows. "Have you forgotten something, my lord?"

"Aye," he said. "A proper farewell from my lady."

His soft, yet commanding tone and the insistent gleam in his eye robbed her of speech. "But don't shinny down the drainpipe as you used to," he added with a chuckle. "My men will think I've handfasted myself to a hoyden."

Horses and riders stirred in the yard. She scanned the faces of his soldiers; they were all watching. And waiting. Waiting for her to confirm his declaration. Or was she doomed to make a fool of herself?

Marriage to him was what she wanted, part of the plan she'd come halfway around the world to carry out. But Malcolm had maneuvered her into a corner, prodded her into playing the lovestruck bride. Which, heaven help her, she was. With Paradise hanging in the balance, what choice did she have? None.

Loathing herself and loathing him more, she smiled brightly and motioned for him to wait. Then she dashed across the room, snatching a shawl as she went. At the foot of the stairs she slowed, securing the wrap around her shoulders and telling herself that her heart was racing because she'd run down the steps. But when she pushed open the castle doors and saw him waiting, she accepted the galling truth that she wanted his kiss.

Twisting in the saddle, he grasped her beneath the arms and picked her up. Leather creaked and the white stallion snorted, but she paid little attention; her mind focused on the strong hands of the formidable man who held her. Her feet dangling in air, her pulse pounding, she wrapped her arms around his neck. The smell of sandalwood surrounded her, but even though he wore an exotic fragrance from a faraway land, Malcolm Kerr seemed as rooted to the soil of Scotland as the ancient rowan trees in the yard.

When they were nose to nose, he whispered, "How is your wrist?"

Unaccustomed to tender solicitations, she made light of the injury. "'Tis better already."

His gaze scoured her face and her unbound hair, then settled on her mouth. She felt buoyant and wondered if the potion was to blame. But no, she hadn't swallowed enough of the drink.

"Have a care while I'm off hunting, Alpin. Look to Alexander for your needs."

The evening fell away, and suddenly she remembered sitting on the rim of the old well, her breasts bared to his hands and lips. "All of my needs?"

Amusement gleamed in his eyes. With an endearing grin, he whispered, "None of your intimate ones. Save those for your husband."

Then he kissed her, a searing, branding kiss of possession. Murmurs spread through the yard, and rather than inhibit her response, the knowledge that his men looked on induced her to surpass his passion. She gloried in the feel of his lips and the power of his embrace, and with a boldness so new it shimmered like tinsel inside her, she opened her mouth wide and deepened the kiss.

A growl of appreciation rumbled in his chest, and as his hands clutched her tighter, his tongue plunged into her mouth, then retreated, inviting her to follow his lead. The heady challenge and the assurance that he was leaving spurred her to greater adventure. Relying on intuition rather than experience, she drew his tongue into her mouth and gently suckled him, tasting the lingering flavor of the berry juice and knowing the potion still had him in its spell.

His chest heaved, and his fingers started to tremble. Thinking she might have gone too far, she pulled back. Applause from the soldiers buzzed in her ears.

His eyes flew open. "Sweet Saint Ninian," he swore. "You've made a raging beast of me."

Absurdly pleased and a little frightened by the fervent glimmer in his eyes, she stared at his clan badge. "I'm afraid you'll let me fall."

As if she were a pennyweight, he lifted her higher. Their eyes met again. "Have I ever let you fall, Alpin?"

Suspended in the cool night air and physically at his mercy, she wondered how much true sentiment she should read into the probing question. Uncertainty made her say, "No. But I used to be much smaller and more nimble."

A crooked grin gave him a reckless air. "You're still small. And nimble, I'll wager, in ways we've yet to explore."

At a loss for a reasonable response, she cleared her throat. "Why are you leaving now?"

"Because the roe deer feed at night, or have you forgotten?"

She hadn't, but she suspected the nocturnal habits of wild game were only a part of his reason, and since he didn't seem willing to volunteer more information, she didn't press him. His absence would allow her to search for proof of his interference in her life.

"How long will you be gone?"

With a grunt of satisfaction, he lowered her to the ground and quietly said, "Not long enough for you to forget that you'll soon be mine. Move your things into my room and sleep there—until I return."

He was speaking of the handfast marriage, but he made it sound as if he owned her. She looked at the crowd of mounted clansmen. They all stared at Malcolm, blatant respect in their eyes.

Her independent nature surfaced. "Where will I sleep after your return?"

He chuckled and devoured her with a hungry gaze. "You won't. Except in snatches."

Embarrassment chilled her. She gave him a bland smile, pulled the shawl tighter. "Enjoy your *sport.*"

"You and I will, I assure you."

"I do live for your assurances, my lord." She turned away.

A stupefied Dora stood on the castle steps, a wineskin and a sack of provisions in her hands.

"What is it, Dora?" Alpin asked.

"Miss Elanna said I should give these to Saladin."

Alpin waved the maid into the yard. Entering the castle, she heard Malcolm urge his horse onward; then the thunder of hooves signaled his departure. She hesitated in the foyer, her mind awhirl with conflicting thoughts. She wished he would never come back. She prayed he wouldn't go at all.

The doors slammed shut.

"Is it true, my lady?" Dora said, her voice a squeaking whisper. "That you and his lordship are handfasted?"

Exhaustion claimed Alpin. "Aye, 'tis true, Dora."

The girl clasped her now empty hands. "Lady Miriam'll be so happy."

Bully for Lady Miriam. Alpin's happiness lay half a world away, but at the moment even the thought of returning to Paradise seemed a poor substitute for the unfulfilled yearning in her heart. A pity she couldn't have both.

The next morning, secure behind the locked door in Malcolm's study, Alpin searched his desk. She found a bundle of letters from Charles, but the loose string and the old knot binding them told her that some of the correspondence had been removed.

She sorted the letters by date. The oldest had been written not to Malcolm but to his father, Lord Duncan Kerr, who had given Charles the money to buy Paradise Plantation over twenty years before. Lord Duncan had offered the funds as Adrienne's dowry.

So, Alpin thought, *that* was the debt of honor Charles had cited in his will. That was the reason he'd bequeathed the plantation to Malcolm.

But wait, the value of Paradise had increased tenfold over the last two decades. Due to *her* hard work. Surely honor alone didn't warrant so generous a repayment. Not even the greediest of usurers could term the transaction a fair return on investment. Still, Charles could not have been called astute in business matters.

Hoping there was more, she read the other letters, and found only a single missive to Malcolm, dated four years earlier. Amid a rambling dissertation on the virtues of the long deceased Adrienne, Alpin discovered a jarring passage: "I must reiterate my thanks for your generous offer and your unselfish solution to the problem of dear Alpin's welfare. It does ease my troubled heart."

Her hands shook, blurring the words. Malcolm had been concerned about her, had made a generous and unselfish offer. Of what? He certainly hadn't given her any money to live on, nor had he freely offered her a home in Scotland. She'd had to haggle with him to earn both. He hadn't expected her to come to Kildalton after Charles's death. He'd been genuinely surprised by her arrival here, and when she'd made the remark that she belonged to him, he had smiled and called it a truly interesting turn of events. Had she incorrectly read pleasure into his statement, or had he been hiding some ulterior motive?

Either way, Malcolm's reaction explained why her guardian had been lax in providing for her future. But at the time this letter was written, Charles had already transferred ownership of Paradise to Malcolm. According to the will, the transaction had occurred one year before the date of this letter. Charles had never intended to leave the plantation to her.

Hurt but convinced that Charles saw little of the world around him, she read the passage again. One word took her attention: "Reiterate."

Suddenly chilled to the bone, she realized she'd found the key that would unlock the puzzle of Malcolm's involvement in her life. But when had his interest in her welfare begun? And for mercy's sake, what form did it take?

She scanned the rest of the page, but read only of the soul-deep despair of a man who had lost his will to live and prayed for the day when he would be reunited in heaven with his beloved Adrienne.

Guilt and sympathy swamped Alpin. She'd never understood the depth of Charles's pain, and by comparison her trouble seemed trivial. She, at least, could control her destiny.

Upon her arrival in Barbados, she'd witnessed a love that had made paltry work of even the most romantic poet. Then fate had wielded its ugly hand and snatched dear Adrienne away.

For the next ten years Alpin had watched poor Charles waste away. The sad memory reinforced her belief that the price of enduring love was too high. Oh, she intended to go through with the handfast marriage to Malcolm and hoped to conceive a child, but she would never risk giving him her heart. She would persuade him to give her the plantation. Then she would return home.

The yearning she'd suppressed throughout the night stemmed solely from physical need. Malcolm had stirred her long-repressed passion. Sleeping alone in his massive bed had heightened her need. When he returned, she would join him in the sporting aspects of love, but her participation would end there. She would keep his castle and manage his servants. Then as soon as she had the papers she would return to Paradise and leave Malcolm behind. Her conscience would be clear.

That settled, she went back to the letters. To her disappointment she read only more of heartbreak and hopelessness. A further search of the desk yielded little for her cause but great insight into the daily life of the laird of clan Kerr.

Eager to investigate Malcolm's suite of rooms, she cleared the desk.

A bell clanged. Alpin yelped and jumped like a kicked puppy. Too terrified to breathe, she stared at the door. She expected Malcolm to break it down. Then she relaxed. As his housekeeper and steward she had every right to be here.

He was off hunting. The letters were back where they belonged. Even if he did return early, he'd never know she'd been snooping.

Besides, the gonging sound had come from within this room. Saladin's Mecca bell. Of course. Chuckling at herself, she wiped her damp palms on her skirt and willed the tremor from her hands.

How silly of her. But why had the bell rung? Of time-dulled brass, it still lay on its side on the high shelf, same as before. Curious, she moved the footstool and climbed up on it. Just as she stretched out her arm, the bell clamored to life again.

She shrieked and drew back. Arms flailing, she teetered, balancing on the balls of her feet at the edge of the stool. In desperation, she threw herself forward and grasped the nearest shelf. With a knock-knocking sound, the stool rocked to a stop on the floor. Her heart pounded like a drum. Her fingers curled in a death grip. Her sore wrist shook under the strain.

She took several deep breaths. When she'd calmed herself, she planted her feet on the stool and relaxed her hands. Then she reached again for the bell.

And saw the string. One end was tied to the clapper; the other end disappeared into a tiny hole in the side of the bookcase.

Seized by an ugly suspicion, she put the bell back in its place and jumped to the safety of the floor. Recently she'd stood in the dark tunnel behind this bookcase and eavesdropped on Malcolm and Saladin's conversation. Years ago she'd made the tunnels her home.

As if it were yesterday and she a desperate child of six seeking shelter from her cruel uncle, she reached for the wall sconce and turned it to the left.

Metal scraped against metal. One section of the bookcase swung away from the wall, exposing the main corridor of the tunnel system. Once she had traversed the tunnels with the speed and agility of a doe on the run. Today she moved cautiously into the maw.

Two feet above her head she saw a row of rusted fishhooks that served as guides for the string. A warning signal?

She snatched up the lamp and followed the path of the string. It ended at the top of a door twenty-five feet away. Her teeth clenched, she grasped the handle and pulled. The portal opened, exposing the lesser hall with its high bank of shutterless windows and double row of tables and benches, deserted in midmorning. The massive throne, carved from a giant oak and emblazoned with the symbolic Kerr sun, sat empty. As a child she had climbed onto the chair and in the quiet darkness pretended to rule this kingdom.

Behind her she heard the bell, but from this distance the clanging sounded more like a tinkle. If the bookcase door had been closed she wouldn't have heard the signal at all. And worse, whoever occupied the study would have fair warning that someone lurked close by.

The contraption had been devised by a conniving mind and employed by a worthless scoundrel. She had been its victim, quaking in fear at the mention of rats and snakes and trip wires. Oh, how Malcolm and Saladin must have laughed.

Keeping a lid on her simmering temper, she pondered the current mystery. Who had opened the door moments ago?

Determined to find out, she retraced her steps, secured the bookcase, and followed her instincts to the kitchen.

She found Dora squatting on the floor and stroking the arched back of a brindle cat that seemed more interested in lapping up a bowl of cream than receiving the ministrations of the maid.

The mouser. Alpin had told Dora to find the cat and put it in the tunnel, but that was before she'd discovered that the story about rats was Malcolm's attempt at intimidation.

Cursing her poor memory, Alpin chided herself for quailing like a nervous nellie.

"Good morning, Dora."

The maid sprang to her feet. "Morning, my lady. This poor starvin' mouser cat prowled those tunnels all night with nothin' to show for it. An' her with a hungry litter of kits mewlin' in the stable."

"You just let her out?"

"Aye. I'd no more'n opened the door in the lesser hall than ol' Delilah here came runnin' out."

That explained the ringing of the bell. It didn't excuse Malcolm, though, for Alpin could have fallen off the stool and broken her neck.

"I knew there weren't no rats in there, even though his lordship told you 'twas so. Mrs. Elliott'd turn to sinnin' in the Rot and Ruin tavern before she'd let Kildalton fall to vermin. Taught all of us maids her tidy ways, too."

"You did very well, Dora." Alpin took a scone from the warming pan and sat at the table. "As soon as Delilah's had her cream, take her back to the stables and give the farrier a pound of butter for lending her to us."

"Aye, my lady. Will there be anything else?"

"Have you seen Elanna this morning?"

"She's still abed. Shall I wake her?"

"No. But I'd like you to clean the windows in the upstairs solar."

Her tail as stiff as a ship's mast, Delilah wound herself around Dora's ankles. The maid snatched up the cat. "Straightaway." She headed for the door.

Her appetite gone, Alpin called the maid back. "How long does Lord Malcolm usually stay away?"

"He'll be back in a week, was what he told Mr. Lindsay."

A week. He hadn't even seen fit to tell his handfast bride. It seemed like both a reprieve and a sentence to Alpin. She could use the time to search for the missing letters. Surely they would tell her why he'd taken an interest in her life as long as five years ago. A part of her hoped that affection had been his motive, but she was too sensible to believe in such a sentimentality.

Dora was eyeing her expectantly.

"Let's just hope he's successful," Alpin said and returned the scone to the pan. "There's hardly enough meat in the larder to last through the harvest. By winter you'll be starving."

"Me?" She shook her head, jostling her mobcap. "Lord Malcolm wouldn't let any of his people starve."

Alpin had accidentally excluded herself. Dora couldn't know Alpin planned to leave, but she must watch her words. "Of course he wouldn't."

Dora cuddled the cat and swayed like a lovestruck girl holding her hopes to her breast. Giggling, she said, "You and his lordship'll be livin' on love."

Come winter, Alpin would be in Barbados toiling in the tropical sun and enjoying her independence. Let Dora see romance in the handfast marriage; it made no difference to Alpin. "I'm sure we will."

When the maid had left, Alpin went upstairs to Elanna's room. She found her friend sitting before the mirror brushing her hair.

"You slept well?"

Elanna reached for a length of cloth and began wrapping it around her head. "Like a lizard in the sun."

Her false gaiety didn't fool Alpin, and the undisturbed
linens suggested that Elanna hadn't been to bed.

Curious, Alpin asked, "What was in the sack of provisions
you had Dora give to Saladin last night?"

This time Elanna's smile was genuinely cunning. "Food
for his mighty Muslim principles."

Vindictiveness lurked behind that grin. "And . . . ?"

Tucking her headwrap in place, Elanna offhandedly said,
"And a little of my squat-in-the-bushes sauce."

"What?" Alpin didn't know whether to laugh or curse.
"Oh, Elanna. He'll be purging his bowels instead of felling
stags."

"Betcha that."

But ten days later, up on the return of the hunting party,
Alpin suspected the plan had gone awry.

10

"Saladin is dying," Malcolm said.

Dumbstruck, Alpin craned her neck to stare up at him. His mount sidled, pivoting on prancing front hooves. She snatched the reins to steady the horse. Thinking a hunting accident was the cause, she found her voice. "Oh, no."

Dark circles under his eyes, darker misery in his bearing, Malcolm tapped his teeth together and stared at the arched doors of the castle. "Aye, 'tis true."

Alarm barreled through her. "How did it happen?"

"For the last few days he complained of a sour stomach. He went to sleep last night and hasn't awakened."

Elanna's potion. But the drink wasn't supposed to induce sleep. "You tried to rouse him?"

"Aye, we burned feathers and put them 'neath his nose. Rabby yelled his name loud enough to bring down the angels. It's no use. He's still unconscious."

"Oh, Malcolm, you mustn't give up hope. Where is he?"

Malcolm jerked his head toward the gates. Riders, three

133

abreast, entered the yard. "A few minutes behind us in the wagon. Rabby's driving it."

Her senses reeling, Alpin dropped the harness and yelled for Alexander. When the soldier joined them, she held up her hand to Malcolm. "Come down, Malcolm." His hand slipped into hers. She felt his tremor of fear. "I promise you, he'll be fine."

He huffed in disagreement. "We never should have gone on that hunt, and he ought to eat the same bletherin' food as the rest of us."

Alpin prayed that he'd merely ingested too much of Elanna's purge. She squeezed Malcolm's hand. "What did he eat last night?"

"Some roots and berries. Dandelion greens. The same rabbit's food he always eats."

The creaking of wheels signaled that the wagon was nearing the gate. "What roots? Could he have chosen wrong and harvested a poison?"

"I don't know," he growled through clenched teeth. "It makes no sense. He's been eating plants all his life. He knows what to eat and what to avoid."

"What did he drink last night?" Alpin held her breath.

Looking dazed, Malcolm glanced back at the dray. His shoulders slumped. "We all drank from the swineherd's well, some of us from his beer barrel. But not Saladin, of course. He took some of that orange water he favors. Nothing tainted or unusual."

That's what he thought. Alpin knew better. As sure as the bearded fig tree grew in Barbados, Elanna and her potion had snuffed out Saladin's life. It was Alpin's fault, though. If she hadn't brought Elanna to Scotland and suggested she bring her potions, Saladin would be alive and well.

Common sense intruded. If Elanna had made him ill with her potions, she must make him well again.

Alpin gave his hand a final squeeze. "You and Alexander take him inside and put him in his bed. I'll get Elanna. Don't worry. She'll know what to do for him."

As Alpin raced across the yard, she thought of the horrid

turn the day had taken. An hour before, in the sun-drenched tiltyard, she had leaned against the post that housed a well-battered quintain. Beside her lay a keg of rum and a canvas bag containing lengths of sugarcane and a machete.

The children of Kildalton had crowded around the globe of the world she'd brought from Malcolm's study. The little ones had spun the orb and searched with eager fingers to locate Barbados.

Banishing the memory, she barged through the castle doors and raced to the kitchen. Elanna sat at the table plucking the feathers from a fat goose.

Two days before, Elanna had dipped into their supply of sugarcane and given a stick to the potboy as a reward for weeding the kitchen garden. Curiosity over the treat had spread through the castle community and prompted Alpin to conduct the morning's geography class.

But as she approached Elanna, Alpin thought only of her childhood friends.

"Saladin is ill."

Elanna glanced up, careless disregard giving her a queenly air. "Sorry, sorry."

Alpin slapped a hand on the bird, pinning the carcass to the table. White feathers flew. "You may have killed him. I suggest you delve into your medicinals and find a cure. Plenty quick, girl."

Her eyes wide with shock, Elanna sprang up from the table. "Killed? Where is he? How is he?"

"He's unconscious. He's been that way since last night. Malcolm and Alexander are bringing him inside. They think he's dying."

Raking feathers from her fingers, Elanna dashed to the wooden bucket and began washing her hands. "What did he eat?"

"He *drank* that orange concoction you tainted."

"What else?"

From the foyer Alpin heard the shuffle of booted feet. She pictured them carrying Saladin to the stairs.

"What did he *eat!*" Elanna shouted.

"Berries, roots, and I think dandelion greens."

Elanna froze, then swung her head slowly toward Alpin. "Dandelions? Blackamoor ate *dandelions* last night?"

Alpin's hopes plummeted. "Yes. Is that bad?"

"Bad combination, dandelion greens and too much squat-in-the-bushes sauce. Very bad." Not bothering to dry her hands, Elanna went to the hearth, wrapped her apron around the handle of the steaming kettle, and swung it off the fire.

Racked with regret and impotent anger, Alpin stalked her friend. "Will he die?"

"I do not know. I'll feed him a little boiled sea-grass root. If he wakes up, we pour mighty big doses of plain orange water down his gullet."

Alpin clasped her hands together. "I pray this works. I'll get your medicinals and meet you upstairs."

Five minutes later Alpin stood with Malcolm at Saladin's bedside. Against the white linens the Moor's swarthy complexion looked dull gray.

"He looks bad," Malcolm said. "He's hardly breathing."

Alpin stepped in front of him. The despair in his eyes made her chest grow tight. "Please don't worry, love," she whispered and reached up to cup his unshaven cheek. "Elanna will do everything she can to make him well."

He sighed and gave her a halfhearted smile. "I wish I had your confidence in her. Since I don't, I'll send for the midwife."

She wanted to tell him the truth, but self-preservation held her back. The midwife wouldn't know the cause of Saladin's ailment. Alpin had to persuade him to let Elanna do the healing. Hating herself, she conjured up a bald-faced lie. "No, you mustn't call the midwife. She might kill him. You must have faith in Elanna, Malcolm. People all over Barbados do. The governor will allow no one else to treat his gout." The hope in his eyes spurred her on. "She's cured everything from heart ailments and impotence to yellow fever and dropsy."

A hint of a smile played on his lips. "Dropsy? I shudder to think of the treatment for *that* ailment."

Footsteps sounded in the hall. Moving again to Malcolm's side, she said, "I don't know the treatment either, but Elanna has the healing touch. You could ask her yourself."

"Ask me what?" Elanna said, entering the room carrying a tray laden with a pitcher, a stack of folded cloths, and a steaming mug.

"Never mind," Malcolm said, his mood again grave. "Just treat him with the same care as you do the governor of Barbados."

Elanna's mouth dropped open. "What?"

"Malcolm's worried," Alpin rushed to say. "I told him how everyone in Barbados praises your healing skills. Even the governor." A man Elanna had never set eyes on.

She put the tray on the nightstand. "Betcha that." Head down, she hastened to Saladin.

She's suffering from guilt, thought Alpin, feeling wretched herself. "What's wrong with him?"

"Lookie-see first." Elanna leaned over the bed and with her thumbs lifted Saladin's eyelids. The contrast of her mahogany skin next to his now gray complexion gave vivid proof of just how ill he was.

Malcolm began to fidget. "Do something, for God's sake."

Alpin put her arm around his waist. His muscles felt tense beneath her hands. "He'll be as good as new."

"I pray 'tis so. He's my best friend, and I love him well."

With a businesslike air that Alpin knew was forced, Elanna placed her fingertips under Saladin's jaw and felt down the length of his neck. She applied slight pressure under his arms. Next she unbuttoned his shirt and laid her head on his chest.

"Well?" said Malcolm.

"Don't fret for him," Elanna said. "Blackamoor's heart beating strong like a jungle drum. This island girl will wake him up"—she glanced grimly at Alpin—"plenty quick."

Elanna stirred a spoonful of dried green herbs into a steaming cup of brown liquid. Easing her weight onto the mattress, she slipped her arm beneath Saladin's neck and lifted his turban-clad head. When she reached back for the cup, Malcolm picked it up and handed it to her.

"You swallow this easy and nice," Elanna said, then threatened her unconscious patient, "or I'll soak a rag in it and stuff it where your mighty Muslim dignity hides."

Her gruffness didn't fool Alpin; she knew Elanna cared deeply for Saladin, and her brusque manner was merely her way of curbing her anxiety.

Malcolm put his arm around Alpin's shoulders and drew her closer. "I think that I just figured out the treatment for dropsy," he murmured. "It involves a soaked rag and a man's hidden dignity."

"Saladin is strong. He'll survive with or without his dignity. He has to. Elanna won't have it any other way." Alpin held her breath.

Curling her arm around his head, Elanna massaged the Moor's Adam's apple. Amazingly, his throat worked involuntarily, and he began to swallow. When the cup was empty Elanna put it aside and bathed his face, neck, and chest with a cool, damp cloth.

"He will awaken?" Malcolm asked.

"Soon, soon, and very soon," Elanna replied.

"If he's still unconscious, how did you get him to swallow?"

Elanna shrugged. "Ashanti holy man call it a body spirit. I say it's a mystery, same as new infant smacks for its mother's breast."

"I'm not sure I understand," Malcolm said. "But I suppose it doesn't matter."

The minutes dragged by. Only the rise and fall of Saladin's chest gave proof that he lived. Silent despair filled the austere room. Outside the open window, activity in the yard crawled to a halt. None of the children sang or squealed in their game of hide-the-harp. Only the farm animals seemed unaffected by the tragedy of Saladin's strange illness.

Alpin drew strength from Malcolm's friendly embrace. He needed her, too, and that notion brightened her spirits. She made him a silent promise then: she would forbid Elanna to use her potions and ask her to confess her feelings for Saladin—if he rallied.

"The people of Kildalton love him, don't they?"

"Aye," Malcolm said.

Saladin coughed, and his eyes fluttered open. His mouth slack, he looked at his surroundings, then at each of the people by his bed. He focused on Malcolm and gave him a pained smile.

"Hallelujah!" Malcolm said on an exhaled breath.

Saladin turned his attention to Elanna, who had begun to cry.

Releasing Alpin, Malcolm rushed to the other side of the bed and knelt.

Elanna buried her face in the damp cloth and sobbed. Near tears herself, Alpin moved behind her friend and patted Elanna's back.

"What is this," Saladin said weakly, "a deathbed vigil?"

Elanna sobbed harder.

Malcolm grasped Saladin's hand. "That all depends, my friend, on how you feel."

The Moor licked his lips and swallowed. "I'd swear you tied me up and dragged me all the way home. How did I get here?"

"We brought you in the wagon."

Saladin rubbed his forehead, pushing his turban askew. "Why's that African woman crying? And will someone get me a drink? My mouth tastes like the moat at Gordon's stronghold smells."

Elanna sniffled and raised her head. "You one sassy blackamoor."

"Ungrateful, too," Malcolm said.

Saladin grinned, revealing the space between his teeth. "I'm also thirsty. Did you use your Ashanti powers to yank me back from the claws of death?"

If only he knew, Alpin thought, that it was Elanna who put his life in danger.

Elanna poured orange water and helped him drink. His eyes never left her face. When he'd emptied the glass, he said, "Did you save me?"

She nodded and busied herself refilling the glass. When she held it out to him, he wrapped his hand over hers.

Staring first at Malcolm, then at Alpin, he said, "Leave us."

Alpin saw Elanna stiffen and was surprised that she didn't bolt. Thinking her friend was afraid to be alone with him, Alpin said, "Perhaps we should stay, Saladin. You might need us."

"I don't think he does. He has everything he needs." With a final pat to Saladin's arm, Malcolm rose. "Behave yourself."

"I'm too weak to break bread. My angel of mercy is safe from ravishment."

Malcolm led Alpin from the room. "God, I'm exhausted," he said, leaning on the banister and staring at the entryway below.

Alpin understood; she was so relieved she wanted to giggle. "Would you like a bath?" she asked.

Looking at her over his shoulder, he chuckled. "Why? Do I need one?"

She twitched her nose. "Not unless you enjoy smelling like damp wool and lathered horse."

He turned and picked her up. "Oh, Alpin, I thought we'd lost him," he murmured against her breast.

Then he swung her around. The doorways, the chandelier, and the ancient battle shields on the wall spun in and out of her vision. She clutched his hair and closed her eyes. Saladin's recovery absolved her guilt. Sweet reality took its place. Malcolm was back. Mere hours from now he would make her his wife in the physical sense. Under common law she would belong to the man who had surely deceived her.

Perhaps it was the recent brush with death, perhaps it was resignation, but whatever the cause, Alpin couldn't let go of him. She wanted him, his comfort, his companionship, and his passion.

By the time he put her down, they were both dizzy. Like regular patrons of the Rot and Ruin tavern, they staggered down the stairs. While the now jubilant Dora filled the tub in the scullery, Alpin served Malcolm a plate of scones, cheese, and cold mutton. Leaving him at the kitchen table, she went to his room to fetch him a fresh tartan and a clean shirt. When she spied her reflection in the mirror, she put down his clothes and chose a fresh dress from the wardrobe to which she'd moved her clothes. Then she tidied her hair, washed her face, and pinched color into her cheeks.

After Malcolm finished his bath and dressed, they went into the yard and spread the news of Saladin's recovery. Soldiers, tenants, and children joined them on their stroll through Kildalton.

When they entered the old tiltyard, Malcolm spied the globe near the quintain. "What's that doing there?"

The irony of her morning role as teacher made Alpin smile. As a girl she'd been illiterate and envious of the children here, for unlike her uncle's tenants, the lads and lassies of Kildalton had been provided with an education. During the year she'd lived here she'd been a stubborn six-year-old, too prideful to set foot in the school. Malcolm had excelled in history and mathematics; Alpin had mastered pranks and survival.

Young Gibby Armstrong dashed in front of them. Walking backwards so he could face them, his fair hair flopping against his forehead, he chirped, "She gave us island candy and let us spin the globe."

Brows raised, Malcolm said, "Did you find Scotland, lad?"

Gibby almost tripped over his own feet. Rabby Armstrong scooped the boy up and gave him a ride on his shoulders.

"Aye, my lord, and Barbados," piped Gibby, his fingers tangled in Rabby's hair. "That's where Lady Alpin grew the candy."

Malcolm took her hand and threaded his fingers through hers. "I'm curious, Alpin. How did you *grow* candy?"

Feeling oddly at home, surrounded by people who had once scorned her for a wicked child but who just this morning had praised her for a generous soul, Alpin squeezed his hand. "I gave them sugarcane. I also showed them a machete. Elanna tapped a keg and passed out cups of rum."

"You gave spirits to Gibby and the other bairns?"

The accusation in his voice jarred her. "No, of course not. Just the men." She pulled away.

Malcolm pulled her back. "I was teasing, love. Now tell me you missed me."

She had missed him, and loneliness had made her restless. To combat the anxiety she had led the servants in a cleaning frenzy. From the tower steps to the dungeon cells, Kildalton had been swept, scrubbed, and polished.

"I was too busy to miss you."

"Ah, I see. How, besides teaching geography and plying my men with rum, did you keep busy while I was away?"

"We slaughtered the hogs and did some remodeling."

"Remodeling of what?"

"I'll show you." She pulled him past the walled garden and into the rear yard.

Malcolm halted in his tracks. Before him stood a new building constructed of fieldstone with a thick thatched roof. "You built a new springhouse?"

"I didn't. Alexander and his men demolished the old one. The wooden beams and roof supports are smoldering over there in a charcoal pile. The stonemason took over from there."

Alexander joined them. "Building a larger springhouse was Lady Alpin's idea, my lord. She worked as hard as any of the lads."

"Well, well, my lady"—Malcolm eyed her from head to toe—"perhaps I should leave Kildalton more often, although 'tis a mystery to me how I could drag myself away."

Murmurs of agreement spread through the men in the crowd.

Feeling trapped by his engaging display of devotion and uncomfortable as the center of attention, she bristled. "An excellent idea."

Dora stepped to the front of the crowd. "That ain't all she done, my lord. She had us clean the castle from top to bottom. Even Mrs. Elliott wouldn't find fault with Lady Alpin's housekeeping ways."

"'Twould seem I've made a bonny bargain, then. I'll have to work hard to uphold my part."

The men chuckled. The women tittered. The children cheered.

Flustered by his heated gaze, Alpin opened the springhouse door. "You'd better inspect it first."

He ducked inside. A moment later he called out, "There's enough cheese and fresh ham in here to last till spring. Bless Saint Ninian! With the game we felled and this bounty, we'll spend the winter eating like kings."

Alpin's high spirits sank. Before winter she would return to Barbados. She'd never see the castle folk or the soldiers again. She'd be only a fond memory to the children. While Malcolm and his tenants toasted their feet by the fire and savored the crumbly cheese and salty ham, she'd be tending her own estate and providing for her own people.

Guilt over her deception nagged at her conscience, but she justified her actions with the knowledge that she had helped Malcolm's people. She'd left her mark and would be remembered kindly.

He, on the other hand, had deceived her, and although she hadn't found the missing letters or uncovered solid proof of his interference in her life, she knew in her soul that he had schemed to take Paradise from her, had lured her to the Borders, and had put her squarely under his thumb.

Only the reasons for his actions eluded her.

But she'd find out, for he couldn't keep his secret forever, not if they were living together as man and wife. At that uneasy thought, she renewed her vow to guard her heart.

When he emerged from the springhouse he gave her a courtly bow. "Good work, Alpin. You're a Scotswoman at heart." To Alexander he said, "Go to the Rot and Ruin. Tell Jamie to tap a laird's keg of ale. We'll drink to our bounty and toast our bonny new lady and Saladin's recovery."

The crowd roared and moved en masse toward the tavern.

Malcolm held out his arm. "Shall we, Alpin?"

She shouldn't feel all bubbly inside. His eager expression shouldn't make her heart trip fast or cause her to make wishes that would never come true. But Alpin couldn't resist wanting him, couldn't pass up the chance for the intimacy he offered. At seven and twenty, she might not have another chance to discover the mysteries of physical love.

She hooked her arm in his. "Are you planning to get me drunk and make sport of me?"

He leaned so close his breath tickled her ear. "Oh, nay. Not that kind of sport. I want you alert when I take you to my bed tonight. I want you besotted only with me."

"I don't besot easily."

"We'll see about that."

The enticing and familiar smell of his sandalwood soap was enough to make her tipsy. His nearness set off other, more delicious sensations in her body. Her legs grew weak, a tightness coiled in her belly, and her breasts ached for the touch of his hands, the feel of his mouth.

Like a lovesick miss, she sighed with longing.

He kissed her cheek and whispered, "Remember that thought, love."

The urge to surrender chipped away at her will to resist loving him.

"And tell it to me later," he added, "in vivid detail."

That overconfident comment sparked her courage. She'd sooner grow fins than reveal herself so completely. "How much game did you bring home?"

He chuckled and tapped her on the nose. "You'll have to dissemble better than that to get my mind off making love to you."

"Love? I thought 'twas bed sport you wanted."

"Do *you* want bed sport?"

She told a half lie. "I don't precisely know what I want."

He nodded, sagelike, the picture of a Scottish chieftain. "'Tis usually the case with virgins."

"Are you so sure I'm a virgin?"

"If not, you'd better tell me."

Miffed that he had grown to such an impressive and respected figure of a man, Alpin demanded, "What will you give me in return for my innocence?"

"Hum." He stared at her mouth. "I'll give you gentleness, every scrap of my attention, and a night of loving you'll never forget."

His promises thrilled her, and deep inside she feared that any attempt at resisting the charming Malcolm Kerr would end in a battle she was bound to lose. She felt like a shallow-rooted sapling swaying to the breeze of his desire.

Still, she couldn't let so cocky a remark go unanswered. "As Elanna would say, you one sassy man."

"Come morning, we'll see who's sassy."

11

Saladin decided that if Elanna called him stubborn one more time he would dive for his scimitar and whack a chunk out of the bedpost. And if she didn't stop fidgeting, he'd tie her to the chair even if he was too weak to wiggle a finger.

In the half hour since Malcolm and Alpin had left, Elanna hadn't said a dozen words to him. He suspected the reason. He just didn't understand how their tryst ten days ago in the walled garden had begun with sweet kisses and ended in a bitter brawl.

"You saved my life, but you won't talk to me. Why not?"

Poised before the bookstand, she thumbed through the pages of his illuminated Koran. "Muslim plenty smart enough to know."

He found himself staring at her narrow waist and the graceful fall of her skirt. The soft cotton fabric, in vertical stripes of daffodil yellow and midnight blue, accentuated her unusual height and complemented her rich brown skin.

The matching head wrap concealed her hair and drew attention to her long neck.

His loins took fire, but to his dismay he was too besotted to govern his lustful urges and too weak to act on them. But as surely as the mountain came to Muhammad, Allah had sent this woman to him. Understanding her and winning her, however, must be the Prophet's way of humbling Saladin Cortez.

"Why did you save my life?"

She turned. Her lips thinned; tried patience glimmered in her eyes. "Dumb question."

Communicating with her was as difficult as explaining the teachings of Allah to a Christian zealot. Perhaps directness would work. "Then explain why you were as bold as a sultan's first wife the last time I saw you. Now you're distant. If you'll recall, you asked me to kiss you."

Her hands flew to her hips, and the square bodice of her gown stretched tight across her breasts. "This African princess cares more about dung flies than playing push-me, pull-you with some stubborn Muslim."

Sadly, Saladin realized he lacked the strength to draw his sword from its scabbard, even if she destroyed his remaining copy of the Koran. "Push-me, pull-you? That sounds interesting." He patted the mattress. "Come here and tell me what it means."

She wandered to the foot of the bed and stopped at the trunk that housed his winter clothes. "Same as what the missionaries call pro-cre-a-shun."

At least she was moving closer to him, major progress under the circumstances. "A manner of speaking, then."

"Manners?" Her chin went up, and her swanlike neck stiffened. "Not you. Dirt-eating Akwamus more polite than plant-worshiping Muslims."

He could envision her leading a tribe, with hordes of the beautiful Ashanti people paying homage to her. He wanted to again offer his own brand of tribute, but how could he when she refused to admit her part in that last disastrous meeting?

He held out his hand. "Come closer, princess."

She eyed the mattress. Yearning shone in her eyes.

Oh, Allah, he thought, what deed have I done to deserve so great a blessing as this woman? Whatever it was, Saladin intended to make the most of his good fortune.

He sought a cheerful subject. "Talk to me about your potions."

"Nothing to tell." She stared at his scimitar. "Just plenty good medicine."

He sought a way to warm her heart. "Thank you for saving me. I'm in your debt."

"No debt." Distant and defensive, she trailed her long, graceful fingers over the aged wood of the chest. "You already paid. So tell it farewell."

His stomach rumbled and his head throbbed. Although he'd never tasted alcohol, he now understood how Malcolm felt after a night of too much ale.

He sought a way to draw her out. "You think I got ill because I acted like a rutting beast?"

With the flippancy of a saucy concubine, she said, "How should Ashanti princess know what almost turned you to duppy dust?"

"Duppy dust?"

"What the jungle leaves of a man. Dried bones. Dust in a Muslim's coffin."

Mother earth constituted a Muslim's coffin, but he doubted that explaining the practices of his religion would aid his immediate cause. "In my culture some believe a man must enslave himself to the one who saves his life."

"Slave taking bad, very bad."

He cursed himself for broaching the one topic that would alienate her. Softly he said, "What about enslaving the heart?"

She headed for the door. "No time for that."

He had to make her stay. Using the cheapest of ploys, he coughed, then groaned.

She nearly flew to the bed. Propping him up as she had before, she put the glass to his lips. "Here. Drink slow, slow. Don't choke."

He swallowed, but barely tasted the orange-flavored water; his senses were fixed on the pillow softness of her breasts and the hint of cleavage the bodice revealed. She smelled of sweet herbs and earthy musk, an enticing combination.

When she took the glass away, he whispered, "I'm sorry I ruined your dress."

She opened her mouth, closed it. Then she sighed. "I sing you a sorry, sorry song about your book."

He could sing her a song, too, about a lonely man who'd overcome the needs of his heart and body to live in a foreign land with people he admired. She challenged his decision of long ago, and for days he had searched his soul, trying to understand his sudden discontent. "I don't know what got into me that day in the garden. I was possessed, as if I'd drunk a love potion. Have you bewitched me?"

"I ain't no witch!" She moved away so fast that his head plopped onto the pillow. The room began to spin. He gripped the edge of the mattress and closed his eyes. This time his groan was real.

He heard the soft rustle of her skirt; then he felt the heat of her skin, the rush of her breath. "You one stubborn blackamoor. When you sing better, better song, this Ashanti princess will tell you a secret."

Exhaustion threatened to draw him back into sleep. He opened his eyes. She was so close he could count her eyelashes. "Will I like your secret?"

She beamed. "Betcha that."

He ached to draw her down for a kiss, but his arms felt like deadweight on the mattress. "Tell me now. I might not wake up."

"You'll wake. Gods throw you back one time. Gods throw you back again."

The color of her lips reminded him of the berry juice. The memory made him smile. "Why?"

"Because you one stubborn Muslim."

As he drifted off to sleep, Saladin wondered if Ashanti men beat their women.

* * *

Amid a chorus of cheers and good-nights, Malcolm led Alpin from the tavern. After the close and friendly atmosphere, the brisk night air cooled her skin, and the silence rang in her ears. The quarter moon rode high in a blue-black sky riddled with stars.

She started toward the keep. He pulled her in the opposite direction. "Where are we going?" she asked.

"Wait and see." He guided her to the edge of the lane near the merchants' buildings.

The detour surprised her; she had assumed he'd be eager to consummate their handfast marriage. His carefree stroll through the castle yard seemed more important than making good on his lustful promises. He wanted exercise; she was eager for love. Aside from ending her curiosity about the physical aspects of marriage, their union would surely move her one step closer to gaining possession of Paradise Plantation.

She stubbed her toe and almost tripped. Malcolm steadied her. "Be careful. Watch where we're going."

Lanterns dotted the battlements, but little light reached the yard. In the darkness her other senses sharpened. As they passed the tanner's shop, the smell of leather filled her nose. The banked forge at the smithy gave off waves of dry, warm air.

Thinking he meant to check on his birds, she said, "Are you worried about the owlet?"

He stopped. "Nay. Should I be?"

During his absence she'd gone to the mews to find escape from troubling thoughts of him. She'd also relived fond memories of her youth. "No. I cared for the bird."

"I thought you would. You never could turn your back on a sick or wounded beast."

In the aftermath of so pleasant an evening, his congeniality was contagious. "No, I never could. Your little one's only need is for food, and the mother's wing is on the mend."

"I'll have to set them free soon."

Resignation dragged at her high spirits. Same as the wild birds, she would leave him, but she wouldn't let thoughts of the future spoil her wedding night. The observation did surprise her, for until this moment she had thought of her departure in terms of returning to Barbados rather than leaving Kildalton.

"What do you think of the Rot and Ruin?" he asked.

She laughed at herself and at his question. "I liked the tavern very much, but who gave it such an odd name? It's a family gathering place, not a tumbledown rum shop."

"Do you remember Lady Alexis?"

"I do." Alpin remembered a dark-haired older woman surrounded by infamy. Years ago, by way of the hidden tunnels, Alpin had sneaked into the noblewoman's room and made use of her toiletries. "She was your stepmother's friend and some relation to Queen Anne, wasn't she?"

"Aye." He put his arm around her and steered her under the awning at the fletcher's shop. "A cousin. She named the tavern."

"What happened to her?"

"She married my father's sergeant-at-arms, Angus MacDodd. They live at Traquair House."

It was the ancient home of the Stewarts, but Alpin knew little else about the royal residence. "Is it near here?"

He stopped in front of the stable. "A few days' ride to the north. Wait here. I'll be right back."

She watched him disappear through the door, a shadow slipping into a blacker maw. The sweet and pungent odor of hay rushed out from the stable. Horses nickered inside. He spoke to them in comforting, melodic tones, and the fading of his voice marked his progress deeper into the building.

Looking back the way they'd come, she saw the tavern door open. Three soldiers came out and went their separate ways. One man carried a lantern. The light swayed as he walked down the lane, then up the stairs to the battlements.

Next came Rabby Armstrong and the maid, Emily, hand in hand. They headed toward the market. The maid giggled. The soldier spoke in dulcet tones.

The horses nickered again. Alpin's pulse began to race, for now Malcolm would take her home and—She halted the thought. Paradise was home. Paradise. Not this quiet castle yard with its battlements outlined against the night sky and the yellow lights glowing in the windows of the keep.

"Close your eyes and hold out your hands."

He sounded playful, like the Malcolm of old. She felt a twinge of regret, then the deep stab of pity, for her, for him, and for the events that had brought her to Scotland twenty years after she had sworn never to see this land again.

She held out her arms. A warm, downy softness brushed her wrists and palms; then she felt weight and movement.

"Do you know what it is?" he said.

An animal. But which one? She hugged it to her breast and stroked the soft fur. Not a mouser, for this creature was too gentle, too docile. Then she felt the ears, noticed the flat back feet.

"A rabbit."

He put his arm around her. "But not just any breed of hare. This one had a special ancestor."

Hattie, another of God's crippled creatures that had been Alpin's only friends. Happiness bubbled inside her, and tears filled her eyes. Her uncle had forced her to give her pet to Malcolm years ago. He'd set Hattie free to multiply in the wild.

Choked with gratitude, she cuddled the living keepsake of her past, and leaned against the man who'd given it to her. "You went to Sweeper's Heath," she said, completely awed by the tender gesture.

"Aye." He stroked the rabbit's ears. "I told you the place was overrun with Hattie's offspring. We call them Alpin's friends."

In one instance, she had been remembered with fondness here. "I don't know what to say."

"The happiness in your voice is thanks enough." He hugged her.

"I am *very* happy." She was more than happy; at that moment she felt the strong pull of love for Malcolm Kerr.

"'Tis a shame it's so dark. I doubt you can see her," he said. "She looks just like Hattie."

"I need no light to remember Hattie or her get. It's as if I left her here yesterday."

"Nay," he said fiercely. "Forget our yesterdays, Alpin, every one of them. Think only about now, about how much I want you and how good we'll be together."

Eager to comply and explore her new feelings, she stood on tiptoe and kissed his cheek. He turned and lowered his head so their mouths met.

His lips were soft and seasoned with the fresh taste of the ale he'd drunk and the honest plea he'd made. She, too, yearned for an end to the troubles between them, and as he tilted his head to the side and deepened the kiss, she knew passion would banish their differences, if only for a time.

The warm, furry creature, nestled snugly and quietly in her arms, formed a symbolic bridge between them, spanning the years of separation, obliterating the turmoil of their youth and gloriously embellishing the good.

When his arms moved lovingly over her back, and a hum of satisfaction rumbled in his chest, Alpin felt renewed and cherished. From a peaceful corner of her mind, a voice whispered that at last she had embarked on the real road to contentment and true joy awaited her at journey's end.

Pulled along by the silent pledge of fulfillment, she leaned into him. The rabbit squirmed.

Malcolm drew back. "Do you realize, love," he murmured, "'tis the first time you've ever willingly kissed me."

"Given the chance, I'll willingly do it again."

"I assure you, the moment we reach my bed"—he took the rabbit from her and tucked it into the sash of his tartan—"you'll get no protest from me. Unless you dally."

Clasping hands, they strolled the well-worn thoroughfare that led to the castle steps.

"You owe me a horse," she said.

"The gray?"

"Yes. Rabby and Emily are between the market and the tanner's shop."

"Playing kiss-the-freckle?"

"Well, it's a little dark for that. They're just kissing."

"The horse is yours. I'll talk to Rabby."

Once inside the keep, he guided her up the stairs and into his bedchamber. In the soft glow of the oil lamp, she watched him release the brown rabbit. Unlike its three-legged ancestor, this rabbit leaped agilely over a footstool and nosed its way behind the drapes.

Then Malcolm was before Alpin, cupping her cheeks and brushing his lips back and forth across hers. The angel-soft touch of his mouth and the dreamy pleasure in his eyes set her senses astir with excitement and her body aflutter with need. Eagerness made her hasty, sent her hands to clutch his waist and feel the sinewy ropes of muscles there. Touching him only whetted her appetite for the banquet of riches he had sworn to lay before her.

"Go slowly, love. Follow my lead."

His simple words spoke to the heart of her inexperience and supplied the resolve she needed to sate the hunger that raged within her. The moment her hands relaxed and her mind took control, she caught a glimpse of the wondrous place he intended to take her. Her heart soared.

He must have seen the elation in her eyes, for he smiled and murmured, "Aye, 'twill soon be ours."

His gaze roamed her face, and with the patience a saint would envy, he drew her closer and laid his mouth fully on hers. Moist and warm and honey sweet, his lips worked a scintillating magic so expertly controlled, it soothed and tingled, provoked and appeased. He beckoned her passion in stages: a little in the kiss at the corner of her mouth that made her breasts ache, a little more in the slow swipe of his tongue across her teeth that made her nipples contract, still more in the gentle suckling of her bottom lip that sent a jolt of desire straight to her belly.

Feeling all of a piece, she said, "It's as if you're kissing me everywhere."

He chuckled. "I shall, in due time." His hands left her face to roam her neck and settle on her breasts. "You feel the desire here?"

Covering his hands with her own, she applied enough pressure to make herself moan. "What do you think I feel?" she asked.

Taking her hand, he drew it down over the soft wool of his tartan past his tasseled sporran to the manly bulge beneath. "I think"—he sucked air through his teeth—"I'd better get you out of those clothes."

Against her palm, he felt robust, the perfect fulfillment to her own emptiness. Her mouth watered at the relief his words and his body foretold. "What about *your* clothes?"

A grin as big as Bridgetown spread across his face. "I'll leave them to you."

For the first time, she felt confident in taking the lead. "Then I'll exercise my right as a lady and insist on going first."

His eyebrows shot up in surprise. Spreading his arms wide, he said, "Then divest me, my lady, but do it quickly."

Remembering his earlier plea, she decided to move at her own pace. With her right hand on the evidence of his need, she used her left to unfasten the clan brooch that secured the flap of his tartan at his shoulder. Understanding flickered in his eyes, and his hands returned to her breasts.

Clutching his most vulnerable part, she waved the silver pin. "Here, hold this."

He took it in his right hand while she unbuckled the sporran belt that rode low on his hips. Another belt, wide and worn and snug at his waist, held his tartan in place.

"I believe this is yours," she said.

His sly grin sent shivers down her spine. He gave her breast a last gentle squeeze, then snatched up his chieftain's pouch.

Leaning back to admire her handiwork, she thought him rather gallant, his arms spread wide. "How does it feel to have your hands full of Kerr regalia?"

He surged against her palm. "How does it feel to have *your* hand full of Kerr regalia?"

She laughed and grew bold in her exploration, sliding her hand up the length of him and then down again. "Is the wool chafing your skin?"

He stared open-mouthed, his forehead dotted with perspiration, his coal black hair damp at the temples. Nostrils flaring, brown eyes glittering with anticipation, he said, "Oh, aye. You'd better get my tartan off now."

"You're teasing."

"Me?" he choked out. "Good God, Alpin, you keep stroking me like that and you'll drive me to ravish you."

With absolute confidence, she continued her intimate ministrations. "Impossible. You can't a ravish a woman who wants you."

He quickened with new vigor. His sporran hit the floor, and his fingers curled around her wrist, stilling her hand. "Wanting me is one thing, Alpin. Satisfying you is something else."

Suddenly out of her depth and self-conscious, she stared at the placket of his shirt. "I don't understand."

"You will," he said lightly, encouragingly. "I promise. Now do something constructive with those buttons and that belt you find so enthralling."

Somewhat mollified, she unfastened his shirt and freed the belt at his waist. He pulled her hand away, and his tartan fell to the floor, leaving him naked from waist to boots.

She gasped at the sight of him, unadorned and magnificent in his male beauty. Her fingers itched to touch him again, but other, more intimate parts of her vied for the same privilege.

"What are you thinking?" he asked.

She blurted, "You've changed."

"Aye, and so have you."

She thought of the day at the Roman wall when he'd bared her breasts and first ignited her desire. Suddenly her clothes felt heavy, suffocating. "But you've seen me."

"Then look your fill, Alpin, but I warn you, you'll be disappointed in our loving if you touch me there again."

She remembered something he'd said. "Because I'm a virgin, you think you have to move slowly."

"I *know* I have to move slowly, and you'll have to trust me."

"I do." And she meant it, but she was still curious.

When he didn't move and her yearning grew to unbearable heights, she concentrated on the nest of jet black hair that narrowed like an hourglass at his navel, then fanned out to spread across his chest.

Her hands were drawn there, to the impressive musculature and short, silky curls that clung to her fingers and tickled the sensitive skin in between. He seemed so controlled, so intimidating, so overpoweringly experienced that she grew timid, an odd feeling for one who'd fended for herself since childhood.

Then she stared at the base of his throat and noticed the hammering pulse and the steel-tight tendons in his neck. Swallowing hard, she looked higher and saw his jaw firmly set and his normally sensual mouth now drawn in a stern line of determination.

Of their own accord her hands slipped beneath the fabric of his shirt and raked it off his shoulders. He stepped out of the pool of plaid cloth, pitched the silver brooch into a chair, and reached for her.

"It's my turn," he said.

Her belly constricted. "But you still have on your boots."

"Later."

His ominous tone wreaked havoc with her newly mastered control, and when he turned her around to free the buttons on her dress, she thought she might slither into a puddle at his feet. A tremor shook her shoulders, but his hands grasped her and he leaned close to whisper, "Just this moment I'm interested in exploring you."

Dampness blossomed between her legs, and she became aware of a wholly feminine, highly sensitive spot that swelled and cried out for his touch. With an enlightened maturity, she came to a startling realization.

"You're trembling. What's wrong?" he asked sharply.

She leaned into him, and since he stood behind her and couldn't see her face, she spoke freely. "I just learned something. You and I, our bodies, are alike and yet different."

Reaching around her, he slid his hand between her legs. "A notion," he murmured against her neck, "that brings me extraordinary delight."

She sighed in pleasant exasperation. "You're much bigger than I, but nature designed us to fit together."

Cupping her, he pulled her back and pushed forward. "I believe that is the gist of the procedure."

Inordinately pleased with her own deduction and his spirited demonstration, she grew brave. "But not if you dally at my buttons."

In reply he peeled her dress off her shoulders, then reached for the straps on her chemise.

"You certainly know the ins and outs of undressing a lady."

"At present," he said, "the word 'in' holds particular appeal."

A revelation struck her. "You mean . . ." At last she understood the concept of consummation, but words failed her.

"I mean *this.*" He stripped off her remaining clothing, then carried her to the bed and laid her down. Bracing himself on stiff arms, he loomed over her, blocking out the light, obstructing rational thought.

"Spread your legs, Alpin."

She did and watched as he slid his knees between hers. The hair on his legs tickled her thighs, and the sight of his manhood poised at the brink of her feminine void heightened her anticipation of what he would do next.

Instinctively she lifted her hips.

He drew back. "Not yet." Watching her closely, he relaxed his arms, lowering himself until his lips found hers and their bodies touched from shoulder to knee. The rasp of his chest hair on her nipples turned her skin to gooseflesh, and the hard planes of his belly flush with hers made her womb contract and her hips undulate. The gentle persuasion of his kisses and the insistent stabbing of his tongue incited a riot of deliciously wicked sensations.

With eager hands, she stroked his back and the taper of

his waist, and when he moaned, she curled her fingers and lightly raked her nails over his ribs. A tremor shook him. His arms quivered, and he wedged his hips deeper into the cradle of her womanhood.

His chest heaving, his body radiating a blazing heat, he dragged his mouth from hers and trailed damp kisses down her neck, across her collarbones, then to the side of her breast. In anticipation of his touch, her nipples contracted and her hands clutched his head to better guide him. The instant his lips found their mark, she gasped and arched against him. The gentle suckling sounds became a faint noise compared to the desire roaring in her ears.

She squirmed and tried to draw him upward, only to hear him murmur, "Soon, love. Very soon."

With mind-torturing slowness, he slid down the length of her body, peeling off her stockings as he went. Then he knelt between her legs and reached for her ankles. The glow of the lamplight illuminated the rippling muscles on his arms and chest and accentuated the intense concentration in the set of his jaw and the pursing of his lips.

Completely open to him, she heard herself say, "I'm cold."

He glanced up, a shock of midnight hair falling over his brow, a mischievous gleam in his eye. "Truly?"

Crouched as he was, his manhood a thick spike against his belly, he seemed a hungry beast ready to pounce. Eager to become his prey, she said, "Yes."

He pulled off her shoes, sent her stockings sailing across the room, then quickly removed his boots. "Would you like a blanket to warm you?"

"Yes, but only if it's you."

He grinned and repeated the word she was coming to hate: "Soon." Like an artist posing a subject, he bent her knees and positioned her feet flat on the mattress; then his hands skimmed her inner thighs in a feather-light touch. His tender ministrations kindled a flame of wanton desire, and she stared, enthralled, as he grazed her most intimate place.

Chills of fire scurried over her skin, but when he slipped a finger inside her, Alpin gasped and clawed the velvet counterpane.

"Shush." He soothed her with sibilant sounds and a comforting hand on her belly, all the while fondling her in a way that melted her loins and weakened her knees.

"Yield to the pleasure, Alpin," he whispered, adding his thumb to the fray. "See it in your mind and let it take you away."

Like an old shawl, her control unraveled. Rational thought fled, and she squirmed, writhing beneath his expert touch, aiding his seductive exploration, and enhancing her own maiden voyage into the erotic. Then the pleasure he'd spoken of coiled like a tightly clenched fist, ready to burst open, and the instant it did, she felt a shattering explosion of relief. She coddled the ecstasy, let it dart from her spinning head to the tingling tips of her fingers and toes. To her absolute delight, in its wake, she experienced countless aftershocks that calmed her racing heart and imprinted on her mind the completeness she felt.

Once she'd settled, a new dilemma gripped her, a hollow feeling that made a mockery of her recent joy. Sweet heavens, she felt empty.

Her eyes flew open, and the answer, the fulfillment, in all his masculine glory, loomed above her. She welcomed him, and as his hardness nudged for entry, she gripped his arms and pulled him down until their foreheads touched. He grimaced and his hips pushed forward, slowly, carefully, making good on his promise to treat her gently. But her own need to complete the mating quickly and again live the glory, pushed her on. She lunged upward.

A searing pain knifed through her. She cried out and tried to move away. He groaned and buried his face in her hair. Their cheeks touched, his skin burning her like a flame, his agony torturing her heart. Then his hands moved to her hips and clutched her.

"Do you remember," he said in an exhausted whisper, "the first time you slid down the drainpipe?"

Baffled that he would bring that up now, she said, "Aye. I took the skin off my hands."

Chest heaving, he gulped in air. "Because you held on too tight. Do not," he said roughly, "hold on too tight to your innocence."

"Or I'll hurt myself?"

"Nay, sweetheart. I'll do the hurting."

"I think I understand."

"Good. Just relax, hold still, and think about how I made you feel a few moments ago."

Reliving the rapture was easy, but it had one flaw: she had been alone. She hadn't thought about him, about whether or not he'd achieved satisfaction. Now she knew he'd been unselfish while she'd experienced euphoria at his hands.

"You'll find joy this time, too, won't you?" she asked.

Vulnerability and his own waning control made Malcolm shiver. "Aye, Alpin, but only if you trust me."

Turning her head to the side, she kissed his cheek and settled beneath him. "I do trust you," she whispered.

Gathering the ragged ends of his patience and beating back the desire that cramped in his gut and lower, he pushed inside her. She was tight and warm and bravely yielding. His heart soared, and he clutched her narrow hips as firmly as he dared; then he drove forward, inch by heavenly inch, until at last she captured him fully. A groan of relief passed his lips.

Perilously close to losing the battle between his weary mind and his randy loins, he shut out the painful throbbing and turned his attention to her. She'd kept her word; she lay still, hardly breathing. She'd also been correct in her observation about nature making their bodies to complement each other, for as he felt her stretch to accept his invasion, he noticed an easing of the tension in her hands and legs.

"Better?" he asked.

Again she lightly scored his sides with her fingertips. "Yes. Is it better for you?"

"Oh, aye," he breathed and began to move inside her. "You feel like my own private paradise."

She stiffened, and assuming he'd hurt her, he slowed again, giving her time to adjust. When she stilled, he resumed the rhythm that was as old as time, but strangely new and different with this woman. He pleasured her slowly, drawing out her passion again, then pausing to let her enjoyment build. Rather than dissuade him from the course he'd set, her groans of frustration and her murmured pleas for release only inspired him to further master his own needs so he could intensify hers.

When her slender legs gripped him and her delectably feminine muscles contracted around him, he threw off the shackles of control and set his passion free. His release was sweet and pure and somehow worthy, unlike any he'd ever experienced.

The observation baffled him, as did his attraction to the panting, satisfied woman beneath him. Because of his inability to sire a child, even on proven breeders, he'd always been left with an emptiness, a sense of failure.

Not so tonight. The outpouring of tender emotions frightened him, for of all the women he should have cared for, Alpin MacKay least deserved his affection. Yet he knew he needed a mate like her, and Saint Ninian help him, he wanted her again. He wanted her forever.

Withdrawing from her, he rolled onto his back and tucked her into the curve of his arm. Her sigh of contentment stroked his male pride. Still, his conscience nagged at him. She'd fulfilled her part of the bargain and more. He'd tricked her into a handfast marriage that would never bear fruit.

But whose fault was that? Hers.

Doubts about a lifetime of carefully organized revenge pressed in on him, but he cast them off and thought about her comfort. Staring at the crown of her head, he asked, "Are you thirsty?"

"No."

"Sleepy?"

"No."

"Hungry?"

"No."

So much for talking and cuddling after bed sport. She was unlike other women in that, too. She didn't beg for words of affection. Suddenly he took her reticence as a challenge. He did, after all, have many unanswered questions where she was concerned. But more than curiosity, he had a driving need to get to know her better.

"Tell me," he said, stroking her arm and admiring the way the lamplight glowed on her sun-browned skin, "how did you entertain yourself all those years in Barbados?"

12

Alpin stared at the exquisite embroidery on the canopy and couldn't help comparing it to the plain netting that draped her own simple bed at Paradise Plantation.

"You speak bitterly about your life so I'll feel sorry for you," Malcolm had said. "I am sorry, Alpin, that you had to steal food, but it's not my fault."

Malcolm's candid words rang in her ears. He had defended his wealth and accused her of judging him unfairly for living in the lap of luxury. He'd been correct, and now she understood her mistake. She couldn't help having been an orphan. He couldn't help having been born into the nobility. Still, she didn't think he'd be interested in the everyday struggles of her life.

"Are you suddenly shy about your life on the island?" he asked.

"No. I learned to bat mosquitoes and imagine snow."

Against her temple, he said, "Don't jest, Alpin. Tell me truly. What are the people there like?"

They were selfish, greedy men who encouraged their slaves to breed, or took it upon themselves to impregnate the women, then ignored the agony on the mother's face as her children were dragged to the auction block. Money was all the planters cared about. Alpin longed to explain the cruelty of the slave system, but Malcolm would only mock her beliefs, as he had that day in the barracks when she'd convinced him that he should not sell Paradise Plantation.

Now she was his handfast wife. Soon she would persuade him to give her Paradise. But she would guard her dream of liberating the slaves. "The men on the island aren't much different from my uncle. He was cruel, negligent, and unloving."

"Baron Sinclair was ill equipped to care for so large a family. He thought it his duty to take in every poor relation." He spat a curse. "I'm sorry, Alpin. I shouldn't have said that."

"You needn't apologize for telling the truth. I *was* a poor relation. But if you're going to defend my uncle, don't bother. He didn't care for me, but he taught me something in a crosswise fashion. I learned that a child should be watched over, loved, and respected."

Malcolm reached for a lock of her hair and curled it around his finger. "He refused to let you go to a workhouse."

His unexpected observation confused her. "What do you mean? What does that have to do with nurturing a young mind?"

"Well, for all his shortcomings, the baron took you in after your mother died. He didn't have to. He already had a houseful of responsibilities and no money to provide for them."

Alpin hadn't considered the baron's situation. At five years old she'd been eager for love and desperate for comfort. She'd received neither at Sinclair Manor. Now, lying naked in Malcolm's arms, her body still aglow with the aftereffects of their loving, she felt vulnerable. Acquiescence seemed the best road. "I suppose the baron did what he thought was right."

"'Tis odd," he said, glancing down at her, "that your father was from so large a clan as the MacKays and yet you came to live with your mother's family. Why was that?"

The question had often plagued Alpin. She thought it cruel that her father's people hadn't wanted a little girl, even if she was half English. "I don't know. My father died at sea before I was born. I have only vague memories of my mother."

"Do you favor her?"

When she thought of her mother, Alpin felt a deep loss, as if she had once held on very tightly to something and then let it go. Had she held the hand of her dying mother? She didn't know, for the event and her mother's face were both a blur in her mind. "I cannot recall much about her."

"You never thought to try to find your father's people?"

A familiar coldness invaded her soul. The MacKays hadn't bothered about her; she wouldn't give a rotten mango for the lot of them. Malcolm needn't know that.

"You're forgetting. I was sent off at age six. How could I search for the MacKays from Barbados?" She laughed. "Besides, I don't even know where they live. Do you?"

"Aye. They still hold the far northwest corner of the mainland. Now that you've made your home with me in Scotland, I assume you'll want to locate your family."

His silence demanded a reply from her. She couldn't tell him she had no intention of staying in Scotland, but if she didn't go along with his assumption, he might suspect her plans.

"I would like to know them," she said. "But what if they don't want me?"

"I'm certain they do."

"Then why didn't Baron Sinclair contact them when my mother died? He must have known who they were. He read my mother's papers before he buried them with her."

"That's not Sinclair's way. It was natural for him to assume responsibility for you, just as he did your other cousins who had no resources."

She really didn't care but felt obliged to address the

subject since it was so important to Malcolm. "The baron could have at least written to the MacKays."

"Nay, he couldn't back then. Remember, he's English and has no ties with the Highlands clans, and he was at war with my father back then. By the time peace had been established in the Borders you were happily settled in Barbados."

True, and she had to get back there. "What do you think I should do about the MacKays? Let them know I'm here?"

"Aye, I think you should. Their chieftain swears allegiance to my friend, the earl of Sutherland. He could help you find your father's kin."

Being an earl himself, Malcolm probably rubbed shoulders with all of the highest ranking noblemen. She wanted nothing to do with them; one nobleman in her life was enough. To guard her privacy and lighten the conversation, she pinched his ribs. "Are you trying to get rid of me?"

He chuckled and slapped his hand over hers, then began moving it in slow circles. The hair on his chest tickled her palm. "By all means," he said offhandedly, "that's why I—"

Her heart skipped a beat. "Why you what?"

Pulling her over him, he hugged her to his chest and cupped her bottom. "Why I can't keep my hands off you."

Ignoring the delicious feelings he inspired, she concentrated on his slip of the tongue and his attempt to disguise it with a compliment. Was his flattery a lie or only a half-lie? He desired her physically, of that she was certain, but lust wasn't the only reason for his interest in her life. The letter from Charles proved it.

Hoping to distract him further, she nuzzled his neck and slipped her legs between his. Against her belly, his manhood stirred.

"Wait," he said, stilling her hips.

"For what?"

"'Tis too soon. Surely you're sore."

Getting information from him concerned her more than the minor discomfort she felt. "Not in the least," she lied.

He huffed in disbelief, but below the waist he seemed to like the idea of another mating. She couldn't bring herself to call what they'd done, what they would do again, making love, not when she had so many doubts about his motives.

"We'll see about that." He moved her to the side, got out of bed, and walked to the basin.

She watched him soak a cloth in the water, then wring it out, the muscles in his forearms bulging. Grudgingly she admired his male beauty, his broad shoulders and thick neck, made strong by years of swordplay in the tiltyard. Her gaze wandered lower, to his trim waist and lean flanks, and the part of him that most captured her interest appeared very enamored of her.

A thrill of anticipation coursed through her. During his hunting trip she'd entered this room dozens of times each day, to tidy up, to explore, to search for proof of his perfidy. She hadn't found the missing letters or the documents concerning Paradise, but she had found some unusual personal items, including what Elanna identified as a contraceptive sponge his mistress had left behind in a bottle of rose water.

When he came toward her, his gait as lazy as his smile, Alpin wondered how soon she would conceive his child or if she already had. Would she tell him? No, not if it meant staying in Scotland. She had responsibilities: to free the slaves of Paradise Plantation; to establish the security of her own future.

"You look faraway," he said, kneeling on the bed and blocking out the light. "Have you grown bored with your new husband so soon?"

Oddly, she felt secure in the situation; she had time to learn his secrets, and if she roused his suspicions she'd lose her chance to gain her independence. Stretching, she said, "Only if my husband has grown bored with me."

Malcolm stared down at himself. "If you call that fellow bored, you've still a lot to learn about the male anatomy."

His boldness took the edge off her assurance. "What's the damp cloth for?"

"For this." He spread her legs.

Realizing what he intended to do, she scooted to the

headboard. The movement made her wince. "I can wash myself."

"True. You can also admit that you're still tender"—he pointed to her lap—"in certain places."

"Oh, all right, but you needn't be so tiresome about it or come at me with an icy rag."

"And you needn't be so stubborn. I'm your husband, Alpin, and I very much enjoy looking at you."

He probably thought ogling her was his right as her lord and master, and she did like the way he made her feel, liked being held in his arms. But she'd give up her claim to Paradise before she'd admit it.

Summoning bravado, she eased down and folded her hands behind her head. "If playing the lady's maid tickles your fancy, then who am I to quibble?"

"You're a very wise woman." His devilish smile and casual tone portended retribution. Then he tucked the cloth between his thighs and lay down beside her.

"What are you doing? I thought—"

"Hush." He shook his finger at her in reproof. "You're quibbling again, my beautiful bride. I'm doing two things— warming the towel and cooling my ardor."

A clever reply eluded her. She spared a glance at his "ardor" and found it suddenly tamed. "Oh."

"But in the interim," he said patiently, "I'm certain you won't mind if I tickle my fancy, as you so aptly put it."

She raised her eyes; challenge brimmed in his. He couldn't possibly shock her; she'd lost her virginity, after all. Striving for nonchalance, she waved her hand.

It was her last casual gesture of the night. He suckled her breasts until she thought she might go mad with renewed wanting. He tasted her from earlobes to navel and would have continued had she not put an end to his depravity.

"Oh, very well," he said peevishly. "I'll save that dessert for another time."

Then he produced the warm towel and redefined her understanding of titillation. Teeth clenched against a barrage of carnal sensations, she managed to lie still until he said, "Thank you, Alpin, for the gift of your innocence."

The honesty in his voice went straight to her heart, and for one of the few times in her life, Alpin felt valued. And awed that she should feel so much pride in such an intimate situation, and with Malcolm Kerr, the man who had shattered her peaceful life. But at the moment she couldn't summon disdain, for her body yearned for him, and he deserved the praise for that. "You said you would be gentle. You kept your word."

He pulled her beneath him. "Gentleness then, thoroughness now."

Wild with need and aware of the satisfaction that awaited, she opened herself to his passion. By the time she fell asleep hours later, she decided thoroughness was a badge of virility for him and a blissful state of mind for her.

Needles of pain shot up her arm and yanked her from sleep. Opening her eyes, Alpin found herself teetering on the edge of the bed and staring at the floor. Her arm was numb from sleeping on it. Certain she would tumble off the bed, she tried to roll over, but encountered an immovable male. Malcolm lay on his stomach, his legs and arms spread wide, so that he took up most of the bed and all of the covers.

She picked up his hand to move it. He stirred, slipped the arm around her waist, rolled to his side, and pulled her against him. Uncomfortable with their nudity and fearful that she had awakened him, she pretended to be asleep. Through slitted eyes she studied the room.

The lamp still burned, but the level of oil in the glass base had dropped. The sun hadn't risen; darkness shadowed the edges of the closed drapes. She could hear the mantel clock ticking, but the high backs of the chairs before the hearth obstructed her view of the dial.

Fatigue threatened to draw her back into sleep, yet a part of her mind stayed fixed on the warm naked flesh of the man beside her.

Malcolm. Her handfast husband. Her lover.

Serenity rippled through her, and a tenderness between her legs reminded her of their hours of lovemaking. He made a low, contented sound and nestled closer. A large, work-roughened hand gently cupped one of her breasts. Tucked up against him, safe and secure, Alpin had never felt so cherished, so protected.

Without thinking, she caressed his arm and closed her eyes.

When next she awoke, she was again lying at the edge of the mattress, completely exposed, her arm numb. Malcolm's hand rested at the small of her back as if he were pushing her away.

Peeved at his physical rejection of her, she eased from the bed. His breathing never altered. Drawing her waist-length hair over her shoulders for warmth and modesty, she turned to look at him. As before, he lay on his stomach, covered with a tartan blanket from the waist down, his face turned toward her. His sun-browned skin and thick black hair contrasted sharply with the white linens. In repose, he appeared older than his years and bore a striking resemblance to his father. They shared the finely shaped jaw and the elegant straight nose typical of the previous earls of Kildalton who were depicted in portraits in the great hall. But Malcolm's sensuous mouth was uniquely different from those of his Kerr ancestors. The memory of his lips, his endless kisses, made her stomach go tight with yearning.

Standing naked before him, she accepted the bittersweet truth that she could easily come to love him. Perhaps she already did.

The prospect terrified her. Eager to get away, she donned a work dress from the wardrobe and brushed her hair. Then she located the rabbit, snoozing behind the drapes, picked it up, and walked to the door. Malcolm still lay sprawled face down, oblivious to her leaving.

When she entered the kitchen she saw Dora squatting before the hearth and stoking the fire.

"You're up early, my lady." The maid sprang to her feet and wiped her hands on her freshly pressed apron. Spying the rabbit, she beamed with joy. "Ain't she a bonny one. Alpin's friends always are."

Complimented anew, Alpin moved the rabbit to her shoulder and patted its back as she would have done to a babe. Its twitching whiskers tickled her neck. "She is indeed, Dora. But I'm sure she's hungry. Will you bring up some carrots from the root cellar?"

Dora dashed to the back door and picked up a pail. "I did that first thing. I also thought I'd look for extra greens at the market today."

Warmed by the maid's thoughtfulness, Alpin said, "Thank you, Dora. That's very kind of you."

The maid flapped her wrist. "'Tweren't nothing, my lady. His lordship's even having the carpenter build a hutch. That's what they was whisperin' about in the Rot and Ruin last night."

Malcolm had spoken to so many people in the tavern that Alpin had lost track of the names. It seemed everyone except her had known about the gift of the rabbit. "Be sure to give the carpenter something from the food stores in addition to what Lord Malcolm pays him for his labor."

"Aye, my lady. Fraser has a taste for haggis, but his wife won't make it for him."

"Then haggis it is. Here." Alpin handed over the rabbit. "You take care of my new pet until we have a safe place to put her. I'll be in the kitchen garden collecting seeds for next year's plants." She would be gone in the spring, but the people of Kildalton wouldn't suffer for her leaving.

Dora stroked the rabbit's ears. "Were you surprised, my lady?"

Alpin smiled. "I certainly was."

"His lordship said you would be. When he thought it up, he was so pleased, he slapped his leg and splashed water all over the scullery floor."

Alpin rather liked discussing Malcolm's generous nature. "When did he do that?"

"Why, yesterday when he was bathing. You were upstairs getting him fresh clothing. He had me send Rabby to Sweeper's Heath straightaway to fetch this pretty hare. Lord Malcolm was beside himself with worry over the Moor, but then when Saladin got better, his lordship couldn't do enough for you."

So the rabbit had been a gift of gratitude, not a token of affection. Alpin felt a stab of disappointment. She had assumed Malcolm missed her during his hunting trip and had brought the hare as a romantic gesture. She'd been as fluttery as a lovestruck girl last night; she'd even felt the stirrings of love. So much for sentimentality on his part. So much for romance on hers. Damn him for making her care.

"Is something wrong, my lady?"

Nothing she intended to share. "Of course not, Dora. I was just thinking about all the work we have to do today."

Dora drew herself up. "I'm ready for my assignments."

Disillusionment clouding her thoughts, Alpin reverted to routine. "I'll fetch the dirty linens from the barracks while you boil water for the laundry. Elanna started plucking a goose yesterday. You finish it."

"What about caring for the Moor?" Dora asked.

Alpin had been so wrapped up in Malcolm Kerr she'd forgotten about Saladin. "I'm sure Elanna will look after him."

Screwing up her face, Dora said, "I don't think so, my lady. Not after last night. Besides, she's gone fishing."

Fishing? Elanna had never fished in her life—and for some very interesting reasons. "You're sure she said 'fishing'?"

"Aye. She asked me for directions to the loch. Probably best she did, after the fight she had with Saladin last night."

Alpin needed trouble in the castle about as much as she needed another handfast husband. She'd been certain Elanna would feel guilty for having given Saladin the potion. She'd expected her to wait on him hand and foot. "Tell me what happened."

"Well . . ." Cheeks flushed with embarrassment, the maid stared at the rabbit in her arms. "They had a bonny row while you was at the tavern. I was cleaning up the scullery, but I could hear them yellin'. Saladin wanted his prayer rug. The African miss said he was too sick to grovel on the floor.

When he demanded the rug, she tossed it out the window and told him to stay abed."

Elanna had always scoffed at traditional religions and blamed missionaries for bringing diseases to her tribe. Alpin could hear the African woman belittling Saladin's faith, especially if it interfered with her healing regimen. The fishing expedition was a means to make amends, since Saladin would eat fish although he avoided meat. "Find the rug and take it to him along with his morning meal."

Dora curtsied. "Aye, my lady. But I'll need the key to the walled garden. That's where the rug landed."

Saladin's room was on the second floor overlooking the garden. "The keys are on the bottom shelf in the scullery."

"Straightaway."

After collecting the dirty sheets from the barracks, Alpin fetched a basket of gardening tools and cloth pouches for storing and drying the seeds. Then she went to the kitchen garden in search of solitude. She had just picked the last of the basil seeds when she heard the tramp of boots on the pebbled path. Instinct and the pounding of her heart told her it was Malcolm.

He sauntered toward her, strutting like a cock who thought the sunrise would await his call. She couldn't help admiring him, dressed as he was in a flashy red and green Kerr tartan, the sleeves of his soft cotton shirt billowing in the late morning breeze. Even the jaunty pitch of his bonnet bespoke a man born to rule.

"You should have awakened me."

Her first impulse was to rail at him. She chose sarcasm instead. "A clan war couldn't have awakened you."

He squatted beside her and plucked a basil leaf. "Out of sorts this morning, are we? That's odd, for I feel like conquering the world." He tickled her cheek with the leaf.

The sharp smell of basil filled the air. "You tried to kick me out of bed."

The herb floated to the ground. "What?" he blurted, loud enough for the soldiers on the battlements to hear.

She snatched up the leaf and put it in her basket. Then she

glanced around to see if they had drawn an audience. Assured they hadn't, she began harvesting seeds from a marjoram bush.

"Last night you almost pushed me off the bed," she said.

He laughed and slapped his knee. "Why would I do that after I tried so hard to get you into it?"

She didn't really care about the episode in bed; either they would learn to sleep together or she'd take a separate room. But she did care, and mightily so, that he'd lied about going to Sweeper's Heath himself. Feigning indifference, she shrugged. "I wouldn't presume to read your mind. Perhaps you just don't like sleeping with me."

A horn blared, signaling the arrival of a visitor, but Malcolm kept his eyes on her. "I must admit that sleeping was not my first priority."

The warmth in his voice melted her resentment. She thought of a way to tease him. "You also snore," she lied.

He drew back as if she'd struck him. "That's absurd."

"No, it's not," she said reasonably. "It's ear-shattering."

"If I'm such a rude bed partner," he grumbled, "then why has no other woman ever told me so?"

Damn him for throwing his past lovers in her face. Damn her for feeling jealous. If it was the last thing she did, she'd make him forget every one of those women. Putting on a sweet smile, she patted his cheek. "Probably because none of them liked you enough to be honest."

His eyes narrowed with suspicion. "And I suppose you're willing to admit that you like me?"

Placing a hand over her heart, she batted her eyes. "I'm fair smitten, my lord."

"I see." He took her hand, and with his thumb, drew lazy circles on her palm. "Then perhaps we should go back to bed and explore your feelings. Given time, I'm certain I could change 'fairly smitten' to 'completely smitten.'"

He could seduce a nun, Alpin decided. He could connive his way into a cloister and have a whole order of religious brides renouncing their vows.

Feeling cross at herself for wanting him, she fought

against the cravings he inspired. "What if you fall asleep and try to push me off the mattress again?"

His hand moved up her arm to her neck and, with the slightest pressure, began tugging her slowly toward him. "We'll just have to make certain I don't."

Knowing she was losing the battle with desire, she dragged her attention from his mouth and stared at the feather in his bonnet. "How?"

When their lips were inches apart, his hand stilled. "Use your imagination."

Over his shoulder she saw Alexander coming toward them. At his side walked a stranger in a subdued plaid of green, black, and yellow that she didn't recognize. Knowing that Malcolm couldn't see the men, she grew brazen. Wickedness forced her to say, "I could tie your arms and legs to the bed."

He raised his eyebrows and leered. "A truly adventurous proposition. I'd be helpless to prevent you from visiting any number of eroticisms on my naked body."

A delicious shiver coursed through her. "You're scandalous, Malcolm Kerr."

"Me?" he said, as innocent as a babe at christening. "'Twas your idea, and a truly inventive one. I must say, I can't wait to try it."

The men drew closer, but Malcolm gave no sign that he heard them. Alpin couldn't resist saying, "The concept of being my love slave excites you?"

Laughter rumbled in his throat. "Take a peek up my kilt and you'll see just how much the idea excites me."

The challenge in his voice spurred her on. Knowing his body shielded her from view of the approaching men, she slipped her finger inside his boot and lightly scratched his calf. "I'd rather take off your kilt, but . . ."

He sucked air between his teeth, and his hand tightened on her neck. "But?"

Alexander cleared his throat. Malcolm stiffened and glanced over his shoulder.

"But unfortunately," Alpin continued, her voice dripping with honeyed regret, "there's no time. You have a guest."

Ignoring the intruders, Malcolm leaned close and whispered, "You're a wicked lass, Alpin MacKay."

Her heart thudding against her ribs, Alpin looked up at their audience. Alexander shuffled his feet. The stranger, a stocky man with red hair and a piercing gaze, stared at Alpin.

"Do you know what happens to wicked lassies?" Malcolm asked.

Swallowing back fear because she knew she might have goaded him too far, she licked her lips. "No, I don't. Tell me."

"I'll show you." He gave her an arch look. "Tonight."

He rose and by way of greeting said to the visitor, "Your visit had better be about the next shipment of salt. Come with me."

Leaving Alpin sitting in the garden, Malcolm and his guest walked to the castle. She glanced at Alexander, who frowned at his departing laird.

"Who is that man?" she asked.

The soldier pretended to spit on the ground. "A troublemaking Gordon, and no one you need concern yourself with."

"Why does he make trouble, Alexander?"

He pursed his lips, as if he'd said too much. "'Tisn't important, my lady."

"If it's not important, then why won't you tell me why he's here? And why was Malcolm so curt with him?"

Raking off his bonnet, Alexander rubbed his balding pate. "He buys Kildalton salt. I hear Fraser's making a hutch for your rabbit. I'll just see how it's coming along." He touched his forehead. "Good day, my lady." He marched off.

From his change of subject and abrupt departure she knew she'd have to learn the answers herself. A scan of the battlements showed no additional soldiers, so she assumed the stranger wasn't a threat to the security of Kildalton Castle. What, then, about his arrival had so disturbed Malcolm? Surely it wasn't salt.

Curious, she left the garden and went to the great hall, which was empty. She took a moment to admire the eight life-size portraits of the former earls of Kildalton, including one of Malcolm's father, the fair-haired Lord Duncan. Even now his hazel eyes looked down on her with kindness.

Then she went to Malcolm's study. The door was closed. She heard the muffled sounds of an argument, but they spoke in Scottish. If she sneaked into the tunnel to eavesdrop again, her entry would set off the warning bell. If she stood here, one of the servants might see her.

So she went to the staircase and examined the battle shields of the clans that had aligned themselves with the Kerrs.

The shield of the Gordon family was conspicuously absent.

13

Wondering when his guest would get to the point, Malcolm sipped his beer and watched John Gordon of Aberdeenshire pace the study. Arms clasped behind his back, he peered at the shelves of Roman helmets, spear-heads, and pottery that Malcolm and his father had un-earthed from the ruins near Hadrian's Wall. With a casual air, he perused the standing globe, gave it a departing spin, then moved on to the wall of paintings.

For a man planning the overthrow of one of the world's great monarchies, the Highlander seemed indifferent to the danger he courted and unaffected by the lives he risked. How, Malcolm wondered, could a man act so blasé while contemplating a declaration of war? Probably because the Gordon chieftain had spent most of his life in the scheming mews of Jacobite politics.

Whatever the case, Malcolm had no intention of broach-ing the subject first. His mind kept straying to Alpin. One night in his arms and she'd awakened a minx. He intended to give her every opportunity to explore her role as seductress—after his guest stopped prowling and started parleying.

"I don't remember Kildalton being so prosperous when your father ruled," Gordon said in Scottish.

Saladin dispatched their letters, and on occasion Malcolm traveled north to the Gordon stronghold in Aberdeenshire, but the last time this chieftain was invited to Kildalton, Malcolm had been a lad. "Times have changed in the Borders," he said. "My stepmother brought us peace."

His guest stopped before the most recent of the family portraits. "The Moorish lad told me Lord Duncan went to Constantinople with Lady Miriam. Have they returned?"

Gordon was making small talk; he couldn't have cared less about the diplomatic missions. "Nay," Malcolm said.

His guest laughed and shook his head. "I pity the Persians. According to Lord Lovatt, Lady Miriam can swindle a man out of his family jewels and call it diplomacy."

Malcolm's stepmother had a special gift for bringing warring men to peace, and twenty years ago, while preoccupied with negotiations, she had forgotten to guard her heart. Malcolm's father had won her love and in marrying her had given the people of Kildalton a prize of immeasurable value.

Affection for her made Malcolm smile. "I'll be sure to pass along your compliment," he said ruefully.

Gordon went back to studying the portraits.

In his stepmother's absence Alpin had assumed responsibility for Kildalton. She was making her own mark on the citizens; her leadership and involvement in their day-to-day activities had inspired respect and a new camaraderie among the soldiers and the castle folk. How, Malcolm wondered, had he managed without her?

Gordon belched loudly. Leaning close to a portrait, he stared at Malcolm's sisters. When he squinted, his roughened skin looked like old leather. He tapped the canvas. "This lass with the red hair. Your father could do something profitable with her."

Gordon was asking about Malcolm's youngest sister. At fourteen years of age, Anne had one passion: to build an estate vast enough to shelter every orphan in London. She would take to Alpin like an archer to a new bow. "Anne has a mind of her own."

"He hasn't betrothed her yet?"

So much for pleasantries. "My parents don't use their children as pawns in the game of politics."

"A pity. An alliance with the Lochiel Camerons would serve both clans well."

It was so typical and disgusting a remark, Malcolm couldn't let it pass. "Servicing the Highland clans is not a priority with this family."

"Aye. 'Tis why Scotland stands divided. You Border clans may enjoy the role of conquered people, but the Highlanders never will."

The old argument rose before them. Malcolm strove for logic. "The Highlanders don't share a border with the English."

All bravado, Gordon waved a clenched fist. "We'd vanquish them if we did."

"The same way you vanquish one another? You can't stop fighting among yourselves long enough to present a unified front. Until you do, James Stewart has no one to lead or rule."

Unmoved by the reasoning behind Malcolm's statement, Gordon continued to examine the gilt frame. "I take it," the Highlander said, "your fancy piece hasn't returned."

Even though he knew to whom Gordon referred, Malcolm refused to acknowledge the slur. He'd almost forgotten about Rosina. "My fancy piece?"

With a last glance at the portrait, Gordon settled his bulk in one of the chairs facing Malcolm's desk. "Rosina."

"What makes you think she hasn't returned?"

"Two things. First, if she had come back, you would have sent the Moorish lad north with the reply from our friends in Albano. Second, you're not the kind of man to bed two women at once. You're like your father in that."

His guest's lack of taste repulsed Malcolm, but reminding Gordon of his bad manners would only prolong the visit. Malcolm chose another facetious answer. "I never was able to hide anything from you, John."

Gordon gave Malcolm a leering wink. "You concealed your Scottish lass well enough. Who is she?"

The Scottish lass. It was odd to hear someone refer to Alpin in that way; Malcolm had never thought of her in terms of her heritage. She had lived with her English uncle. She'd always been simply Alpin. Now she was *his* Alpin. A situation he found exceedingly enjoyable, especially after last night. He wanted to explore his feelings for her, and he would, the moment his guest returned to his northern lair. "She's no one you'd know."

Gordon shrugged and picked up his tankard. "She looks familiar."

That, too, was odd. "What about her is familiar?"

"'Tis those unusual eyes and her mahogany-colored hair, but I can't place where I've seen them before. What'd you say her clan was?"

Instinct and the curiosity in Gordon's eyes told Malcolm to equivocate. "She's a local lass, and exclusively mine."

"Protective, eh?" Gordon chuckled. "Can't say I wouldn't covet the lassie, were I in your place. She's a wee thing, with a bonny set of attributes."

The memory of her attributes rose clearly in Malcolm's mind. His randy body followed suit. Uncomfortable, he picked up the pitcher. "More beer?"

"Aye, 'tis a fair brew." Gordon emptied his mug and refilled it, then emptied it again. His eyes shone with challenge. "I'd also like a commitment from clan Kerr."

It was always the same with Gordon. "Then you've made a useless trip, for my position hasn't changed, John. I'll ferry your messages to Italy, but I won't be a party to treason."

The tankard hit the arm of the high-backed chair. "Dammit, Malcolm, time is running out. You cannot keep standing on both sides of the border."

"Aye, I can, since I own the land on either side. My

English mother, by way of her dower lands, saw to my interest in both sides."

"Your father had no business taking an Englishwoman to wife."

Malcolm's good intentions fled. "Then I'm sure you jumped with joy when she dissolved the marriage by dying before I was weaned."

Unaware of or uninterested in the tragic events of Malcolm's life, Gordon said, "Either you're with the clans or we'll call you enemy. Which is it?"

A tempest of anger churned in Malcolm's gut. Striving for calm, he picked up a lead pencil and rolled it between his fingers. In English he said, "Watch your words, John. They're beginning to sound like bloody sedition."

Gordon leaned forward, his complexion turning as red as his hair. "You're sounding more like an Englishman every day."

So much for bandying words. "I am half English, as are many people in the Borders."

"We've never held that against you."

"Bide your tongue, especially when you're gorging yourself on beef from my cattle in Northumberland and seasoning it with salt from my English mines."

"'Tis commerce, nothing more. You're well paid."

Knowing the discussion was going nowhere, Malcolm reined in his temper. "You and I have better things to do than to sit here wasting our time citing the differences between Highlanders and Low."

"Aye, 'low' is the word," Gordon growled, radiating stubbornness. "Because you're the one who's determined to draw a line between my people and yours."

"I didn't draw the Highland line. Your ancestors did it centuries ago."

"We did it to protect ourselves from Lowlanders who'll kiss the feet of any foreigner who squats himself on the throne. Answer my question, man. When the time comes, will you or will you not side with your brethren in the north?"

"That does it." Malcolm lunged to his feet, marched

around the desk, and stood before Gordon. "You and I will settle this in the tiltyard now. Have you a broadsword, John?"

The Highlander stood, his shifty eyes peering up at Malcolm. "You're a braw lad, and when it suits you, you're like your Kerr grandsire, the Grand Reiver."

Over the years, a few people had made the insulting comparison. Malcolm's paternal grandfather, the Grand Reiver, had been a violent man who considered himself above the law, much the same as Gordon. Kenneth Kerr had left a legacy of strife and poverty in Kildalton.

In his reign as the eighth earl, Malcolm's father, Lord Duncan, had used kindness and compromise to right the wrongs of the seventh earl. Today everyone reaped the benefits of the peace his father had won.

Because of his size and his dark hair, Malcolm was sometimes compared to his grandsire. But like his father, Malcolm would sell his soul to Satan before he'd put the people of his Borders in jeopardy.

"Likening me to the Grand Reiver is another unoriginal condemnation."

"Condemnation?" Gordon laughed. "Your grandsire told the English what they could do with their laws and their taxes. The comparison would be a bonny compliment, did you live above the line."

Above the line, below the line. Highlanders, Lowlanders. Malcolm grew tired of the divergence, but Gordon and his ilk thrived on pitting Scot against Scot. Peace to them was a truce drawn of necessity and ended out of boredom.

"What's it to be, Gordon? Swords or silence?"

Excitement glimmered in the chieftain's eyes. "You'd like to goad me into a fight, wouldn't you?"

Absolutely. But not for any reason Gordon understood. Frustration over the encounter with Alpin lay at the core of Malcolm's anger. Gordon and his petty affronts had only intensified it. "Me, goad you? If you think to come into my home and insult me, you're daft."

"Must I remind you," Gordon continued, "that I'm ten years older and ten times slower than you?"

If the laird of clan Gordon lacked physical strength and youth, he excelled in cunning and experience. But Malcolm had learned verbal finesse from a master, or mistress in his case, for his stepmother had been his mentor.

Thinking of the patient and clever Lady Miriam, Malcolm relaxed and sat on the edge of his desk. "Then harness that bloody tongue, John, and think about the real problems facing your people and mine. Show me you're willing to do something to benefit the future of every Scot, above and below the line."

His mouth quirking in a satisfied grin, Gordon again settled in the chair. "Very well. I'll give you my daughter."

Thanks to Saladin, Malcolm had expected the proposal. Even so, the political consequences of such a match gave him pause. Uniting half of Scotland would be tantamount to declaring war, especially when the king had voiced his disapproval of this same alliance when Malcolm was a lad and had done so in none too gentle terms.

Well aware that he was being tested, Malcolm said, "I thought you had betrothed her to Argyle's son."

"You don't want her?"

He was really asking if Malcolm would defy the Crown. He'd asked it numerous times since Malcolm became laird of clan Kerr, but never within the walls of Kildalton. It was interesting that he'd come at a time when Malcolm's parents were out of the country. That aspect angered Malcolm more than the audacity of the offer.

"I will not turn Kildalton into a battlefield."

"Look, lad." All cordiality, Gordon turned his hands palm up. "We have to fight the English sometime."

The Gordons always wanted to fight someone, and what better reason for bloodshed than returning a Stewart to the throne? "Speak for yourself. I will not engage an enemy I cannot defeat."

"But you *can* defeat the English. King Louis will provide a fleet and twelve thousand French regulars. With the Bonnie Prince aboard, they'll put ashore near London and catch the English by surprise. When those Hanoverian cowards flee to the north, you and I will be waiting for them.

We'll hold the Borders until James comes to claim his crown."

Military aid was a French carrot dangled before the exiled Stewart for the sole purpose of riling the Hanoverian who occupied the English throne. Unfortunately Gordon and a few other Highland chieftains were so eager to see the reign of James III that they believed the empty promises of Louis XV.

In some ways Malcolm pitied the Jacobites their naïveté. "I do not believe the French will fight a war for the Scots. Nor do I see much honor in having others wage our battles."

"The other Scots'll join in, just you wait and see," Gordon wheedled. "Once they set eyes on our Bonnie Prince, they'll rally to him."

In other ways, Malcolm despised their stubbornness. "Why don't they support him now, if they're so determined to see a Stewart on the throne?"

"'Tis James. He thinks to reconcile the Scots and the Brits, person by person. That'll take years, and when has an Englishman been reconciled by peaceable means?"

Ruefully, Malcolm said, "I believe George the First was the most recent converter of souls." When Gordon frowned and looked away, Malcolm added, "William and Mary also claimed the crown in a bloodless revolution."

"They claimed an *English* crown."

Patience dwindling, Malcolm tapped his teeth together. "George claimed the Union of Crowns, same as Queen Anne." He couldn't help adding, "If you'll recall, she was a Stewart."

"An Anglican," he spat.

As the absurdity of Gordon's argument grew, Malcolm wondered if there would ever be peace in the Highlands. "Oh, so now 'tis a religious war you'll fight?"

Gordon pounded his fist on his kilt-clad thigh. "'Tis a fight to preserve the royal house of Scotland."

Malcolm almost retorted that, thanks to the largess of the pope, the Stewarts and their vast entourage of exiled Scots were quite well preserved in both their Italian villas. Instead, he calmly replied, "Uniting our clans through marriage is impossible, John, for I'm handfasted."

"To the Italian piece?" Gordon clutched the chair arms. "What kind of agreement have you worked with the Stewarts?"

Ah, so he thought Rosina was some link into intrigue rather than a mere messenger to the exiled royal family. An interesting assumption and so typically Jacobite that Malcolm pursed his lips to keep from grinning.

Another irony gripped him. He had never imagined that his marriage to Alpin would have an advantageous effect on his life or a positive impact on Scottish politics. Paradoxically, she had always occupied a separate yet integral part of his life. Now her presence could save him from insulting the Highland clans by unconditionally refusing to unite the Kerrs with the Gordons.

"Well?" Gordon demanded, peevish in his skepticism.

"'Tis not Rosina but the Scottish lass you saw in the garden."

"What's the wench's name?"

Malcolm sidestepped the question. "She's related to my English neighbor, Baron Sinclair."

"Aye. You said she was half Brit," the Highlander said, as if the words were bitter.

"Aye. The same as me."

Chagrined, Gordon sighed. "Who is she?"

With an end to the conversation in sight, Malcolm cast off his better judgment and viewed the situation objectively. On the positive side, if Gordon did know Alpin's family it would be easier for him to locate them. Her reason for coming to Scotland glared in Malcolm's mind: she had no place else to go. Last night she'd been tentative about locating the MacKays. She'd said she didn't believe they cared about her. Her reaction seemed natural; all her life Alpin had been shuffled from one relative to the next.

No matter how much he wanted to keep her in his bed,

Malcolm hadn't the heart, or the right, to prevent her from exploring her Scottish heritage.

"Her name is Alpin MacKay."

His gaze fixed on the edge of Malcolm's desk, Gordon rubbed his forehead. At length, a cunning smile blossomed on his craggy features. "I thought I recognized her. Well done, Malcolm!"

When Malcolm and his Gordon guest hadn't emerged from the study by midafternoon, curiosity got the best of Alpin. Who was the fellow, and why had Alexander been so closemouthed? Malcolm had mentioned salt, but why would so ordinary a commodity cause him such distress?

She thought he might be angry with her over the episode in the garden. Yes, that was it. He was using the man's arrival to distance himself from his handfast wife. But Alpin shied away from that conclusion; if it was true, she risked losing the little ground she'd gained.

Desperate for answers, she went to the kitchen.

From Dora she learned that Malcolm had requested a tray of food shortly after twelve o'clock.

"Do you know who that man is?" she asked the maid.

Dora sloshed turnip greens in a pail of water. "All I know is he drinks enough beer to fill a moat. After the second pitcher, Lord Malcolm came himself and fetched the keg to the study."

"When was that?"

"Over an hour ago."

"Are they still arguing?"

"Nay, my lady, but his lordship looked fair toilworn."

The question loomed larger. Was he upset with her because she'd been miffed and teased him, or was his guest the source of his unhappiness? Hoping it was the latter, Alpin made a pitcher of orange water and went to the one person who might tell her the significance of the visitor.

Lounging in bed, a wall of pillows at his back, a sharpening stone and his scimitar in his lap, Saladin looked like a sultan on his throne.

She poured him a glass of the drink. "Your color's back. How are you feeling?"

"Better, thanks to a bounty of tender ministrations."

Remembering Dora's story of his argument with Elanna last night, Alpin decided to hasten the peace between them. "Elanna doesn't understand your religion."

He sent her a meaningful look that dripped skepticism.

"She's terribly sorry she threw your prayer rug out the window. That's why she went fishing today."

He put down the stone and folded his arms across his chest. "Am I to assume that in her twisted African mind going fishing is some sort of atonement?"

Alpin smiled. "It's actually punishment. In her culture an Ashanti princess never forages for food—not even for a tribal chief. She'd starve first."

On a half laugh he said, "I don't doubt that."

"It's really a tremendous concession on her part, Saladin."

Staring at the ceiling, he stroked his beard. "Then for my part I will be dutifully humble as she picks out the bones and feeds me the tenderest morsels."

"Oh, she'll never do that."

Seeing his raised brows and unconcealed confidence, Alpin had second thoughts about having broached the subject of Elanna's fishing trip. Doubts turned to assurance when he said, "She will feed me and thank her pagan gods for the opportunity."

Prudence dictated that Alpin concentrate on her own troubles. She told Saladin about the visitor. "Do you know who he is?"

Saladin eyed her cautiously. "Why do you care who comes to call?"

Alpin wasn't sure of her motives, but intuition wouldn't let the matter rest. "Because his arrival upset Malcolm."

"And you are concerned about his lordship's moods?"

"Of course I am. We're handfasted."

His brow furrowed, exposing the tip of a widow's peak beneath his turban. "This arrangement pleases Malcolm?"

Alpin tamped back maidenly modesty. "He seems pleased so far. But it only happened last night."

A sly smile gave Saladin a boyish look, one she remembered well. "Do you share his joy?"

She would babble the intimate details of her wedding night if she didn't watch her tongue. "I'd be more pleased if I knew why the identity of his visitor remains such a secret." Hearing peevishness in her own words, she rushed to say, "I don't know whether to lay an extra plate at table and prepare a room or hide the maids from this man who remains a mystery."

Saladin went back to honing the blade. "I'm certain your husband will let you know his desires in the matter."

The swish of stone against steel sliced into the silence. Her wits dwindling, Alpin decided to take a direct approach. "Do you or do you not know why that man is here?"

He tilted the blade to better view the edge. "What makes you think I know all of Lord Malcolm's business?"

"Will you stop answering my questions with questions? I want an answer."

"Then ask your husband."

"You'd think that Gordon fellow was either a criminal on the run or a deviant plotting some dangerous scheme."

Appearing as calm as the glassy waters in Harmony Bay, Saladin put aside the stone. "Do you think so?"

"I don't know what to think."

"Then perhaps you shouldn't think of it at all."

Alpin threw up her hands in disgust and walked to the door. "You're as stubborn as Elanna says."

"Elanna will change her tune."

More curious than before, Alpin hoped the soldiers would tell her what she wanted to know. She went in search of Rabby Armstrong. Unfortunately he stood outside the barracks talking to that tight-lipped Alexander Lindsay.

She went to the smithy.

After exchanging small talk and congratulating Alpin on her handfast marriage to Malcolm, the blacksmith told her the stranger had a finely honed sword.

She stopped at the Rot and Ruin and peered through the windows. The barkeep was busy serving ale to a group of rowdy clansmen wearing the same plaid as the stranger.

At the stable she learned that the stranger rode a well-shod mount and that Lord Malcolm had found himself a bonny bride.

The weaver complimented both the stranger's tartan, which she already knew was a Gordon plaid, and Malcolm's good fortune in winning Alpin, which made her feel guilty for prying.

Crossing the lane, she headed back to the keep. Since she had to pass the tanner's shop, she decided to stop. He supplied the first new information: judging from his chieftain's pouch, the stranger was laird of clan Gordon, an important man. "And a foosty scunner," added the tanner with a wink, "for keeping our laird from his bonny new bride."

Flushed and feeling happier than she had since last night, Alpin almost floated up the front stairs. The doors flew open.

Malcolm's grip was firm but gentle on her arm. "Where have you been?" he demanded, pulling her inside.

So much for wedded bliss. Her euphoria vanished. Smiling up at him, she jerked out of his grasp. "I've been in the barracks telling all of your men how melodiously you snore."

He put his hand to his mouth to cover a laugh, but his shoulders shook and his eyes twinkled with mirth. "I suppose I deserved that."

He was supposed to be shocked, not amused. "Oh, you deserve much more than that."

"I swear"—he slapped his hand over his clan badge— "I'm eager for my comeuppance."

Rising on tiptoe, she said, "Don't be glib with me, and don't dissemble."

Leaning down so their noses almost touched, he replied, "As always, you started it."

She smelled sandalwood and remembered the delicious

taste of his skin. Appalled at herself and afraid he would discern her lustful thoughts, she grew defensive. "Dora said you were drinking with a man named Gordon."

"Only a wee dram, my bonny bride. I want to be completely sober when you tie me to the bed."

She gasped and realized she'd misjudged his mood. He wasn't angry; he was elated. But about what? "I'm mortified that you'd take me seriously."

"I'll take you anywhere, Alpin, anytime."

She had no intention of playing the wanton again. "Well, I'm not going upstairs with you now, so you can wipe that lecherous grin off your face."

"I'd rather put a grin on yours."

His charming ways robbed her of protest. "All right, I'll grin." She did.

"I'm sorry I tried to push you out of bed." His brown eyes glowed with sincerity. "I assure you it wasn't intentional."

Warmed by his honesty but still curious as to the source of his high spirits, she said, "I accept your apology."

"I hoped you would, for I thought to give you a wedding gift today."

The only gift she wanted was the same thing she'd always wanted. A home. Her home. Paradise Plantation. And the chance to lift the bonds of slavery from the people who had trusted and depended on her for the last twenty years.

Straight-faced, she said, "I want the one thing I don't have."

He hitched up his belt. "I know you too well, Alpin. I've learned to decipher your evasions. I know why you came to Scotland."

The bottom dropped out of her stomach. Oh, Lord. He'd found her out. "You do?"

As serious as a sorcerer on Allhallows Eve, he said, "Aye. I remembered what you said last night about Barbados. You must have felt exiled there."

The old bitterness fired her temper. "I *was* exiled there."

He cocked his head. His hair brushed his shoulder. "In a moment you'll never again have to think about Paradise Plantation or your life there."

Sweet Jesus, he'd sold her home to that rascally Gordon. She stood paralyzed, her heart thumping in great hollow strokes. Then she grasped his arm. "What have you done?"

"'Tis a surprise." He took her arm and led her across the entryway. "Come with me."

14

Fear assailed Alpin. She felt trapped. The grip of his hand on her arm squeezed like a slave's manacle. The quizzical expression in his eyes held her captive. Was the sale of Paradise the reason for the stranger's presence?

Oh, God, no. Please, no.

With every step across the room, she felt her terror grow. As a defense her mind darted around the awful possibility that he had shattered her dreams, her hopes for the future that had sustained her for years.

Male laughter drifted from the corridor leading to the lesser hall. The men of the night watch were gaming, passing the time until sundown. Had Dora put out enough food for them?

Halfway across the foyer, Malcolm stopped. "Alpin, you're trembling. What's wrong?"

Nothing she cared to ponder, not if she intended to keep her fears at bay. If she could get away from him, she could think of a way to stop him. "I was just wondering if the soldiers had enough to eat."

"I don't believe you. Tell me what you're thinking."

She darted a glance at the closed door that led to the kitchen—and sanctuary. "I was concerned about your guest. I wouldn't want him to think poorly of Kildalton hospitality. You do pay me handsomely . . . and just because we're handfasted doesn't mean I'll become a layabout and shirk my duties."

"Alpin . . ." he warned. "You're babbling."

Oh, God, he saw through her, but she could think of nothing else to say.

"Look at me."

Reluctantly she did. Impatience tightened his mouth.

She gave him a quivery smile. "Yes?"

His knuckles grazed her cheek. Tenderly he said, "Talk to me, and please don't equivocate."

Why did he have to be so blessed nice? Because he had no idea how much she distrusted him and no inkling to how desperate she was to save the people of Paradise. "About what?"

"About what you're thinking right now."

A diversion flashed in her mind. Fluttering her hand, she laughed nervously. "I'm thinking about how much I hate surprises."

He gave her a confident, arresting smile. "You'll like this one. 'Tis a gift from your husband. Trust him to know what's best for you." Then he ushered her into his study.

The man named Gordon stood before one of the family portraits, his face pulled into a frown. Wrinkles distorted the square pattern of his tartan, and a bulging belly lapped over his low-slung belt. An elaborate chieftain's sporran dangled at his knees, rather than at his groin, giving him an unkempt look.

She glanced at Malcolm, and although her heart tripped fast in anticipation, she had to admire his well-muscled yet lean frame and the neatness of his Scottish attire.

Appreciation turned to puzzlement. If Malcolm had truly discovered her reasons for coming to Scotland and had sold the plantation, why would he wish to have an audience when he told her? To punish her. Aye, his kindness and consideration had been an elaborate act of cruelty.

He cleared his throat and moved his hand to the small of her back.

The visitor turned and stared at her, cataloging her from head to foot.

"Alpin," said Malcolm, urging her farther into the room, "May I present John Gordon, my fellow Scotsman and laird of his clan. He's also the earl of Aberdeenshire, although he shuns the title."

Not taking his eyes off her, Gordon sneered. "'Tis a rank the English bestowed and not worth a Carlisle shilling."

Having no relevant comment, she made a curtsy. "How do you do, my lord."

In answer, he stepped closer and walked before her in a half circle, inspecting her as an overseer would a newly acquired slave. "Eyes from heaven," he murmured.

Insulted to her soul, she lifted her chin. "Are you enjoying your stay, my lord?" When he gave her a blank stare, she added, "I mean, I hope your trip to Kildalton has been pleasurable."

He looked up at Malcolm and nodded. "'Tis now. She's a MacKay; there's no disputing that. The hair's true enough, but her eyes confirm it. She's of Comyn's line."

Feeling left out, she stepped away from both men. "Of course my name is MacKay. But what does that have to do with the price of salt? What's going on here, Malcolm?"

"John knows your father's family," he said, as if it were some great revelation.

An eerie feeling crept over her. She clasped her hands. "So?"

"'Tis my gift to you, the one thing you never had—a family."

Hearing her own words only intensified the bleakness of her situation. What she had considered a clever evasion had come back to jeopardize all she held dear. She had a perfectly fine family in Barbados—dark-skinned women who'd given her rag dolls to make her smile, men who'd carved stately faces in coconuts and left them outside her door to ward off evil spirits. People who missed her, people who needed her.

Crushed by despair, she forced back tears. "You thought I wanted a family?"

Confused, Malcolm battled disappointment. She looked appalled at the idea. Or had she expected some other gift? "What did you think I would give you?" he said.

An instant later, relief blossomed on her face. "I couldn't imagine it at all." On an exhaled breath, she rushed to him and took his hand. "See? I told you I was dreadful at surprises. I always act like a ninny and never say the right thing."

Alpin, the quick wit? She invariably had a clever retort. Her skill at verbal evasion could rival Lady Miriam's. But Alpin had expected some other gift from him. But what, and why had it made her so anxious that she had dawdled in the foyer and carried on about household chores? Surely she wasn't like his other women who had wanted jewels and gowns.

"Malcolm, please don't be cross with me. We have a guest."

He'd forgotten about John. The Highlander had perched himself on Malcolm's desk, his smile reflecting his amusement at their disjointed exchange.

"Please?" she implored.

The appeal in her eyes went straight to Malcolm's heart. She had evaded his questions about her life in Barbados, told him little about herself. He should celebrate her new openness. Selfishly, he should rejoice in his own good fortune.

He studied her hair and her unusual eyes and thought again of the advantages she would bring him. "I'm not cross with you."

"'Twould be a mistake to treat the lass poorly," said John, waving his mug. "Comyn MacKay is peculiar about the women in his line. Coddles them."

"I've never heard of anyone named Comyn MacKay,"

Alpin shot back. "So I can assure you, he has never coddled me!"

"He spent years looking for his lost granddaughter. So don't *you* be hasty, lass," warned John Gordon.

"Don't you dare presume to tell me who I am or what I ought to do."

She wasn't dissembling. But she *always* dissembled. Confused, Malcolm watched anger overtake her. Hoping to quell it, he said, "Aren't you curious about your father's people?"

"Here's how curious I am." She pivoted on her heel and faced the wall, her skirt twirling about her ankles, her back stiff.

Gordon whistled. "She's a MacKay, right enough. I'd stake the future of Scotland on it."

She faced them again, fire blazing in her eyes. "You can stake Comyn MacKay's hide on it for all I care."

"What's wrong with her?" Gordon asked. "She should be glad. The MacKay takes care of his own."

She opened her mouth, then looked at the floor, but Malcolm knew she had plenty to say. "Go ahead, lass," he encouraged. "Say what's on your mind."

Her bearing bespoke hesitancy. "It was—" She took a deep breath. "It was kind of you, Malcolm, to want to reunite me with my father's family, if indeed these people are my relatives. But please don't bother telling the MacKays that their long lost chick has come home to roost. I wouldn't walk across the lane to greet them." A tentative smile curled her lips. "I have all the family I need."

Gordon sent Malcolm a shocked look.

If Alpin was Comyn's missing granddaughter—and Malcolm wasn't convinced of that fact, either—she'd eventually change her mind about her family. According to John, Comyn had spent years scouring the Highlands for her. Malcolm wished his stepmother were here; Lady Miriam knew Comyn MacKay and could confirm the resemblance. For now Malcolm thought it best to honor Alpin's wishes. "My lady has spoken, John. 'Tis up to me to coddle her."

Her nervous gaze flitted to his chin. "Thank you," she said.

Malcolm wondered what she was thinking. Turning to Gordon, he said, "If you'll excuse us . . ."

Frowning, Gordon said, "I'll just gather my men and be on my way. You'll send the Moorish lad north when—"

"Of course," Malcolm interrupted before the Highlander could reveal their arrangement. "As always, Saladin will bring your salt."

When the door closed and they were alone, she rushed into his arms. "I'm sorry I got angry, but I truly want no more family."

Malcolm couldn't ward off a twinge of jealousy. Twenty years ago, in a childish prank, she'd taken away his chance for a family. Since manhood he'd held a grudge, but now he rethought his view.

The woman couldn't be held responsible for the act of the child. She hadn't meant to damage him permanently, couldn't have known the far-reaching effects of her prank. She'd known nothing about procreation back then. For chrissake, she'd believed a woman got a child by spending a night alone at the inn in Bothly Green. She couldn't have known the stings from the hornets had poisoned his seed and sentenced him to a life devoid of heirs.

Blame aside, who better for him to marry? Perhaps that was her penance. When she didn't quicken with their child, she'd be called barren. Husbands were seldom held accountable. Some people in Kildalton might scorn her. They'd scorned her as a child, but in barely a fortnight she'd won them over. Given enough time, she would prevail again. And all the while she would belong to him.

Feeling her snuggle against his chest, he began to see her in a different light. He saw the courageous front she'd worn years ago, the mask she'd donned against the cruelty of the world. As a child she'd blustered to hide her hurt feelings. As a woman she'd made the best of her life. It was his destiny to make the best of her future.

A sense of peace spread through him. He'd write to Lady

Miriam and tell her about Gordon's visit and the growing dissension among the Highland clans. But he'd save his personal news and his suspicions about Alpin's Highland relatives and tell both of his parents when they returned.

Starting tomorrow he'd try to win Alpin's trust and learn her secrets. For now he would simply hold her in his arms.

Saladin found them that way, standing in the study, locked in a healing embrace. Allah desert him, but he envied their accord. Still, no two people deserved to find joy in each other more than these childhood adversaries turned adult friends.

Malcolm looked up and grinned. "Welcome back to the world of the living, my friend."

Elanna's words rose in his mind—"Gods kick you out one time; gods throw you back again"—but Saladin kept them to himself. His feelings for her were too raw to expose, even to Malcolm. "I came to offer my congratulations," he said.

Alpin stepped away from Malcolm; he pulled her back. "Don't be shy. 'Tis just Saladin. He'd never embarrass you or tell you what to do."

"I know. But I'd best see about supper." She gave Malcolm a parting smile and hurried from the room.

Saladin said, "You should tell her the truth."

Malcolm began to pace. "I know, but not now. What is it you always say about lying? I have it: 'One evil which creates one hundred truths is better than one truth which creates one hundred evils.'"

"I don't follow your rationale for deceiving Alpin into a handfast marriage. You should have wed her outright."

"I know, and I will."

Saladin was only five years older than Malcolm, but the philosophical differences between them were vast. A Muslim would never take a decent woman out of wedlock. Saladin couldn't abide such deceit in Malcolm. "How can you justify tricking her?"

Malcolm rubbed his forehead. "Gordon and the other Jacobites are ready to move against the king. They're demanding I join them. Marriage to Alpin gives me an option because the MacKays are moderates."

Another difference arose. Malcolm's methods in dealing with the Highland clans tried Saladin's patience. "Using a woman to settle a dispute is dishonorable. Why not use your sword?"

"Because in our culture we value our women for more than childbearing. We give them freedom."

Saladin couldn't resist saying, "But Alpin's conceiving a child is a moot point."

"Dammit, Saladin. I know I cannot give her a child. But I need a tie to a Highland clan, and she needs a home."

Feeling guilty, Saladin said, "You're certain she's kin to Comyn MacKay?"

"Now that I picture them both? Aye. I should have noticed the resemblance before now, but I haven't seen Comyn in over a decade and I've had other things on my mind."

So much distress was surely born of emotions rather than politics. "I think you love her."

He chuckled ruefully. "Maybe I do." Perching on the arm of a chair, he grew serious. "I spent years blaming her. 'Twas all senseless. She couldn't have known the harm her prank would cause. I couldn't be bothered with her feelings. God, Saladin, she must have been lonely. Can you imagine being six years old, alone, and boarding a ship to Barbados?"

Such a voyage would have been a holiday in Saladin's childhood. "Yes, my friend. I can."

Malcolm clasped Saladin's arm. "I'd forgotten your wretched childhood. I'm a selfish man, and sorry to my soul."

One of Malcolm Kerr's finest qualities shone through: though quick to anger, he was quicker to forgive, except in Alpin's case, but at last he'd done the right thing by forgiving her.

The joy of their seasoned friendship made Saladin smile. "Don't apologize. Lady Miriam rescued Salvador and me from the slave block. Our life is as Allah willed it."

"I wonder what your brother would say if he knew Alpin and I were handfasted."

Saladin laughed. "He'd probably forgive her for breaking his ribs all those years ago."

Malcolm shook his head, his eyes brimming with fondness. "God, she was a hellion." Quietly he added, "She's changed."

Thoughts of his twin brother brought a lightness to Saladin's heart, a relief he sorely needed. "So has Salvador."

"Aye," said Malcolm. "Knighthood has altered his life."

"But not his *way* of life."

"We know him too well. He'd rather play the scribe for Lady Miriam than parade his achievements about the court."

Saladin laughed. "This is so. It also prevents him from keeping his vow to find our mother."

"What about your part of the pact? Will you ever seek out your father?"

Indifference consumed Saladin. He cared less than nothing for the worthless man who'd sired two fine sons, then boarded his ship and sailed off without a word. But Malcolm's engaging grin warranted a positive reply. "I'm certain I will someday, but I think I had better wait until you've persuaded the Jacobites to forget about putting James Stewart on the throne."

"Well said, my friend. Well said."

From that day on, a cloud of happiness settled over Kildalton. Alpin was the openly affectionate bride, Malcolm the dutifully attentive groom. For the next month Saladin watched them revel in the state of matrimony. As summer came to a close and harvest time grew near, no one dreaded the hard work ahead. Meetings were held to assign crews to particular farms. If the crops weren't harvested, the people would starve. Every able-bodied person joined in.

The joy of the laird and lady was contagious.

Only Saladin was immune to the festive atmosphere. At times he even doubted his faith, and all because of an

Ashanti princess with bizarre beliefs and too much pride for her own good.

To escape the torment her presence caused, he distanced himself. She had destroyed his palm-sized copy of the Koran, but like all good Muslims he knew the book by heart; still he kept to his room and set about making another copy.

Solitude offered little comfort, for Elanna came to him each evening after his prayers. She plied him with delicacies to please his palate; she tempted him with kisses to spoil a saint. He always proposed marriage; she inevitably, and often ungraciously, declined.

Life couldn't, he decided, get any worse. On a particularly balmy evening as he stood near his desk he changed his mind.

Elanna appeared in the doorway, her hair brushing her shoulders. A tightly belted robe the shade of old ivory covered her from neck to ankle and served as a perfect contrast to her brown skin.

Lust flooded his groin, but he was becoming accustomed to that torturous reaction. He could bear the frustration; the ache in his heart and the loneliness in his soul overshadowed the needs of his body. Even from across the room, he could feel her warmth.

Past pretty speeches and small talk, he put away his ink and quills and prepared for another round in their ongoing battle of wills. But she brought the art of seduction to new heights when she leaned against the doorjamb and held up a flagon. "You will invite me in to . . . visit?"

Her idea of a visit was to try to lure him into making love to her. But she confused love with lust. "Have you come to play push-me, pull-you?"

Her eyes brightened and she started to enter the room but stopped. "No." She settled against the jamb again. "I just want to talk."

And he was a eunuch with air between his legs. "Since when do you make social calls in your robe?"

She curled her fingers beneath the edge of the garment and moved her hand to her waist, giving him a peek at her breast. "I just had a bath. My skin is slick with oil from the coconut."

"Yes. I can smell it from here."

"You invite me in, yes?"

A fool would tell her no. A wise man would insist she leave the door open. An optimist would expect her to accept his proposal of marriage. "Close the door behind you," he said.

"Betcha that." She breezed inside and secured the bolt.

He watched her find his drinking cup. Looking inside, she frowned, then drank the contents. "I bring you berry juice."

Bearing gifts was her forte, but never the prize he wanted. "No, thank you."

She filled his cup anyway. "You drink it. You liked it before."

"You drink it. I'm not thirsty."

"But it's for you, and there is no more."

"Call me unselfish, because I insist you share it with me."

Reluctantly she put the cup to her mouth and drank. The dark juice appeared transparent on her lips, for they were the same shade of red.

She glided toward him, the cup in her outstretched arm. Eve. Forbidden fruit. The Christian comparison was too suitable to deny, too appealing to refuse. He took the cup.

"You have a handsome neck," she said. Her fingers touched his neck and followed the movement of his throat as he swallowed.

Her smile portended trouble for his scruples. Her hands promised disaster, for she untied the robe. It fell to the floor.

His body turned to stone. His poor beleaguered mind rattled through every helpful tenet of his faith while his eyes were fixated on her dark button nipples and his memory told him how perfectly they fit into his mouth and how delicious she tasted.

The curve of her waist drew his attention; the cradle of her hips lured his more intimate parts. In a voice pinched by lust, he said, "If this is your idea of talking, you have an odd vocabulary."

She toyed with the primitive cord she always wore about

her waist. "This Ashanti princess come to make you sing happy, happy song."

Anger dulled the sharp edges of his desire. In the last month he had denied her, ignored her, even physically removed her from his room. But he couldn't put her out of his thoughts, so he decided to take a different tack. "I can't think of anything I'd like better."

She swayed, her dark eyes luminous with triumph, her lips pursed and damp, ready for his kisses. "You one smart Muslim tonight. Better you forget that polite, polite song and play push-me, pull-you with Elanna."

She radiated heat, desire, and willingness. Allah help him, but he wanted more than one night of love. He wanted her for his wife. "I thought my proposals of marriage *were* always polite, and rather eloquent."

She stopped only inches away. Stubbornness brought an elegance to her high cheekbones and a pout to her full lips. "Proposal no good."

The crux of their problem rose between them. "Because I've never seen the face of my father?"

She tapped her breastbone. "Because this Ashanti princess never look into the eyes of your father."

He stepped back but lowered his gaze to her finger and the rise of her breasts. "That's an absurd tradition," he said. "You can't refuse my noble offer because I do not know my father, then demand I make love to you."

"It's Ashanti way."

Her careless disregard for his feelings robbed him of patience. "May I remind you that you are not among your people."

She leveled him a scornful look, then gave him her back. He wanted to yell at her, but found himself staring at her narrow waist, her high rounded buttocks, and the sleek line of her flanks. His loins grew heavy and ached with need. Humility, he decided, was a state of grace he had yet to achieve.

He held out his hand. "Come here, princess."

She turned. Determination shone in her eyes. "Tell your principles farewell. Gods send you this princess. Enjoy her."

Softly he said, "What about enjoyment of the heart?"

"Elanna sing you sorry, sorry song, but she must save her heart for her forever mate."

"Forever mate. You've said that before. I want to be your forever mate."

"Never, never." She sat on the bed and fluffed his pillows. "Ashanti princess choose you as now-time mate."

Incensed, he said, "Am I supposed to be flattered?"

She grinned. "Yes, yes."

He turned away. "No! No!"

The mattress rustled as she stood up. Then she was behind him, her arms circling his waist, her hips undulating against him. "I make you sing happy, happy song."

He'd heard the statement every night for the last month. The ignoble offer still stung his pride. "So you would have us mate at will, here in this bed?"

She eyed the mattress. "Quick as you sing yes, yes song and get naked." Her hands made fast work of the buttons on his shirt; her fingers made stones of his nipples.

Amazed by her persistence but unwilling to let the matter drop, he turned in the circle of her arms and held her wrists. "But we needn't trouble ourselves with promises of lasting devotion or, Allah forbid, vows of marriage."

Like a child getting her way, she beamed. "Betcha that."

His fingers coiled around her fragile bones. He stepped back. "Find yourself another rutting beast, princess. I'm unavailable."

She arched her eyebrows in query. "Same stupid principle?"

If ever a female deserved a man's wrath, it was she. Were he a violent man, he'd go searching for a rod. He released her and put a safe distance between them. "Decency and honor are hardly stupid principles."

With a sad smile she said, "You make mighty big mistake."

"Then help me unmake it."

She put her hands on her hips and swayed. "I'll help you."

He closed his eyes. "No."

Her breath fanned his face and set off an explosion of

desire. "You want to." When her lips touched his, he couldn't help himself, couldn't deny the need that burned in his soul. He tore into the kiss. She tasted of sweet berries and bitter torment. Her tongue plunged past his lips, made a sweeping raid on his misgivings, then retreated. Knowing he must stop or cast his honor to the wind, he set her away from him.

"Oh," she moaned, her mouth open and ripe, her eyes wide with desperation.

Conversation seemed prudent. He touched the cord at her waist. "What's this?"

She sighed so profoundly that her breasts jiggled. "You always ask. I always say it is Ashanti business." She flung her arms around his neck and went for his mouth again.

Unable to resist, he reveled in the kiss until she touched him intimately. Jolted by a desire that made his senses spin and his head light, he untangled her arms. "Then I'll say good night."

She glared at him as if he were an inferior. "You want this Ashanti princess."

"No, I don't, not in the way you say it must be. However, I do want to know why you always wear this belt around your waist."

She stared at his groin and smiled. "You want me, and mighty bad. Your body sings to me."

He stretched the truth by a Highland mile. "My body doesn't rule my mind."

"I'll tell you about this cord, but Muslim won't like what he hears."

All he could hear now was lust ringing in his ears. "Tell me anyway. I insist."

"It's a princess belt, and I wear it until I'm a queen."

More tribal custom. Oh, Allah, how many of these primitive obstacles must a weak mortal climb? "How do you become a queen?"

She rolled her eyes. "Simple, simple. Ashanti queens give birth to Ashanti princesses."

He understood; only by giving birth could she become a queen. He reached for her. "I'll give you a princess."

As always she came willingly into his arms. "Give me joy."

Compared to the emotions her kiss evoked, joy was blandness.

Her hand found his groin. "You want me plenty, plenty bad."

"Saying I am ready and capable of giving you a child is an understatement. Don't you agree?"

"Tricky question, Muslim." She caressed him in the intimate way he'd taught her weeks ago. "Child, yes. Princess, no. Only forever mate can make Ashanti princess a queen."

In her twisted pagan way, she had said something he didn't like, for the negative reaction registered in his mind. But his body was too far gone to listen. A voice in his soul cried out for him to grasp her meaning. When logic plowed through the morass of desire his mind had become, Saladin's patience snapped. There would be no marriage between them.

Disgusted with his abundance of morals and her lack of them, he accepted the sad truth that she would never be his. Removing her hand, he pushed her toward the door. "Go, and take your primitive beliefs with you."

Tears pooled in her eyes. "You hate me."

"No, Elanna. I love you."

"You cannot love me!"

He needed relief, but even ten thousand prayers would not get him through this night. Under the circumstances, religion and principles made poor bedfellows. To ease his torment, Saladin chose a path he knew he would regret.

15

The dream began the same way.

Weary from a long afternoon in the cane fields, Alpin entered the water shed, a small building between the plantation house and the slave quarters. She stripped off her damp cotton dress and stepped into a tub of rainwater. Her heated skin cooled, and the clean smell of vanilla, her favorite fragrance, wafted around her. Sloe-eyed Sally, a sweet faced and sweeter natured child of six, pulled the pins from Alpin's hair and let it cascade to the floor. Small nimble fingers danced on her scalp, tripped over her temples, and massaged the strain from her neck.

Just as the remnants of the day's sweaty labor floated away, Alpin became aware of the eerie silence.

Her skin prickled with alarm, for the dream was going bad.

She tensed and called to the laundress. But it wasn't Marguerite standing in the shadows. Dry-mouthed, Alpin watched a skeletal figure with empty eye sockets and a grotesque grin emerge from the gloom and shuffle toward her. The creature extended a hand. Blackened bony fingers curled around a bloody mass of pulsing tissue.

The heart of Paradise Plantation.

A silent scream stalled in Alpin's throat. The voices of Marguerite and Sally rose in harmony, pleading for Alpin to deliver them from evil.

She leaped from the tub and ran for the door. She must save them all—Mango Joe, the fleet-footed messenger; Scabby, the best cane man on the island; smiling Bumpa Sam, who could call down the angels with the magical rhythm of his drum.

The people were hers to rescue. She had to reach the clearing where they gathered around an evening fire and sang songs about mother Africa.

The well-worn path cushioned her footfalls. Banana leaves and fan-tailed ferns slapped against her naked arms and legs. Deathly silence drove her onward.

Like a fist in her chest, a thumping noise brought her up short. She rejoiced. It was Bumpa Sam, bringing the plantation to life with his drum. She started to sway to the beat, but the cadence was all wrong.

"My lord! You must come."

Alexander's voice, urgent and thunderous.

No drums. No Paradise. A pounding on the door.

Shaking off sleep, she stared, stunned, at a bar of yellow light pouring beneath the door. She wasn't in Barbados caring for the people who needed her. She was in Kildalton Castle, still stymied in her efforts to get home and deeply in love with the man beside her.

The rapping came again, pulling her fully into reality. No one had ever disturbed them in their chamber. She rolled to the center of the mattress and called to her bedmate. He murmured her name and reached for her, nestling her naked body next to his.

Alexander knocked again, this time loud enough to rattle the wall sconces on either side of the door.

"Malcolm!" she yelled, jostling his shoulder. "Wake up."

Moonlight poured through the open windows and showered him in a silvery light. His eyes drifted open, and he smiled. "Hello, love. Have I tried to push you off the bed again?"

He had, but she'd leave it for now. "Something's wrong. Alexander is banging on the door and calling for you."

He blinked and slapped his cheeks.

"My lord! Come quick."

"You stay here." Malcolm gave her a smack of a kiss, bounded from the bed, and threw open the door.

Alexander stood there, a lantern in one hand, the other braced against the wall. The light threw his face into sharp relief and turned his frown of concern into a grimace of pain.

Although her husband appeared as a black shape framed in a rectangle of light, she saw him tense. "What's happened?"

Alexander spoke quietly. Alpin deciphered only a few words: "trouble," "Rot and Ruin."

"Sweet Saint Ninian!" Malcolm swore and whirled back into the room. "Wait there. I'll get dressed."

Alarmed, Alpin wrapped herself in a blanket and scooted to the edge of the bed. "What is it?"

Malcolm thrust his arms into the sleeves of his shirt. "'Tis nothing for you to bother with. Go back to sleep."

He was excluding her, a practice she abhorred. "If someone is hurt or ill, I should get Elanna."

He pointed at her, his arm stiff, his hair in disarray. "Absolutely not."

"Then I'll come with you."

"Don't get testy, MacKay."

Blast that family and Malcolm's affinity for bringing them up. "Forget the MacKays. I'm just Alpin."

"You're just testy."

She had been irritable, and why not? Time was running out. She had failed in her efforts to save Paradise Plantation. And she had fallen in love with Malcolm Kerr.

Heartbreak made her stomach float. She had no business loving this man.

Seeking a diversion, she demanded, "I want to help."

"Nay." He snatched up a tartan, wound it around his waist, and flipped the end of the cloth over his shoulder. After buckling on a leather belt, he gathered his boots and came to sit beside her on the bed. "You cannot help, Alpin, and considering how hard you worked to please me a few hours ago, you should be exhausted. Just go back to sleep."

Alpin had grown accustomed to his frank references to the intimate aspects of their marriage. What she couldn't accept was his unwillingness to share his troubles. "But I'm wide awake."

With a grunt, he pulled on his boots. "Then I'll sing you a lullaby when I get back."

"Do not patronize me. Tell me what's going on."

"I hardly believe it myself. You stay here."

He stomped from the room, not bothering to close the door. Side by side, he and Alexander tromped down the hall, the light fading in their wake.

During the last month she had seen her hopes grow dim and her heart turn traitor. He had purchased her home, stolen her well-planned future, and replaced it with a life she had no right to live.

In her role as his wife, she had watched him rule his earldom with a fair and firm hand. Some days he seemed as industrious as a second son scrambling to acquire his fortune: inspecting the ripening fields, distributing holdover grain to those in need. Other days he became the benevolent earl: rewarding a winning archer or fawning over a new babe.

He was available and affectionate to a fault. Preparations for the harvest occupied much of his time, and finding buyers for his herds of Spanish cattle consumed much more, but the nights he saved for her.

By candlelight he worshiped her in a way that made dry prose of the poets' romantic tales. Where once he had named her hellion and tossed the events of the past in her face, he now called her clever and remembered their youthful times with understanding and a compassion that eased her troubled soul. He spoke often of their future and encouraged her to reconsider her indifference to clan MacKay.

"The MacKays couldn't find you, Alpin," he often said. "They wanted to care for you. Give them a chance to love you now."

Even the memory of his tender concern couldn't alleviate her restless spirit, for he had changed since her arrival. When the right opportunity presented itself, she would find out why.

She paced the room, stopping to comb her toes through the tangled fringe on the rugs. She occupied her hands with tidying the tables and sweeping the hearth. She folded their scattered clothing and put it away. She made the bed.

An hour passed. When the crooked rows of books on the shelves cried out to be straightened, she lined them up like soldiers on parade.

The clock chimed the hour of two, and he still hadn't returned. Worried, she dressed and headed for the tavern.

On the battlements directly above the Rot and Ruin a cluster of torches gave evidence that the soldiers had abandoned their posts. A milling crowd blocked the front of the building. Curiosity ruled the onlookers. Emily was lifted onto the blacksmith's shoulders so she could peer through a gap between the window frame and the top of the tavern's drawn curtains. Alpin couldn't hear the maid's words, but knew she reported to the crowd. In response they murmured among themselves.

When she reached them, Alpin saw Alexander standing guard outside the door. She plowed through the throng. "What's going on?"

Arms folded, he glared down at her. "Saladin demanded ale and took to gaming with the barkeep."

The information spawned new grumblings. Saladin drinking alcohol? Alpin stifled a gasp of disbelief. She must take control of the situation. She held up her hands. "Go home, all of you. There's nothing more to see."

Someone yelled, "MacGinty had no business serving the Moorish lad. He took advantage of him."

"We ain't leavin' till Saladin's home safe," another man called out.

"Aye," yelled his supporters.

Fearful that their concern would make matters worse, Alpin clapped to get their attention. "I promise you I'll see that Saladin gets back to the keep."

A female voice yelled out, "Lady Alpin'll straighten out the laird and the Moor right enough. To your beds, lads."

Their concerns satisfied, the grumbling crowd dispersed. She turned to the soldier posted at the door. "There's more to it than that, Alexander. Tell me."

He stared at the departing castle folk. "Saladin and the African miss had another row. He sought to drown his troubles in drink. He started rolling the dice and won enough ale to sot a lord. Then his luck went bad, and he lost his scimitar to MacGinty."

Twenty years ago the sword had been Saladin's most prized possession. Once he sobered he'd be devastated by the loss. "Spirits and manly pride," she murmured, "make poor companions." Then she wedged her way around Alexander and through the door.

At the bar she stopped in her tracks. The low-ceiling and rough-hewn beams intensified the closeness of the room. The scent of stale beer and woodsmoke perfumed the air. Scattered candles provided precious little light, but enough for her to see the jeweled scimitar atop a keg of ale near the bar.

The proprietor busied himself scrubbing tables. The other two occupants didn't notice her.

In the far corner Saladin Cortez, usually the most devout of Muslims, lolled in a chair, his turban askew, a drunken grin on his face.

"Push-me, pull-you," he said, slurring his words and causing the candle flame to waver. "Do you know what that is?" His face fell, and his pointed beard accentuated his woebegone appearance. "It's poison, my friend, pure poison wrapped in ebony skin and sent here by Allah. I've failed the test of my faith."

Seated across the table, his back to the door, Malcolm put down his tankard. "Hardly. I think you're supposed to convert her. That's what the Prophet intended."

Awareness flashed in Saladin's eyes, but quickly faded. "Then I'm a sorry excuse for a believer." His elbow slid off the table.

Malcolm caught his arm and propped it up again.

Saladin grabbed Malcolm's wrist. "What's this?"

It was a scarf tied around Malcolm's wrist. Alpin wanted to tie it around his neck. Helping Saladin get drunk was a poor role for a friend.

Saladin snorted. "Your woman's afraid you'll escape her bed, eh?"

"Actually"—Malcolm untied the scrap of silk and tucked it in his belt—"'tis to keep me there."

Embarrassed to her teeth, Alpin stepped back and bumped into Alexander.

"Then it failed." As his stupor grew, so did the melodrama. Closing one eye, Saladin steered his tankard toward Malcolm's. "For you're here with your old friend, sharing a bracing cup at last." His aim was off the mark. Ale sloshed onto the table and dribbled onto the plank floor.

"You'll have an aching head tomorrow," Malcolm said.

Saladin laughed without humor. "It'll match the pain in my heart. Oh, why, my friend, did you meddle in Alpin's life and bring those women here?"

Bewildered, Alpin rolled the statement over in her mind. Malcolm had intentionally meddled in her life. Charles had termed Malcolm's interference a solution to the problem of her welfare. But why did Saladin call it meddling?

"'Twas fate, Saladin." Malcolm hiccuped. "Pure and simple."

"My lord!" Alexander called out.

Malcolm swung his head her way. "What are you doing here?"

Alpin had had enough. She marched up to them. "I'm putting an end, pure and simple, to this celebration."

Saladin attempted to shake his finger at her in reproof, but his aim was still poor and his eyes unfocused. "Naughty girl, Alpin," he said to Alexander, who had moved to her side. "You should be ashamed of yourself for tying my friend to the bed."

Alexander choked back a laugh and winked at her. "I think I should cart him home."

"To a place of peace and happiness?" Saladin banged his fist. "I have no home."

Who better than Alpin MacKay could understand his frustration? "Then we'll find you a bed."

"No," he snapped. "I shall make a pilgrimage to Mecca."

"First thing tomorrow," piped Malcolm, a slight slur to his words. "We'll all go."

"No women in mosques," Saladin declared. "There ought not be any women at all—anywhere. At least not if they smell like coconuts. My friend," he said to Malcolm, "have you ever tasted coconut on a woman's skin?"

Malcolm had the good manners to say, "Nay. But I'm sure 'tis a delight."

Saladin groaned. "A delight. No, a disaster. Why did that Ashanti princess come to Scotland?"

"This Ashanti princess will wash the feet of her captors before she begs that stupid Muslim to come home." Seated on a bench in the entryway of the castle, Elanna looked more like a queen than the reigning Caroline.

Alpin took five deep breaths and prayed for patience. Malcolm had gone to bed. She would deal with him in the morning, but now she had to make Elanna see reason.

Moving to stand before her friend, Alpin said, "Did it ever occur to you that Saladin's religion is as important to him as your customs and traditions are to you?"

"Bah!" Her chin went up. "Religion makes weaklings of kings."

"How can you accuse Saladin of being weak when you ply him with love potions, then grow angry when he refuses to bed you? He sounds strong and admirable to me."

Elanna's jaw worked, and her nervous gaze darted from

the front doors to the urn of fresh heather at the base of the stairs. "Silly, silly man."

Alpin tapped her foot. "He has principles."

Elanna held up her index finger. Her dark eyes snapped with conviction. "One stupid principle."

Patience gone, Alpin snapped, "You are full of yourself. I should never have freed you."

Elanna swallowed hard and wrung her hands. "Never say that. I owe you my life."

"You owe me nothing except to listen to my opinions. But you owe Saladin respect."

Remorse lent an earthy quality to Elanna's ebony beauty. "What can I do?"

Alpin sensed a possible compromise. "Go to the tavern and sit with him. He's never taken alcohol before in his life, and everyone knows he's broken faith. He also lost his sword in a bet. He'll be embarrassed, Elanna. As embarrassed as you were that time Charles put a bow in your hair and paraded you before the Ladies' Social Club."

"Very bad time." She shook her head slowly, and her eyes filled with pain. "Very bad."

"Then you know how Saladin feels. You've driven him from his home. Go to him. Talk him into coming back where he belongs."

Long, dark fingers gripped the chair arms; then she pushed to her feet. "You one smart white woman, Alpin MacKay, and I think you are happy with your Scotsman."

Echoes of the dream still tormented Alpin. She scanned the room and the stairs to be sure they were alone. "Others need me. Good people who helped me have a happy life. I promised them I would return to Barbados. I cannot forsake them."

Elanna walked to the door. Over her shoulder she said, "You will not forget them, Alpin MacKay. They know this."

Alpin smiled. "Sing Saladin a sorry, sorry song."

"Betcha that. After I sing *your* name to the gods."

It was the greatest compliment Elanna could pay, and Alpin acknowledged it with a respectful nod. Then she went up to bed to rest and devise a way to deal with her own stubborn man.

Hours later, like a patient cat with a trapped mouse, Alpin watched Malcolm stir. His sooty eyelashes fluttered, the pitch black color a perfect match to the stubble that shadowed his chin and jaw. The red silk scarves securing his wrists to the headboard gave him a particularly vulnerable look.

He emitted a groan, writhed; then his eyes popped open.

She pounced. "What did Saladin mean when he accused you of meddling in my life?"

Bloodshot eyes focused on her, then closed. "Why are you sitting on me, and what time is it?"

Her knees hugged his ribs. She glanced at the clock. "It's time for you to answer me. Did you trick me into coming to Kildalton?"

He sighed. "You must be tired, Alpin. Come lie down and go back to sleep."

She hated his placating tone and lordly arrogance. He shouldn't look so appealing after a night of selfish indulgence. "Answer me."

"You came to me. You said I was your best friend. Now untie me."

He would have to bring that up. Well, she could be clever, too. "I thought you liked being tied up. You said as much last night."

Through gritted teeth he said, "That was then; this is now. Get off my belly or you may regret it."

"You're bluffing. How will I regret it?"

"I may throw up on you. Untie me."

Her own stomach roiled, and she edged her bottom down to the cradle of his hips. His manhood stirred.

His eyes flew open. "Jesus, Alpin. You wouldn't dare torment a man fighting the demons of too much ale—and getting a tongue-lashing from his wife."

She squared her shoulders and didn't bother to dignify the absurd statements with a reply.

"Would you?" he asked weakly. Misery wreathed his face.

She felt herself weakening.

"That's a lass," he crooned. "Let me up and we'll discuss what's bothering you. We're both intelligent, compassionate people. Let's act like it."

He was too blasted reasonable. She shifted. He smiled in triumph.

"Not so fast. I want an explanation."

"I was besotted, sweetheart. 'Twas the ale talking, and you cannot hold me responsible."

Like boiling cane dripping sugar, he oozed charm. "Oh, yes, I can. Stop changing the subject. Did you or did you not meddle in my life?"

"You wanted to return to Kildalton. You came to me because I was your best friend. That's what you said. Remember? Please let me up, Alpin. I must go to Saladin. He probably feels as wretched as I."

"That's no answer."

"'Tis so."

"'Tis not. Why do you want me here?"

He grew still. "Because," he said quietly, "I love you, Alpin, and I think you keep looking for reasons not to love me."

Her mind skidded to a halt, and her heart soared. She hadn't expected him to declare his love, not with so much unsaid and so many things unsettled between them. "That's an unfair answer, Malcolm."

"Loving you is unfair? Why?"

"Because you said it to distract me."

"Then turnabout is fair play, for you often distract me. You're beautiful."

"No, I'm too short, and my skin is unfashionably brown."

"Your skin is lovely, and you're a tireless helpmate."

"How would you know if I'm a tireless helpmate? You keep me busy in the kitchen and the scullery."

His brows rose and he made a meaningful examination of the bed.

Flustered, she said, "Well. Once we're out of this room you never ask my opinion on important matters."

"Such as?"

"Such as when you moved that herd of sheep from Farleyton to Sweeper's Heath."

He stared at the canopy. "I always move the ewes to the heath in fall."

She hadn't intended to pour out her complaints, but couldn't seem to stop the flow of words. "Had you asked me, I would have pointed out that it would be more practical and economical to put the herd in the outer bailey. You pay the Fraser brothers to cut the grass. The sheep will do it for nothing."

"True, but how will the Frasers make a living? They're proud men."

"Of course they are, and hard workers, too. They can learn to shear sheep, or better yet, you can teach them to raise a herd of their own. The Frasers are not young men, and they have no land. What will happen to them when they're too old to swing a scythe?"

Her practicality confounded Malcolm. He had admitted his love, but she'd accepted his devotion as if it were no more than a daily chore. To hide his disappointment, he took refuge in addressing her flawed theory. "I take care of my people, including the Frasers."

"But that's charity. I doubt they would be happy old men living off your generosity."

She was thinking about her own life, about being a poor relation. It was another valuable insight into a woman who assumed responsibility with the same glee as other women accepted a new dress. It was also another reason why he loved her. "I admit yours would have been the better plan. We'll bring the ewes here next year, and you'll be the one to tell the Frasers about their new life."

The light of excitement faded from her eyes. "Very well."

"Thank you for the suggestion. Now can we agree that you like me a wee bit?"

She studied his bare chest. "You could say that. But I'm still angry because you told Saladin that I tied you to the bed."

How did he explain to a woman the working of a lifelong friendship between two men? "Last night Saladin told me the secrets of his heart. I felt bound to return the favor by telling him one of my own."

A confused frown furrowed her forehead. "It was your idea," she grumbled. "Not mine."

He longed to kiss away her troubles and ask what was really bothering her. Using the silken restraints had been her idea; she'd suggested it in the garden weeks ago. But Malcolm knew he had to foster her affection, for she held on to it the way a miser guarded his gold. Arguing wasn't the way. Besides, he had a full day of work ahead and the effects of a longer night to contend with. Still, creating harmony with Alpin came first.

He knew of one topic that would stimulate her interest and put a spark in her eyes. "Since you've shown such ability with the Frasers' welfare, you can advise me on the sale of Paradise Plantation."

She flinched as if he'd slapped her, and instead of a spark in her eyes, he saw an explosion of fear. "What do you mean, sell it?" she demanded. "When did you decide that?"

She might have been honest when she said she wanted to return to Scotland, but Malcolm knew that Alpin MacKay had unfinished business in Barbados. He was desperate to know the details, but he'd just vanquished her morning irritation and wouldn't risk alienating her again. He had to win her love; only then could he learn her secrets.

"Codrington sent me a list of prospective buyers. They have the funds and are eager to strike a deal."

"Who? What are their names?"

"I cannot recall, but I'll show you the letter. Now will you either untie me or make this captivity worth my while?"

An endearing blush crept up her cheeks. "I thought your stomach was troubling you."

His randy body responded with a vigor only Alpin MacKay could inspire. "The ache is a wee bit lower now."

16

I love you.

Standing in the crowded market later that day, her hand poised over a mound of freshly cut leeks, Alpin heard the echo of Malcolm's words. Around her, feminine chatter faded and movement became a soft blur. All that mattered was the soaring of her spirit and the low twinge of excitement deep in her belly.

I love you.

His words had become tangible, so real she had the absurd desire to string them on a daisy chain and hang them from the castle gates for all to see.

I love you.

A pledge that answered every prayer she had whispered in the loneliness of her life. A promise that fulfilled the soul of an orphaned child, a banished girl, and a solitary woman. A tribute that would alter her future and the life of every person she held dear. One other life would be affected: the life of the child she carried.

The sharp odor of leeks made her mouth water and her

222

stomach pitch. She now understood why she'd been irritable earlier. That and the absence of her menses told the tale: she had conceived Malcolm's child.

Amid the turmoil her life had become, she felt a solidity, an anchor, and she thanked the hand of fate that had brought her to Scotland. Her sojourn here had not only sweetened the bitterness of her youth but had heaped a bounty upon a woman who had expected much less out of life.

Malcolm's child. Malcolm's love.

Guilt tripped on the heels of her happiness. He'd come along too late for Alpin MacKay; she'd already committed herself to a future and a people thousands of miles away. But the boy or girl tucked safely in her womb would have a better chance. This child wouldn't go begging for love and security. This child wouldn't look expectantly into the faces of strangers and hope for a smile or a word of kindness, only to receive indifference or a cuff on the jaw for having bothered them.

She dropped a handful of onions into her basket and moved on to the other produce. Just as she reached the apples, she felt an awareness prickle her skin. Sensing she was being watched she turned and saw a group of women staring at her, smiles wreathing their faces.

She knew them: Mrs. Kimberley, who helped with the baking; Miss Lindsay, Alexander's maiden aunt; Nell, the barkeep's wife; and Dora's mother, Betsy, who managed the market. Alpin couldn't call them friends. They were Scots, cruel critics from her past, unsuspecting players in her destiny.

Alpin had elected to go to the market herself today; Malcolm's admission of love had given her the strength to storm this bastion of female authority.

But as she looked from one face to the next, she was unexpectedly reminded of another group of women an ocean away, women with ebony-hued skin and a dream of freedom. Slave women who would rejoice at the news of her impending motherhood. Indentured women who depended on her, women who honestly enjoyed her company.

The clock of time turned back, and the little girl in her braced for the disdain that always came from the women of Kildalton.

Betsy stepped forward. "We're so glad you're handfasted to Lord Malcolm. Some of us believed him when he swore never to wed until he found the perfect mate."

A knot of tension inside Alpin began to ease. The smiles and the concern of these women were real. They had even confided a truth about her husband. He could have made a dynastic marriage, but he'd wed for love instead. For that gift she said a prayer of thanks and absolved the women of their cruelty years ago.

"You've made him very happy, my lady," said Betsy.

This one experience was so different from the encounters of her youth and the camaraderie was so intense that Alpin felt tears pool in her eyes. Too choked up to speak, she shrugged self-consciously.

The stately Miss Lindsay elbowed her way to the fore. Her arms folded primly at her waist, her bonnet ribbons tied in a lopsided bow near her cheek, she was the image of a dignified spinster. "Betsy, you should be ashamed of yourself for embarrassing her ladyship so." She executed a perfect curtsy. "Contrary to what Betsy would have you believe, we were not gossiping about his lordship's private affairs. I was just saying how he has a fondness for cobbler, wasn't I?"

"Cobbler?" squeaked Nell. "You was talkin' about—"

"As I said," Miss Lindsay interrupted, glowering at each of them, "we were discussing how Lord Malcolm favors cobbler. None of us would stoop to gossiping about what a blessing it was that he chose you rather than that Cameron heiress."

Nell harrumphed. "Your own nephew says the Highland clans are pressing for an alliance with the Borders. Lord Malcolm could've wed the Gordon lass. Her father came to call, or have you forgot?"

"I haven't forgot the visit by John Gordon. His clansmen left a pretty penny in your husband's pocket for all that ale they drank at the Rot and Ruin."

"I say," a beet-faced Betsy declared, "politics is an unnatural subject for ladies."

A dozen questions blazed in Alpin's mind. Sensing the conversation might turn to banal matters, she looked to Alexander's aunt for answers. Playing the innocent, as she had with the lawyer Codrington, seemed wise. "I'm terribly confused, Miss Lindsay. Why does Lord Malcolm need an alliance with anyone?"

"Because someday those troublemaking Jacobites will start another war."

Caught off guard, Alpin said, "War?"

A stern-faced Miss Lindsay nodded. "Aye. They still want a Stewart on the throne."

Betsy sighed and rolled her eyes in exasperation.

Alpin remembered Malcolm's anger at the unexpected arrival of John Gordon, a Highlander. If these women hadn't dabbled in politics, Alpin would never have known about warring Jacobites, who really didn't interest her, or Malcolm's need for a tie to the northern clans, which interested her very much.

Had his declaration of love been a political ploy?

All contriteness, Miss Lindsay rushed to say, "Do not give those Highlanders a thought, my lady. Lord Malcolm tolerates them when he has to."

Alpin had a niggling suspicion that his desire to reunite her with her father's family stemmed from selfish motives. To test her theory she said, "But aren't the MacKays Highlanders?"

"Certainly," said the spinster. "They're probably the most reasonable of the lot, according to Alexander. But they've naught to do with you. You're from around here, my lady. We've known you since you were a girl. There's no link between you and the Highland MacKays, however advantageous for Lord Malcolm that match might be."

Oh, yes, there was a substantial link: Comyn MacKay.

"They couldn't find you, Alpin," Malcolm had said of the MacKays. "They wanted to care for you. Give them a chance to love you now."

Understanding snuffed out the flame of her euphoria.

Love. She'd been foolish to believe in so tender an emotion. The methods of her paternal relatives and her handfast husband were suspect in the extreme. As always, she must look out for herself. For weeks she had shelved the issue of her security. But no more. She would wait for a break in the storm of his male power. When a calm arrived, she would make use of it.

"Well," she declared, waving a hand toward the baskets of produce, "since we've used our feminine logic to settle all of the man-made strife in Scotland, I think I should worry about feeding my husband."

Eyes twinkling with mirth, Mrs. Kimberley put a hand on Alpin's arm. "Right you are, my lady. Those apples'll cook up fine and juicy in a cobbler," she said. "Shall I bake you one?"

"She makes the best cobbler in Kildalton," declared Miss Lindsay. "Everyone says so."

Alpin set down her basket. "Yes, please, and I insist on buying enough apples so you can make a pie for your own family."

Miss Lindsay hummed her approval and nodded to the others.

Mrs. Kimberley started sorting through the pile of fruit. "Thank you, my lady. I'll bring it 'round before dark."

Her basket filled with Malcolm's favorite foods, her heart racked with doubt, Alpin headed for the keep. In the crowded lane, the people of Kildalton respectfully noted her passing. She exchanged small talk, but her interest kept straying to the tanner's wife, who stood with her husband outside their shop, her belly swollen with an advanced pregnancy. The man's tender expression bespoke pride and devotion.

Had hers been an ordinary marriage, Alpin would have sought out Malcolm, thrown herself into his arms, and told him that she carried their child. Once again, however, his dishonesty demanded she keep her news a secret and redouble her efforts to get home.

Disappointed to her soul, she went to the study to search for the letter from Codrington. Malcolm had offered to let her read it, but he'd gone back to sleep after making love to her this morning. Bristling with energy, she had dressed and begun her duties for the day. When he awakened, he'd roused Saladin and gone to Lanarkshire to deliver a herd of Spanish cattle.

Alpin looked in the drawer that contained the other correspondence. The old letters were there, but nothing new. A further search of the desk and the room proved futile. Thinking he might have left it upstairs in his traveling pouch, she went to their room.

In the leather satchel she found an accounting from a squire in Kelso, an invitation to a wedding next month in Carlisle, and an offering of stock from a tobacco concern in Glasgow. Recent correspondence. Nothing from Barbados. She felt certain if she found the letter from the island lawyer she would find the other missing correspondence too. Where had he hidden it, and why?

A more worrisome question plagued her. What would she do when faced with indisputable proof of Malcolm's duplicity? Misery compounded her trouble, but she knew what course she would take. She would hide her heartbreak and do the same thing she had always done. She'd look out for herself.

She must be careful, though, for if he suspected her motives or learned of the child, he'd use all of the powers at his disposal to keep her here.

She must persuade him to transfer ownership of Paradise to her. Inadvertently, Miss Lindsay had given her a new reason to succeed.

In the sunny solitude of the upstairs solar, Alpin refined her plan and rehearsed her words. Sometime later a knock sounded at the door.

"Come in."

Elanna entered the room. Agony dulled her eyes and pinched her mouth.

Seeing her friend so forlorn, Alpin said, "Ashanti princess got big trouble."

"Betcha that." The reply lacked its usual impudence.

Alpin put her own problems aside. "What happened?"

Elanna paced aimlessly around the room, trailing a hand over an embroidery frame, then riffling through a basket of spare buttons. When she pricked her finger on a needle and didn't seem to care, Alpin grew alarmed. "The sooner you tell me what's bothering you, the sooner you'll sing a better, better song."

Elanna looked up. "You cannot help this stupid island girl."

During his sober periods Charles had criticized Alpin for spoiling the slaves and indulging Elanna. Alpin had never viewed her actions in that light; she believed in respecting individuals. In the protected atmosphere of Paradise her actions had seemed proper. Away from that secure world she wondered if she might have been wrong to allow Elanna the eccentricities of an Ashanti princess.

"Please talk to me, Elanna."

Her shoulders sagged. "That Muslim forgives me."

Alarm shot through Alpin. "Did you tell him about the potions?"

"Never, but I threw them down the privy shaft. He forgives me for driving him to drink."

"Why are you upset if he forgave you?"

Head down, Elanna appeared the antithesis of her African birthright. "This woman plenty much afraid. That man put a scare in my soul. The gods now laugh at this Ashanti princess."

Alpin had no culture to call her own, no heritage save a batch of uncaring relatives who'd been eager to ship her off to Barbados, where she'd made a good life and better friends. "I doubt the gods are laughing because you fell in love. My guess is they are rejoicing."

She shook her head slowly. "Ashanti princess sing sorry, sorry song."

"Saladin is a fine man. You cannot regret that you care for him."

"No regrets. Wise Ashanti queen say it's better to feel heart aching than not to feel heart at all."

As much as it pained her, Alpin had to agree. "I think we should go home."

Excitement flickered in Elanna's eyes, and her innate poise returned. "How you get Paradise back from Scotsman?"

Alpin related her plan to get Malcolm to transfer ownership of Paradise to her.

Brows lifted in surprise, Elanna smiled. "You plenty clever white woman."

"This white woman is also pregnant."

Elanna's mouth fell open. Fist clenched, she spat what could only have been an Ashanti curse word. "I should have given you careful-woman sauce."

"No. I want this baby."

"Scotsman never let you leave."

"He will never know, unless you tell him."

Elanna raked a hand across her lips. "Secret yours and mine—until we get home. Then you tell Bumpa Sam so he plays his drums for your child. Old Romeo will build a cradle." Cupping her hands over her ears, she added, "Marguerite will howl and burn twigs for her Asebu gods."

All of Alpin's friends would be happy. They would fuss over her, praise her, and vie for the right to spoil her baby. "I expect they will. I want you to pack only one change of clothing and your valuables. We must be ready when the time comes."

'When will we go?"

"Soon, Elanna. Very soon."

"What about money for the ship?"

Alpin applauded herself. "As Lord Malcolm's steward, I pay everyone's wages. Even my own. And now, Elanna, I think this clever white woman should make herself beautiful for her husband."

"Betcha that."

At Alpin's insistence they dined in the study. After the meal, she poured Malcolm a glass of brandy and sat on the arm of his chair, her hand touching his shoulder.

"When will the harvest begin?" she asked.

Looking like a pampered husband, he stretched out his legs. With the bowl of the glass cupped in his palm, he swirled the contents. "Next week, and I cannot say I relish the prospect."

"Have you enough men to do the work?"

He tipped his head back and gave her a stern look. "If you're thinking of helping, you can forget it. I will not allow you to work in the fields, Alpin."

Did he suspect she had conceived, and was he concerned for her welfare and that of the child? No. He was just being stubborn, a trait she knew well. "Allow me? That sounds despotic."

A smile curled his lips. "Call it what you will, but I'd rather have you pampering my palate than blistering your hands."

He shouldn't be so considerate, not after coercing her into a sham of a marriage. Never mind that it had been her idea; she had a right to her anger. How else could she bear his false promises of love and keep her mind on her mission?

"I do," she conceded with forced regret, "enjoy satisfying your appetite."

His eyes smoldered with meaning. "A circumstance," he murmured, caressing her thigh, "that makes me crave you all the more."

His touch inspired memories of their lovemaking, but she fought her desire and concentrated on his deceit. "Malcolm Kerr! You could turn a how-do-you-do into an indecency."

"You were rather indecent yourself this morning. I, if you will recall, was merely your bound victim."

Appalled, she looked away. "I untied you before—"

"Before what? Before you mounted me and rode my docile manner to exhaustion?"

She laughed. "If you're docile, the pope's a Jew. Stop changing the subject. We were discussing the harvest. According to the ledgers, the yield was poor last year."

"How did you know that?"

She stared at the crown of his head and the play of lamplight in his blue-black hair. Would her child have such glorious hair? Would it be a strapping boy with a thirst for knowledge? Or would her child be a girl with brown eyes and her father's engaging grin?

"Alpin?"

She put aside her motherly speculation. She had plenty of time to think about her child. "Because I compared the harvest totals with the entries for the last two years."

He walked his fingers to her knee. "Why?"

She stifled a shiver of longing and concentrated on what he'd said. Had she made him suspicious? No, he was only curious. "Because I was interested. Remember, I'm your steward and your housekeeper."

"And my wife."

His temporary wife. Fighting regret for what could never be, she took up the conversation. "Precisely. What concerns you concerns me."

He gave a contented grunt and sipped the brandy. "This year our profits should be greater. We had ample rain and plenty of fertilizer from the cattle."

She seized an opening. "What if someone inquires about purchasing some of the animals while you're away?"

"I doubt anyone will, but you can tell them to come back next month."

Small talk was getting her nowhere. Finesse was what she needed. "I suppose you think I couldn't sell a cow."

He began working her skirt up to her knee. "I *suppose* you could sell a coal mine to Newcastle."

If she owned a blasted coal mine, she wouldn't be pregnant and in love with a man who wanted her only for bed sport and political gain. "You're just flattering me because you managed to get out of shopping for a proper gift for your bride."

He almost choked. "I knew you wanted something from me, other than a reunion with the MacKays. What is it?"

He was the one who wanted the meeting, not Alpin. Following her plan, she made light of the question. "It was a jest, Malcolm. I have all I need, except enough work to keep me busy."

"That'll change soon, for all of us."

He referred to the harvest. "Not for me, if all I have to do is cook and turn away cattle buyers." She snapped her fingers. "Oh, I almost forgot. You were going to show me the

231

letter from Codrington." She held her breath, hoping he would take the bait.

"What does that have to do with keeping you busy?"

"Well . . ." She rubbed his neck. "Since I know more about the plantation than you do, you could give Paradise to me for a wedding gift."

His hand went still. Her skirt fell back into place, covering her knee. "Why do you want it?"

Honesty came easy. "I was raised there, Malcolm. I know the slaves as well as you know your soldiers. I couldn't live with myself if the new owner mistreated them."

"They were kind to you?"

She tamped back a burst of homesickness and love. "Very much so, and I'm afraid a stranger would take advantage of them. You can't imagine how wretchedly some slaves are treated."

"Then tell me."

"The women are encouraged to breed, and not always with other slaves. On some plantations the children bear a striking resemblance to the master."

"That's disgusting."

"Yes, but it gets worse. Oftentimes little children are taken from their mothers and sold. Imagine a man siring a child, then selling it to his neighbor."

"Aren't there laws dictating humane treatment of slaves?"

"White men make the laws and the profits. But those abominations have never occurred at Paradise, and if you'll give me the authority and the responsibility, I'll keep it a decent place."

"You never could abide any creature being mistreated, could you, Alpin?"

She tucked the compliment away; she'd have a lifetime of lonely nights to remember his words of praise. "There's another reason." Again she waited, for this was her most persuasive argument.

"I'm listening."

She had rehearsed the words; distancing herself from the sentiment they evoked posed a challenge. "You once told me that I resented you because you were born to wealth and position and I was born to poverty. At first I denied it, but now I have to agree that you were right."

An eerie calmness surrounded him. "You no longer resent me for my birthright?"

Borrowing one of his rejoinders, she said, "You could hardly call my attitude toward you this morning resentful."

He chuckled. "True, and in light of what you've told me, I'll give you Paradise for your wedding gift."

She had to bite her lip to keep from shouting with glee. Paradise would be hers. With the papers in hand, she would return to the safety of her island home. No one could stop her. No one could take her property away again. With the help of her friends, she would raise her child there. Malcolm could wed his Highland heiress.

She fought off a stab of jealousy. "Perhaps I'll have a daughter someday. The plantation could be her dowry."

He jumped from the chair, almost knocking her to the floor. "'Tis a bit early for such talk."

Gaining her balance, she stood, transfixed by his odd behavior. He seemed distant, enraptured by the family portrait on the far wall.

At length she said, "But the subject of children is important. What if I do not conceive? You'll still be obligated to provide Kildalton an heir. What will become of me then?"

He whirled to face her, a hard edge to his features. "We needn't discuss this now."

"Quite the contrary."

"Leave it, Alpin," he growled.

Baffled by his sudden anger, she forced herself to be reasonable. "Look, Malcolm. If I had my own means, you wouldn't be troubled to look after me."

"By 'means,' you refer to the proceeds from the sale of Paradise plantation?"

She had no intention of selling it, but he needn't know that. Once he'd signed over the property to her, she could relax. The day the harvest began, Alpin MacKay would begin her own voyage—home.

Her plans made and her destiny within reach, Alpin said, "Yes. Having resources of my own is important to me. Can you understand that?"

"Aye. You shouldn't feel like a poor relation in this marriage."

Actually she felt like a pawn, but she would exit this marriage with her future assured and the wonderful gift of a child. "Will you draw up the paperwork now? That way I can answer Codrington's letter tomorrow." If she couldn't devise a way to escape quickly, she'd write another letter, to the governor of Barbados, informing him of the transfer of ownership and her plan to return to the island.

"If it will make you happy, Alpin, I'll do it." Malcolm left the room.

Too excited to move, she counted his departing footsteps, heard the smooth rhythm of his bootheels on the stairs. But she had looked up there, searched their room from top to bottom. Curiosity overrode her enthusiasm, and she raced to the door. Peeking around the corner, she saw him disappear down the hall leading to his parents' bedchamber. So that was where he kept the papers. She hadn't thought to look there.

Then she realized it didn't matter where he'd hidden the documents; only getting them in her possession did.

He returned with a box under his arm. The wooden surface had been richly worked in marquetry. Easing into the chair behind his desk, he handed her Codrington's letter, then began penning the official transfer. He looked troubled and she wondered why, but she was too excited to dwell on his mood.

According to Codrington, activities on the plantation were going well under the supervision of Henry Fenwick. Alpin relaxed.

Once the deed was written, he offered her the quill.

"Why are you nervous?" he asked.

Concentrating hard, she willed her hand to stop shaking long enough to sign her name. "Because I've never owned anything before."

"Well, you do now." His smile was forced, his voice stiff.

From the box he produced several tally sheets she herself had written over the years. Charles had insisted the accountings were for his own use. Now she knew he'd begun sending them to Malcolm five years ago after he transferred ownership of the plantation.

She held the papers loosely, although she wanted to clutch them to her breast and dance around the room.

"Alpin, there's something I want to tell you."

He seemed so serious. Thinking he would lecture her on the responsibilities of being a landowner, she put the papers on his desk. "Not now, Malcolm. Let's toast our marriage."

He tapped his teeth together, a sure sign that he was troubled. "'Tis important to our marriage, what I have to say."

"And bad news, from the look on your face. Leave it for now. Please. Let's celebrate our good fortune."

He stared at the other documents in the box, his indecision obvious.

Her heart bursting with joy, she sat on the rug before the hearth. "Come sit beside me," she said, "and bring the brandy with you. I'm eager to hear all about those cattle you sold today."

"'Twould bore you to tears, Alpin."

He seemed miles away, even as he crossed the room and dropped down beside her. Or perhaps it was just that she was so happy.

Determined to cheer him up, she said, "Then tell me how Saladin plans to get his sword back from the barkeep."

"MacGinty never intended to keep it. He was afraid Saladin would use it on someone. God, he was a sight drunk, wasn't he?"

She elbowed him in the ribs. "You made quite a picture yourself."

He glanced down at her, challenge glittering in his eyes. "I wasn't that drunk."

"Of course not. You always stumble up the stairs and fall asleep in your clothes."

"Did you take them off me?"

"Yes, and it took me ever so long to get you naked."

"Was that before or after you tied me up?"

"I'm not telling."

"I could make you."

"How?"

He pulled her across his lap and leaned close. "I could start by carrying you upstairs and stripping *you* naked."

Desire swirled inside her. She would leave him soon, so why not enjoy his passion while she could? She could also examine the contents of the box. Surely Charles's letter was there. Inhibitions gone, she wrapped her arms around his neck. "Let's sleep here. Then you cannot push me off the bed."

"I'm sorry, Alpin."

"Apology accepted. Just lock the door."

"No one will come in without first knocking."

"No one?"

His intense gaze roamed her face. She saw herself reflected in his eyes and wondered if he would truly miss her. Her heart ached at the thought that he might not.

He smiled that endearing grin she hoped God would bequeath to her child. "No one," he murmured, "except my family, and we needn't worry about them."

Then he kissed her, his lips soft and persuasive, his arms a strong and comfy cradle. The kiss inspired a new intimacy, a contentment born of two souls searching for oneness in this space in time. Then she felt a familiar yearning that seemed to bind her fully to him and spawn dreams of a future that would never unfold. She threaded her hands in his hair, mapping the shape of his head, committing to memory the rich texture of his hair, his high brow, and the slight indentation at his temples. Even as her need for him grew and she anticipated the pleasure they would share, her mind envisioned the child they had created.

No longer fettered by the constraints of an uncertain future, she felt free to explore him, to take the lead. With the same attention to detail he'd practiced on her since the first night they'd made love, Alpin hugged him close and spread kisses over his face, his neck, and the shell of his ear.

His breathing turned raspy. Against her cheek, he said, "If my gift inspired such wifely devotion, I'll be certain to give you presents every day of the year."

Ignoring the reference to a permanence they would never achieve, she whispered in his ear. "It wasn't your generosity, but you. Please love me, Malcolm."

He groaned and removed her clothing with the skill and speed of a man with no time to lose. Then he laid her down on the soft rug and lavished her breasts with slow, wet kisses, teasing the sensitive sides and grazing the nipples with his tongue and the tantalizing edge of his teeth. When at last he set to suckling her properly, she cried out and hugged him to her.

The familiar ache deep in her belly turned to a raging need. Reaching down, she rucked up his tartan and, with both hands, caressed him, learning the different textures of his sex, the soft, weighty sacks, the velvety skin that encased his steely maleness, the crowning glory that had touched her intimately.

His mouth went still on her breast. She looked down at him and beheld a man deep in the throes of absolute pleasure. His eyes were closed but not tightly shut, his mouth was open but not slack. Seeing him thus and knowing she'd brought him to such a state of arousal, she grew bolder in her handling of him. She coddled him with her palm and brushed him with the pads of her fingers; she lightly grazed his length with the tips of her nails.

He gasped and his eyes flew open; then his luminous brown gaze focused on her. "I think," he said, "you had better stop."

Feeling spunky, she winked. "But I like it."

He grinned. "Have your way with me, then, Alpin, but be forewarned: I shall retaliate in kind."

The picture wouldn't form, so she continued her ministrations. "Wouldn't you rather kiss me than threaten me?"

"Oh, aye, love. But—"

Then his eyes did squeeze shut and his jaw went tight with tension, and instinctively she knew he was fighting the demon that was himself, the demon that she had aroused.

Suddenly he jerked away and tore at the buttons on his shirt, almost ripping the fabric.

Lying naked before him, lazily watching his frantic movements, Alpin felt a devil invade her mind. "I feel like a lusty proclivity."

He laughed. "Oh, you are. No doubt about that, and as soon as I get out of my regalia, I'll show you how much I appreciate your new station in life."

As innocent as a virgin, she said, "But we haven't had dessert. It's on the table."

Still clothed from the waist down, he paused and shot her a look that promised retribution. As if he had all the time in the world, he forgot about removing his garments and knelt between her legs. "Nay, mine's right here."

Then he caressed and loved her in a way that defied her imagination and made child's play of her preconceived notions about physical love.

She fell asleep in his arms, his tartan wrapped around them for warmth and modesty.

Through a heavy blanket of sleep, Malcolm felt a raspy wetness on his cheek. Instinctively he drew up his arm to shield his face. Alpin lay nestled against his side. The floor of the study felt solid at his back. He heard an impossibly familiar whimpering and sensed movement in the room.

Flint struck steel. Light blossomed behind his desk, followed by a female gasp. Craning his neck he focused on the dog. His heart sinking with embarrassment, he lifted his gaze to the woman who stood before him.

Lady Miriam MacDonald Kerr.

Her blue eyes flamed with motherly outrage. "That naked brunette had better not be Jane Gordon."

17

Malcolm cast off the last shackle of sleep and awakened to the reality that he and Alpin lay naked on the floor with only his tartan covering them. Over him stood his stepmother and her dog.

"That naked brunette had better not be Jane Gordon."

He tried to decipher her warning. Politics often dominated his stepmother's life. She never meddled in his private affairs. He had written to her of Gordon's visit. He had hinted at the unrest among the Highland clans. He had been specific about Gordon's offer of his daughter's hand in marriage.

His conclusion drawn, Malcolm quietly said, "She is not Jane Gordon."

"Good. I feared he would go to any lengths or depths to press the suit." She picked up the marquetry box and clutched it under her arm. "I was looking for this."

As always, Lady Miriam was a victim to her own logic and dedication to work. The box contained Malcolm's notes

239

taken from the months of correspondence between Gordon and the exiled Stewarts.

Alpin stirred beside him. Placing his hand over her ear so as not to wake her, he whispered, "Wait for me outside, Mother, and take that slavering beast with you."

"Yes, of course. I'm terribly sorry." She put her hand against her cheek, a cheek that was as smooth as that of a woman half her age. "I just didn't expect to find you here at this hour. I mean, I did expect you to be awake by now, but not here and with—Oh, Malcolm, why couldn't you have locked the door?"

Alpin moved again, and this time her knee brushed his groin. Dodging an arrow of desire, he clenched his teeth and said, "Apology accepted. What time is it?"

She stared at the array of male and female clothing scattered on the floor. "Almost six."

He glanced at the drapes, but the heavy fabric blocked out the light. "Leave the lamp. I'll join you in a moment."

She snapped her fingers. The huge sleuthhound, aptly named Redundant for his resemblance to his grandam, trotted to the door. In a swirl of green silk and stately elegance, Lady Miriam glided out of the room.

Malcolm closed his eyes and breathed deeply, giving his dignity a moment to recover. He spent most of his time at Kildalton Castle, but he had always kept his women at Carvoran Manor. He had younger sisters here and their sensibilities to consider. He also respected his parents too much to parade his lusty proclivities before them.

But he was past his desire for mistresses; the woman in his arms was all the female he needed and more. Her frankness and the reasons behind her asking for the property in Barbados spoke volumes about how much she wanted their marriage to succeed.

It was unfortunate that she would never have the opportunity to present her newly acquired dowry to a daughter or bequeath her money to a son. He had wanted to tell her the truth last night, but she'd been too excited about becoming a woman of means, and too eager to exercise her new independence. Spontaneity had been their watchword last night, happiness the result.

Yet their marital bliss stood on shaky ground, the bedrock cracked with a lie.

He intended to make a full confession, just as soon as he'd spoken to his stepmother.

Feeling lighter for having made the resolution, he pulled Alpin onto his chest. "Wake up, you slugabed."

She moaned and cuddled against him. "What time is it?"

"'Tis nearly six o'clock."

"Oh, my goodness." She bolted to a sitting position, taking his tartan with her. "Dora will need her instructions. We were to make candles this morning, and the floors in the barracks are a muddy mess from the rain yesterday."

She looked delightfully mussed, her expression still endearingly sleepy, her hair a mass of chestnut-hued ringlets trailing to her waist. How could anyone term her glorious hair brunette? The word sounded too ordinary. It must have been the dim light.

"Wouldn't you rather forget Dora and dirty floors and give your husband a good-morning kiss?"

Saints condemn her; she actually pondered the question. Pride stinging, he said, "Unless you don't care to know the name of the very special person who arrived here a few moments ago."

She leaned over him and rubbed her nipples across his chest. "Good morning, husband mine."

Her hair formed a warm curtain around them, and when her lips settled on his, he thought he might just have to make love to her again. His randy body confirmed it.

He hugged her close, allowing his mind to drift to the softness of her skin, and the way she fit perfectly against him. He enjoyed savoring this woman and nurturing her passion, but he couldn't banish the idea of a quick loving.

She drew back. "What's so funny?"

"I was thinking about one of the coarser terms for lovemaking."

Curiosity sparkled in her eyes. "Tell me."

"'Tis called the rooster rut."

Her carefree laugh was the second sweetest sound he'd ever heard her utter.

"What is the rooster rut?" she said.

"'Tis something that happens very quickly. Are you interested?"

She stared at the ceiling, her teeth toying with her bottom lip. The delicate column of her neck and the perfect planes of her shoulders drew his attention. Her dainty size was misleading, for she possessed an abundance of womanly charms.

She glanced down at him, a wicked gleam in her eye. "Instead of nipping me on the neck and calling out my name when you . . . you know . . ."

Enjoying her discomfiture, he smiled. "You mean when I'm trapped in the throes of passion."

"Yes. Instead of enjoying what you usually do, I'm eager to see you tuck your thumbs in your armpits, wag your elbows, and cock-a-doodle-doo."

They both laughed, and he embraced her again, feeling cozy and content. His desire subsided, replaced by a deeper need for harmony and trust with this very special woman. She warmed his heart. She made him long for day's end and the time when they could be alone. She made him regret all of the years he'd spent scheming for revenge against a crime committed by an innocent lass who'd never known love and security.

A shadow of doubt passed over his happiness. What if she couldn't forgive him?

"Who is here?" she said.

What if he couldn't make her love him? Malcolm shied from the possibility. "Lady Miriam."

Alpin scooted away again. "Truly?"

"Aye, she arrived a little while ago."

She scratched her forehead, then gathered her hair and pulled it over her shoulder. "Where are my hairpins?"

"Scattered, I'm sure, as are your clothes."

"She mustn't see me like this."

He didn't have the heart to tell her just how much Lady

Miriam had seen. "Take the tunnel up to our room. Do you remember the way?"

She snatched up her stockings and petticoats. "Yes, I think so." Once she had dressed, she scooped up the papers and the lamp and disappeared into the tunnel.

As he dressed, he wondered what Lady Miriam would say when he told her about his handfast marriage.

"Congratulations, Malcolm," she said. "Who's the lucky lass?"

She stood at the base of the main staircase, her tapestry valise at her feet, the enormous sleuthhound at her side.

"Welcome home, Mother."

A warm smile brightened her face, and she hugged him fiercely.

The embrace brought to mind how much she had enriched his life. A woman of extraordinary character, a world renowned diplomat, Lady Miriam MacDonald Kerr had changed the course of British history and affected the life of everyone in the Borders. By example she had taught him to fight for his dreams and hold his principles dear. In the latter he had failed her.

Her dog barked and wedged a cold nose between them.

"Redundant, get back!"

The dog, which weighed a pebble shy of six stone and sported front legs as thick as Malcolm's forearms, immediately sat. Aside from being the only creature able to snap Malcolm from a sound sleep, the sleuthhound could smell a rabbit from a hundred paces and track it for miles without tiring.

"Well?"

Lady Miriam's arrival spawned dozens of questions. "My news can wait," he said. "Tell me when you got back."

She huffed impatiently. "My ship docked in London three days ago."

" 'My'? Singular? Where's the rest of our family?"

"Malcolm! I'm as curious as the widow MacKenzie. Who is your bride?"

Although the top of her head barely reached his chin

Lady Miriam was truly a formidable presence and an expert in the art of intimidation. The only problem was, she often failed with family members. "You go first," he said. "What happened in Constantinople?"

She put down the marquetry box and began pacing. "'Twas an unremarkable treaty punctuated with passages from the Koran and concessions from both sides. I drank an ocean of fruit juice and ate a mountain of rice and greasy mutton. The sultan wanted to house me and your sisters in the seraglio. Your father bedeviled me by pretending to contemplate the arrangement. Saladin would have been in heaven there. Salvador despised every moment and had the nerve to fashion tiny icons into the illuminated border of the sultan's copy of the treaty. Mahmud came to terms with the Persians. As we speak, both sides are scrambling to find ways to break the agreement. I expect that effort to keep them busy for a couple of years."

She stopped and bowed from the waist. "So there, my inquisitive son."

She rattled off matters of state as if they were a list of household chores. Her flawless memory and attention to detail had been the bane of kings and carpenters, the torment of bootboys and bishops.

"Did you tell that to King George?" Malcolm asked.

"I told him nothing. He's in Hanover trying to make a mistress of the Countess von Walmoden."

"But you saw the queen or Walpole?"

"Both, unfortunately." She removed her lace-worked coif and shook her head. Her shoulder-length hair fell perfectly into place. "That's why I'm a day late getting here. The prime minister insisted I attend a reception commemorating the opening of his house on Downing Street. The queen was there. We stood in a broom closet while I gave her my report on the mission."

He laughed. "You expect me to believe you convened a meeting with the queen in a broom closet?"

"You always were a skeptical lad. Now. I've told you everything about my trip. Will you please tell me everything about your bride?"

He felt as proud as he had the day he'd learned to wield a broadsword. "She's Alpin MacKay."

Surprise enhanced her youthful appearance; caught off guard, Lady Miriam could have been mistaken for her eldest daughter. "The baron's Alpin MacKay?" she said. "That's who you were with just now?"

Possessiveness consumed him. "She's *my* Alpin MacKay, and she's gone upstairs to change and comb her hair. She's nervous about seeing you again after all these years."

Now that she'd regained her composure, she scrutinized him like a mother reunited with a wayward child. "How long has she been here?"

"'Tis a long story, and you look exhausted. Let's sit down."

She stuffed the delicate coif into her pocket. "You're such a comfort to a vain mother."

Ignoring her gibe, he led her to her favorite room, the lesser hall, which was empty. Redundant trotted to his favorite spot at the base of the Kerr throne and plopped down with a thud.

Malcolm held out a chair at the table near the windows, then sat across from her. The first rays of sunlight accentuated the strands of silver that salted her red hair. At eleven years old, Malcolm had fallen in love with her, thought she was the only woman in the world for him. At twenty-eight, he thought the world a better place for her presence in it.

"Now that you've seen to the comfort of my rickety old bones, you can tell me how Alpin MacKay came to Scotland and ended up naked on the floor with you."

A fresh bout of embarrassment seized him. He cleared his throat. "She arrived from Barbados a couple of months ago."

"Why didn't you write it to me in your letter?"

At the time he'd written, he had justified the omission by telling himself the news would have complicated her mission in Constantinople. In actual fact, she was too skilled to be distracted, but the point was moot, for his plans for Alpin had taken a different turn.

Thinking of his handfast bride and how he'd acquired

her, he decided one small lie would create a hundred truths. "I wanted to surprise you."

A frown marred the ivory smoothness of her forehead. "I am surprised. I thought you disliked her because you believed she made you sterile with those hornets years ago."

He'd wasted too much time on that emotion. "I love her to distraction, and now that you're home, I'll set a date for the wedding."

She gave him a rueful smile to let him know she hadn't missed his evasion about the hornet incident. Hell, his stepmother's perception was rivaled only by her perfect memory.

"Does Baron Sinclair know she's here?"

"Nay. He hasn't returned from Ireland and the company of his grandson."

"You'd never know he once abhorred children, especially Alpin," she said. "Why did she come back to Scotland?"

If half-truths were blessings, Malcolm had a foot in heaven's door. "Charles died."

She winced. "Oh, I'm sorry. Your father said the poor man never recovered from the tragedy of his wife's death." She stared at the Kerr family throne, a faraway look in her eyes. "Twenty-two years ago, Duncan gave Charles and Adrienne the money to escape Scotland and build a new life on that plantation. They were happy there, and they prospered, despite their disappointment over Adrienne's many miscarriages. They actually thanked us for sending them Alpin. She must be heartbroken."

Lady Miriam didn't know Malcolm acquired the plantation. The transaction had been a private matter, and she never interfered in his business. "Alpin's healing, Mother."

Her lips curved in a wry grin. "The men of clan Kerr have innovative ways of distracting their women. I'm glad you've put the past behind you. She didn't hurt you intentionally, and as I've said before, I doubt that you're sterile."

He was accustomed to her bluntness. He just didn't share her optimism on the matter of his siring children. "'Tis obvious you are wrong."

"Oh, posh. You never were one to dally 'round with the maids, and you cannot count mistresses, especially the ambitious Rosina. She, by the way, has turned her attention to a pair of Italians who look like throwbacks to the days of Roman centurions."

That didn't surprise Malcolm, considering the woman's appetites. He was pleased, though, that she'd found entertainment elsewhere.

But how would Miriam know? "Who told you about Rosina?"

"We were talking about Alpin. She was such an independent sprite. She didn't mean to hurt you."

A wave of guilt engulfed him. "I know. I'm just sorry it took me so many years to figure it out."

She gave his hand a motherly pat. "Your father will be very sad about Charles."

"Where is he?"

She drummed her fingers on the polished surface of the table. "He's in Italy—he and your sisters."

So that's how she'd found out about Rosina. "Why are they in Italy?"

"Because your beautifully rhetorical letter reached us a week before we left Constantinople. I thought it best to pop in on the prince across the water. I tried to talk young Charles out of coming to Scotland to reclaim the crown in his father's name."

The ramifications of such a venture were staggering. Malcolm glanced about the room to be sure they were still alone. An invasion could endanger the life of everyone from Cornish fishermen to the shepherds of the Orkney Islands. "I cannot believe the Bonnie Prince wants to come here."

Her lips tightened. "Believe it."

"But he cannot."

Pained tolerance squared her jaw and stiffened her neck. "So I advised him."

"And he didn't listen to you? Either he's half-witted or you're slipping, Mother."

She cocked an eyebrow at him. "He's more stubborn than

a sultan. That taste of battle he had last year at the siege of Gaeta made him eager to rouse his brother Scots. Then his mother died. I think he's angry at the world."

Through a haze of denials, Malcolm saw red. "What language does he intend to use to rally his countrymen? Italian? We speak that tongue often in Scotland, you know."

"A clever sarcasm, Malcolm." She glanced out the window. "Your sister Anne is teaching him Scottish."

Malcolm's temper exploded. He stood, knocking his chair to the floor. "That twit. How could you let her do such a thing?"

The sleuthhound bolted across the room to Lady Miriam's side. "Everything's fine, boy. Lie down." She stroked the dog's long ears and burnished red coat. "Redundant is very protective of me."

Regretting his outburst, Malcolm picked up the chair and sat down again. "He looks a bit thin."

Tears misted her eyes. "Redundant is not the traveler my Verbatim was."

Everyone in the family had loved the old female dog, and when she died they all had grieved, but none more than Lady Miriam. To ease her pain, Malcolm said, "Of all her offspring only Redundant inherited her tracking skills."

"Aye," she said, casting off sorrow as easily as another woman would throw off a cloak. "He's even better on a scent than she was. Poor thing. He's been confined for months."

"I'll take him hunting."

"Good. Where were we?"

"As if you'd forget," he chided. "You were about to tell me why my impetuous sister Anne is tutoring Charles Stewart."

"You needn't take up the office of outraged older brother. Your father is chaperoning them." She laughed. "You should see him standing over them, his hands clasped at his back, his posture as stiff as Dora's apron. Duncan's quite righteous in the role of duenna."

Malcolm chuckled, which he suspected was her plan. "I'll be sure to tell him you said so."

"If you do," she warned, "I'll tell Alpin about the time

Angus MacDodd caught you spying on him and Alexis Southward. He scared you so badly you wet your breeches."

Shame, as only a mother could inspire it, made him cringe. "I yield to the more devious mind, and propose a truce."

She held out her hand. "How novel and original of you to propose a treaty to me."

She had spent her childhood at court and her adult life in the diplomatic corps. But still she had a sense of humor. "What can I do to help with the Stewarts?" he said.

"Pray that the impetuous prince changes his mind or that his father forbids him to make war."

"Have you spoken with James?"

"Yes. He sided with me, but I fear Lord Lovatt and Murray are too influential with our young Stewart warrior."

"What will you do?"

"I'll go to the Highlands and talk with Gordon and the other clan chiefs. If I cannot dissuade them, I'll go to France and speak with King Louis. He's listened to me before. I'll try to change his mind about financing a Stewart invasion. 'Tis unthinkable, truly."

"Does Queen Caroline know?"

"I'm certain she's unaware of it now, but there's much intrigue among the Jacobites in Italy. I wouldn't be surprised if someone leaks the news to her or Walpole."

"You'll make John Gordon see the error of his ways. I have complete faith in you, Mother."

"Thank you, but I'll tell you a secret, Malcolm." Her businesslike mien faltered, and he saw a glimpse of the loving mother who had tended his scraped knees and brightened life's disappointments. "I'm weary of spending my time preventing arrogant men from doing their worst. 'Tis the ordinary people who suffer for the arrogance of the nobility."

She did appear tired. Faint circles shadowed her eyes, and she lacked the vibrancy that was her hallmark. "How long since you had a good night's sleep?"

"Since I last saw your father." She sighed and, with a skill that never ceased to amaze him, rose above her exhaustion.

"I insist"—her hand slapped the table—"that you tell me more about my new daughter-in-law."

He could have talked for hours, purged his soul of sinful lies, and expounded on the rewards of romantic bliss. Who better to hear his confession than the only mother he'd ever known? His conscience answered: the only woman he'd ever loved.

He chose the information about Alpin that would most interest Lady Miriam. "John Gordon is certain that Alpin is Comyn MacKay's long lost granddaughter. He says she looks just like him."

Interest sharpened her keen gaze, and he realized she was looking not at him but over his shoulder. "That would certainly explain the baron's dislike for her and his eagerness to send her to Barbados. He hated anything and everyone Scottish back then. I'll tell you this, Malcolm. You had better wish on your lucky star and pack away the breakables," she said quietly, "when Comyn MacKay sets eyes on her."

Malcolm swiveled and saw Alpin standing in the doorway, her hair perfectly plaited and coiled at the crown of her head. She wore a lavender gown that turned her eyes to twinkling amethyst jewels.

His heart bursting with love, he beckoned her to them. Then he turned back to Lady Miriam. "Do you also think she looks like Comyn MacKay?"

Her gaze trained on the approaching Alpin, his stepmother whispered, "Is the King German?" Then in a louder, casual tone, she feigned friendly conversation. "Verbatim did love to travel. . . ."

18

As Alpin neared the table she heard Lady Miriam say "verbatim." It was the first big word Alpin had learned. At the time she had been awed by the beautiful lady who knew so many fancy words she could give them away to dogs.

But Alpin was no longer an impressionable illiterate child. She was a woman who had succeeded in her mission. Neither her handfast husband nor England's most illustrious ambassador could prevent her from returning to Paradise.

Reaching the table, she saw the marquetry box in Lady Miriam's possession. After Malcolm had fallen asleep last night, Alpin had read the contents. Although she didn't understand all of the notes begun by Lady Miriam and continued in Malcolm's distinctive hand, she knew trouble was afoot. John Gordon of Aberdeenshire was behind it. The Kerrs were trying to foil it. Alpin MacKay wanted no part of it.

She curtsied. "Hello, my lady."

Malcolm's stepmother rose and embraced her. "Please, call me Miriam. The Kerrs never stand on ceremony." Leaning back, she smiled fondly. "We have always considered you one of us."

The rhetoric stung. As a child Alpin had lived on the fringe of this family. When life at Sinclair Manor turned unbearable, she always sought shelter here at Kildalton. Before being discovered, she had knelt by her straw pallet in the windowless tower room, said her prayers, and promised to be a good girl if only God would give her kind people of her own. He had; they were waiting for her half a world away.

Pasting on a smile, she stepped back and dished up some rhetoric of her own. "You're very kind, Miriam, but you always were—even when I least deserved it."

"Like most bright children, you were headstrong." She glanced pointedly at Malcolm. "And your pranks were harmless."

"Who are you making excuses for, Malcolm or me?" Alpin asked.

"Both, and welcome to our family."

Alpin looked at her handfast husband, who gave her a bland smile. A sooty stubble shadowed his cheeks and jaw, and his hair begged for a brushing. His shirt was wrinkled, his tartan hastily donned. He hadn't even bothered to put on his sporran and his clan badge. He didn't need the accoutrements of power; he possessed them naturally.

He snaked an arm around her waist and drew her to him. "Well, Mother, what do you think of my bride?"

"I think she's lovely." She winked at Alpin. "Why, I wonder, would she burden herself with a slovenly troll like you?"

"I am not a troll." With a gentle squeeze, he said, "Tell her the truth, Alpin. I'm a generous soul, and you adore me."

Even disheveled he looked too handsome for his own good—or for hers. Peeved by her attraction to him, Alpin patted his head. "I have always adored wounded beasts."

"Oho!" Lady Miriam clapped her hands. "She knows you too well."

Feeling decidedly self-conscious with their familiar banter, Alpin said, "Dora's preparing your room, Miriam, and a bath."

His mother smiled apologetically. "You mustn't go to any trouble, for I'll be leaving within the hour."

Considering the contents of the notes, Alpin thought the decision wise. But she'd keep the knowledge to herself. "So soon?" She looked to Malcolm for his reaction.

He shrugged. "I tried to talk her into staying, but she never listens to me. The king's business, you know. Here. Take my chair." He stood. "You two get reacquainted while I change clothes."

"Malcolm," said his stepmother, "perhaps you'd like to ride with me as far as Sweeper's Heath."

She made the offer in a light-hearted tone; yet her eyes held his for a long moment.

"'Twould be my pleasure, Mother." Giving them a courtly bow, he left the room.

Alpin sat, her eyes straying from the box and the dangerous information it contained to the unshuttered windows and the traffic in the lane, her mind dwelling on her husband's departure and how she could make use of it. She would devise an excuse to leave this afternoon. She'd write Malcolm a note and be on her way. Her heart constricted at the thought of never seeing him again, but, as always, life had given Alpin MacKay few options. When pitted against the welfare of eighty people, one woman's heartbreak seemed a small price to pay.

"You could join us if you like."

The politely worded offer lacked sincerity; Lady Miriam wanted to speak privately with her stepson.

"Thank you, no," Alpin said, terrified of their dangerous game. "We've candles to dip and barracks to scrub." And treason to avoid.

"I'm deeply sorry about Charles's death."

Caught off guard, Alpin said the first thing that came to

mind. "It put an end to his suffering. He's where he longed to be."

Alpin worried that she'd been too frank, but Lady Miriam smiled and said, "Thank goodness he had you to care for him. Tell me, Alpin. Did Duncan make the right decision years ago when he persuaded Baron Sinclair to send you to Barbados?"

Tears clogged Alpin's throat. "Oh, yes. I had a good life there."

"And you're happy now, as Malcolm's wife?"

Lady Miriam looked hopeful, her blue eyes glowing with motherly love, her lips curving in a tentative smile. The truth, bittersweet as it was, came easy to Alpin. "I love Malcolm, and I'm proud to be his handfast wife."

As if relieved, his stepmother leaned back in the chair. "Forget the handfasting. He's ready to call in the parson."

Girlish dreams soared, then settled like a rock in Alpin's stomach. A real marriage? But that was impossible—unless they knew she carried his child. She had to find out. "I thought formal vows were exchanged when the woman conceived."

"And you will, my dear. I'm certain of it."

Alpin relaxed and found herself blushing.

"Did Charles leave you a dowry?" Lady Miriam asked.

The old hurt resurfaced. "No. He left me a stipend."

All business, Lady Miriam propped her elbow on the box and rested her chin in her palm. "We'll correct that, once you're countess of Kildalton."

She was talking about exchanging permanent church-sanctioned vows. If Alpin pledged her troth to Malcolm, she would become his property, as would Paradise. She'd just become the lawful owner and refused to give up her land to a man who couldn't be bothered with the plight of the slaves. "I'd rather wait until I conceive. Malcolm needs a son to carry on the Kerr name."

Eyes narrowed, her chin stubbornly set, his stepmother, said, "Daughters are as valuable as sons. Anyone who tells you otherwise is a pigeon-brained fool who cannot rub two sticks together to make a fire."

Her defense of their sex was so fierce that Alpin felt herself swell with pride. Still, she had to steer the conversation away from Malcolm Kerr. "Speaking of fools, some of the white men in Barbados would turn your stomach. They ride around like kings and treat their gamecocks better than they treat the females in their keeping. One fellow in Bridgetown harnesses bare-breasted slave women to his carriage on Sunday mornings."

"That's how he gets to church?"

Hatred fueled Alpin's need to return and begin freeing the slaves in Barbados. "Yes."

Lady Miriam's face grew flushed with anger. "Self-serving men without common decency and respect for the law?"

"Yes. The island's overrun with them." Alpin poured out her heart as she never could with Malcolm.

"I think I shall visit there when—" Her zeal gave way to resolution. "When I can. Now tell me this, Alpin, and forget Malcolm's needs and feelings. Will you be disappointed if you do not conceive?"

As if determined to prove her a liar, her traitorous stomach fluttered. Alpin stared out the window. Saladin passed by, his prayer rug tucked under his arm. "I cannot answer that," she said truthfully.

"'Tis too soon, I'm sure. Has Malcolm given you any money?"

"I receive a salary as housekeeper. I maintain the ledgers and pay the staff."

"You're his steward, too?"

Alpin felt her hackles rise. "Yes," she said defensively. "I prefer staying busy. I haven't the temperament for sewing and chitchat."

Lady Miriam seemed pleased rather than surprised. Chuckling, she said, "We are alike, then, you and I. 'Tis just as well you're industrious, considering I took most of the staff to Constantinople."

"We've managed."

"I can see you have, and admirably so." She grew serious again. "Let's talk about Comyn MacKay."

The words fell like boulders into the conversation. Alpin tensed. "What about him?"

"More to the point, what do *you* think about him?"

In conversation, Malcolm's stepmother was as slippery as a ribbonfish. Alpin could be crafty, too. "Why is everyone so sure we're related?"

Instead of answering, she asked, "Do you remember your father's name?"

Alpin delved into her memory, but it was like stumbling blindfolded through a maze. "I seem to remember a common name. James or Charles. It wasn't Scottish."

"Both are names of Scottish kings, as are Comyn and Alpin. The MacKays always name their firstborn after a member of Scottish royalty."

Alpin wouldn't be swayed. "It's a coincidence, no more."

"I disagree, Alpin. Why else would a man name his daughter after a Scottish king?"

She felt the old hollow ache and despised Lady Miriam for causing it. "My father did not name me. He was lost at sea before I was born."

"So your mother, an Englishwoman, thought to name you after a Scottish king."

Phrased that way, it did seem farfetched.

"Have you any papers," Lady Miriam asked, "letters or the like, that belonged to your father?"

"They were buried with my mother, or so Baron Sinclair said."

"He'll be sorry he did that, Alpin. I assure you."

Alpin believed her. But her heritage didn't matter. "Do whatever you wish, but not on my account. I have no need for more relatives."

"Even if your marriage proved advantageous?"

"To whom?"

"To you of course. As an heiress of the MacKay clan you'll be entitled to the dower lands your grandmother passed to your father."

Alpin wanted only one plot of land, the land she now owned. "How can you be so sure I'm an heiress?"

"The MacKays are wealthy."

"Let them keep their money. I don't want it."

"Then think beyond yourself, Alpin. What if the people of Scotland will benefit from your being one of the Highland MacKays?"

Alpin didn't care a broken seashell for Scottish politics. But of course Lady Miriam did. "I doubt I could be of any value, for I wouldn't know those people if they walked through that door."

"Oh, aye, you would. I know that clan well, and the resemblance is too strong to deny." She stared at Alpin's face and hair. "In the north, they call your unusual eyes 'eyes from heaven.' Comyn *is* your grandfather."

Would she never let the matter drop? Patience gone, Alpin braced her palms on the table and pushed herself to her feet. "Well, I'm past needing a grandfather, thank you very much."

Lady Miriam grasped her wrist. "He tried to find you, Alpin. I heard about his search years later. He couldn't know to look for you here in the Borders, but they say he scoured every glen and brae above the Highland line and every port on the western coast."

Her soft, cajoling voice and pleading eyes reached out to the lonely child in Alpin, but the woman in her balked. She had made a vow to the people of Paradise. She must fulfill her promise. "That's very admirable, and I appreciate your concern. But I am not interested."

"You'll have to deal with the MacKay, for I can assure you John Gordon has told him where you are."

Her assurance chipped away Alpin's determination to remain civil. "Gordon came here over a month ago, and we haven't heard a whisper out of this Comyn MacKay. You're overestimating his devotion."

She smiled a smile that any orphan would have cherished. "We'll see, my dear, but I advise you to prepare yourself. John Gordon doesn't do anything unless and until it benefits him. When it's to his advantage to tell Comyn about you, he will. I simply think you should be forewarned."

Lady Miriam's caution was an exercise in futility. Alpin was leaving Scotland today.

At sunset Alpin and Elanna sat in the public room of the Barnacle Inn near the docks of Whitley Bay. At high tide they would sail on an English flute, its bulging belly loaded with whiskey and wool. This ship would take them to Southampton, where they would book passage on an East Indiaman for the long voyage to Barbados.

A fire crackled in the blackened hearth, spilling warmth into the near empty room. Feeling listless, Alpin sipped the honeyed milk and hoped the drink would settle her queasy stomach. She hadn't been able to stay in their rocking cabin; she would have retched until the ship sailed at two o'clock in the morning. So she'd taken a room here, but doubted she could sleep.

In her note Alpin had told Malcolm she'd gone to Carvoran Manor to pay the servants there and inventory the stores. She had wished him pleasant dreams and said to expect her home by afternoon the next day.

Home. Once the word had held a wealth of meaning to her. It had represented security, a sense of self-worth, the ultimate happiness. Now a part of her, the part that Malcolm had nurtured with love and captured with passion, saw this journey and her future as an obligation.

Had he given her one inkling of support on the subject of freeing the slaves she would have told him about her beliefs and torment. She would have sought his counsel. But he had made a joke about the issue.

The earl of Kildalton couldn't be bothered with the plight of Bumpa Sam, Mango Joe, and the seventy-eight other people who were her responsibility. Malcolm was too busy intriguing in Scottish politics.

Her lover had his cause; she had hers. She couldn't help lamenting over the poor timing of their romance. Under different circumstances they might have had a happy future. But that was a fool's wish, and dwelling on what might have been would only make her feel more miserable.

"You left your rabbit behind," said Elanna.

"I know." Same as her last departure from Scotland, she was leaving with little more than the clothes on her back. Years before, she had left a menagerie of nature's forgotten creatures in the care of Lady Miriam. But this time Alpin was leaving her heart.

Solace came in thoughts of the child she carried. She'd have a part of Malcolm to cherish, a little person to warm her heart and share her life, a true family to bring joy to her waning years.

"Will he come looking for us?" Both fear and hope shone in Elanna's eyes.

Alpin knew well those conflicting emotions. "No. I told him if he did, I'd never get my work done. I also invited Alexander and his aunt to sup tonight, to keep Malcolm company."

"You plenty clever, Alpin MacKay. Let's just hope the lucky gods ride on our shoulders until that ship sails."

If he did come after her, he'd be angry, and Alpin had no desire to feel the brunt of his wrath. She preferred to take with her the memory of their good times together.

"Do you think Saladin will come for you?"

Elanna folded her arms on the table and stared into the fire. The light threw her high cheekbones into relief. "Muslim tied to his principles."

"Are you sorry we came?"

"Never, never. He say his Prophet willed it so. I believe Ashanti gods respect this Allah and send me to his servant." She sighed and shook her head. "Muslim too stubborn to know what's good for him."

The door opened. Alpin jumped and jerked around to see a man and woman dressed in traveling clothes step into the inn. The newcomers stared, shocked, at Elanna. Fighting panic, Alpin picked up the saddle pouch that served as her valise. She had sewn the deed to Paradise Plantation into the lining of her cloak. She draped the garment over her arm. "I think we had better go up to our room until time to board the ship."

259

Accustomed to having people gawk at her, Elanna calmly gathered her meager sack of belongings and food for the voyage; then they made their way to the room. They shared the narrow bed and tried to sleep.

The blast of a horn awakened Alpin: the signal that the tide was on its way in. In painful silence they left the inn and walked to the ship.

The *Lydia Jane* rode low in the water, lanterns dotting her decks and crewmen scurrying in the rigging like green monkeys in a fruit-laden fig tree.

Alpin's footsteps rang hollow on the gangplank, a fitting sound to the emptiness in her heart. A sailor respectfully averted his eyes as he offered her a hand onto the deck. She felt the other men watching her and her unusual companion and speaking quietly among themselves. Like everyone else, they were intrigued by Elanna.

The ship rocked gently. Ropes creaked, and the tide lapped against the hull. In the narrow companionway, the air felt close and smelled of damp wool. Alpin's stomach churned, and she swallowed hard, praying that the sickness would not accompany her to Bridgetown.

Their assigned cabin was the third on the left. The louvered door stood open. Light from inside poured into the hallway. Alpin stepped across the threshold and froze, for there, lounging on the narrow bunk, his arms folded behind his head, his legs crossed, was Malcolm Kerr.

Her heart catapulted into her throat. Elanna bumped into her and muttered words that sounded like crusty mustard seeds and hollowed-out logs.

Malcolm drilled Elanna with a devil of a stare and tipped his head toward the hallway. She clutched Alpin's arm and pulled back, but Alpin's legs wobbled like saplings in a gale and her feet felt nailed to the teetering floor.

She waved Elanna back. "What are you doing here, Malcolm?"

He didn't bat so much as an eyelash.

"How did you find me?"

A bland handsome stare was her answer.

Anger seemed her best defense in what appeared a defenseless position. "You want me only because of who my grandfather is."

"If you will recall, sweet wife," he drawled, "I handfasted myself to you before John Gordon laid eyes on you."

He had her there, if she believed him, which she didn't. Scraping up every last bit of gumption, she lifted her chin and glared at him. "I think you knew all along that I was related to Comyn MacKay. You were desperate for an alliance with him. That's why you meddled in my life and made sure I had nowhere else to go but here."

"Do you honestly believe that rubbish?"

She hadn't even thought of it until a moment ago. She'd been too preoccupied with her pregnancy and too worried about the people at Paradise. But now, as she recalled his excitement in telling her she was Comyn MacKay's granddaughter, the conclusion made sense. Malcolm had probably known for years. She felt used, manipulated by him, all in the name of love.

The liar.

"I believe it implicitly," she said. "You took Paradise and brought me here under false pretenses."

"Why would I take the plantation only to give it back to you?"

Because she had outsmarted him. "It's a mystery to me how your loathsome mind works."

"I assure you, Alpin," he murmured ominously, "you have yet to learn the true meaning of 'loathsome.'"

He could frighten her, but he'd never make her cower. "What will you do, beat me?"

"The law gives your husband that right, among others."

"Such as what? Locking me in a dungeon? Whacking off my hair?"

"You've been reading the law." He swung his legs off the bunk and sat, his fingers gripping the edge of the mattress, his broad shoulders taut with tension. "How industrious of you."

"I'm not afraid of you, no matter how many laws you have

on your side. You cannot keep me here to salve your wounded pride."

"I do not intend to keep you *here*. You'll walk off this ship of your own accord. You'll mount the horse that awaits on the quay. You'll return to Kildalton and fulfill your part of our bargain."

The walls seemed to close in on Alpin. "I'll do nothing of the sort."

He seemed so embittered, looked like a battle-hardened soldier. What had happened to the laughing, joking Malcolm? The Malcolm who had professed to love her? Sadly she knew the answer. He'd gotten what he wanted, a tie to an important clan.

He should have grown up to be an admirable man, not a selfish schemer who destroyed other people's lives to achieve his own goals. Power had been his birthright, but instead of wielding it for the betterment of those in his keeping, he used his position to batter anyone who stood in his way.

"Either you'll walk or I'll carry you. The choice is yours."

"Why are you doing this? You don't really want me."

"I welcome the opportunity to show you just how much I want you, but unfortunately I have crops to harvest, and Captain MacMarcil has a tide to catch."

So coldly polite was his tone he might have been declining an invitation to sup with a tiresome acquaintance.

She could be chilly, too. "I suppose you know the captain."

He smiled without humor and waved a hand toward the door. "After you. I intend to be home before sunrise."

She glared at him.

He shrugged. "Make no mistake, Alpin, I *will* carry you. If it comes to that, I insist that you kick and scream. I would so like to send these seafaring men off with a tale of gossip on their lips."

As always, she had no choice but to obey a man. Too angry to speak, she whirled and edged past the waiting Elanna. Marching down the gangplank, she spied Saladin and four horses near the dock. Beside him lay the enormous sleuth-hound. The dog must have led Malcolm to her.

Sunrise greeted them at Kildalton. Malcolm lifted her off her horse. She tried but failed to stifle a yawn.

"Go to bed, Alpin, and get some rest."

Surely he was as exhausted as she. "What will you do?"

"I'll pull a man from the haying crew and assign him to guard the paddock. If you leave again, Alpin, you'll have to walk." He looked at the cloud-filled horizon. She saw vulnerability in his eyes, but the next instant it was gone. "Then I'll return to the fields and pray the storm passes us by."

Too tired and heart-weary to argue, she turned and walked into the keep, vowing with every step that next time she'd take ship at the larger port of Tynemouth or at South Shields. She would even ride all the way to Southampton if she must.

Her opportunity came the next morning when the men returned, toilworn, from the fields.

Standing with Elanna on the deck of a merchantman ready to depart the harbor at Tynemouth, Alpin heard the thunder of approaching riders. Two clansmen bearing torches came into view. In front of them loped the sleuth-hound; behind them rode a stoic Malcolm Kerr. Saladin and Alexander, each leading a riderless mount, brought up the flank.

Alpin shivered with frustration. This time he didn't even dismount. He sat astride that white stallion looking like a king whose word was law. She could feel his anger. Unfortunately her own rage matched his.

The ship's captain hurried down the gangplank. Malcolm spoke but never took his eyes off Alpin.

The captain returned. "Lass, you'd best go to your husband."

"But, sir, I've booked passage."

He gave her back her money. "Go. There's no place for

you or the African woman on my ship or any other leaving this port."

Hating herself, she clasped her hands together. "But he'll beat me."

The captain laughed. "The laird of clan Kerr fights off the women, not the other way 'round."

All the way home she glared at Malcolm's back, damning him and damning herself for a fool. She and Elanna had escaped through the postern gate and walked to the village of Weber's Glen. There they had borrowed horses. The hound had led Malcolm to her again. As she planned her next escape, she considered her mistakes.

Later that day a courier arrived with a letter for Malcolm from his stepmother. Alpin gave the man tuppence, then locked herself in the study. She gently lifted the seal and read the message: "Wish on your lucky star and pack away the breakables. I return soon."

Alpin's hand trembled. The confusing message made no sense, except the last words. Lady Miriam was coming back. Alpin had to leave.

A knock sounded at the door. She resealed the missive and put the letter with Malcolm's other mail. Then she released the bolt. Elanna stood on the threshold.

Once inside, she said, "I'm the reason he keeps finding you."

Elanna was part of the problem; an African in Scotland stood out like a Chinaman in Barbados. But Alpin would not leave her friend behind, and they must make haste. Disguises seemed the most logical solution. That and divert the attention of the nosy sleuthhound.

"She's done it again, my lord."

Like too much whiskey, angry resolve spread through Malcolm, intoxicating him, dulling his senses.

He secured the reins and jumped down from the hay-laden wagon. The whistling of sickles ceased. The field-workers and clansmen stared. The persistent crows swooped down to feast.

Looking at Alexander, but seeing his own hands clutched

around his wayward bride's neck, Malcolm ripped off his gloves.

"Did you lock the postern gate?"

"Aye, sir. I also put an extra guard on the paddock."

"Then how the devil did she get away?"

"She was wearing breeches and a hat. She told the guard she was there to exercise the gray. Since she was alone and pretending to be a lad, the guard saw naught amiss."

"She left without Elanna?"

"Nay, sir. The African left the grounds half an hour later through the west gate. Said she was off to collect the Moor's supper."

"Saladin's supervising the haying at Sweeper's Heath. Send Rabby to fetch him."

"Aye, sir."

"Where's Redundant?"

His eyes teeming with regret, Alexander stared at Malcolm's bonnet. "At Farley Green hooked up with Wiley's bitch. Even if you could get 'em apart, the hound's nose is ruint for now."

"Shit!"

"'Twill make a fine litter of pups, my lord."

Malcolm glanced sharply at the soldier. Alexander gave him a weak smile. "We'll get her back."

Worn out and heartsore, Malcolm found himself laughing at her cleverness. By putting Redundant with a bitch in heat, she had taken away his surest means of finding her.

Twenty years ago Alpin had lived unnoticed for weeks at Kildalton Castle. No one was more familiar with the passageways and exits of the keep. He'd have to pull a crew of men from the fields and set them to guarding the gates and grounds.

The real reason for her flight eluded him, but he suspected it was pride. He had longed to tell her about the perilous state of affairs in Scotland, to impart to her his fear that war loomed ahead. But he couldn't confide in a woman who scorned Scottish politics and didn't care if the fields were harvested. He didn't trust himself in the presence of the woman he loved, the woman he'd tricked into coming to

Scotland in the first place. He couldn't abandon the harvest to spend his days playing her jailer. As laird, his duty lay with his people.

Now Comyn MacKay was on his way to find the lost member of his flock. Lady Miriam's message had been clear. Malcolm shuddered to think what the Highland chieftain would do if he arrived at Kildalton eager to see his long lost granddaughter and learned that Malcolm had driven her away.

He had to keep her, but not for the alliance. He wanted her for himself and the love he couldn't deny. Once the Jacobite plot had been foiled, he would bare his soul to her.

First he would get her back, and he had no doubt that he would, for he was several steps ahead of his clever wife. On his orders, the blacksmith had forged notches into the shoes of the horses at Kildalton. If she managed to get away on one of the mounts, Malcolm could easily follow the distinctive tracks.

That was just what she had done.

Like footprints in the snow, the hoof marks led him unerringly to the docks at South Shields. Standing on a hill, he gazed at the port the Romans had discovered over fifteen hundred years ago. No visible signs of their presence remained, but an industrious explorer could dig beneath the mounds of earth and uncover the tools and remnants of a civilization of builders and engineers.

Wishing he were on such an expedition, Malcolm guided his mount down the hill. He found the horses in a field near the orphanage. Then he went to the quay.

"Have you a blackamoor among your passengers?" he asked captain after captain.

"Nay, my lord" was the response of the day.

A glance at the passenger list gave him an idea. "This widow. Is she veiled?"

"Aye, sir. All proper like, she is. Grieving, I'm sure, poor lady. Ain't said but two words to me, and odd those were."

Malcolm was already studying the next ship. "Oh?"

"I asked her if she'd like her meals sent to her cabin. She

said, 'Betcha that.' My money says she's Welsh. They've got a strange speech about them."

Applauding himself and Elanna's slip of the tongue, Malcolm fetched his bride and deposited her on the steps of Kildalton.

"The gates are locked, Alpin, and I've put extra guards on the grounds. You cannot get away."

She gave him a fake smile. "Watch me."

Her next ruse was even more clever, and his second trip to Tynemouth proved amusing in the extreme. If, that is, he ignored the fact that his wife had deserted him again.

"Tell me about this masked leper and the sister of charity," he asked the first mate on a barkentine destined for Calais.

"They come in a cart, my lord. Ain't heard a peep out of the poor wretch or the nun with 'im."

A nun in Scotland? Improbable. "She was wearing a habit?"

"Peculiar, it was, now that you mention it. Looked more like a monk's robe to me. Bonny thing she is, though. 'Magine a sister 'o mercy with eyes like fancy purple stones."

Ten minutes later when he led her off the ship, Malcolm thought her fancy eyes were shooting daggers. "You cannot get away, Alpin. Give it up."

Two days later when he fetched her back a second time from Whitley Bay, humor fled.

"You put Elanna in a coffin?"

"I'd rather see you in one," she spat.

"We were speaking of Elanna."

"It was her idea. She assured me she'd be fine. I was going to let her out as soon as we set sail."

The last thread controlling Malcolm's temper snapped. He scooped her up and marched not to her gray gelding but to his stallion. Unceremoniously he tossed her onto the saddle and mounted behind her.

"Let me go, you wretched toad!"

Ignoring her, he slapped a hand to her back and gave the

horse his head, leaving Saladin and the others at the dock. In a frenzy, the Moor used his scimitar to pry the nails out of the coffin containing the woman he loved.

Alpin yelled, "If you don't let me off this horse, you'll be sorry."

He was already sorry—sorry he'd fallen in love with her and disgusted with himself because he couldn't let her go.

"Malcolm, for God's sake, stop. I'm pregnant!"

19

Malcolm's mind became a dark cave with one word shaping the light at the opening: "pregnant." He eased back on the reins and shook his head. Alpin, pregnant. The horse stopped. His wife had conceived.

Hope blossomed in his soul and obliterated the darkness. He was going to be a father. At last.

Alpin had been a virgin, no mistaking that. His stepmother had been correct: he could sire children. Hallelujah! Alpin would give him a babe.

He dismounted and lifted her to the ground.

"You miserable cur." She put her hands over her stomach in a protective gesture. "If I lose this babe, the sin be upon your head. Oh, God, why won't you let me go?"

"Go where?"

"Back to Barbados, where I belong."

Reality set in, and with it a coldness that chilled him to the bone. He understood the reason behind her escape. Suddenly he couldn't stand still. "Who's the lucky father?"

Stupefied, Alpin watched him pace. He had tossed her

around like a sack of oats. Fear of a miscarriage had forced her to reveal her pregnancy. "What did you say?"

The ocean breeze tousled his hair. He squinted into the wind. "I asked you the name of the man I should congratulate."

He appeared so calm she wanted to slap his stoic face. Over the snorting of his horse, she said, "What do you mean? *You're* the father."

"Oh, I doubt that."

Incensed, she marched up to him. "Well, it wasn't an immaculate conception!"

He looked down, but didn't seem to see her. "Obviously not. Who is he, Alpin? Rabby, or one of the other men on the night watch? Were you wallowing in the sheets rather than stripping them off the beds?"

The strength went out of her legs. She dropped to the ground and stared at his bare knees and the hem of his kilt. He had hurt her before with his false words of love, but this latest cruelty bruised her to her soul. "I know you're angry because I left you again, but you cannot, out of lost pride, name me an adulteress."

"I can and I will."

Saladin, Alexander, and the others joined them, Elanna looking none the worse for her captivity.

Malcolm leaped into his saddle and sawed on the reins. The horse reared.

Alpin rushed to him. "Malcolm, wait!"

"Help her mount, Alexander," he yelled over his shoulder. "And take your time getting home."

He left a trail of dust for them to follow. Crushed by his cruel accusation and determined to get back on that ship, Alpin called out to Saladin. But the Moor couldn't take his eyes or his attention off Elanna.

"How do you feel?" he asked her.

Elanna pouted. "Feel bad, very bad. Better I should ride with you."

He glared at her. "Better I should beat you."

In a blatantly seductive move, she ran her fingers over her

shoulder and her neck. "You would mark this skin, Muslim? You like this skin, remember? You say it tastes like ambrosia."

His heated gaze followed the path of her hand. Then he tipped back his head and stared at a passing cloud. At length he said, "See them home, Alexander."

Then he, too, raced down the well-traveled road.

Alpin stared with longing at the dock.

"Doona think about it, lass," said Alexander. "The captain wilna take you aboard."

By the time they reached Kildalton, Alpin had cursed, cried, and called Malcolm Kerr every vile name she could think of. She had also devised a new method of escape. She and Elanna would book passage in Tynemouth, then cross the river Tyne to the port of South Shields and book passage there, too. While her husband waited for her in the first city, she'd be taking ship in the next. The plan was so simple she berated herself for not thinking of it sooner. She would outsmart her sorry excuse for a husband.

He was waiting for her in their bedchamber. Standing before the bookcase, he barely spared her a glance, but the revulsion in his eyes made her want to weep again.

Marshaling her defenses, she put away her cloak and the saddle pouch, then washed her face in the basin. The room seemed lifeless, not at all the place where they'd loved and laughed and reminisced about the past. Had they truly lain naked in the wide bed and in the aftermath of loving discussed grain harvests and a future for the Fraser brothers?

Malcolm hated her now. Paradise legally belonged to her. She could at last tell him why she must return to Barbados.

"You might as well tell me the name of your lover."

She yanked up a towel and tossed off any notion of unburdening her soul. "You might as well go to hell."

"Oh, come now, Alpin." He drew a book from the perfectly straightened row and stared at the spine. His large hands dwarfed the tome. "I'll find out sooner or later."

"Very well." When he looked up, his eyes all attention, she added, "I call him a sniveling cur."

He gave her a flat, unamused smile. "Considering your creative disguises of late, I expected more originality from you. You mustn't think I'll harm him. Quite the contrary."

"Why should I believe anything you say?"

Violence flared in his eyes. He threw the book across the room. "Because he can sire children and I cannot. Thanks to you!"

Baffled, Alpin watched the copy of Thomas Fuller's *History of the Worthies of England* crash against the mantel and slide to the floor, taking an ancient Roman vase with it.

Alpin clutched the damp towel. "That's the most ridiculous thing I've ever heard you say. You cannot disavow this child just because its mother hates you."

He stalked her then, his face stone-hard with rage, his eyes glittering with menace. "Despise me if you will, Alpin. Call me the cuckold I am." He grasped her upper arms. "But tell me the bastard's name."

Alpin held her ground and ignored the fact that he could crush her bones with a flick of his wrist. She considered reasoning with him, but her pride wouldn't allow it. "It's you, you beef-witted pinhead, although you hardly deserve to be a father."

Like butter in the sun, his rage melted. "Oh, hell." He released her and plopped down in a chair. "I am not the father of your child, Alpin. You destroyed my seed. So do not expect me to give that bastard in your belly the Kerr name. If that was your intention."

More confused than ever, Alpin searched his face for some sign of madness. "Destroyed your seed? What on earth are you talking about?"

"I'm referring to the deviltry you worked years ago with that jar of hornets. My parents kept the result quiet. Only Saladin knows." His unguarded expression revealed a man at peace with failure. "I have never sired a child, even on proven breeders, and believe me, I've tried."

Alpin didn't know whether to laugh at him or sock him in the jaw. The riddle of why he'd interfered in her life was now solved. She saw through his meddling, understood the reason behind his love words and false affection.

It was all lies. It was all for revenge.

Their marriage had borne fruit, but she didn't care if he believed her. "That's why you talked Charles into giving you the plantation. That's why you brought me here."

"Your logic knows no bounds."

The sheer evil of his plan hurt worse than his sarcastic denunciation. She had been shunned during her childhood by adults who couldn't or wouldn't see past her hoydenish ways. As a grown woman she had been despised outright by insensitive plantation owners who refused to give up their hold on a race of defenseless people.

Today those occasions paled, for no one had treated her so maliciously as Malcolm Kerr. The man she loved.

Her chest constricted and her tears flowed freely, but Alpin didn't care if he saw her weep. He'd made his decision years ago and plotted his life accordingly. "Tell me this, Malcolm. When did you make your startling discovery?"

He glanced up, but looked away again. "Does it matter?"

How dare he be so blasé when he'd ruined her life and cast the fate of her friends to the wind. "Was it in your fifteenth year, when the milkmaid did not conceive?"

"I have never taken advantage of a servant."

She let that lie pass. He didn't care enough about her to remember that she was his housekeeper. "Did your parents take you to London where you found a willing shopgirl? Was she ripe for your affections?"

"Stop it, Alpin."

"Or were you one and twenty and on your grand tour when you decided that a six-year-old girl had ruined your life?"

All of his interest seemed fixed on the drapes. "I hardly think a litany of my amorous adventures will prove anything."

"No?" She thought of those women, probably bright-eyed and eager for the affection of so handsome and well fixed a man as Malcolm Kerr. Had he cared about any of them?

She cared, because she knew well the pain of being at the

mercy of men. She knew better the pain of loving Malcolm Kerr. "How many hearts did you break to prove your theory?"

"I know what you're thinking, Alpin. But you're wrong. I have never mistreated women."

"Until now."

The signal horn blared. A visitor had arrived, probably Lady Miriam. Alpin's bad luck was holding true.

He strummed his fingers on the arm of the chair. "I'm sure you will not believe me, but I refused to make a dynastic marriage, knowing that no dynasty would follow."

She laughed to keep from sobbing. "How noble of you to save your common deceptions for me."

"I was angry."

"You were eager, too. You wanted the handfast marriage because you thought nothing would come of it. What did you expect to do with me when I didn't conceive? Had you decided to give me fifty pounds and send me on my way?"

When his gaze met hers, she saw regret and resignation. In a reasonable tone he said, "That night we slept in the study I tried to tell you, but you wouldn't let me. You were too eager to have me sign over Paradise Plantation to you. Will your lover join you there?"

"I was a virgin, damn you."

"Aye, you were, I'll grant you that. I even thanked you for the gift of your innocence. How long after that did you take a lover?"

He maintained that she'd been unfaithful. Through a fog of misery, she thought about the sponge that his last mistress had left behind. Rosina hadn't wanted his child. Alpin might have felt sympathy for him if he hadn't been so cruel to her.

Reaching into the wardrobe, she grabbed the bottle and threw it at his feet. Glass shattered, and rose water perfumed the air. The sponge skidded to a halt at the edge of the carpet. "I cannot explain why your other women never conceived, but there's the reason your Rosina didn't. I've had no man but you. For pity's sake, Malcolm, I'd never even been kissed before."

Her piece said, her heart a shambles, Alpin collected her cloak and marched out of the room.

Malcolm heard her leave, but couldn't take his eyes off the contraceptive device. Impossible, his pride said. Consider it, his mind countered.

There were no milkmaids in his past; he had not been the sort of son to dishonor a servant in his father's house. There were no shopgirls; he had not been the kind of youth to take advantage of an innocent. He had always chosen experienced women, women who'd already borne children. He'd even gone so far as to scorn the notion of conception.

Experienced women. Women who had earned their keep pleasing him. Had he, by hedging his bet that they would not conceive, given them license to prevent it?

Like the broken bottle, a lifetime of conviction shattered. A vision of Alpin rose before him, tears streaming down her face, her lovely eyes filled with pain.

And the truth, for he believed her.

Damning himself, he got to his feet and kicked the sponge across the room. God, how he'd hurt her. He had flung accusations as if they were weapons. He'd been a fool, but no more. He'd go to her, make her listen. She still cared for him, of that he was certain.

Sweet Saint Ninian, she would blossom with their child. Joy tightened his chest and brought tears to his eyes. She would give him a bairn of his own, a bonny lass he could swing into the air and spoil to his heart's content, or a laddie he could teach and mold into a fine man. Whatever the sex, the child would be a product of the love he and Alpin had shared.

The love they would share again.

He would woo her. If it took the rest of his life, he'd win back her affection. Starting now.

His course set, his heart buoyed by love and hope for the future, he dashed from the room and ran down the stairs. Hearing voices in the lesser hall, he followed the sound. In the doorway he stopped, stunned, at the sight of his handfast bride in laughing conversation with Saladin's twin brother.

Saladin had been blessed with the features of their

Moorish father, but Sir Salvador Cortez had inherited the straight black hair and olive skin of their Spanish mother. Even their choice of clothing reflected their differences. Salvador preferred modern dress; he wore a fashionable jacket and breeches of green velvet, a stark white shirt, and knee boots.

But the greatest contrast between the brothers Cortez was evidenced in their views of and practices toward the fairer sex. Where Saladin had taken a vow of chastity until marriage, Salvador practiced the popular art of seduction.

To Malcolm's way of thinking, he was practicing his art now. Why else would he be holding both of Alpin's hands and making her blush?

Possessiveness gripped Malcolm. He stepped into the room. "Am I interrupting something?"

Alpin's breath caught, and she jumped back as if burned.

The ever-affable Sir Salvador turned smoothly toward Malcolm. "Only a happy reunion, my lord." He bowed from the waist.

"If you'll excuse me." Her head down, Alpin took the longest route to the door.

Malcolm blocked her path. To Salvador he said, "Is the family with you?"

"No." His dashing countenance vanished. "I've come with a message for Lady Miriam, but Alpin tells me she's not here."

Hope of a speedy reconciliation with Alpin faded, for if Salvador had come alone and looking for Malcolm's step-mother, trouble was afoot.

"Wait for me in my study, Salvador."

His brows raised in casual query, Salvador nodded and left the room.

Malcolm closed the door.

Alpin gave him her back. "I have nothing to say to you."

Braced for the difficult task of earning her forgiveness, Malcolm said, "I know. But I have much to say to you."

She stiffened, as if shoring up her defenses.

Malcolm wanted to hold her, but he knew it was too soon.

He found himself staring at the wisps of curling hair at the nape of her neck and thinking how delicate she was. Because of her size, he'd underestimated her. She might be small, but his wife possessed the strength and courage of a gladiator.

Daunted at the prospect of conquering her, Malcolm spoke from the heart. "I'm sorry for the hurtful things I said to you."

"I'm sure you are. Hadn't you better see what Salvador wants?"

He had to break through the shell of her indifference. "I'd rather hear what you want."

Her hand touched the arm of the family throne. "I want to go home to Barbados."

Kildalton Castle was her home; he would make it so. "You would take my child?"

She turned toward him then, righteous anger blazing in her eyes. "It's *my* child. Before I let you use it as a political pawn or wreck its life, I'll raise it in a ditch."

She looked so defiant and so proud, and Malcolm had never loved her more. He had to ball his fists to keep from reaching for her. "As I wrecked yours?"

"You flatter yourself. I can make my own way and provide for my child."

Given time, he would rekindle her affection. But with Salvador here and half the crops still in the fields, Malcolm wondered when he could begin his quest for her heart. "We will provide for our child together, and we'll do it here, Alpin."

Alarm smoothed out her features. "You would force me to stay even though I loathe you?"

"You loved me once. If you give us a chance we could have a good marriage."

"I want no part of your Scottish dynasty. Now let me pass. I have work to do."

Unfortunately, so did he, and the responsibility weighed heavy on his soul. "What work?"

"The soldiers will be hungry, and I'm sure Salvador would prefer linens on his bed."

Malcolm felt a glimmer of hope. She must care for him. Why else would she be so eager to resume her duties? "Until later, then."

Before he joined Salvador, Malcolm sought out Alexander. "Take all of the men you can spare from the haying crews and put them on the watch. Station guards at all the exits. Have them inspect every conveyance before it leaves the grounds."

"Aye, my lord, but what excuse shall I give for the search?"

"Tell them that Alpin's pet rabbit has gone missing."

"The lass'll not get away again, my lord."

Standing at the windows in the upstairs solar, Alpin had an unobstructed view of her husband. *Husband.* The word stirred her ire anew. She'd handfasted herself to a stubborn, selfish man who would say or do anything to salve his great Scottish pride.

What was he saying to Alexander? She opened the window, but they were too far away and there was too much noise in the yard.

As if he hadn't a care in the world, Malcolm returned to the keep. With sinking dread, she saw Alexander go into the barracks. When he emerged, he was followed by a dozen clansmen. He barked orders, and in pairs, eight of the men scattered. The remaining four marched to the main gates.

She stood there a moment longer. To her dismay, the soldiers began searching every wagon and cart leaving Kildalton. She pictured guards at every exit.

Since escape seemed impossible, she needed leverage. Hoping to gain it, she entered the tunnel through the wardrobe in her bedchamber and made her way down the dark stairs to the corridor near Malcolm's study. Approaching from a different direction, she didn't have to worry about the alarm bell.

Leaning close to the door, she heard Salvador say, "What do you think?"

Paper rattled. "I think Father has been married to a

diplomat for too long. 'Tis rubbing off on him, for he pens rhetoric as well as she does."

"Where is Lady Miriam?" Salvador asked.

"Trying to dissuade John Gordon from going abroad."

Alpin shivered, remembering the coarse Highlander and the way he'd stared at her and proclaimed her the grand-daughter of Comyn MacKay.

"Then she's made a useless trip," Salvador said.

"What do you mean?"

"Read on, my friend. It's all in your father's letter."

After a brief silence, Malcolm said, "Sweet Saint Ninian. He actually wants to come to Scotland?"

John Gordon lived in Scotland, so they couldn't be speaking of him. Who was this "he"? Alpin wondered.

"He wanted to, but your father talked to his father, who changed the lad's mind. At present he wants to go to Aix-la-Chapelle."

Why wouldn't they say the man's name?

"Why does he want to go there?" Malcolm asked.

"Who knows how his mind works? That's why Lady Miriam must come back with me. Lord Duncan thinks she'll have better luck dissuading him."

Alpin had no idea of whom they spoke, but obviously the man and his travels were a source of great concern.

"Now that I've delivered my merry message . . ."

Malcolm laughed, but the sound held more pain than humor.

"Will you tell me," Salvador continued, "why your old nemesis Alpin MacKay is back in Scotland."

"My nemesis? Have you forgotten the time she broke your ribs?"

Salvador groaned. "No, but I deserved it. I told the baron about the wounded vixen Alpin had found. He made her watch while he killed it and hung the hide on the stable door."

Alpin remembered, too. She had vomited for days. But at least she had saved the fox's kits.

"The bastard," Malcolm spat.

"At least he's changed," said Salvador. "He loves children now."

"Aye. He's still in Ireland with his newest grandson. God, he was wretched to Alpin."

"Speaking of her, what's she doing here with you?"

"We're handfasted, and she carries our first child."

"What?"

Alpin couldn't listen to any more. She made her way to the kitchen, where she found Dora churning butter.

After instructing the maid to add another chicken to the pot and prepare a chamber for Salvador, Alpin said, "Where's Elanna?"

"She went to Sweeper's Heath to take Saladin his lunch."

Poor Saladin, thought Alpin. His romantic straits were as dire as hers.

The horn sounded again, warning of another visitor. Surely this time it would be Lady Miriam.

The need for solitude drove Alpin to the mews, where she fed and watered the birds, then sat on the three-legged stool and berated herself for telling Malcolm that she carried his child. But as always, where men and the important matters in life were concerned, she'd had little choice.

"If you give us a chance," he'd said, "we could have a good marriage." But that was an impossible dream, for she was already committed to Paradise and the uphill battle that awaited her there.

The owlet peeped. Alpin fed it a strip of meat. She pictured Malcolm escaping the responsibilities of his kingdom to care for these birds. The image seemed wrong. How would a selfish, scheming man find sanctuary in this dark and peaceful place? How could she want him so?

Damn Malcolm Kerr for keeping her here so long and tearing her life apart. Damn her for not wanting to leave him.

A commotion outside sent the kestrels to pacing. Reluctantly Alpin left the mews. Shielding her eyes from the sun, she started back toward the keep. Two dozen soldiers had gathered at the gate. The men on the battlements all faced toward the north road. A sense of anticipation filled the air.

Would Lady Miriam's arrival cause such a stir? If not, then who? Alpin thought about the evening meal and wondered if there would be enough food to go around.

She stopped herself. This was not her castle to worry about, and she would not go out of her way. To keep Malcolm off guard, she would perform her duties. She would deal with the household problems as they arose. No more, no less.

Just as she reached the steps, the door opened. First Rabby, then a frowning Malcolm stepped outside. He had donned his bonnet and his broadsword.

When he saw her, he hurried down the steps. "I was just coming to find you."

Something was wrong. Craning her neck, she looked up at him. "Why are you wearing a weapon?"

He turned to Rabby. "Go to Sweeper's Heath. Bring Saladin back with you."

When the soldier walked away, Malcolm took her arm. "I'm wearing this sword because I may need it. Come with me. We have guests."

She dug in her heels. *"You* have guests, not I. I only work for you."

"Alpin," he growled, his hand tightening on her elbow, "this visitor very much concerns you."

Behind her she heard the rumble of approaching horses. "Nothing and no one in Scotland concerns me."

He stared past her. "Not even Comyn MacKay?"

20

Four abreast, the mounted Highlanders streamed through the gates of Kildalton. The bright sunshine of early afternoon reflected on swords and battle shields. At the head of the sea of soldiers, clad in sedate black and green tartans, rode the chieftain. He alone wore three eagle feathers in his bonnet, but the ornamentation was unnecessary; in the set of his shoulders, the tilt of his head, Comyn MacKay exuded leadership.

Alpin trembled inside, for here was another man who thought it his right to dabble in her destiny. First her uncle had snatched her from the jaws of poverty, only to banish her for a troublesome child. Then Charles, weak-willed and broken in spirit, had left her adrift and at the mercy of a more dangerous adversary.

Melancholy weighted her soul, for her lover's crime had been the greatest; he had altered the course of her life and, in the process, stolen her heart.

She felt fragmented, terrified, and alone.

Malcolm put an arm around her shoulders and drew her close. "Which chamber shall we put him in?"

His question jolted her. She stood at another of life's crossroads, and Malcolm wanted to discuss accommodations. Furious with him, she tipped her head back until their eyes met. "You can house him in the stables for all I care."

Concern softened his features. He gave her a gentle squeeze. "He's just a man looking for his granddaughter. But I'm the man who found her."

He had taken her mind off the uncertainty and made her think of the everyday. She found solace in his answer and loved him a little more for it. "I shall give him the suite next to Saladin's."

He winked. "The perfect choice. I believe, as they say, we have our ducks in a row."

His sword rattled, inspiring a question of her own. "You do not fear him?"

He stared at the gates. "Nay, for I expect you'll deal with him, Alpin. 'Tis his army that troubles me."

She faced the visitors and estimated that at least fifty soldiers had passed through the gates. Her gaze was drawn to the leader, and she found herself looking into a pair of very familiar eyes.

Comyn MacKay dismounted and marched toward them, spurs jingling, his arms swinging, his step as quick and light as that of a man half his age. Alpin's heart tumbled in her chest, for he was studying her with an intensity that matched her own.

He wasn't a tall man, compared to Malcolm, but he was spry and trim and carried himself with dignity. He wore his tartan as Malcolm did, the sash thrown over his shoulder and secured with a silver brooch bearing a hand holding a dagger erect. His sporran was made of a prize badger hide with intricate stitchery and fine golden tassels.

When he doffed his bonnet, he revealed a shock of curly white hair, yet his brows and full beard still held sprinklings of dark red. In Highland fashion, he sported narrow braids at his temples.

Her grandfather.

He stopped a yard away. His eyes, the same shade as hers, narrowed, then went glassy with tears. "Do you know who I am, lass?"

Misgivings fled like cowards from a battle struck. She couldn't stop her bottom lip from quivering. "Yes."

Arms spread wide, he chuckled. "Then step away from that foosty Lowlander and give your grandsire a hug."

The pull of his affection was strong, and when Malcolm slid his hand to the small of her back and gave her a push, she went willingly.

Comyn MacKay drew her to his chest and hugged her tight. He smelled of a forest at dusk, and if welcome had an odor, she thought she'd discovered it, too.

"Lassie mine," he said, "you've been out of the fold for too long."

In that instant a thousand girlish dreams came true. The MacKays had wanted her. No awful flaw in her character had caused them to desert a little girl. Fate had sent her to Baron Sinclair, and he had separated her from her father's people by sending her to Barbados.

Malcolm cleared his throat. "Shall we take our reunion inside?"

Comyn held her at arm's length for a moment, then drew her to his side. She looked at Malcolm and found him shaking his head and glancing from her to the man who held her. "Lord, you two are a pair of MacKays. She's your kin, Comyn. There's none to deny that."

"Sure as the king's another Hanoverian," Comyn said with disdain. "I expect the bastard's German blood to boil when he learns you've taken one of my Highland lassies to wife."

Once again Scottish politics intruded in Alpin's life. By marrying her, Malcolm would anger the English king and make an ally of this Highland chieftain. Her grandfather.

He stepped away from her. "You've not finished your haying, I see," he said to Malcolm.

"Nay. I've had a few interruptions from your granddaughter." He shot Alpin a meaningful look.

"She is that right enough—the very image of my mother." Comyn slapped Malcolm on the back. "Call your next man. My soldiers can swing a sickle as good as any."

"Thank you, sir," said Malcolm. "We could use the extra hands." He yelled for Alexander.

When the soldier approached, Malcolm and Comyn left her and joined the newcomers in the yard. The MacKay singled out one of his soldiers, presumably his own next man. Introductions were made; then Alexander and Malcolm conferred, the others gathering in a circle around them.

Forgotten for the moment, Alpin watched their male camaraderie and thought Barbados had never seemed so far away. She was homesick for her friends and her stable, orderly life. She was drawn to the grandfather who'd held her in his arms and spoken of his own mother. She'd fallen in love with a man who used her as a stepping stone to power.

Now she faced the daunting task of housing and feeding not only the soldiers of Kildalton but Comyn MacKay's men too.

With that diversion in mind, she marched up the steps and into the kitchen. Dora was pitting cherries, but from the stains on her mouth, Alpin saw that she had eaten her share.

"Go to the butcher. Tell him we need enough beef to feed one hundred men for supper."

Dora squealed in dismay. "What'll we do for vegetables?"

"Get all the peas and tatties from the market. Ask your mother and Nell to help you clean and cook them. Tell the baker we'll need a mountain of bread. Take all the cherries to Mrs. Kimberley and have her turn them into pies. When Elanna gets back, she'll help you."

Alpin turned to leave, then remembered the accommodations. "Have Emily and her sister come and prepare every guest chamber."

"Aye, my lady. But what about food for the morning meal?"

Alpin felt torn. If she were smart, she'd use the arrival of the MacKays to cover her escape. Once Malcolm was asleep, she and Elanna could make way for Tynemouth. On the one hand she was curious about Comyn, but on the other she felt disloyal to Bumpa Sam and the other kind men who had for years fulfilled the role of grandfather in her life. She missed their kindness, their freely given affection. None of them would care who had sired her child or think of the benefits the babe would bring them; they would simply adore it. Once, that is, she returned.

If she shirked her duties to Kildalton now, however, Malcolm might grow suspicious and double his efforts to prevent her escape.

Plagued by indecision, she drew a pitcher of beer, gathered up some mugs, and went to the lesser hall. Salvador stood at the windows watching the activity in the yard.

No sooner had Alpin poured the drink, than Comyn MacKay strolled in with news that the watch had spotted Lady Miriam's carriage approaching from the Aberdeen road. Alpin wondered if her arrival would prove to be a curse or a blessing.

Bless Lady Miriam, thought Malcolm as he helped her from the carriage. "Let's take a walk." He guided her past the front of the castle and toward the walled garden.

She scanned the soldiers in the yard. "I saw some workers in the field near Otterburn. They were wearing MacKay colors. I take it Comyn has arrived."

"Aye, he's inside, but he can wait." He told her about the letter Salvador had delivered. "Father has persuaded James to forbid his son the trip to Scotland. Now Prince Charles wants to go to Aix-la-Chapelle."

Her only sign of agitation was the vigor she used in slapping dust from the skirt of her velvet gown. "That's very close to Hanover and King George."

Malcolm hadn't considered the geography. "If the king gets wind that a Stewart prince is encroaching on his German playground—"

"He'll dispatch his Hessian mercenaries before you can say 'king across the water.' Bonnie Prince Charles will find himself languishing in the Tower."

His stomach sinking with dread, Malcolm nodded to the guard at the wooden door as he ushered Lady Miriam inside the walled garden. The gurgling of the fountain and the chatter of wagtail larks made a peaceful contrast to the tumultuous events of the day. "Perhaps martyrdom's what Charles wants."

"Nay." She walked to the fountain and sat down on a bench. "Aix-la-Chapelle is a favorite retreat for Scots and English. I'm certain he thinks to mingle with them and gain their support. He has sworn to take the crown for his father. This trip is only a first step toward returning to Scotland."

Malcolm still went cold inside at the thought of a Stewart prince on Scottish soil. "Let's just hope no one in London knows of the prince's travels."

"We cannot count on secrecy," she said. "Walpole seems to know the Stewarts' every move even as they make it, and news travels fast between London and Hanover."

"That's why Father wants you to return with Salvador."

"I will," she said, "in a day or two. What else has happened?"

Problems of the realm vanished. "Alpin's pregnant."

"Oh, Malcolm!" She grasped his hands, her blue eyes twinkling with joy. "I'm so very happy for both of you."

He thought about the flimsy hold he had on Alpin. Fear of losing her burned like a hot coal in his gut. He told his stepmother about her attempts to escape.

Lady Miriam studied her hands. "You're certain she's upset because she thinks you want her only for a dynastic marriage?"

Malcolm almost laughed. "She's more than upset, Mother. She's obsessed with the notion of returning to Barbados."

"I'm not surprised. What decent person could stand by and watch the slaves being treated badly?"

"She told you that?"

"Yes. In vivid detail. Hasn't she told you?"

She had tried to convey her thoughts on the cruelty of human bondage, but Malcolm had made light of the subject. "I haven't been listening."

"You? I don't believe that. You're a generous man, Malcolm."

Her confidence pricked his guilty conscience. "You're prejudiced."

"Surely you can patch up things between you. Where's that Kerr charm?"

"I'm afraid I threw it out the window when I accused her of being unfaithful. But I just didn't believe the child was mine. I should have listened to you." Then he told her about the contraceptive device Rosina had left behind.

She squeezed her eyes shut and rubbed her temples. He stared at her supple fingers and thought of the times she'd felt his forehead for a fever or patted his cheek in affection. She was more than a mother to him and the love of his father's life; Lady Miriam was a trusted, cherished friend.

"Well." She rose and turned toward the garden exit. "What will you do?"

No experience in his past had prepared him for the task that lay ahead. Yet instinct told him honesty was the place to start. "I often think about what her life has been like and wonder about the friends she's made. I just wish she would talk more about the years she spent in Barbados. She's a passionate, exciting woman."

"I'm sure she is, considering I've a grandchild on the way." Shyly, she added, "I am delighted. You're father will be thrilled."

On reflection, Malcolm knew he hadn't tried hard enough to make a friend of Alpin MacKay. He'd been more concerned with the physical aspects of their relationship. Perhaps it was time to seduce her mind.

"That look in your eye bodes ill," Lady Miriam said.

Then he remembered he had a castle full of guests and fields to harvest. "Romance will have to wait."

"Nonsense. Your happiness affects all of the people, and I'll wager they've warmed to Alpin—even Miss Lindsay and her market cronies. What's more important than happiness?"

"Nothing," he said, and knew it was true.

His stepmother gazed at the castle, a faraway look in her

eye. "I used to think I had no place here. Your father was so settled in his role as earl and so much a part of this land. Because I'd spent my life in Queen Anne's household, then traveling on her behalf, I couldn't picture myself settling down at Kildalton."

Her presence in the Borders had bettered the life of everyone. "Father changed your mind."

She laughed. "With help from the Border Lord."

Only a handful of people knew that Malcolm's father had donned the disguise of the legendary hero. "I'm glad he did, Mother, and I wish I had a romantic persona at my disposal."

"Oh, but you do, Malcolm. You're kind and generous and not afraid to show your feelings. Just remember, no one will begrudge you the time to win your wife's love. The people of Kildalton will expect you to make a happy marriage, and in a way you owe them that."

She was right. "Harmony begins at home." He echoed one of her tenets.

"Exactly, and tonight while you're wooing your bride, I'll get to know Comyn MacKay. Then tomorrow I'll negotiate a dowry worthy of her."

His bride had been so proud of owning Paradise. Now she would be an heiress of the MacKay clan with all the wealth and influence that came with the territory. His stepmother would see to it.

"When will you return to Italy?" he asked.

"In a couple of days. But right now I'd like a long bath and a nap in my own bed. I'm tired, Malcolm, of matters of state interfering in my life."

He understood completely.

Conviviality was the order of behavior in the lesser hall that evening. Seated at one of the banquet tables, her husband and her grandfather on either side of her, Alpin vacillated between guilt and euphoria. Across the table, Lady Miriam conversed with Saladin and Elanna.

Throughout the evening, Alpin had been the victim of a dual assault. Malcolm and his stepmother had asked a continuous stream of questions about Alpin's life in Barbados. Their ploy was as transparent as the glass in the windows. With Lady Miriam's help, Malcolm was trying to make amends for accusing her of cuckolding him. And why shouldn't he? He thought he was about to wed a wealthy heiress with ties to a Highland clan.

In addition to a verbal barrage of cordiality, Malcolm touched Alpin constantly. If he wasn't holding her hand, he was wrapping an arm around her shoulders or dancing his fingers on her thigh. Little kisses, winks, and looks smoldering with sensual promise punctuated his every word.

For hours he had lavished her with attention and chipped away at her anger.

"I think," he whispered in her ear, "I hear my sweet tooth calling."

She fought the urge to smile and lean into him. "There's pie left in the kitchen. Shall I dish you up a piece?"

"Too big. I was thinking about a wee morsel."

Alpin felt herself color. "A sugarplum?"

"Too rich. I'm hungry for a treat to soothe my palate."

Knowing smiles from the other occupants of the room rained down on them, increasing her embarrassment. Still, he'd been at her all night, murmuring one innuendo after another. "A spoonful of honey?"

"Oh," he breathed. "As a garnish? Aye, I'd like that."

Laughter bubbled up inside her. "You're indecent."

"Not yet, love. But I intend to get that way."

"Tell me, Elanna," said Lady Miriam, "how does it feel to be a free black woman in Barbados?"

Alpin jumped at the chance to cool Malcolm's ardor, for if he continued to press her, she feared she might lose her composure and giggle like a love-struck girl.

"Good, good, but lonely." Elanna gazed fondly at Alpin. "I'm the only free black in Barbados, thanks to my mistress."

Alpin could feel Malcolm watching her. Lady Miriam leaned forward, seemingly waiting for Alpin to comment. Honesty was easy. "No man or woman has the right to own another."

"I'll drink to that." Saladin held up his mug of orange water.

Pewter clanged against pewter as everyone joined in the tribute.

Comyn drank, then looked at Alpin. "I propose a toast to John Gordon for reuniting me with my granddaughter." Again the mugs touched. He added, "Although I thought he'd be here already."

Malcolm stiffened beside Alpin.

"Oh?" Lady Miriam appeared the picture of the serene woman, but her eyes were keenly fixed on Comyn. "He's coming to Kildalton?"

"Aye. When he sent me word that I'd find Alpin here, he told me he'd join us by midweek." He glanced at Alpin. "He'll probably arrive tomorrow and take all the glory for finding you."

Today was Thursday, so John Gordon was late, and if Alpin's hunch was correct, the information sat ill with Malcolm and his mother.

Comyn emptied his mug and slammed it on the table. "Are all of the women in Africa as bonny as you, Miss Elanna?"

She stretched her long neck and squared her shoulders. Her dark eyes glittered with pride. "Betcha that."

Alpin couldn't help teasing her. "Even the mosquito-eating Equafos?"

"Oh, yes," piped Saladin. "Tell us what you truly think about those people with bones in their noses."

Elanna pursed her lips and stared at the ceiling. At length, and in perfectly clipped English, she said, "An Ashanti princess must be tolerant of the more primitive cultures."

Only Alpin and Saladin laughed.

"You're a princess?" Comyn asked, his face blank with shock.

"Of course she's a princess, and you can close your mouth, my lord," Lady Miriam said. Then she turned to Alpin. "Tell us about your schooling on the island."

"Don't be shy, Alpin," Malcolm coaxed. "Tell us."

Unwilling to spoil the happy atmosphere, Alpin told the

truth. "When I was little, Adrienne taught me. Then we took on an indentured servant who'd been a tutor and an estate manager." Later, when Charles had taken to drink, Henry Fenwick had become her dependable right hand.

Malcolm said, "An Englishman?"

Henry was a private man, and it had taken Alpin five years to learn why he'd left Northampton. Out of habit and respect, she was reluctant to discuss his personal business. She picked up the pitcher. "Yes, he was English. Would anyone like more beer?"

Malcolm held out his mug. As she refilled it, he leaned close and whispered, "Not too much, love. I wouldn't want to spoil my appetite or dull my sweet tooth."

A familiar thrill went through her at the thought of his lovemaking. But she couldn't forget his anger or forgive his scorn of the child she carried.

She was saved a reply when Lady Miriam said, "I'd love to live in Barbados for a few years. I'm interested in meeting that fellow who uses slave women for horses."

"I suspect you'd make him see the error of his ways," Saladin said.

"I'd do my best. And now that Alpin's all settled in at Kildalton, I'm not needed here. What say you, Alpin, will you sell me Paradise Plantation?"

Bewildered, Alpin studied Malcolm's stepmother, looking for some sign that she was joking. Her proposal was the solution to the problem of caring for the slaves. But if Alpin severed her tie with Barbados, she would have nowhere else to go.

The old fear gripped her.

Malcolm could be assured of keeping her in Scotland and feathering his political nest. Had he and his stepmother cooked up this scheme for the same reasons they showed an interest in Alpin's past? Having no answer, she hedged. "The lawyer may have already committed us to a sale."

"Business can wait," Malcolm said, getting to his feet and holding out a hand to Alpin. "I dearly hate to leave good company, so I'll take mine with me. Good night, all."

As she stepped over the bench, Alpin held his flattery

close to her heart. Perhaps she had judged him too harshly. Perhaps he deserved the benefit of the doubt.

Then she saw a man standing near the door leading to the tunnels.

A guard. Another clansman sat on one of the benches in the main entryway, the sleuthhound curled on the floor beside him. Looking up the stairs she saw still another watchman. They had been at their posts since early afternoon. Their counterparts stood sentinel at every exit, and not because the castle was full of Highland guests. Malcolm's men had followed her all day, even when she fed her rabbit or went to the privy.

The reminder of the day's scrutiny jangled her nerves.

Were the outside guards still on duty?

"Wait here," she said, drawing away. "I'll be right back."

He reached for her. "Where are you going?"

To see if you're still keeping me a prisoner, she wanted to say. Instead, she took a lesson from him and winked. "I heard there was a sweet tooth prowling the castle."

His eyes grew luminous. "Will you feed the beast?"

What choice did she have? None, as always. She put on a smile. "If I don't, he might devour me."

"He might anyway."

"I'll meet you upstairs."

He cupped her chin and leaned close. "I'll light a fire and turn down the bed." Then he gave her a kiss of promise. "Hurry."

In the kitchen she found Rabby Armstrong standing near the back door. He smiled apologetically. "A fine meal, my lady. All of the MacKays said so. We told 'em the laird knows how to pick a bride."

She shrugged but felt betrayed by his loyalty to Malcolm, for she'd come to know him well. She had a right to happiness and peace of mind, same as he.

Spitefulness made her say, "How is your mother?"

"Walking better since you brought her that poultice for her foot."

"Give her my best, Rabby." She dished up a slice of pie and tucked the honey jar under her arm.

In the entryway, she gave the plate to the guard.

His eyes downcast in shame, he stroked the sleuthhound. "Thank you, my lady."

She climbed the stairs and ignored the sentry who stood outside the chamber she shared with Malcolm. Once inside, she paused.

Barefoot and grinning like a king on coronation day, her husband lounged on the bed. She smiled, too. What woman wouldn't have, when faced with the prospect of making love to so handsome and powerful a man? He bent one knee, causing his kilt to bunch up in his lap. In the shadowy folds of the cloth, his maleness stirred to life. Curiosity drove her to the foot of the bed where she enjoyed an unobstructed view of his loins.

She tried to govern her lustful thoughts, but her mind seemed determined to taunt her with the pleasure this man could inspire. She gripped the honey jar with both hands.

Although fully exposed and completely aroused, he appeared comfortable with his masculinity.

"See what you've done to me?" he said.

Even at a distance of fifty paces she couldn't have missed his ardor. "I haven't even touched you yet."

"Nay, but watching you caress that honeypot stimulates my imagination and brings to mind any number of wickedly delicious endeavors we could undertake. I doubt the night is long enough to explore them all."

The lusty words delivered in a seductive tone sent her own fantasies soaring, yet she couldn't ignore his real reasons for wanting her. "Am I more appealing to you, now that I bring you a tie to a Highland clan?"

"Forget the alliance, Alpin. 'Tis unimportant, and I promise you clan loyalties will never come between us."

If only that were true, but as always he was speaking of his obligations and ignoring hers. She had a responsibility, a clan of her own.

"Put down the jar for now, Alpin."

Weary of the strife over problems that had only one solution, she knelt and set the crock on the floor. When she stood again, her head felt light, an odd counterpoint to the heavy desire that pulled in her belly and captured rational thought.

He murmured, "Undress for me."

Her fingers felt as clumsy as toes on the buttons of her dress, and as she worked her way down the placket of her bodice, she watched him watch her. His eyes grew glassy with desire, and a sheen of perspiration glistened on his forehead and upper lip. The rise and fall of his chest set a tempo for his pulsing maleness. She knew the cadence well, for it thrummed in all her secret womanly places.

Awash in an ocean of sensual promises, she heard the signal horn blare.

His concentration wavered, but only for an instant. "Show me your beautiful breasts."

Mouth watering with wanting, she pulled her arms from the sleeves of her dress and peeled the straps of her chemise off her shoulders. Slowly she drew the garment down to her waist, exposing herself.

His breathing turned raspy.

Her nipples turned to stone.

He folded his arms behind his head, stretched out his legs, and crossed his ankles.

It was a pose she remembered well. Only he hadn't been languishing in an elegantly outfitted bed with passion on his mind; he'd been lounging on a narrow ship's bunk with anger in his heart.

She shivered with vulnerability.

He cocked his dark eyebrows. "Don't stop now. I ache for the sight of you and the feel of your body next to mine."

In spite of his honest plea, she couldn't shake the picture of his coldly despotic behavior or shut out the echo of his angry words.

"My lord!" Alexander pounded on the door.

"Go away," Malcolm yelled.

"But, sir—"

"Begone, Alexander." Malcolm held out his hand to her.

Her feet seemed determined to disobey her brain. Loving

him meant trouble and heartache. Leaving him promised loneliness and grief. Comfort came with the knowledge that she could heal her wounds among friends in a land she knew.

She tipped her head toward the door. "It might be important."

"Nothing," he murmured, "is more important than you."

The words soothed, cajoled her to forget the obstacles between them and to accept the passion he offered. She already carried his child. What harm could come from sharing another night of pleasure in this cozy room?

"What are you thinking?" he asked.

That we're not in a bower, she wanted to say. This room, this castle, was her prison, and the father of her child, her warden.

"Alpin," he said, "I promise you, we will not be disturbed." Grinning, he added, "I rule here, you know."

His conviction fired her independence. He might command the people, but Alpin knew she held sway over his desire. She gave him a saucy smile. "I'm thinking that I haven't finished undressing for you."

His gaze slid lazily from the top of her head to the tips of her shoes. He pulsed with renewed vigor. "I'm all eyes, and you're a wicked temptress—"

"Malcolm, you must come." It was Lady Miriam's voice.

"Damn!" He closed his eyes and balled his fists in the velvet counterpane. Alpin watched his desire for her subside.

Disheartened, she thrust her arms into the dress and buttoned it. "It would seem that 'never' has arrived."

He sprang from the bed and took her in his arms. "I'll be back; you have my word on it."

"Of course you will." She believed him, but a greater truth weighted her soul. She and her interests would always come after the politics of Scotland.

"Keep the bed warm." He kissed her deeply, possessively.

Then he pulled on his boots, snatched up his sporran, and marched out the door. She stood where he'd left her, her thoughts darting from the sad state of their affairs to the identity of the new arrivals.

Inquisitiveness got the better of her. She opened the door. The guard stepped back. Her jailer. Now furious, Alpin made her way to the upstairs solar and drew back the curtains.

She gasped at what she saw.

21

In the darkened yard below, Alpin saw Malcolm, Lady Miriam, Saladin, Salvador, and Alexander walking toward the open gate. The twin brothers carried lanterns.

Not far beyond the wall, in the inner bailey, she saw two riders carrying torches and galloping toward the castle walls. The men wore bonnets and the distinctive plaid of the Gordons. Behind them rode their red-haired laird and half a dozen more of his clansmen. One of those men drew her eye. His fair hair flowed beneath a smartly cockaded hat. He was dressed like the others, but he seemed out of place.

Turning her attention to the welcoming party, Alpin was surprised to see Lady Miriam on the receiving end of Malcolm's wrath. He towered over her, his face taut with rage. Her red hair blazed in the lamplight, and she stared up at her stepson, her expression pleading, her hand on his arm as if to contain his obvious anger. Lady Miriam let go of him just as the Gordon outriders passed beneath the gate and approached the keep.

Alpin eased open the window, but the noise from the horses drowned out Malcolm's words. The visitors dismounted. Malcolm and the others stepped forward. When he reached the fellow with the plumed hat, Malcolm nodded in an oddly formal fashion, as did Alexander. Lady Miriam rushed forward, took the young gentleman's hand, and led him into the keep.

More puzzled than ever, Alpin dashed to the stairs. She heard Lady Miriam speaking French, but her tone was too low for Alpin to make out the words. The tramp of boots followed, and from the direction of the sound, she knew they'd gone to Malcolm's study.

As she made her way back to her room, Alpin saw her grandfather emerge from his chamber and stomp down the stairs. The guard outside her door paid no attention. Disgusted anew, Alpin went into her room and locked the door.

Then she opened the panel at the back of the wardrobe and stepped into the tunnel. Cool, stale air brushed her cheeks, and pitch darkness loomed ahead. Bracing her hand on the wall, she carefully made her way along the corridor to the circular steps that led down to the first floor. A guard had been posted in the tunnel earlier today. He was still there.

Cursing to herself, Alpin retraced her steps. Once in her room, she paced in agitation. Her grandfather had said John Gordon was on his way, so why did his arrival distress Malcolm? She didn't for a moment believe his ill temper stemmed from the interruption of their lovemaking. Then what had caused it? And why was her grandfather involved?

For the next hour she ransacked her memory, but she uncovered only scattered pieces of a puzzle. Treason had often been mentioned, but she didn't know enough about Scottish politics to draw a conclusion.

Why should she care? It amounted to another broken promise, another deception from her husband.

Wondering if Elanna was still awake, Alpin unbolted the door. The corridor was empty. Where had the guard gone? Probably to the privy.

She knocked on Elanna's door. It opened immediately. "What's going on?" Elanna said.

"I don't know. I thought you might."

"Muslim told me nothing except 'I'll be back.' Curse his committed soul."

An affronted Elanna had been cause for celebration among the slaves at Paradise; they swore that outrage stripped her of her royal air. Alpin agreed. "The guard is gone," she said.

Elanna stepped into the corridor and led Alpin to the stairs. "Shush," she said, tiptoeing down the steps.

The entryway was empty, too.

Excitement burst inside Alpin. Escape seemed possible. A part of her fought the notion, pleaded for her to stay. But the voices of the island called again and reminded her of the lies her husband had told. He had apprehended her before and seemingly with ease. She would probably fail in this attempt, too, but heaven help her, she had to try.

She pulled Elanna close and whispered, "You go into the kitchen and see if Rabby's still standing guard. I'll check the lesser hall."

Hope flickered in Elanna's eyes. "Maybe we go home?"

Love dragged at Alpin's heart. Duty and obligation pulled her another way. "Maybe so."

Elanna hugged her. "Bumpa Sam and the others, they need you."

"I know. Now hurry."

The merchantman *Brittany Bull* lumbered low in the water, the outgoing tide dragging at the mooring lines. Alpin and Elanna stood on deck near the gangway, their nervous gazes focused on the road leading to the neighboring port of Tynemouth. They'd left there two hours ago after booking passage on a ship bound for Calais.

They had escaped without a hitch. A full moon had aided their flight, and its reflection now shimmered on the surface of the sea.

Alpin's heart thundered in her chest, and her hands grew

clammy on the rail. Any moment now the hands would cast off the lines and the ship would catch the tide.

Would Malcolm come for her? Surely he would. He'd throw his heart at her feet and ask again why she was trying to leave him. But this time he would truly want to know. She'd tell him of her commitment to the people of Paradise. He would listen and understand the dilemma that even now was ripping her apart. He'd sail with her to Barbados, call it a honeymoon.

"What's that?"

At the sound of Elanna's voice, Alpin again stared toward the road.

"Back there—in the water."

Alpin whirled and saw a frigate easing into port beside them. Hundreds of smartly uniformed soldiers filled the deck. Their voices carried across the water, but she couldn't understand their words, for they spoke in a foreign tongue.

As she listened to them, she was reminded of the cobbler in Bridgetown, a German.

Eager for a distraction, she crossed the deck to get a closer look. Not ten feet away, on the deck of the other ship, stood an officer wearing a battery of medals and braids. He unfurled a map and spread it on a barrel. One of his subalterns held up a lantern. They conferred.

Then she heard the man say, "Kil-dal-ton, here!" and point a gloved finger at the map.

Kildalton. Why would armed German soldiers go to Kildalton? Perplexed and suddenly frightened, she watched the officer bark out orders. The hold was thrown open. Horses were led on deck.

One thought kept flashing in her mind: her escape had been almost too easy, as if Malcolm wanted her to get away.

John Gordon had come in the middle of the night. Malcolm had been angry. Who was the young man in the cockaded hat? Why had there been no guards on the battlements? Why had the stables been left unattended?

Like icy fingers on her neck, danger gripped her.

"We're going back."

"What?" Elanna said.

"We must go back to Kildalton."

Now that his rage had simmered to gnawing disgust, Malcolm leaned back in his chair and watched his step-mother work her diplomatic magic.

Charles Edward Louis Philip Sylvester Casimir Maria, better known as Bonnie Prince Charlie, sulked, albeit with grace, in one of the wing chairs. Since Lady Miriam had worn his hostility down to a nub, John Gordon merely prowled the room. Comyn MacKay still fumed, but quietly.

For the benefit of the prince, Lady Miriam spoke in French. "I'm sure you will agree, Your Royal Highness, that while eagerly awaited by many, your visit seems ill timed for a precious few."

At age fifteen, the prince possessed an odd maturity. His calculating gaze skittered from Gordon to MacKay, then back to Lady Miriam. "They will support me in the Highlands."

Comyn MacKay shot to his feet. "You'll hang before you get there. How dare you come to Scotland with only John Gordon and a dozen of his clansmen?"

The prince smiled. "But you brought fifty of your soldiers for my escort."

"I did no such thing. I came here to find my granddaughter." He glared at Gordon. "And I resent being coerced and having the lass used for your purposes."

The lass. Loneliness twisted in Malcolm's gut. He quelled the ache with the knowledge that at least she was safely away from the trouble brewing at Kildalton.

"Now, gentlemen," Lady Miriam said, "we've already settled that. As I recall, Comyn, you accepted John's apology and perhaps taught him something about valuing women in the process."

Alpin's grandfather sat down again, but he was still plainly miffed at his fellow Highlander. Resentment shimmered in his eyes, and his back grew stiff with disdain. Malcolm was so reminded of Alpin that he grew melancholy again, and as Lady Miriam convinced the Stewart prince that a return to Italy was in his best interests, Malcolm damned himself for a fool and wished with all his heart he could have another chance to get her back. He had vowed to befriend her, but the moment they were alone his good intentions had yielded to his body's need for her. Letting her go had been the hardest thing he'd ever done. But she was safe.

The door banged open, and the object of his thoughts burst into the room.

All eyes turned toward her. Malcolm bolted to his feet.

"Malcolm!" Out of breath, her cheeks pink from the cool night air, Alpin rushed to his side. "Soldiers are coming here—German soldiers. They came by ship. To South Shields."

"Who is she?" said the prince.

"She's my wife," Malcolm said.

"The lass is my granddaughter," declared Comyn MacKay.

The danger came rushing back. Malcolm took her hands. They were ice cold. He rubbed them between his own. "Catch your breath, sweetheart. Mother, get her a drink."

While the men murmured, Lady Miriam poured Alpin a glass of brandy. "Here, Alpin."

She drank, but only a swallow. Clutching the glass and still panting, she said, "Why would German soldiers come here?" She surveyed the men in the room. "What have you done?"

Gordon cursed. The prince grew stiff with fear.

Comyn said, "I told you no good would come of this."

Lady Miriam said, "There's a perfectly good explanation."

"Oh, aye," said Comyn. "They've come for the Bonnie Prince, and they'll take all our heads as souvenirs."

"The prince?" Alpin frowned. "What prince?"

Malcolm said, "May I present Charles Edward Stewart." Then in French he said, "My lord, meet my wife, Alpin MacKay."

"Tell us about these soldiers," the prince said.

To his surprise, Alpin answered in French. "I know little,

303

actually, Your Grace. They have a map, but I do not think they know exactly where they're going. I expect they're several hours behind me."

Real fear widened Charles's eyes, and he suddenly looked like the fifteen-year-old lad he was. "What will I do?" he asked Malcolm.

Malcolm had no intention of challenging the king's Hessians. Perhaps someday the battle to put a Stewart on the throne would be struck, but not now. The clans still fought among themselves, and until they unified, any attempt to dethrone the Hanoverians would be senseless.

Malcolm went to the door and called out to Alexander. He explained the situation. "Post a score of riders on the road to South Shields. I want to know exactly where those Hessians are at any moment."

"Aye, my lord." Alexander pivoted and marched away.

Malcolm stepped back inside his study and closed the door. "You must return to Italy," he said.

Prince Charles nodded. "But how?"

Lady Miriam stepped between them. "You're easily recognized even in that Gordon plaid."

"He could wear a disguise," said Alpin.

Malcolm pulled her into the circle of his arms and silently thanked a wayward prince for bringing her back to him one last time. "As a master of disguise, what do you recommend?"

She colored and shot him a look that promised further discussion, which he relished. Then she studied the prince. "We must be clever, but we must also get you away from here quickly. What about one of Mrs. Elliott's dresses?"

The war-trained prince nearly choked. "I cannot travel as a woman."

Lady Miriam beamed. "Yes, you can. 'Tis the safest way." She turned to Gordon. "John, go to the stables and have them ready my carriage." When he left, she turned back to the prince. "Come with me, your Royal Highness."

"Mother," Malcolm called after her, thinking of what his father would say about her plan. "'Tis too dangerous. Let Gordon take him."

"Do not worry. I've been in more perilous situations."

She probably had, but Malcolm couldn't bear the thought of risking her life. "I'll go with him."

"Nay," she said. "Salvador and I were to return to Italy anyway, and I know Whitley Bay and the people there. Any one of a dozen fishermen will take us willingly."

She had a point. "I've never won an argument with you anyway," he said, grumbling.

"'Tis the way it should be twixt mother and son."

Malcolm watched her lead the last Stewart prince out of the room.

Comyn planted his hands on his hips. "I'd like to know what you were doing in South Shields, lass."

She grew still. "I was going home to Barbados."

"Barbados?" he said, looking bewildered. "You're soon to be properly married, and you said you were selling that plantation."

Malcolm could feel her slipping away, but God help him, he had to defend her, even if it meant losing her. "I believe she was happy there before I meddled in her life and forced her to handfast herself to me."

Comyn's beard quivered. "You forced her?"

"Stop yelling over my head, both of you." Alpin stepped to one side.

Malcolm braced himself for the heartbreak of a lifetime. When her eyes met his, he saw torment and strength.

"I was happy there," she said quietly, reasonably, yet her fists were knotted. "I had a good life with people who loved me and depended on me. I promised to free them, Malcolm, and I will, no matter what."

So, he thought, loyalty had been her driving force. He'd been absolutely wrong in his treatment and his judgment of her. Now he must make amends. "Will you excuse us, Comyn?"

Her grandfather touched her shoulder. "You're loved here, too, lass. I'll be at *your* side, no matter what."

She gave him a tentative smile. "Thank you, Grandfather."

Comyn glanced sternly at Malcolm, then left the room.

305

"You let me go this time, didn't you?" she said.

"Aye, but I didn't want to."

"Then why did you?"

"Because I love you."

She stiffened. "That's not the only reason."

"Nay, I feared for you."

"Because of that prince?"

He couldn't help but smile, for she relegated the hopes of the Jacobites and the pride of Scotland's greatest dynasty to a nameless title. "Aye. He wants to start a war in Scotland and take the crown for his father, James."

A frown marred her brow. "I hate Scottish politics."

With absolute honesty he said, "As do I."

The tension left her shoulders, and her hands relaxed. "Truly?"

He put his hand over his clan badge. "My word as a Kerr. However, I find myself interested in the politics of Barbados."

"You do?"

"Aye. Since it concerns you."

She began to pace. "I must free the slaves."

"Then you will. What can I do to help?"

She stopped and studied him, hope and doubt sparkling in her eyes. "Would you go there with me? Help me fight for their freedom?"

With two questions she had opened the door to their future. Malcolm held out his hand. "Is tomorrow soon enough?"

She lunged into his arms. "Oh, Malcolm. You'll like everyone at Paradise. Just wait till you meet Bumpa Sam and the others."

He listened as she spoke lovingly of the island folk and told stories of her life with people who obviously cherished her and depended on her.

Never had Malcolm felt so complete, so right with the world. He hugged her close. "I have only one stipulation. I refuse to name our firstborn son Bumpa Sam."

Her laughter sealed their fate and vanquished their foes. He pictured the sons and daughters she would give him; he imagined her guiding their children with kindness and love, molding them to be decent, honorable people. No man, he thought, had ever been given so rich a bounty as this slip of a woman with amethyst eyes and a heart as big as Scotland.

"Will you marry me in the church, Alpin MacKay? Will you stay with me through lean times and fat?"

Her palms felt warm on his cheeks and her eyes were luminous with adoration. "I'll love you always, Malcolm Kerr."

He kissed her then, and the promise that flowed between them foretold a future bright with laughter and warmed by enduring love.

Twenty minutes later they stood arm in arm on the castle steps. The carriage awaited. Salvador had said his good-byes and was already inside. A dozen Kerr clansmen, with Alexander at the head, milled around in the yard. Riders had been dispatched along the road to watch for the approaching soldiers. According to the last report, the Hessians had taken a wrong turn and were still hours away.

"I wish John Gordon could take the prince," Alpin said.

Malcolm realized that she, too, was concerned about Lady Miriam's safety.

"Salvador will be with her, and for all his courtly ways, he's as deadly with a sword as Saladin is."

Malcolm heard the rustling of fabric and turned. His stepmother and Bonnie Prince Charlie emerged from the keep.

Seeing the pride of Scotland dressed in a maid's gown of drab brown muslin, a coif pulled low over his forehead, Malcolm didn't know whether to laugh or weep. A stern look from his stepmother advised him to do neither.

"Come here, Mother." He held out his free arm.

She hugged him. "Worry not, son. I'll send Alexander back as soon as we've found a boat."

She seemed almost excited by the challenge ahead. Malcolm kissed her. "I love you, Mother."

She gazed fondly at Alpin. "You'll be here when I return?"

Uncertainty glimmered in Alpin's eyes. "Malcolm and I

plan to travel to Barbados. He's going to help me free the slaves."

Lady Miriam grasped Alpin's hand. "Wait for me. I want to go with you. I've a hankering to dabble in island politics."

Malcolm pitied the men of Barbados, for his wife and his stepmother would make a formidable team.

Alpin glanced up at him, her brows lifted in question.

"'Tis up to you, sweetheart."

"We'll wait," she said.

"I love you both." Lady Miriam kissed them, then sailed down the steps and into the carriage.

The prince extended his hand. "Another time, my lord."

"Another time, my lord."

Fumbling with the unwieldy skirts, Charles Stewart lumbered into the carriage.

"Hold!" Saladin dashed outside, Elanna hanging on to his arm. "I'm going with you."

"You one crazy Muslim. This Ashanti princess forbids you to go."

Alarmed, Malcolm said, "You needn't go, Saladin. Salvador and Alexander will protect them. And if it comes to a fight, the prince is an expert swordsman."

Dislodging Elanna's hands from his shirt, Saladin wrapped an arm around her. "I do not go for that reason alone. This condescending, spoiled African princess will not marry me until she looks into the eyes of my father. I intend to find him."

Elanna hugged him. "I ask the gods to ride on your shoulders. You come back safe, plenty quick."

"I'll do my best." He extended his hand to Malcolm. "Keep her out of trouble until I return."

She huffed. Malcolm nodded and watched his longtime confidant salute the woman he loved, then climb into the carriage.

Alpin laid her head on his shoulder. "Won't the German soldiers be suspicious when they see my grandfather's soldiers here?"

Under normal circumstances the gathering would have been cause for alarm. But political woes were the farthest thing from Malcolm's mind at the moment. "Not if we invite them to the wedding."

She leaned back, and their eyes met. "What if the king protests our marriage?"

"Then we'll leave this place in my father's keeping and languish in Barbados until the king changes his mind."

Her arms circled his waist, and she sighed. "I love you, Malcolm Kerr."

As he held the woman he adored, he thought of the many roles she had played in his life and the parts she had yet to fill. A bright future unfolded before them, a time of peace and understanding, of companionship and enduring love.

POCKET STAR BOOKS
PROUDLY PRESENTS

TRUE HEART
Arnette Lamb

**Available
from
Pocket Star Books**

**The following is a preview of
True Heart. . . .**

Prologue

"You didn't for a moment think I believed you asked me into the stables to show me a new horse."

Even after all these years, Juliet brought out the rogue in Lachlan. He took her hand and pressed her palm against his cheek. "What I have in mind is infinitely more entertaining than a foal."

Her interest engaged, she lifted her brows. Her fingers traced his mouth. "Which is why you brought me to the loft."

Her familiar scent softened the robust aroma of freshly mown hay. Her touch did more earthy things to his sense of decorum. "Why I brought you up here is a surprise."

"I see." She licked her lips. "You *intended* to wrinkle my dress and muss my hair?"

"Aye. The first before I ravished you, the second *while* I ravished you."

Always the grand skeptic, she said, "A husband cannot ravish his own wife. . . ." She had more to say, but she'd make him wait. Juliet had helped Lachlan raise Agnes, Sarah, Lottie, and Mary. But respect and love for his four bastard daughters only scratched the surface of her generosity. She'd given him four more daughters and an heir. He loved Juliet more today than when she'd placed his son in his arms. At sunrise next, he'd love her more still.

Touching her was a pleasure he couldn't deny himself now that they were alone. "In the event you've lost the gist of the conversation, you were holding forth on the issue of whether a husband may ravish his wife."

"The word 'holding' distracts me." She glided her hand down over the placket of his breeches and made a carnal image of the ordinary word. "Tell me why there is a satin pillow beneath the hay." She flicked her very arresting gaze to the spot where roof met wall.

Lachlan chuckled. "If you hope to tease me with conversational detours, you'll go wanting for that, love. Not even a bolster of gold could distract me at the moment."

Her supple fingers began a dangerous rhythm, and her voice softened to an enticing purr. "Pondering two things at once is surely manageable for a man of your invention."

Desire thrummed in his chest, rang in his ears. On a shallow breath, he said, "You, on the other hand, are not completely captivated."

With her free hand she cupped his neck and pulled him closer. "I've been captivated since the winter of sixty-two."

The occasion of her entry into Lachlan's life and the genesis of his true happiness. For hours he'd anticipated this time alone with her. Their eldest,

Virginia, was betrothed this very day to Cameron Cunningham, a lad they favored. Their son Kenneth would foster soon with Cameron's parents, Suisan and Myles. Lachlan's elder daughters were seventeen years old and planning their own futures.

For now, time alone with Juliet was a luxury to Lachlan, but in a few years he'd have her all to himself. This afternoon's tryst was a gift he intended to savor. Teasing her was a part of their lovers' game.

He plucked a straw from her hair. "But coherent thought is ever your constant companion, no?"

"Not always."

"Let's see about that." Gaze fixed to hers, he kissed her. Her brown eyes glittered with pleasure and desire smoldered in their depths. A sense of belonging swamped him, and as he deepened the kiss, he wondered for the thousandth time what great deed he'd done to deserve this woman. With a sweetness that always thrilled him, she returned his ardor and fired it with her own.

In the distance he heard the happy sound of childish laughter. Juliet heard it too, but that was the way of mothering with her. Even in the crowd at Midsummer Fair she could discern the voices of her own children.

"Which of our brood is so joyous? Cora?" He spoke of their youngest daughter.

"Kenneth. Agnes must be tickling him."

"I'll be glad when his voice changes."

"Will you rejoice when Agnes flies the nest?"

"Aye and nay. 'Tis dear Sarah I worry over more."

"Not our newly betrothed Virginia?"

Juliet's first daughter was unlike any of his other children. She'd been strongly influenced by her four older sisters. From Lottie she'd learned grace and stitchery. At Mary's hand she'd perfected an artist's skill. From Sarah she'd gained a love for books and law. From Agnes she'd learned too much cunning and bravery.

"Now who's distracted?" Juliet teased.

Lachlan moved closer. She winced and shifted.

"Uncomfortable?" he asked.

She gave him a look of tried patience. "No. But a pillow would be nice."

That mysterious pillow again. An odd jealousy stabbed him. He couldn't own her every thought. She was curious about the pillow and wouldn't leave the subject alone. He reached for the item in question and held it so they could both inspect it.

Embroidered in satin thread were the words "We love you, Papa."

Juliet said, "Only Lottie's stitches are so finely done."

Lachlan eased the pillow beneath her head. "Never will I understand the female mind."

"We are cerebral creatures, even in our stitchery."

They'd plowed this conversational field often over the years. "Cerebral." He pretended to ponder it. "For a thinker you're doing some very earthy things with your other hand."

"Then I'll allow you a moment to gather your priorities."

"Gather holds great appeal." Which is what he did to her skirts, moving his hand up her thighs. He found bare skin. "No underthings? You're bold, Juliet."

She fairly preened. "The last time you lured me into the stables you took my underclothing and wouldn't give them back. Agnes made a show of returning the garments to me."

Two months to the day after Kenneth had been born, Lachlan had enticed his wife into the loft.

They'd spent the day loving, laughing, and napping in their pursuit of happiness. She was the sun to his day. The moon to his night. The joy to his soul. The love in his heart.

He pressed her back into the soft hay. "We were also interrupted that day."

The interruption had come when she'd asked him to give her another child. He'd refused. She'd respected his wishes.

"'Twas a rough argument 'tween us." She mimicked his Scottish speech, but beneath the mockery lay regret, for she'd carried his children with ease and birthed them with joy. Five babes of her own had not been enough for his Juliet. Counting his illegitimate daughters, nine children were plenty for Lachlan.

"You're wonderful," he said.

"I thought I was the moon to your night."

"Aye, you are."

"The rain in your spring?"

"And the skip in my step."

She pretended to pout. "The thorn in your side?"

He blurted, "The bane of this loving if you laugh like that again."

She giggled low in her belly, more dangerous than full out laughter. Still in the throes of mirth, she said, "Do you recall the morning I seduced you in Smithson's wood house?"

He did. "Hot house better describes it. Actually I was remembering the time you tied me to the bed at Kinbairn Castle."

"You made a delicious captive, except for that one request you refused me."

Had she been cunning, Juliet could have gotten herself with child that day, for she had ruled their passion. "I prevailed."

"A winning day for both of us, but—" Something caught her attention. "Look." She pointed to the ceiling.

Craning his neck, Lachlan saw a piece of parchment secured to the rafter with an arrow. Printed on the parchment in Sarah's familiar handwriting were the words, "We love you, Mama."

Fatherly love filled him. Knowing he'd bring Juliet here, the lassies had left the pillow so he could see the affectionate words. Mary, the best archer of the four, had secured the note in a spot where Juliet couldn't miss it. Even though she wasn't their mother, they thought of her that way. But the positioning of the messages left no doubt that the girls knew that Lachlan and Juliet were making love in the loft.

On that lusty thought, he burrowed beneath her skirts and feasted on her sweetest spot.

Too soon she tugged on his hair. "Please, love."

He growled softly, triggering the first tremor in her surrender to passion. The beauty of her unfettered response moved him to his soul. But when she quieted, he eased up and over her, wedging himself into the cradle of her loins. His own need raging, he entered her, but not quickly or deeply enough, for she lifted her hips and locked her legs around him.

Lust almost overwhelmed him. "Say you're wearing one of those sponges." The sponges were the second most dependable way to control the size of their family.

Her slow smile struck fear in his heart. She wasn't wearing the sponge. If she moved so much as a muscle below the waist, he'd spill his seed, weighing the odds that she'd conceive again.

With his eyes he told her no.

Juliet's smile turned to resignation, and she mouthed the words, no ill feelings, love. He didn't need to hear the sound of the words; he'd heard them many times in the last three years. She waited until he'd mastered his passion. Then she reached into her bodice and retrieved a small corked bottle. With a flick of her thumb, she sent the cap sailing into the hay. The smell of lilac scented water teased his nose.

To tease her, he plucked up the wet sponge. "Excuse me for a moment." He put the sponge between his teeth, leered at her, and again burrowed beneath her skirts.

Primed, sleek, and ready, she awaited him. In his most inventive move to date, he inserted the sponge, then brought her to completion a second time.

"I want you now," she said between labored breaths.

Obliging her came easy to Lachlan. Just when he'd joined their bodies again and began to love her in earnest, voices sounded below.

"You must let me go with you," said a very disgruntled Virginia.

Lachlan groaned. Juliet slapped a hand over his mouth.

He knew to whom Virginia was speaking: her betrothed, Cameron Cunningham.

Hoping they wouldn't stay long, Lachlan returned his attention to Juliet.

Praying for patience, Cameron followed Virginia into the last stall.

She stopped and folded her arms. "Why can't I go with you?"

The greatest adventure of his life awaited Cameron. Years from now, after they were married, he'd sail around the world with her. For now, reason seemed prudent. "'Twouldn't be proper."

"Proper?" Her dark blue eyes glittered with temper, and her pretty complexion flushed with anger. "We're betrothed. That should be reason enough. Papa knows you will not ravish me. I haven't even gotten my menses yet."

From another female the remark would have sparked outrage, but Cameron had known Virginia MacKenzie since the day of her Christening, ten years ago. His ears still ached when he remembered how long and loudly she'd cried. He'd been eight years old at the time. He'd fostered here at Rosshaven. He'd learned husbandry from Lachlan MacKenzie, the best man o' the Highlands. The announcement earlier today of Virginia's betrothal to Cameron had been a formality. Their marriage, five years hence, would mark the happiest day of Cameron's life. Their parents heartily approved, for the union would unite their families.

He told her a lie and the least hurtful refusal. "You cannot go with me to France." He was sailing for China. She'd learn that truth from her father on the morrow.

"But everything's formal now, and I've made us a symbol of our own. See?" From her fancy wrist bag, she produced a silk scarf.

Fashioned after the ancient clan brooches, the design on the cloth featured a circle with stylistic hearts and an arrow running through.

"The arrow is for your mother's people, Clan Cameron. The hearts are in honor of our friendship and love, which will be timeless. It took me ever so long to think it up and a week of nights here in the stable to stitch it. 'Tis a secret. I wanted you to see it before everyone else."

Cameron voiced his first thought. "'Tis feminine for a man to wear."

Her eyes filled with tears. "That's a wretched thing to say."

Immediately defensive, Cameron stood his ground. "I'm sorry. I was surprised is all."

"Then don't disappoint me again. Take me with you. I'll cancel the betrothal if you do not."

His pride stinging, Cameron tucked the scarf into his sleeve and headed for the door. "Cancel it if you wish. I only agreed to please my parents."

Virginia gave up the fight. He couldn't mean those hurtful words, and by the time his ship sailed tomorrow, she'd be tucked securely in the hold.

Chapter 1

Nine years, eleven months, and thirteen days later, Cameron swung the canvas bag onto his shoulder and stepped on the quay in Glasgow Harbor. Pain no longer accompanied memories of Virginia. Only a deep sense of loss. Since her disappearance, he'd learned to live with an empty soul. The image of the clan brooch Virginia had designed years ago rose in his mind, as vivid as the day he'd first seen the delicate hearts with an arrow running through.

Cameron stopped in his tracks and blinked. The picture became real. Before him loomed a wall of hogsheads. Burned into the wood of each of the barrels was the symbol created almost a decade ago by Virginia MacKenzie.

His heart pounded, and the ale he'd drunk with his crew just moments ago turned sour in his belly. No one else had seen the hallmark. Virginia said it had been her secret gift in honor of their betrothal. By candlelight, she'd embroidered the scarf for him. After her disappearance, when Cameron had relayed to her father the details of that last meeting in the stables at Rosshaven, the duke of Ross confessed that he'd never seen Virginia's hallmark.

Cameron had thought never to see it again.

He put down his burden and peered closer at the design. With only a slight variance, a common heraldic crown over the top, the symbol was the same.

From the ashes of certainty, a spark of hope flickered to life. Virginia could be alive. The thought staggered him.

Mouth dry, hands shaking, he leaned against the stack of tobacco casks. Past disappointments warned caution. But what were the odds of another person combining the arrow of Clan Cameron, his mother's Highland family, with hearts of love? No coincidence appeared before him; Virginia was alive and this drawing was her cry for help.

Stuffing one of the hogsheads under his arm, he located Quinten Brown, captain of the merchantman.

"From where did this hallmark come?"

Brown swept off his three-cornered hat and tucked it under his arm. "Why would you be asking, Cunningham? Ain't the brandy trade enough for you?"

In his place, Cameron would also be protective of his livelihood; any businessman would. To allay the man's worry and loosen his tongue, Cameron fished a sack of coins from his waistcoat. "I've seen this design, and it's very important to me. I've no intention of heeling in on your trade."

Satisfied, Brown pocketed the gold. "'Course you ain't. I'll tell you what I know o' the matter. The cooper at Poplar Knoll always favored the plain crown—even after the colonies was lost to us." He traced the design. "This girlish mark, the hearts 'n' arrow, on their barrels. I ain't seen it afore."

"Then how do you know this tobacco came from there?"

"The new mistress herself come aboard to pay her respects to me." Rocking back on the heels of his bucket-top boots, the seaman clutched his lapels. "Her husband, Mr. Parker-Jones, bought the plantation more'n a year ago. I tell you true, Cunningham, the slaves 'n' servants o' that place are praising God. The old owner and his wife were devils and more."

In his search for Virginia, Cameron had scoured every port in the British Isles, the Baltic, Europe, and even the slave markets of Byzantine. He'd searched Boston, the cities of Chesapeake Bay, and even the Spanish-held New Orleans. "Where is this plantation?"

"Poplar Knoll? The tidewaters of Virginia."

Cameron had sailed those waters, but not in years. With his father serving in the House of Commons, Cameron now favored the shorter European trade routes. "On the York River?"

"No. The James, just west of Charles City."

"The south or the north shore?"

"South, if I'm remembered of it. Fine dock with lovey doves carved into the moorings. Yes, south side."

At the least, the person who'd crafted this hallmark had some knowledge of Virginia. If she were on an isolated plantation, that would explain why he hadn't found her. The lost war with the colonies had limited shipping traffic, and little news traveled out of tidewater Virginia.

Anticipation thrumming through him, he thanked the captain and made his way to Napier House, home of Virginia's sister, Agnes. Now the countess of Cathcart, Agnes was the only family member who still believed that Virginia was alive.

Dear God, he prayed, let it be so.

POPLAR KNOLL PLANTATION
TIDEWATER VIRGINIA

Planting would be upon them soon. From dawn's first light until sunset or rain forced them to stop, they'd hunker in the fields. Virginia shifted on the bench, her back aching at the thought. In the corner of the weaving shed, the strongest of the slaves dismantled the looms used to weave book muslin, the fabric of necessity for slaves and bond servants. Everyone, even the pregnant females worked in the fields until harvest. At first frost, the looms would come out again.

Life would continue for another year. But three harvests hence Virginia's indenture would end. The old bitterness stirred, but she stifled it. She'd tried escape once, nine years ago. For penalty five years had been added to her servitude. Freedom would come. Three years from now, she'd have money in her purse, new shoes and a traveling coat, and passage to Williamsburg. From there—

"Duchess!"

Virginia started. Merriweather, the smartly dressed butler from the home house strolled toward her.

"Wash your hands and face, Duchess. Mrs. Parker-Jones wants to see you."

No one addressed Virginia as Virginia. They hadn't believed her story about who she was and how she'd come to the colonies. When she'd proclaimed herself the daughter of the duke of Ross, they'd laughed and named her Duchess. She'd been a frightened child of ten.

Merriweather cleared his throat. "You've done nothing wrong. The mistress hastened me to say so."

Virginia smiled and put aside the hat band she was tooling. She'd spoken only once to Mrs. Parker-Jones since the woman and her husband had purchased Poplar Knoll two years ago. Did this summons also involve the design Virginia had secretly branded into the hogsheads? Hopefully not, for she'd come away from the meeting with a small victory and an apology. She'd been assured the matter was ended.

Encouraged, she went to the table and washed her face in the bucket of clean water. Then she untied her apron and took the brush from her basket.

As they left the shed and made their way through the servants' hamlet, she brushed her hair and tied it at her nape.

"She'll not be seeing you in the front parlor, your grace."

No rancor hardened his words, and Virginia chuckled. She might be a bond servant, but never had she been a sloven.

She was ushered into the back parlor, where Mrs. Parker-Jones was reading the Bible. Putting the book aside, she waved the butler out the door. "Close it on your way out, if you please, Merriweather."

Although she'd never been in this room, Virginia

refused to gape at the fine furnishings. She'd seen better at Rosshaven.

"Tell me about yourself." Mrs. Parker-Jones indicated a chair. "How did you come to servitude?"

Caution settled over Virginia, and she stood beside the chair. "Three years remain on my indenture, Ma'am. I want no trouble."

"I want the truth. Are you Virginia MacKenzie, daughter of the sixth duke of Ross?"

Something in the tone of her voice alarmed Virginia, that and her knowledge of the specifics of Papa's title. She gripped the back of the chair. "Who wants to know?"

"Cameron Cunningham."

Images of her youth swam before Virginia. Then she saw nothing at all.

Look for
True Heart
Wherever Paperback Books Are Sold